Readers love CATT FORD

I0614352

The Last Concubine

"…full of energy and excitement…"

—Reviews by Jessewave

Lily White, Rose Red

"This story is great for the mystery and the romance reader."

—The Romance Studio

"The combination of truly stunning writing with great characters, a compelling mystery, and hot sex makes this story simply entertaining on all levels."

—Long and Short Reviews

"It's sensual, exciting, and, best of all, it's pure fun."

—Joyfully Reviewed

The Untold Want

"…stands out from the sea of romances for the good writing and in depth characters."

—Long and Short Reviews

Dash and Dingo

"There are many intriguing twists and turns that had me on the edge of my seat."

—Blue Ribbon Reviews

"*Dash and Dingo* has something for everyone, comedy, drama, history and, of course, the romance between the main characters."

—Dark Diva Reviews

By CATT FORD

<u>NOVELS</u>
A Strong Hand
Dash and Dingo (with Sean Kennedy)
The Last Concubine
Lily White, Rose Red

<u>NOVELLAS</u>
Extreme Bull
The Long Way Home
Murder at the Rocking R
Riding Out the Bull
Summer Fever
The Untold Want

Published by DREAMSPINNER PRESS
http://www.dreamspinnerpress.com

BULLHEADED

Catt Ford

Dreamspinner Press

Published by
Dreamspinner Press
5032 Capital Circle SW
Ste 2, PMB# 279
Tallahassee, FL 32305-7886
USA
http://www.dreamspinnerpress.com/

Bullheaded

Cover Art by Catt Ford

ISBN: 978-1-62380-625-5
Digital ISBN: 978-1-62380-626-2

Printed in the United States of America
First Edition
April 2013

Dedicated to the bullfighters who courageously put their bodies on the line to protect the bull riders in danger. You are almost as crazy as the riders.

BULLRIDING 101:

Arena: Bull riding takes place in a sports arena surrounded by steel fences six feet high. At one end, the ring announcers narrate from a platform, giving stats, scores, and opinions. At the other end, a two-story steel structure houses the TV announcers up top, with the chutes down below. A TV reporter is stationed by the exit gate to interview riders coming and going.

Away from his hand: When the bull spins to the opposite direction from the bull rider's hand.

Bonus points: Winners of each round and the entire event receive bonus points and extra money.

Bucked off: When a rider is thrown before eight seconds and doesn't earn a score.

Bull rope: The rope is wrapped around the bull and the rider's gloved hand. A bell is attached to the rope and the weight of the bell pulls the rope off the bull after the dismount.

Bullfighters: A team of athletes who distract the bull to keep the rider safe. The bullfighters' goal is to look like an easier target, and they will take the hit for the rider, or each other, if necessary.

Challenge: A rider can push the red challenge button if he feels the bull fouled or the timing clock malfunctioned. If the challenge is denied, the rider must pay $500.

Change direction: When a bull changes direction laterally, front to back or side to side.

Chutes: A gated box where the rider wraps his rope around the bull and gets ready to ride. There are usually six chutes where riders get ready in turn. When the rider nods his head, the gateman will open the gate.

Cover: When a rider successfully stays aboard the bull for eight seconds, he has covered the bull.

Delivery: The stock owner decides whether the gate will open left or right, as bulls usually perform better in a particular direction.

Dismount: If a rider makes the whistle, he reaches down with his free hand, jerks the tail of the rope to free his riding hand, and tries to get off as safely as possible.

Disqualify: A rider can be DQ'd if he touches the bull with his free arm, loses his grip on the rope, or leaves the chute with his spur caught in the knot of his bull rope.

Down in the well: When the bull pulls the rider down into the vortex of its motion.

Draw: Bulls and riders are randomly paired in the draw. For the championship round of each event, riders choose their own bulls from a list provided to them.

Eight seconds: A qualified ride is eight seconds. The clock starts when a bull's shoulder or flank breaks the plane of the gate and stops if the whistle blows, the rider's hand comes out of the rope, the rider's free arm touches the bull, or the rider falls off. The rider can be upside down, but as long as he's got hold of the rope, he makes a score.

Finals: Points are counted throughout the year, and the top forty riders (and alternates) go to the finals to joust for the World Championship.

Flank strap: A rope loosely tied around the bull's hips so the bull thinks it can kick it off. This rope has no contact with the bull's genitals. You damage the genitals, you aren't getting stud fees from your money bulls when they retire.

Free arm: The rider uses the arm not wrapped in the rope to move his body with the bull. If any part of the arm below the shoulder makes contact with the bull, the rider is DQ'd.

Gateman: The gateman is positioned inside the arena, and when the rider gives the nod, he must open the gate as quickly as possible.

Glove: The thick leather glove that protects the rider's riding hand from rope burn.

Go-around: Each event has several tries for the riders, called long rounds. If they score high enough, up to fifteen riders can advance to the short-go, or championship round, for the event.

Hooked: When a bull hooks a human target with its horns.

Hung up: When a rider is unable to free his hand from the bull rope, he is hung up. The bull will drag the rider until he or the bullfighters can free him from the rope.

Into his hand: If the bull turns toward the rider's riding hand, it is spinning into his hand.

Judging: Four judges evaluate each bull and rider. Bulls always receive a score, even if they buck the rider off. They are judged on the difficulty of their performance and how smart they are at getting a rider off. Riders are judged on technique and control, but only get a score if they make eight seconds. Spurring earns extra points as showing control.

Kindness to animals: Only blunt spurs are allowed. The rider spurs to demonstrate control, but the spurs do not scratch the bull's hide.

Livestock director: The livestock director works with stock contractors to bring the best bucking bulls to the events.

Making the whistle (or horn): An alarm sounds when eight seconds has passed or if the rider makes a violation.

Mean bull: A bull that will actively go after a rider or bullfighter.

Muley bull: A bull without horns.

Rank bull: A challenging bull that is difficult to ride but not necessarily mean.

Reride: If the judges feel the rider didn't get a fair chance they may award a reride. This can be for a foul, if the bull gets hung up in the gate, or if the bull is having a bad day.

Riding hand: The hand the rider uses to hang onto the rope.

Ring usher or safety man: A cowboy on horseback who assists the bullfighters when they have trouble getting a bull to leave the ring.

Safety equipment: Riders must wear protective vests. Helmets are not mandatory. Bullfighters wear different kinds of vests and lots of padding, but no helmets, because they need their peripheral vision. They wear cowboy hats instead.

Shark cage: A round steel structure in the middle of the ring. A TV crew is stationed inside to shoot the action. The clown, or entertainer, can go there for safety. Cowboys will often run there if a bull is after them. At the start of the event, there are two ramps, and as their names are called, cowboys go up, tip their hat, and go down the other side to line up in the ring.

Scoring: Both rider and bull are scored on their performance, with 50 points available for each, making a possible score of 100. It is said no one has ever received 100 points, although urban legend disputes this.

Slap: If a rider slaps a bull with his free arm during the ride, he is DQ'd.

Stock contractor: Individual contractors who buy, breed, and train bulls for the events.

Trip: The type of ride a particular bull offers.

CHAPTER 1:
A Good Ride

IT ALWAYS started this way. He could feel his heart speed up, the insistent pounding in his chest, the steel rail cold under his hand, the restless beast throbbing between his legs, the tightness of the wrap around his hand. He gave the nod.

When the gate opened, the bull exploded out of the chute, bucking and twisting high in the air. Time slowed down for him as the rush of adrenaline shot through his body. It made him feel weightless yet powerful. Energized but floating on air. This was going to be a good ride. He was in the zone, shifting his body expertly, just enough to counter each move the bull threw at him, finding the perfect center of balance. The bull's rage shivered up his spine, but it didn't make a dent in his determination to win. He could almost hear the ticking as each hundredth of a second counted down.

His timing was perfect. He was so concentrated on his ride he couldn't hear the roar of the crowd or the buzzer when it came. His internal clock told him once again he was the victor in the ageless contest between man and beast.

The physical and mental challenge to stay aboard and the ecstasy of conquest rushed through him, electrifying his body. It felt like more excitement than his body could contain, as if he might explode with the insane joy of it any moment.

The sight of the bullfighters closing in told him it was time to bail. He tugged at the rope to release his hand and realized too late he was hung up, leaning too far down in the well and unable to fight gravity any longer. At least he came down on the right side, where he had a fighting chance of staying on his feet as the bull jerked him along, trying to rid itself of the irritant now flopping along behind.

He yanked at the rope desperately but his gloved hand was stuck. Some movement on the other side of the ring drew the bull's attention, and he saw an anonymous hand working the rope up and over. It came loose, relieving the strain on his rotator cuff. The bull kicked hard at the same moment, sending him flying, his body literally soaring through the air. He grinned in the general direction of the hushed crowd and tucked his head into his chest to roll when he hit the dirt, but he just knew there was no way was he going to land right this time. He misjudged the timing, and the crash made him tumble like a rag doll for a few yards before he came to rest on his back.

His triumphant grin vanished when he looked up to find he hadn't rolled far enough away, and one ton of angry bull was about to come down on him. The bull's hooves looked as sharp and lethal as scythes, and he knew even the protective vest couldn't handle that kind of impact.

As he rolled frantically to get out of the way, he barely caught a flash of red by the bull's head, and then the animal twisted away from him, turning to chase the movement.

He made it to his feet and ran for the fence that surrounded the arena. He leaped up on the rails just in time before the bull came back around and crashed into the steel that circled the ring, trying to crush him. He heard Johnny's voice yelling at the bull, and then the full, roaring sound of the arena rushed back into his consciousness. They were chanting his name: "Cody! Cody!" A pretty girl in a tight tank top in the first row stood up and grabbed his face, planting a kiss on his lips. Grinning, Cody put his arm around her waist and pulled her closer to return the favor before jumping down into the ring.

Behind him, the ring announcer was practically having a verbal orgasm. "And that's what makes Cody Grainger so exciting to watch, folks! Just under 90 points on a rank, rank bull. This season, Cody has been in the 90-point club over ten times already! If the other riders don't take him out first, the stock contractors will have a bounty out on this man pretty soon, because he's making their bulls look like milk cows. If he keeps riding like this, he could take the title for the second year in a row! We've never had a back-to-back champion before, but he's way out ahead of the pack on points, and we'll be seeing him in Vegas in October for sure!"

People in the stands were grinning at him, holding their hands through the bars to congratulate him, trying to touch him because in this arena, he was *somebody*. Cody was a draw and he knew it. He slapped the hands of the children closest to him, gave them his famous grin, and peered up at the scoreboard.

He was on top.

A good place to be. Just under 90 points.

"Not bad for a man with a concussion, Cody!" One of the bullfighters came by to toss him his rope. He caught it one-handed and started to coil it.

"Thanks, Reese. It was just a little one."

"Good ride." With a pat on the back, Reese ran off to join his team at the gate.

Jinks the rodeo clown swung by to slap his back. The wide smile painted on his face was stretched even wider by his grin. "How's it feel at the top?"

"Can't complain." Cody grinned and bumped fists. "How's it feel in the barrel?"

Jinks did a little dance shuffle. "A lot safer than on the back of one of those beasts, but to each his own."

Cody limped to the gate where one of the medics stopped him, briskly asking, "Any dizziness? You were slow getting up. Did you black out? Any neck pain?"

"Nope, I'm fine. It's all good." Cody snatched off his helmet and reached for his hat.

He'd stand behind the rails and watch the riders yet to come in the short round to see if any of them could best his score. There were some rank bulls at this event, but he didn't think any of them were ranker than his. However, you never knew. Bull riding was as much a game of luck as any roulette wheel in Vegas. One day you were up and the next you were down.

The ring announcer went on. "Just a review of the NBR 101; a qualified ride is eight seconds. Bull riding is a judged sport with 50 points to the rider and 50 to the bull for a possible 100. The highest score in the history of the NBR was 96.5. We have thirty riders in the long round, but only the top ten riders will qualify to move into the short round. First two rounds are tonight, and the event will finish up tomorrow with two final rounds. Right now, Cody Grainger is top dog in the Leader of the Pack position, but there are still riders who think they can beat him. Next up is top Brazilian rider Juca Matos, who has been snapping at Cody's heels all year. Juca is known for his consistency. He may not score big, but he scores often. You won't see him fall off too many bulls. While he gets ready, let's watch the screen for the replay of Cody's exciting ride!"

Cody looked up with everyone else at the big screen at the top of the arena as they replayed his ride. Looking at the replay, he was surprised he'd managed to hang on for the full eight. He'd even managed to get his outside leg working the spur like mad. He winced watching himself slide off and get dragged along next to the bull, and then gasped in horror when Johnny darted right in front of the bull, getting hung up on the horns and flipped ten feet in the air. Johnny did a spectacular somersault, landed lightly on his feet, and quickly turned to reach over the bull and yank at the rope, setting Cody free while the other two bullfighters got the bull's attention.

During the replay, the audience screamed in fear to see Cody roll onto his back and stare up at the bull about to land on him, when once again Johnny shot the gap to put his body between bull and man. This time the other two bullfighters were right behind him, darting in and out, working like a flawless team to distract the bull and drive it to the exit gate. It was Johnny's quick action that made the bull turn away from Cody's limp body, but it made Cody's blood run cold to see such a close call. The big screen cut away then to show Juca Matos currently getting set in the chute.

With a deep breath, Cody singled Johnny out in the ring by the red shirt over his vest, still out there doing his job, waiting with his team by the gate for the next bull. In relief, Cody gave him a nod and fist pump to thank him for the save, even while his heart was still pounding at the shock of the sight. Sometimes it killed him that Johnny put his life and limbs on the line for him when there was nothing he could do in return to help Johnny if he got in trouble. The flash of a smile on Johnny's beautiful dark face made him feel happy and relieved, which in turn made him feel horny, something they could maybe take care of together later.

He started to peel his glove off and unwrap the tape. There were only three riders still left to go, and so far he'd been the only one in this short round to cover a bull. He didn't mind if the other boys managed to stick for eight seconds as long as he won the round.

Juca Matos made the whistle as usual, but the final two bucked off.

He staggered at the congratulatory slap on his back and caught a flash of red as Johnny ran by him, heading toward the locker rooms.

"Keep that up tomorrow and you'll get another buckle for the collection! Congrats!"

He smiled after the bullfighter and then ran out into the ring, jumped up onto the shark cage in the center for the brief interview, and held both arms over his head in triumph, flashing his famous grin. Lights flashed and confetti rained down as the crowd applauded and shouted his name, even though he'd only won the short round for the first night. Tomorrow was a whole new crapshoot and he loved it. Loved the challenge, the physicality, and the risk of his chosen profession. He just loved to ride.

"CAN'T complain about your work, rookie."

"Thanks, Vern." Pleased with his leader's praise, Johnny felt a smile tug at his lips but tried not to let it out.

"It's okay, you're allowed to pat yourself on the back once in a blue moon." Reese was always quick to tease. "That was a nice save."

"Especially since we haven't been working together as a team that long." Vern backed up the DVD and played Johnny's save of Cody again in slow motion. "Teamwork. It's what keeps us all safe. When you grabbed that bull's attention, Reese was able to slip in and tag him."

"You're the one who played kissy-face with him, boss," Reese said, lazily pointing at the screen where Vern was teasing the bull by putting his hand on its head and staring it down before darting away in the direction of the exit.

"Hey, we're all sporting a big red S like Superman on our chests. A night with no one going to the emergency room is a good night by me." Vern replayed Johnny's aerial somersault again and snickered. "Good thing at least one of us is young and athletic, Reese."

"You calling yourself old?" Reese asked, pretending to clutch his heart in shock. "'Cause I'm not ready for the back pasture yet."

Vern ignored him and spoke to Johnny. "I heard you know Cody outside the circuit."

Answering the real question, Johnny said, "Yeah, I work for him on his ranch. But I hate seeing anyone get hung up like that."

Vern gave a quick nod of approval. "It's a good night when we all get to go home, riders and fighters. I couldn't ask to work with better partners."

Reese wiggled his eyebrows and gave Johnny a wink. "That's like getting a fucking gold star. Better remember it, Johnny. Our fearless leader don't give them out so easy."

"I'll treasure the memory forever," Johnny assured him, and Reese chuckled.

Vern stood up and held out his hands. The other two joined him in a circle and bowed their heads as he said a quick prayer of thanksgiving for their safety in the ring that night. "Okay, see you boys tomorrow. No drinking and staying out late tonight."

Watching the slim, bow-legged man amble down the hall, Johnny asked, "He always bring up about not boozing it up?"

"Nothing to do with you, kid. He's AA and proud of it. Been in recovery twenty years steady. Couldn't ask for a better partner to fight bulls with." Reese picked up his hat and put it on. "Last time he had a drink, he ended up with a broken shoulder in the ring. 'Course, he was younger then. Just wants to make sure we all keep safe."

"Oh, I thought it was because I'm Diné. Some people think we're all drunks."

"Nah. He don't think that way. He knows being a drunk ain't a race thing." Reese tipped his hat. "Get some rest, rookie. We get to do it all over again tomorrow."

"Will do. You too, Reese."

Johnny let the other man precede him into the parking lot and stood still to take in a deep breath of air. Then he grinned to himself. He was beginning to get used to the way Vern analyzed the entire night's action while they watched the DVD after the event. At first Johnny had thought it was his way of keeping them safe by pointing out where they fucked up, but right from the start, the three of them mostly worked together as if they had some kind of ESP. Rider injuries had been fairly minor since he'd come up from the NBR touring division. He'd thought it might be tough stepping into a regular team as a substitute after Chris Bellow got hurt, but from the start it had been an easy transition, thanks to Vern and Reese.

One thing he had noticed, though, was that during the time Vern was yakking at them, all the riders and tour staff went off to the bars, and it dawned on him maybe all Vern wanted was some way out of the inevitable invites that wasn't too obvious.

It was times like these he wished he still smoked. He would have liked the calming effect of taking in a deep drag of the smoke, watching the burning ember arc through the air when he tossed it away to land in a little shower of sparks, grinding the butt out with his heel....

He'd started up at fourteen to look cool, but quit once he began working on a ranch after school. He needed to be fit to ride. And now there was no way he could run and jump and turn somersaults in the ring if he smoked. It was a dirty habit anyway. He hated littering, and the parking lot was enough of a mess without him adding to it. When he used to smoke, he always picked up the butt after stepping on it and tossed in a litter bin because he was kind of a stickler for keeping Mother Earth clean.

He shoved his hands into his jacket pockets and started walking. He would have time for a shower before Cody made it back from the bars.

The sight of Cody's hand stuck in the rope had terrified him. A rider could be hurt bad hung up like that, especially if he couldn't stay on his feet next to the bull. He'd been too far away to reach Cody and yank the tail of the rope, and yet he'd done it. The bull had then sent him flying when Cody finally came loose and rolled to a stop in the dust. When Johnny saw over a ton of beef poised to crash down on Cody, somehow he grew wings on his heels. That was the only explanation for how he managed to run the bull down and then fly over its head to distract it. When Vern played the video of the evening's program, he saw how it happened. He jumped and the bull had gotten under him somehow. The horns got caught in his baggy shirt and flipped him. He laughed when he thought about how simple it was in retrospect.

Vern was right. It was a good night when the riders and the fighters all went home.

The hot shower felt like heaven, beating down on Johnny's sore shoulders. After one final, bone-crunching stretch, he turned off the water. It was good to feel clean again. He loved his job, but after a good night in the ring, gritty dust got stuck in the sweat, and there was the smell of the bulls that clung to you. He corralled his long, wet hair into a ponytail and put on a clean pair of jeans before wandering through the connecting door into Cody's room.

The room was a giant step up from the ratty motels he'd stayed in when he used to work the touring division, clean and luxurious. Cody could afford it, even if he couldn't. Johnny settled onto the couch in front of the TV and wrapped a blanket around his shoulders while he surfed for the sports channel.

The sound of the lock clicking open shook him from a light doze.

"Anything good on?"

"You smell like beer and bulls." Johnny thought Cody looked almost good enough to lick clean, but didn't say so.

"Hey, it's manly. Bull-rider aftershave. Gotta love it." Cody grinned and tossed his hat onto the desk.

"Yeah, well, take a shower anyway and I'll love it even more."

"Okay, babe. Stay awake for me." Cody dropped a quick kiss on Johnny's forehead and went to the bathroom, dropping each item of clothing at his heels as he walked and stripped.

"Fucking slob," Johnny muttered, but he was too pleasantly drowsy to get up and police the mess.

He woke up again when Cody's arm slipped around him.

"Better?" Cody lifted his other arm so Johnny could sniff his pit.

"Fuck you." Johnny batted his arm down.

"Not tonight. Gotta keep a good seat tomorrow." Cody gave him a grinning leer.

"Same here, so don't get any ideas about tapping my ass."

Cody comfortably tangled their legs together. "You're wearing too many clothes."

"I can fix that." Johnny unzipped, and then lifted his hips to slide his jeans and underwear off.

"Better," Cody approved. He rubbed Johnny's thigh with his free hand, trailing his fingers lightly through the hair. "When I was lying there flat on my back after my ride, I thought I saw a flash of red in the air. Was that you?"

"Yep. Took pity on you. Didn't want to see you get trampled in your moment of glory." Johnny chuckled.

"What did you do? A handstand on the bull's back?"

"I ran in front of him to draw his attention and his horn got caught in my shirt. Flipped me up in the air and I did a somersault. Landed on my feet too." Johnny nodded with pride.

"You're a lunatic. I would have been okay."

Johnny's voice was a bit tight. "You weren't moving fast enough. Bad enough getting stepped on, let alone having a bull fall on you from six feet in the air."

"Thanks, babe." Cody pulled Johnny close and kissed him.

"You taste like booze," Johnny commented when Cody released him.

"It's a fine old tradition for the losers to buy a few for the winner after," Cody said promptly. "Listen, I don't want you taking chances like that for me again."

"I do it for everyone. It's my job."

"But that one was too close."

Johnny shook with laughter. "Every now and then you gotta let the bulls think they got a chance. It's the sporting thing to do."

"As long as they don't get you for real."

Johnny reached over and gently started rubbing Cody's dick.

"Are you trying to change the subject?"

"Am I succeeding?"

Cody leered, then dropped his head onto the back of the couch and groaned with pleasure. "I'm too drunk to make it to the bed and too old to fuck on the couch."

"I'm amazed you can even get it up with all you had to drink," Johnny marveled. "Especially at your age."

"Hey! I'm not old!"

"That's not what you just said. But we could just stay here and mess around."

Then Cody's mouth was on Johnny's, his tongue thrusting between his lips. The first touch of his hand made Johnny's hips jerk as they made out. There was something that made him get all weak about being the object in the laser beam of Cody's attention. When Cody wanted something right now, he planned on getting it, and nothing stood in his way. Johnny parted his legs to give Cody better access while reaching for his partner. Cody's dick felt hard and silky in his hand. He spit in his palm and went back to jacking his boyfriend while they kissed.

He tried to hold off as long as he could, but it was so weirdly erotic and intense to sit huddled under the blanket jerking each other off like teenagers with Cody's tongue down his throat, almost hotter than fucking would have been. Cody ground forcefully against him. His hand was moving quickly, and Johnny exploded without warning, gasping as his hips jerked and Cody's fingers grew slick with his come.

Johnny held his spent cock, lazily watching while Cody used his come as lube to finish himself off. His boyfriend's body was lean and tight, narrow hips lifting off the couch as he shot, his eyes closed and mouth open in a pleasurable grimace. Then his muscles sagged in surrender to fatigue and booze, and his head rolled to the side as he fell instantly asleep, giving Johnny a chance to stare at him without feeling stalkerish about it. With a gentle finger, he traced the scar on the square jaw from the time a bull's horn had gashed Cody.

The contented humming sound he heard turned out to be him. Johnny rested his head on Cody's shoulder and closed his eyes.

WAKING up hot, sticky, and with a kink in his neck, Cody peered around the room blearily, looking for Johnny. He was alone. His head hurt. He pushed the blanket off and staggered to the bathroom to bleed his lizard and take a shower.

When he emerged, Johnny was in the room, eating breakfast and watching TV with the sound off. A takeout bag sat unopened on the table. Cody moaned at the smell of sausage and also with the pain of his hangover. "Coffee."

"And aspirin. By your takeout." Johnny pointed with his biscuit.

"You really are a lifesaver, in the ring and out."

They ate in blessed silence, and by the time he finished Cody was feeling a bit better.

"How can you eat when you have a hangover?"

"I didn't drink that much," Cody explained. "Besides, I need the energy. Got a buckle to win tonight."

"You gonna work out?"

"Of course."

"Keep you company?"

"Meet you at the gym."

It sucked, Cody thought, that they couldn't just rock up to the gym together, but it was safer this way. It had only been three months since Johnny came up to the Top Cut to work, but already Cody felt as if it had been years that they traveled together. Bull riders and the fans were a conservative crowd in general. Somehow he didn't think they'd take kindly to one of the stars of the ring keeping house with another guy like a married couple.

On the other hand, watching Johnny walk into the gym put a different slant on things than going in next to him. It gave Cody a chance to relive the first time he ever laid eyes on him. That little kick of possessiveness always reared up when he saw heads turn at the sight of him. Females for sure, but even some guys you'd never suspect stared at Johnny.

Of course, Johnny stood out. He was the most beautiful man there, tall, slim, and strong, with his dark skin and long, lustrous black hair caught back in a braid. Cheekbones you could cut yourself on, glittering obsidian eyes that sometimes looked so dark you'd think they were all pupil. His nose had been broken often enough to be slightly flat with a bump, but Cody loved every scar on his body. There were no other Navajo in the gym, although there were a few Native American riders on the circuit. Diné, Cody corrected himself. Johnny had at least drilled that into him.

"Hey," Johnny said casually as he put his towel down on a bench.

"Hey."

The two men worked out in silence, switching machines for their reps until droplets of sweat glistened on Johnny's coffee-colored skin. Cody couldn't help staring; he wanted to lick them off.

It would have to wait 'til they got home to the ranch.

When they headed to the showers, Cody purposely took one at the other end of the bank of stalls. No peeking in public.

"See you later, then," Johnny said as he left.

"See you." Cody watched him walk away, unaware of the little smile playing across his own lips. They wouldn't see each other again until that afternoon in the arena. Johnny would be doing whatever Zen group thing Vern decreed for the fighters, and Cody would be sitting in a darkened room, visualizing each ride and how he intended it would go.

Also the moment when they handed him another buckle and he held it up for the crowd's roar of approval.

THE bull lunged forward in the chute and almost succeeded in banging
Cody's forehead on the rail. Only Dub's hand on his vest saved him
from another concussion. If he had one. At thirty-two and having
ridden professionally since he was eighteen, he'd had enough of them
to know when he had one, despite what the medic said.

"Fuck. Thanks, Dub." Cody released the rope and the gateman
pulled it free. He'd have to wrap again.

"Bull's in a cantankerous mood tonight." Dub was perched on the
rails of the chute, with a firm grip on the back of Cody's vest. "You can
take him, though."

"Yeah, I hope." Cody exchanged a quick grin with Dub before
lowering himself onto the bull's back again. Normally Grizzly Rain
was calm in the chute and a demon in the ring, but tonight he seemed to
be breathing fire from the moment he was brought out from the back.
Could make for a good ride, though. A little trouble before the gate
opened might make the judges more generous in their scoring.

Patiently, he began the wrap again with the bull shifting restlessly
beneath him. Cody lifted his leg hastily, before the bull could pin him
to the wall. Riders had gotten their legs smashed that way before, and
this was no time for a dislocated knee. He had a buckle to win, not to
mention the fat check that came with it.

Usually Grizzly Rain kicked high out of the gate and then turned
into your hand if you happened to ride left-handed, which Cody did.
From the moment the gate opened that night, Grizzly Rain made it clear
this would not be one of those usual nights. First the bull stumbled,
almost going to his knees, and then hopped into the air as pertly as a
pony. When the bull landed, he ran a few steps forward and then
suddenly jammed on the brakes. Cody only just managed to keep from
flying over the bull's head. He also managed to avoid slapping the bull
with his free arm, an automatic end to the ride. Grizzly Rain jolted to
the side and kicked three times in quick succession. Then, just to keep
things interesting, he stood up on his hind legs. The movement threw
Cody's weight back, but he managed to bend at the hips and stay with

the bull 'til he was on all fours again. The bull never did find his rhythm, mixing giant leaps with nasty kicks, belly rolls, and sudden spurts of speed.

Cody remembered what his dad had told him: keep your chin tucked, your hand closed, and keep trying your darnedest. It wasn't the prettiest ride, Cody could feel that with every painful jerk of the rope, but he would earn a good score for perseverance if he could just hang on until the buzzer.

It turned out he could.

Eight seconds of hell on the back of a brown devil, and the bull seemed to be set on banging him into the rails, so Cody didn't bother to try bailing. He waited 'til the bull charged close enough to the fence and then yanked the tail end of his rope, breathing a sigh of relief when it released smoothly. He didn't want to do last night over again. Cody grabbed on to the top rail and let the bull keep on going out from under him. Instantly the bullfighters were there, chasing the bull to the exit.

He waited 'til the gate clanged shut before dropping into the ring. He was pumped! He felt as though he could have bitten a piece out of the steel pipe he'd been clinging to. That was a ride!

Cody clenched both fists and pounded his chest, his face contorted in a triumphant snarl as he ran madly around the ring high on a rush of adrenaline. He couldn't even hear his own voice because the stands were going wild, confetti falling from the ceiling, the crowd on their feet.

After he'd worked off a little steam, he looked up to catch his score. 91.5! Not a top record for him, but he would most certainly take it. The only place to go was up! And it wouldn't matter if the next rider made his eight seconds standing up on the bull's back while jumping through flaming hoops, with his score they wouldn't be able to catch up to him on points.

The night was his!

Dub whacked him on the back, his face split by a wide grin. "Knew you had it in you, Codes."

"You are the wind beneath my tail," Cody responded.

"Go fuck yourself, you pervert," Dub responded amiably, as only a close friend and competitor of many years could.

"If only I could."

"At least you'd be fucking someone you really love." Dub draped himself over the fence to wait with Cody. "That new fella in red, the bullfighter. He's pretty quick on his feet."

Cody felt heat flood his face and ducked his head to pull off the helmet. He put on his hat before he said carefully, "Saved my bacon, all right. Heard he's replacing Chris while he's out healing."

"If you ask me, Chris is getting a bit past it."

"I didn't ask you," Cody snapped. Dammit. It was like biting down on a sore tooth. He didn't want to hear about anyone getting past it.

He pulled himself up on the fence to get a better view of his competitors, and also so he didn't have to look at Dub's ugly, smirking face.

"You can stop glaring at those cowboys. No one but me can overtake you now," Dub drawled.

"You can try," Cody said, instantly taking the challenge.

"Oh, don't you even dream I'm going to take it easy on you." Dub's grin revealed sharp cuspids. "You're riding for a fall, and I'm just the one to kick your ass."

"You're up next. Just remember, anything you can do I can do better." Despite the jibes, Cody followed Dub to the chute. It was his turn to help Dub get set for the ride. Even with the trash talk and competitive jousting, all the riders knew it was only you and the bull once you were in the ring. The only person you could really compete with was yourself.

As he bent over the rails, hanging onto Dub's vest, other riders slapped him on the back as they passed behind him, as if he'd already won. Cody had to chuckle inside, knowing their congratulations had to be making Dub shoot steam out of his ears.

"Don't steal my check, now," he said.

"Will if I can," Dub answered quickly.

The remaining riders weren't just going through the motions either. Dub was going to have to give it his all, and knowing the bull he was mounted on, Cody knew he'd make the eight seconds, but unless the bull sprouted a jet engine, Dub wouldn't be able to overtake Cody's score. This was his year. His ride percentage was in the stratosphere. The winner's check from this event would make it possible for him and Johnny to stay on the ranch over the summer break, and he was really looking forward to it.

He stayed put on the bars to watch Dub ride. It was a good one. Just not quite good enough. His bull was having an off night and that never made for a high score. When Dub bailed off the bull, he landed on his feet and immediately turned to point at Cody and gave him the number one sign, but judging by the look in Dub's eyes, Cody had a feeling if bull riding wasn't such a family event he might have gotten a different finger.

It didn't matter how often he won. Every time he felt that heart-stopping happiness, as if he might explode with joy. The feeling was electric, and he wanted to run around the ring shouting and pounding his chest. Instead he headed back to the gate.

Stopping at the gate for a brief interview with Rex Durham, the TV reporter who traveled to the events with the NBR, Cody managed to thank his sponsors, family, fans, and the great country he lived in for the chance to do what he loved.

The crowd was already cheering when Cody ran back out into the ring and knocked knuckles with Dub when he passed him. If Johnny had been closer, he might have done the same with him, but the three bullfighters were congregated near the exit gate, applauding him like everyone else.

Leaping up onto the shark cage, confetti showering down on him, laser lights flashing, bursts of flame shooting up in the air, music blaring, Cody held up the buckle and pressed his lips to it lovingly for the cameras before turning in a full circle to display it to the fans. It was far from his first, but each one was a treasured possession, a symbol of hard work and pain and triumph. Somewhere behind the glare of the lights, he knew Johnny was standing there grinning and just as happy as he was.

AFTER a shower and the usual play-by-play breakdown by Vern, Johnny was at last free to join Cody at the bar. He exchanged manhugs with both Reese and Vern on the way out. He wouldn't see them for three weeks until they met up again in Chicago after the short break to work the touring division. As he stood outside the arena, he watched them get into their respective pickups and drive. Probably going home to their wives.

Vern's usual after-meeting made it impossible for Johnny to go to the bar with Cody, but maybe it was better that way. They hung out together enough as it was. No sense starting a train of thought in anyone's mind that led to questions neither of them wanted to answer.

When he reached the bar, raucous laughter and shouting was audible outside. Johnny didn't like to drink much and sometimes a bunch of drunken cowboys could be a handful, but Cody would want him there to help celebrate his victory.

He pushed the door open and went in, stopping just inside for a moment to locate Cody. And there he was, on top of the mechanical bull, naturally, showing off for a bunch of hooting, hollering riders, his charm gun turned up to full blast. He had a beer mug in one hand and held it so he didn't spill a drop as the bull rocked and dipped. When he caught sight of Johnny, Cody's gaze went seductive and sultry. He licked his lips and then laughed mockingly at himself. Luckily, there were plenty of girl groupies around in case anyone was watching.

Dub stopped by Johnny. "Hey, bullfighter. Name's Dub. You had some nice saves tonight. Appreciate it. Can I get you a beer?"

"Johnny," Johnny replied. "No thanks on the beer; designated driver. Water for me."

"You came in on the Top Cut tour when that other bullfighter Chris Bellow got hooked, right?"

"Yeah, Vern had me working in the touring division for a while. While Chris is healing up, I'm holding his place for him."

"Well, you've been doing a great job. The boys are beginning to take notice too." Dub playfully nudged Johnny in the ribs. "See you around. Don't drink too much of that H2O now. Sober hangovers are the worst. Damn that Cody anyway!"

Johnny watched Dub dart off toward the mechanical bull, and nailed his feet to the floor to stop himself from chasing after him. Cody was getting up on his feet to stand on the saddle while the mechanical bull was still moving. Now he was slopping his beer all over, his face flushed red, laughing as the boys standing too close got splashed from his mug. Dub was there to catch Cody when he lost his balance, and with another cowboy, they raised Cody onto their shoulders to parade him around the bar.

His muscles relaxed when Dub rescued Cody and his ego from a stupid fall. When Johnny noticed the fool stunt he wanted to run over and save Cody from his idiocy, but he'd made himself stay put. It went against his instincts to see a cowboy in trouble with a bull, even a mechanical one, but what would people say if he charged through the crowd and pulled Cody down from his perch? And most likely Cody would have started yelling at him for being stupid. A little fall like that wouldn't have hurt him anyway, drunk as he was, and the bar had mats and straw on the floor.

"Always got to show off," Johnny muttered, but then he had to laugh. After all, that was Cody. That was all bull riders, showing off their *cajones* inside the ring and out. If they didn't have that alpha-male gene thing going on, they wouldn't ride bulls. He went to the bar for his bottle of water and settled down in a corner to wait until Cody was ready to call it a night.

"I'M GETTING too old for this."

"Thirty-two's not old."

"Feels like it tonight."

"Because of drinking, or riding?"

Cody draped his arm over Johnny's shoulder now that they were almost to their room in the hotel, using him as a crutch to limp along. "Both. Mostly the drinking."

"Let's see, you might have gotten a slight concussion Wednesday and the beginning of a hip pointer—"

"It's just a little bruise," Cody interjected.

"Whatever. And you're drunk. Takes a real man to hold his booze," Johnny said. "You gotta practice more if you insist on going out and whooping it up when you win."

"Hey, Dub wants to buy me a drink and then everyone else wants to come and watch me drink it and then I get to stand them all a round in appreciation. Or two or three." Cody hiccupped and laughed. "There go my winnings!"

"It's a fine old tradition. You said so yourself." Johnny unlocked the door to their room and they staggered inside. He walked Cody to the bed and let him fall on it and bounce.

"Some traditions are stupid."

"But we still do them."

Cody lifted his head and leered. "Here's a tradition I like better. Take off your clothes."

"If you take yours off," Johnny bargained.

Cody groaned. "You might have to take them off for me. I'm not sure I remember how to work buttons."

"I'm sure a couple parts of you are still operational."

When he saw Cody was actually watching him, Johnny made a show of stripping off his clothes. Once he was naked, he took the rubber band off his braid and ran his hands through his hair, letting it flow freely down his back.

Cody was rubbing himself through his jeans and watching intently. "You're such a skinny fucker it makes your dick look bigger."

"It *is* bigger," Johnny boasted. "Want to suck it?"

"Want to suck mine?"

"Sounds like a win-win. Show me the goods."

Johnny waited until Cody had unzipped his fly and hauled his junk out. Seeing he was barely able to lift his hips off the bed, Johnny grabbed Cody's waistband and yanked his jeans down to his thighs.

"Ow."

Johnny shut him up by kneeling on the bed and straddling him. Bending down to give him a deep kiss, he felt the roughness of Cody's clothing rubbing against his naked skin, something that always got him hard. He had a thing for being naked while Cody stayed dressed. Cody's mouth tasted pleasantly of beer and mints, and Johnny could have made out with him for a while, but he knew his window of opportunity tonight was a slim one, and he was horny.

He switched around so his dick was dangling over Cody's open mouth while he parted his own lips to suck Cody's cock inside. His hips bucked when Cody's mouth closed around him, engulfing him to the root. The taste of precome on his tongue, the stretch of his jaw to accommodate Cody, and the feel of the hard shaft filling his throat were so good. He'd wanted Cody in his mouth all weekend.

His knees trembled when he felt Cody's hands roam over his backside and up his flanks. Somehow Cody managed to toy with one of his nipples, sending a shock of pleasure to his cock. The head of Cody's cock caught his lips as he let it slip out so he could turn his attention to the tight nuts drawn up under the shaft. He slurped both of them into his mouth and hummed, knowing the vibrations drove Cody wild. He went back to licking the shaft, letting Cody thrust up into his mouth while he feathered his tongue around the entire length. He knew how Cody liked it.

A muffled groan told him Cody was close. His hips were moving faster now and Johnny varied the pressure of his lips, covering his teeth with them, letting Cody fuck his mouth.

Cold air on his dick let him know Cody had let him fall out, but it was okay. He wanted to give Cody as much pleasure as he could. After all, he had just won another buckle. Cody had a firm grip on his buttocks, and Johnny couldn't help but whimper when a thumb brushed his cleft and over his hole. He dipped his head to give long, deep strokes and followed by concentrating on the underside of the ridge. He could feel the surge of come move up Cody's cock, and then he was swallowing, sucking to get every last drop.

He let go only when Cody's cock was limp, and lifted his head, taking in a deep breath. "Okay, my turn." He started shifting around when a snore told him Cody had passed out after getting his.

"Tired old fucker."

He stood up on his knees and started stroking off, looking down at his boyfriend. Cody's shirt was rucked up, exposing an impressive ridged abdomen, and his cock and balls were hanging out of his open jeans. The sight of Johnny's helpless prey inspired an erotic fantasy of having his way with some horny drunk cowboy who was probably straight and would pretend to remember nothing in the morning. Of course, it would have been that much hotter if this particular horny, drunk cowboy had been participating, but the sight of Cody splayed out for him was hot enough. Johnny's hand moved faster over his shaft, and he fought his closing eyelids as he brushed his thumb over the head and squeezed.

The tickle of pleasure started at the base of his spine and buzzed upward to his brain, making his hand move with more urgency. He cupped his balls with the other, his hips flexing. He watched as his come landed on Cody's flat stomach, spurt after spurt until Johnny sagged back onto his heels. For a moment he just savored the afterglow, and then he bent to lick his seed off Cody's skin.

He sank down on the bed, laid his head on Cody's shoulder, and yawned. He felt sticky and warm where they touched. Cody moved in his sleep to rest his hand possessively on Johnny's waist.

"G'night, champion."

CHAPTER 2:
Going Home

"It'll be good to get home." Cody tossed his stuff into his bag as Johnny folded his clothes and packed them neatly. "One day to relax, one day to catch up on my healing, then a full summer of training."

"I love how you have everything scheduled out. One day to relax—full speed ahead! One day to heal, and if that hip isn't better by the end of the day, dammit, it's going to hear something about it from you!" Johnny chuckled.

"Hey, gotta keep paddling. A ranch doesn't run itself."

"There's work to be done," Johnny said, saying the words at the same time as Cody.

Cody had to laugh. "You know me too well, but I can't slow down now. I've got too much to do in life. Got to win the finals this year, get the young stuff trained up and get them contracted out. Ride in a few exhibitions over the break. Meet and greets with sponsors and fans over the summer. I don't have time for injuries. Ain't nothing going to slow me down."

"The ranch is pretty slow. And your parents don't push much—"

"They were pretty high-powered in their day. I get my competitive drive from Mom and the need to get stuff accomplished from Dad. They would hate it if I turned out to be a slacker."

"Nothing to worry about on the slacker front. You just keep on trucking."

"I'll get the desk to call us a taxi."

"We could take the hotel shuttle."

"I got it handled, babe," Cody said, taking charge as usual.

It irked Johnny a little when Cody opted for the more expensive route, but he had to admit it was more comfortable. They both traveled light, but light for a cowboy meant several suitcases full of safety equipment and extra clothing. It was a dirty job for both of them. But it meant Cody was paying. Again.

Of course Cody flirted with security at the airport as he pulled off his boots, put his stuff on the conveyor, and stepped through the metal detector. He made a big deal of pulling off his belt and showing off the buckle to the pretty security girl. Silently, Johnny passed through the detector after him, reflecting that at least this time he didn't have to watch Cody flirt with a male guard. Cody's charisma seemed to hypnotize anyone he met into smiles, and then he would pass it off to Johnny as good PR.

"Fucking airport security. Fucking boots." Cody clamped onto Johnny's shoulder to stamp his boots back on.

"Maybe you should wear sneakers." Johnny snickered, relishing the idea of Cody in sneakers.

"I'd have to bend over to tie them."

"Looks like the terrorists won if all they wanted was for us to get stuck in stupid annoying lines," Johnny said.

"Whatever. I can't wait to get home. I'd rather have some time alone with you before they show up than be on the road." Cody picked up his bag and started to walk to the gate.

"Before who shows up?" Johnny hurried to catch up, slinging the strap of his bag over his shoulder.

"Didn't I tell you? Sam Wells is sending a few boys over for lessons. Some kids from the touring division. He says they need a little help to get them up to Pro Cut standards."

"Shows he appreciates your talent," Johnny said.

"Yours too. You, me, couple of the hands. Maybe between that and contracting my bulls to ride, I might be able to make us a living."

"Could be fun. Could be a disaster." Johnny decided to ignore the crack about earning a living. Cody had a hard time talking about retirement. If he could have his way he never would.

"Don't worry. I won't let 'em near one of my bulls 'til I know if they got any glue on the seat of their pants," Cody assured him. "Those bulls mean too much to me."

Johnny laughed. "Not the bulls. I meant for the riders. What if one of them breaks a leg or something?"

"Never too early to get broke in," Cody said with a grin. "Pain is just a by-product of bull riding, and they better get trained to it young. They got health insurance. Sam wouldn't send them out if they didn't."

"When'll they get there?"

"We'll have the ranch all to ourselves for three days before they show up." Cody stared at Johnny's groin and licked his lips. "The first class will go a week, unless they all drop out. Then if Sam likes our style, he might send another bunch of riders our way. After that we have to work the two-year-old bulls. The more I can get out bucking this year, the better."

"I was thinking of working through the break. Vern asked me if we could keep the team together for the summer tour," Johnny started. "Said as a team we're clicking and—"

"You don't want to do that," Cody said authoritatively. "You guys already work like you've been together for years. You need a break as much as I do. Stay home with me." He wiggled his eyebrows suggestively. "I'll make it worth your while."

"I'll think about it, but it's a great opportunity—"

"Great," Cody said with satisfaction. "It's all settled. We'll work out and get in really good shape for September."

"And then you'll win the top prize," Johnny teased.

"I try to plan ahead," Cody said modestly. "A few of the other guys might have the same idea. I'll do my best but it's not in the bag yet."

"Yet."

Cody held up a finger as the loudspeaker blared. "They're starting to board our flight. It'll be great to get home."

WHENEVER they returned to the ranch, Johnny felt more relaxed at each stage of the journey. He was no star, but Cody was, and the strain of monitoring every expression and impulse to touch was tiring when they were at an NBR event. He enjoyed the flight on the prop plane to the Santa Barbara Airport. It was a small plane, and no one took any notice of the two cowboys sitting with their broad shoulders pressed together. Someone from the ranch would have left Cody's truck for them, and all they had to do was find it in the lot.

Cody would always drive, or possibly speed was a better way of describing it. Maybe it was good they spent so much time on the road, or Cody would have spent it in traffic school instead. After following Route 101 toward Santa Rafael, Cody would turn onto the winding road that led up into the hills where the ranch was. He always drove with one hand, the other hanging out the window, steering past the row of houses where the ranch hands lived with their own families, over the log bridge, and right up to the big house. Even though they lived in the bungalow a couple hundred yards farther on, Cody still thought of the place where his parents lived as home, and stopped there first.

Johnny got out and stretched, feeling stiff more from being confined in the airplane than the ride from the landing field. "It's nice to be back."

"You're allowed call it home."

Cody held out a hand to him but Johnny didn't take it. They'd been together for two years, but he wasn't used to touching Cody in front of anyone yet, let alone his parents. Johnny was still on public behavior.

"I'm still getting used to the idea."

"I bet Mom has supper ready."

"I miss her cooking."

Letting his shoulder nudge Cody's as they walked to the screen door, Johnny felt the final stage of relaxation come over him. Being on the road with Cody was great, but he had to watch himself. Here it didn't matter so much if he made a gesture that might come off a little too feminine. Even Cody's dad didn't seem to care or notice.

Through the front screen door Johnny could see straight down the hallway to the back door, which also stood open to catch the breeze. The smell of chili and cornbread made his stomach grumble and reminded him how hungry he was.

Cody let the screen door slam, and the tall, thin figure of his dad loomed into the dim hallway at the sound. "Val, the kids are home."

"Just in time for supper. Wash up, boys, or no dessert," a female voice called out.

Cody grinned and whispered the words, "Can't wait for dessert," before going to the kitchen to hug his parents.

The kids. It was their calm acceptance that made Johnny feel secretly at home, although he wasn't quite able to say it aloud just yet. It still felt weird. He paused to look into the living room. The furniture was just ordinary ranch stuff, but on a custom stand by the fireplace stood the King trophy saddle Cody's mother had won at her last rodeo over twenty years ago.

"Want to bow down and kiss it?"

"I thought that was just for when you want to make Cody swear on it." Johnny let Valerie Grainger pull him down to plant a kiss on his cheek.

She slipped her hand into the crook of his arm and stood there admiring it with him. "That saddle is better than a Bible for swearing on. It's how I taught Cody to always tell the truth."

"It's a beautiful saddle."

"It really is. Cody used to think it was silly I made a shrine to it, but he's just the same now about his buckle collection." She waved a hand to the wall-mounted display case filled with gleaming metal. "It's good to have you home again, dear." Val patted his arm and released him. "Supper's on the table. We'd better get in there before the boys vacuum it up."

The kitchen was a big room, fitted out for hands who had worked hard to relax in and eat without worrying overmuch about manners or tracking dirt in. Val herself dressed like any ranch worker in jeans and a worn plaid shirt that suited her athletic frame, her long hair caught back in a careless ponytail as she loaded food into serving dishes.

The lamps were lit even though it was still light out, giving a warm, homey glow to the room. At the long table, Davis Grainger was seated at the head, while the two top hands sat on a bench on one side, leaving room for Cody and Johnny on the other.

After washing his hands and sharing a dish towel with Cody, Johnny sat down and dug in. Even though he didn't have much to say, merely sitting and listening to Cody and his parents talk made him feel comfortable. It was nice they didn't try to make him talk.

The two ranch hands were as opposite as two men could be. Although they were both in their fifties, RJ was huge, a silent mountain of a man, especially next to the slim and talkative Travis. Maybe that was why they got along so well like one big family. In fact, Johnny realized, the Graingers didn't think of them as hands. Even Cody acted as if they were his gay uncles. It was rare Johnny had ever seen any exchange of physical affection between them, but there was some sort of psychic glue that seemed to mark them as a couple. At least, it was obvious to him.

The fact that Travis and RJ were a couple never seemed to fluster Val or Davis Grainger, and maybe accounted for the way they took Cody's homosexuality in stride. Having a gay son, it probably didn't make any difference to them if their hands were also a little light in their boots. Johnny wished his family could have been a bit more like that, but it was what it was.

After serving himself, he shoveled it in while he listened to Davis playfully rag his son about the weekend's performance. Talking over the week's ride was the only time he ever saw Davis get worked up like that. Or maybe he was just excited and relieved whenever Cody came home in one piece.

"What the heck were you thinking getting hung up in the short round on the first night? I taught you better'n that, didn't I? Maybe pick a bull you know you can ride to make the points to move forward, but don't risk getting blown out of the competition by getting injured. Every ride doesn't have to be a brand new Mt. Everest."

"Yeah, Dad, you did, but sometimes the bull can't find a rhythm and you're just hanging on for the ride. And besides, I don't want to bore the fans by picking an easy bull over and over."

"Like you're ever going to pick an easy one."

"I like the rush."

"You weren't using a Brazilian rope, were you?"

"No, Dad, I wasn't, but their rope is just as good as ours, just different—in fact, it gives you a little edge when you pull it from the other direction. Something to lean your hand against on the inside."

"You gotta wrap up careful if you don't want the bull to tear your arm off at the shoulder," Davis interrupted him. "You don't want to end up with a bum rotator cuff." He circled his own shoulder and stretched his neck.

"It all worked out. I got loose and scored the buckle," Cody said.

"Yeah, don't kid a kidder. It was Johnny got you loose. I got eyes and I saw it all on the TV."

"It was a good ride," Travis put in. "I thought the judges shortchanged you a might though. That was a 90-point ride at least. They must have been leaving room for some other cowboy to score high. Trying to be fair to the rest of the pack and not make it look like you walk away with every round."

"I didn't win the long round," Cody pointed out. "But that bull sure was a rank one. Up and down, and side to side. He was all over the place. I think he cleared the fence on the first jump."

"He did on the last one when he almost stomped you into dust," Travis said. "But you made up for it on Sunday, that ride was textbook. Break at the hips, keep the free arm up, and your outside leg raking—"

"Keep it loose. That bull on Saturday knew how to mix it up and not fall into a predictable pattern. But you rode better on Sunday," Davis said. "No one else came close to your score."

"Aw, come on, Dad. There were other good riders there that night. Dub gave me a run for my money."

"He was good, not the best."

While Cody and his father got serious analyzing his ride, RJ turned to Johnny, and as always the quiet Aussie accent took him by surprise. "You did a bonza job out there."

"Thanks." It was nice to get that simple commendation. Cody was a flashy rider and as a mere a bullfighter Johnny was used to not having much notice taken of his performance.

Travis immediately horned in on the new conversation. "See you're still all in one piece."

"Yeah, nothing fell off." Johnny made a muscle and grinned.

"Don't break your neck over Cody, Johnny. He can take a hard fall. We love you too, and we don't want to see you hurt," Val said as she passed a dish to him.

"Oh, don't worry about me." Johnny flashed her a grateful smile. "Too much left to do in life."

She smiled back, but her eyes seemed oddly troubled. When Johnny raised his brows, she just shook her head and focused on the shiny new buckle Cody was showing off. Basking in being the center of attention like always.

AFTER dinner, RJ and Travis disappeared promptly, sticking Cody and Johnny with the dishes. Davis rested his hand on Val's back and smiled down at her as they left the kitchen to watch TV in the living room.

Cody actually didn't grumble too much. Maybe he was glad to be home too, even if it meant washing up.

"Mom's cooking is worth the cleanup," he stated, but he looked at Johnny's ass rather than into his eyes.

"Shut up and dry so we can get out of here," Johnny ordered. The casual brushes as Cody passed behind him at the sink were making him feel like the big top at the circus, if the tent in his pants was anything to go by. Sometimes anticipation was a good thing.

And sometimes there could be too much of a good thing.

He was wringing out the dishcloth when he felt something hard pressed against his ass and hot breath in his ear.

"Think we should sit down and catch up some more with the 'rents?"

Johnny reached back to rub the bulge in Cody's jeans. "Yeah, I do. What if your dad managed to swat a fly today? Wouldn't you want to know?"

"Are you saying they lead a boring life?"

"I'm just saying maybe that kind of hot-off-the-presses news probably can't wait 'til morning." Johnny admired how well he controlled his breathing. No hint of panting here.

"I can't wait to fuck you," Cody murmured and licked Johnny's throat. He pushed Johnny against the sink and worked a hand down the front of his jeans to rub his cock.

"Kind of forward for someone I just met." Johnny managed to keep his voice steady.

"You're too pretty to leave alone."

Cody's lips on his throat made Johnny shiver. He closed his eyes and lifted his chin when he felt Cody's teeth nip his neck. They froze when they heard Davis call from the other room.

"Cody, got some paperwork to go over with you. Get out here."

"Sorry, babe. I'll go see what Dad wants," Cody said. "I'll catch up with you at the house." He gave Johnny an apologetic pat on the back and left the room.

Johnny squeezed his erection through his jeans to get it to shut up, and after a while the pressure worked enough so he could hang up the dish towel without having to be nervous about someone coming into the kitchen and getting an eyeful.

He closed the screen door quietly behind him. Even though they were in the hills, with a good view of the mountains to the east, the ranch was pretty close to the ocean, not that they'd ever gone there. Somehow there was always too much to get done when they were home. The cool breeze blowing over the hills from the west was refreshing after the hot and humid day.

When he stepped into their house, Johnny almost gasped for air. He left the door ajar and opened all the windows, hoping the hot, airless rooms would cool down by the time Cody got there. His shirt was soaked with sweat when he went into the bedroom.

After he dropped his damp clothing into the hamper, Johnny started the water running. While it warmed up, he took the rubber band off, letting his hair swing free. He knew how Cody liked seeing his hair loose. He stepped into the shower, enjoying the water running over his skin, cooling him off. He washed quickly and turned off the taps, then pulled the shower curtain aside, startled to find Cody waiting for him, naked, stroking an impressive hard-on.

"Let me dry off."

"You don't need to." Cody leaned forward and lightly touched his tongue to one of the water droplets sliding down Johnny's chest. His hands came up to rest on Johnny's shoulders, lightly massaging the tight muscle leading to his neck.

Johnny leaned his head to the side and closed his eyes to enjoy the sensation of soft kisses and licks as Cody worked his way down his torso. His hair was cool against his back and a trickle of water dripped from it, sliding down his spine and tickling his crack with anticipatory lust.

He gasped as Cody's teeth sank into his nipple, and again as the soothing sweep of hot tongue wiped away the sting. The tongue went farther down, leaving a wet line that cooled instantly as the saliva evaporated. Johnny jutted his hips forward helpfully, hoping to give Cody a hint, but his lover skirted Johnny's cock standing at attention, instead dropping to his knees to lick at the sensitive furrow between abdomen and thigh, and then he felt the scrape of whiskers on his inner thigh before Cody licked at his balls.

His knees melted as Cody moved him, turning him to face the sink, bending him over. Johnny braced his hands against the vanity and leaned his cheek on the cool stone, widening his stance.

Strong hands spread his buttocks and held them, kneading them. His cock bobbed in front, almost smacking his stomach when he felt warm air on his hole. He could feel his muscles clench, and then the softest, wettest kiss on the delicate skin sent a jolt of exquisite pleasure up his spine.

He arched his back, wordlessly begging for more.

"Let me hear you," Cody murmured, his fingers still working the round globes.

It was hard for Johnny. He was more used to needing to be quiet, but he wanted the feeling so bad, he allowed a whimper to escape from his throat.

The reward was instant. Cody's tongue slid within his crease, lingering over his hole. Johnny moaned, losing himself in the sensation. His hips started a tiny flexing motion.

Cody's tongue lapped gently at the puckered skin, gradually growing more insistent as the point probed his hole and then withdrew, darting around like a hummingbird, keeping him on the edge. All the while, the tension and strength drained out of Johnny's muscles 'til he almost felt that only Cody's hands were holding him up. The coolness of the water drying on his body and the pleasingly damp curtain of hair heightened his sensitivity to the fire Cody was igniting within him. He didn't want to come too soon. He tried to fight off the temptation to allow himself to drift closer to the ultimate pleasure, but then he would force the delicious sensation to dissolve and ebb away, dissipating like a soap bubble until the next time Cody sealed his mouth over his hole and sucked. Teasing him. Making him beg. Waiting for him to ask for it.

"Fuck me," he said softly. "Fuck me."

CODY loved feeling the taut hardness of Johnny's body turn to water in his hands, loved the power of knowing that however he positioned him, whatever he told him to do, Johnny was so lost in the moment, he would submit to his desires.

The tight opening that blossomed under his attentions seemed to beg to be taken. Cody was hard as a rock from eating Johnny out; it was his second favorite thing. The first, of course, was fucking. He wanted to be inside that delicious hole.

He lifted his face and ran his hands up and down the beautiful slim body, trembling now, waiting to be fucked. He opened the drawer, knowing Johnny would hear the sound and know what was coming next. The tearing of the packet, sliding the condom over his hard dick, a squeeze of lube over the latex, another squirt on his fingers. Cody stood up and nuzzled the back of Johnny's neck while he worked a couple fingers into the slick channel.

Johnny moaned again, his eyes closed, all nerves and anticipation as he stuck his ass out, the better to ride the fingers entering him. Cody loved that, the arch of his back, the luscious curve of his ass, the passionate eagerness for him. He'd never had a lover so responsive, but maybe it was because he'd never had a lover who meant so much to him before.

From his kissing and licking, Cody could tell Johnny was ready and pulled his fingers out. He positioned himself behind his lover and pushed Johnny down, pinning him in place. In the past he'd had trouble fucking someone against a wall, but it was as if Johnny was made for him; the exact right height, and the curves of their bodies fit perfectly together. He worked his way in to the music of Johnny's gasps and moans, pushing the head of his cock past the tight ring and then out, teasing him just a little, loving the sight of the of the dark-pink flesh stretching to accommodate him.

The heat was incredible closing around his cock. Johnny's muscles seemed to suck him inside, the channel tight enough to enclose and hold him in a firm grip. He slid an arm around Johnny's waist and turned his head with his other hand so they could kiss while he sank his hard cock inside.

Then he slowly pulled out, pushed deeply in, and held for a moment. Cody started to move in slow, romantic strokes, gliding softly in and out while enjoying the feeling of Johnny's body writhing beneath his. He kissed the back of Johnny's neck and shoulders, moving the damp hair out of the way with his nose.

Cody pulled out and penetrated Johnny once more, burying his length as deeply as he could, enjoying the dance of Johnny's inner muscles clenching and squeezing around his cock in all the right ways. He'd never asked Johnny where he'd learned to do it. Maybe it was natural talent. Back when they first started fucking Cody'd had to tell Johnny what he wanted, but Johnny had certainly been eager to learn.

There was something so vulnerable about the delicacy and strength of the man under him, surrendering to him. It brought up feelings of tenderness, but also a possessive drive rose up in him to mark Johnny as his. Cody bit down on the side of Johnny's throat, an alpha male holding his mate in place while the thrust of his hips grew faster.

Then Cody let go, standing upright to grab Johnny's hips, moving from making love to hard male fucking. Driving his cock in as far as he could, making sure Johnny would feel him tomorrow. And Johnny was into it, he liked it hard and fast as much as Cody did, rearing back to meet each drive with his ass raised, his legs spread wide, his hands gripping the edge of the counter.

Cody yanked on Johnny's hair, tilting his head back for a savage kiss. The familiar feeling was pooling at the base of his spine and his legs were getting shaky. Johnny's hand had gone to his cock and he was jacking himself fast. When Cody felt Johnny's body shudder in a deep spasm and heard the groan that accompanied his release, his cock was gripped so hard he could barely move. He slid in and out only a couple of inches, fighting off his own orgasm until Cody saw the slump of Johnny's shoulders.

Cody changed rhythm, moving slower until his dick began to swell in waves of feeling, and shot with a loud groan until he was only grinding his pelvis gently, enjoying the roundness of Johnny's ass against his hip bones. Letting his head rest on Johnny's back Cody closed his eyes, aware of the lift of each breath. Their fingers were twined together as they came down.

"Love you," Johnny murmured.

"I know," Cody said. "Want to do it again?"

"Hell yeah."

"Maybe in the morning." Cody pulled out slowly and got rid of the condom before wiping himself. He lifted his hand to his mouth to taste his own seed. Then he pulled Johnny upright and laughed at the white ropes of come on his chest. "Good thing you took that shower."

Johnny grinned. "Guess I need another one."

"Maybe in the morning," Cody said again. He bent to lick the come off Johnny's smooth skin, tracing the tattoo that decorated

Johnny's ribs with his tongue. At first he'd thought it was lightning, but Johnny had said it was a cloud ladder, something to do with the sky. Cody always thought of it as his own pathway to heaven. When he was finished tracing the zigzag line with his tongue, he kissed Johnny to let him taste himself in his mouth. "Let's get some shut-eye."

Hand in hand, they went into the bedroom where the breeze was stirring the curtains. They didn't bother to switch on the light, just fell onto the mattress twined together.

CHAPTER 3:

Cowboys Don't Walk, They Have Horses for That

AFTER breakfast, RJ and Travis bounced out of the house immediately.

"Hey, what are we? The dish slaves now?" Cody called after them.

Travis stopped and looked back with a smirk. "If you want, we can do the dishes and you can muck out the barn."

"No, that's okay," Cody said hastily.

"You get the morning off for today," Davis said, walking into the kitchen, "seeing as how you're just back, but there's no vacations on a working ranch. There's work to be done."

"Dad, we've *been* working! Riding bulls isn't a stroll in the park," Cody said, and grinned.

"Don't kid me. You're playing, boy. You love riding and you know it. But you got those boys coming for classes and we got to get ready for them, on top of all the other chores." Davis tilted his head from one side to the other, letting out a series of cracks. "Got to take your mother to town to lay in enough provisions to feed all you growing boys. See you later." He went out the back door.

"You can have the morning to ride around and look at the place," Val said. "If you go up the hill, keep an eye on the fence line and take note if anything needs fixing while you're up there. Then you better get the bunkhouse ready for your pupils."

"Pupils." Cody snickered, but the thought of passing on what he knew excited him.

"I'll hang out towels and sheets on the line to air them, but you'll have to open the windows, sweep and dust, make up the beds, and make sure the place is livable," Val continued.

"Can we take a couple horses out for the morning before we get to our chores?"

"Help yourself, but don't take my Cajun Spice," Val said. "And those dishes won't wash themselves, so get to it before you sneak off." This was directed at Cody, who was making a play of trying to slip out the door.

"Yes, ma'am," Cody said meekly, and came back to the table to stack plates.

"Good boy." Val smiled at him and left the room.

"You weren't really trying to skip out on the dishes, were you?" Johnny muttered in an undertone so Val wouldn't overhear.

"Nope, but she'd have been disappointed if I hadn't tried," Cody said, grinning. "She knows me."

After they'd cleaned up, they walked out to the barn corral to saddle up. Cody made a beeline for the showy black gelding he usually rode, but Johnny's favorite was a mouse-colored grulla that nuzzled his hand when he offered a carrot.

They led the horses outside and mounted up.

"Good to be back," Cody murmured, looking around at the place with a sigh. After running a thousand miles an hour, sometimes it was good to just take a breath.

"You like it better here or in the ring?"

He had to ponder a moment. "Both. I like both."

"I love how quiet it is. How alone you can feel out here." Johnny took in a deep breath. Cody couldn't see his eyes behind his sunglasses, but his lips were curved in a smile of contentment.

"Yeah, nature boy. You're one with the land." Cody couldn't help teasing him.

"My people are one with the Great Spirit," Johnny said solemnly. His snicker gave away that he was joking. "You white guys know nothing."

"How." Cody held up his hand, knowing he was the only person who could get away with it.

Ignoring him, Johnny asked, "Ever think about just staying on the ranch?"

"I love it here, but I'd get bored if this was all there was. I also love it in the ring, the crowd, the challenge, the excitement. I like traveling and seeing new places." Cody shrugged. "Couldn't be anything but a cowboy. I like thinking about the men who rode around the country before there were roads and cell towers."

"You just like thinking about them riding around without women."

Cody leered. "Yeah, that too."

"So when you retire from riding—"

"Ouch! I'm not that old yet."

"You're thirty-two. You're going to have to quit sometime. They'll make you. Or your body'll give out."

"If I could die on top of a bull I would," Cody said fiercely. "I never want to quit!"

Johnny made a movement Cody couldn't read, as if he wanted to reach out to touch him but controlled it. "I hear you."

"I love it! I love getting up there and dominating the bull 'til I win. Can you imagine me working in an office? I need the rush!"

"It sucks being an athlete. You have the desire but—"

"Don't say it!" Cody barked.

"Bull riding is the most dangerous sport there is. The injuries pile up and you don't heal the same anymore. Hell, I know it. I might be forced to retire tomorrow if a bull stomped me good," Johnny said quietly.

"I know, babe. We're in the same boat." Cody looked off into the distance, unable to talk about the pain deep inside him when he was forced to think about giving it up. "I know I'll have to one day. I'll break something so bad I can't heal enough to ride again, or I'll just get too old to stay aboard. But I love the danger. I love the risk, hanging right on the edge…."

"You got hurt bad that one time. You almost got hurt really bad this time out."

He laughed. "That's what makes it exciting. Knowing what can happen and *daring* it, you know?"

"When you have to retire you can still be in the sport. Contract bulls, get a job as an expert announcer, get on the board of the NBR. They'd be happy to have you."

"Yeah, I'll be around the sport, not *in* it. Thank God I don't have to retire yet. I have a few good years left in me." Cody leaned over to give Johnny's thigh a hard squeeze. "And at least I have a place to go when no one wants to watch my sorry carcass flop around on top of a bull. Home is where they can't turn you out, even when they turn you out to pasture."

The bitterness in his voice surprised even himself. Cody was a star, but the time was coming soon when he wouldn't be anymore, and he couldn't bear to think of the loss. So far he was gagging on it.

"I'll still want to watch your sorry carcass, no matter what you're doing."

"Even if I have to quit I'll still have this place. I'm glad my parents are okay with us living here."

"It's a great place," Johnny said softly. "I love it here."

Cody stopped his horse alongside Johnny's. The saddle creaked as he leaned closer to give him a kiss. "Even though I like the circuit, this is one thing I do like better about being here. No one for miles around—"

"Except your parents."

"They don't care, even if they saw us."

"I know."

The sun was warm on Cody's back as they walked their horses alongside the east pasture standing high with grass, almost too warm. When they reached the line of firs, it was a relief to pass into the dappled shade. He led the way even higher, heading for the clearing where he could see the mountains to the east, the ocean to the west, and the ranch a few hundred feet below.

Something always drove him to his favorite tree, an ancient live oak where the remnants of the tree house he'd built with his father still perched in the branches. It made him feel as though he belonged here in a way he'd never been able to express to Johnny, but Cody always brought him here when they got back, as if in some way this spot tied together everything that was most important to him. They ground hitched the horses, leaving them to crop the grass.

When they reached the tree, he ran a hand affectionately over the bark and then turned to plant his back against the trunk, pulling Johnny back against him and wrapping his arms around him so they could both look down on the ranch below.

Route 101 leading to Santa Rafael was visible, but they were far enough away that they couldn't hear the sound of the passing traffic. His mother's horses grazed in one fenced pasture while the bulls occupied another on higher ground closer to the hills. He could see RJ, Travis, and the other hands moving around between the barn and the bunkhouse, doing the morning chores. Tomorrow he and Johnny would be down there with them, giving them a hand, but the first morning home belonged to him and Johnny alone.

THE air felt soft and warm as he heaved in a huge sigh of happiness. Johnny gave a light snort as Cody's arms tightened around him.

"Know what I want to do?"

"Yeah, I think I have a clue."

"What kind of clue?" Cody slid a hand down to rub the front of Johnny's crotch through his jeans.

Johnny ground his ass against Cody's groin. "Something's coming up between us."

"Nothing will ever come between us, baby."

"I love how you can see the ocean from here," Johnny said dreamily. "You ever used to go there or did you spend all your time on the ranch doing chores?"

"I used to surf, dude. I ripped."

"I suppose that means you did something epically good."

"Of course." Cody began to chuckle and shook his head. "And also epically bad. I wiped out a lot, but I learned the most important thing about any sport. Keep your balance. I also found the glory holes in the bathroom and played both sides. I was such a slut when I was younger. I think I spent more time in the restroom at the beach than on the waves."

"What were you doing?" Johnny turned his head to stare, trying to imagine a teenage Cody and how everyone who saw him must have wanted him.

"What do you think? Sucking and getting sucked. It was a playground of free dick back then. And I was kinda cute. I had no trouble hooking up."

"You're still…." Johnny paused as he felt Cody tighten his embrace, obviously waiting for a compliment. "Passable."

"Passable? I was hot young teenage ass. Everyone wanted a piece. They still do."

"How did you, uh, meet people?"

"Meet them? I never asked their names. I'd show them mine, they'd show me theirs. You could tell if they were interested, and they were always interested in me. Sometimes I'd sit in a stall waiting for a guy to tap his foot under the partition."

"That was the secret handshake?"

"It's one of the ways, but it's more attitude and looking south longer than most guys do. You get so you recognize the signs."

"Did your parents know what you were doing?"

Soberly, Cody shook his head again. "Not until a cop brought me home one day and told them what he caught me doing. He didn't want to arrest me because I was underage, but he said it was dangerous and he thought they should know."

"That's how you came out to them? Man, that sucks. What did they do?"

A funny look came over Cody's face, almost as though he wanted to cry, but Cody never cried. "Told me to be careful. And then they hugged me."

"Wow." Johnny didn't think he could have loved Cody's parents more than he did already, but this story did it. It helped him understand their immediate acceptance of him in Cody's life. "They didn't ground you?"

Slowly, Cody said, "I think it would have had the opposite effect of what they wanted. Made me feel trapped and I would have acted twice as bad. This way—I knew they cared about me. It made me take a minute to think about my own safety. Probably saved my ass a couple times."

"So they didn't care you were gay?"

Cody laughed. "Nah. They're love children of the sixties. Anything goes, right? What about your parents? How'd you come out to them?"

Hearing a familiar haunting sound, Johnny looked up and spotted an eagle soaring above them on the thermals and pointed at it. "Look at that. Always wished I could fly like that."

"You do. You can," Cody said, giving him one of those intense looks Johnny was at a loss to interpret but almost always led to sex.

It turned out this was one of those times. Cody got them sitting on a smooth fallen log facing each other, their jeans pulled down, hands on each other's cocks while they leaned into each other, kissing.

Johnny watched the green reflection of the trees glimmering in Cody's eyes until he closed them and lifted his head in ecstasy, coming with a gasp instead of a shout. Then it was his turn to drown in the pleasure of Cody's hands on him.

CHAPTER 4:

So, You Wanna Be a Bull Rider

JOHNNY sighed at the sight of the four kids lined up in front of them. They were so young, probably in their early twenties, and yet already three of them showed off that cocky swagger indicative of extreme youth, insecurity, and the ego of a rider. He wasn't much older, but he hoped he hadn't been that stupid at their age, even though he didn't have too many illusions about how smart he'd been. Add in the confusion about being gay and he'd probably acted even more like an idiot.

"Thanks for coming out here to the Circle G," Cody said laconically. "Bunk house is behind you. You can pick a room and stow your gear, or you can stay in town if you prefer. There's a cheap motel and a couple places to eat. If you want to stay here, we'll give you all the grub you can handle. My mom's an excellent cook."

"Do we have to pay extra for it?"

There was always one, Johnny thought. One guy who thought he was trouble with a capital T and set out to prove it every chance he got. The kid was already giving him and Travis the hairy eyeball. Johnny hoped he wasn't an idiot skinhead.

"Nope. Part of the service. The bunkhouse is sitting there empty anyway, and my mom's never happier than when she's feeding up a bunch of hungry cowboys."

Johnny noticed the quiet one seemed to perk up at being called a cowboy instead of a greenhorn.

"That there is the main house," Cody continued, pointing at the white house. "That's where we'll be eating in the kitchen. Mom will ring the triangle when the chow's ready. We'll get started in the corral tomorrow at ten sharp. If you want to go into town, I'll have someone give you a lift. So, what're your names?"

The cocky one took charge, pointing at himself and then going down the line as he said their names. "Bobby Blue Chandler, top rider. Aubrey Matthews, Tommy Benson, Zane Winslow. We want to know what the program is."

The quiet one with close-cropped black hair, Zane, seemed as though he hadn't signed up for a tour guide, Johnny noticed, and the expression on Aubrey's face when Bobby Blue named himself top rider made him figure they'd be breaking up a fight at some point.

RJ was as imperturbable as always with the ever-present toothpick hanging out of his mouth, but Travis rolled his eyes like the clown he was. Luckily he was behind the boys where they couldn't see, but Johnny was standing right beside Cody, so he had to work to keep his thoughts from showing on his face. The hostile, sneaky glances from Bobby Blue were something he was used to, and Travis probably was too. It aggravated him and he had to hand it to Cody for keeping it so businesslike.

"Tomorrow morning after breakfast, we'll meet up at that ring." Cody pointed it out. "We'll see what you got and what you need to learn. Then we'll go to work. Two hours in the morning, four in the afternoon. After supper if you want to ask about anything, well, me and my men will be around."

The sneer on Bobby Blue's face said he'd never heard of anyone but Cody and he didn't care what any of them might have to say to him, especially Travis or Johnny. Actually, Johnny wouldn't have put a cent on the chances of Bobby Blue even listening to Cody. He seemed to think he knew it all already. He wondered how Sam had managed to strong-arm Bobby Blue into coming.

"So it's your *opinion* we got to listen to," Bobby Blue said.

Aubrey punched him in the arm. "Shut up and get your bag, cowgirl."

"Fuck you! I ain't no girl. And I ain't paying if I don't get my money's worth."

"Great, they're off again," Tommy observed.

Quietly, Zane picked up his duffle without commenting and went to the bunkhouse.

Travis was there to open the door for him. "That one's the best bed," he said, pointing at the last room.

"Thanks." Zane went inside.

Tommy disappeared inside before Bobby Blue and Aubrey jammed into the doorway, jostling for position.

Cody was shaking with laughter as the boys vanished. Travis shut the door behind them and dusted off his hands.

"I bet he's ornery enough to squat on his spurs if you told him not to," Johnny said.

"I don't know. He reminds me of me when I was younger." Cody grinned.

"That Bobby Blue is all hat and no cows," Travis said. "Too slow to catch worms."

"Don't spoil his fun yet," Cody said. "He'll be singing a different tune when he's saddle-sore and banged up some."

"He's probably a city boy, studying up on that-there cowboy lingo. *Ain't* we gonna laugh when he lands on his back in the dust," Travis replied. "Well, which one would you slap a saddle on? I'm taking Tommy."

"Bobby Blue's my baby," Cody said. "If he can get over himself and ride, I think he's tough enough."

"My money's on Zane. He may be quiet but he's taking it all in. Plus he got first pick of the bunks while the rest of them were arguing. Good strategy," Johnny said, quelling his irritation at Cody's amusement about Bobby Blue. The kid was probably good-looking enough, but it was overshadowed by his being a prick.

"That leaves Aubrey for my man RJ," Travis said. "Gentlemen, the bets are down. May the best cowboy win."

"Let's go wash up for supper," Cody said. "And keep a straight face in front of them."

"Straight face, eh?"

"You know what I mean."

Johnny followed him into the big house, where they took turns at the kitchen sink. Cody's limp came back as soon as the boys were out of sight, and Johnny found it secretly entertaining that he'd tried to hide it. But a couple days off from riding had already helped, and Johnny intended to try to keep Cody off a bull's back as long as he could. He knew Cody would have to show off for his students at some point, but hopefully it would come later in the week.

Cody's dad set a pitcher of milk on the table while Val went out to ring the triangle. "What do you think of this lot, son?"

"It's going to be a fun week," Cody said. "Here they come. Hope Ma made enough."

"You know your mother, son. She either made too much or way too much, as usual. I don't think anyone is going to starve."

RJ SAT on the top rail of the fence, chewing on his toothpick and looking bored. Travis leaned against the gate, his arms crossed and his hat pulled low over his eyes. Johnny had his elbows hooked onto the rail, casually leaning back against the fence, looking mighty tasty to Cody.

He had lined up the four boys so they were looking into the sun while he had it on his back. It was all strategy, to see if any of them would shift around so they weren't squinting into the light.

"So, you wanna be a bull rider."

"I *am* a bull rider already." Bobby Blue thumped his chest. "Don't know what you got to tell me that I don't already know."

Ignoring the kid's brashness, Cody went on. "First of all, there ain't a bull that can't be rode and there ain't a rider that can't be throwed."

"Whoa! Say it isn't so! I ain't never heard that old shit before!" Bobby Blue crossed his arms and scowled in disgust, darting a mean glance toward Travis.

"Would you shut the fuck up?" Aubrey exclaimed in exasperation.

"Would both of you shut up! If I wanted to watch you two wave your ropes around, I would just shoot myself," Tommy said. "Or maybe you."

Zane watched quietly but didn't say a word.

Bobby Blue opened his mouth to retort but Cody deftly cut him off. "Just so you know. Inevitably even the rankest bull will be topped, just as sure you'll all be on your faces breathing dust at some point, with the wind knocked clean out of you. Happens to the best of us."

"Yeah, I saw you at Toledo when that pussy bull put you down," Bobby Blue said.

Johnny pushed off the fence, both hands curled into fists as he glared at Bobby Blue, who ignored him as if he weren't there.

Calmly, Cody agreed. "Yeah, I eat the dust plenty of times too. It comes with the territory. Even the greats in our sport spent their fair share of time on their backs with no score to show for it. You can count on being thrown, you just don't know when, so safety comes first. This morning we're going to cover equipment. Safety gear, regular bull rope versus Brazilian, what to do if you get hung up dismounting, and how to fall."

With a groan and exaggerated roll of the eyeballs, Bobby Blue crossed his arms over his chest.

Aubrey opened his mouth but Cody stopped him by pushing a hand out. "You'll all get a chance to tell Sam how much I suck later. Right now we have work to do. My boys'll each take one of you for a little one-on-one attention."

Johnny crooked a finger at Zane, who looked surprised but came over to him. "My name's Johnny Arrow." He stuck his hand out.

With a shy smile, Zane shook. "Zane Winslow. But I guess you knew that."

"I guess I did." Johnny smiled at him. "Tell me about yourself. Where you ride, what gear you prefer. Regular rope or Brazilian?"

It seemed Zane wasn't used to talking much; he was a man of few words. Johnny got them sorted and on with the practical before any of the other men. He was down in the dust showing Zane how to roll when Cody called for everyone's attention.

"I want you to watch this. Johnny's going to show you the best way to roll when you hit the dirt, and believe me, you *will* hit the dirt and hard. It's all about using your momentum to not get hurt. You try to put on the brakes and breaking something is just what you'll be doing."

Despite the sneer, Cody could tell Bobby Blue was interested. "You ever broke anything?"

Cody sniggered. "I been riding over twenty years. I've broken plenty of bones. Last time, it was my femur." He chuckled sheepishly. "Shouldn't be funny, but it kinda was how it happened. And it wasn't the bull so much as the fence, but it's a story for another time. If I can keep you boys from breaking something, it'll probably be better than if I teach you to stay on top of the rankest bull."

"Are we going to see an actual real live bull or don't you have any?" Aubrey demanded.

"Oh, I got 'em, but you won't see them until I'm satisfied you're not going to hurt my animals," Cody retorted. "Johnny?"

Johnny went down again to do a small circle roll to his left and came up effortlessly on his feet. "It's all about using the energy to roll rather than trying to stop your forward motion. There's a lot of power in these bulls and when they buck you off, that energy has to go somewhere—"

Cody cut in. "Your first impulse will be to stick out your hand and stop yourself. Don't. You do that, and you'll be riding in a cast."

"What if I can't roll?" Tommy asked.

"Practice 'til you can. It could save a limb or your career. I'm showing you how and you can practice them as part of your workout," Johnny said.

Cody horned in again. "Even if you can't make it look as good as Johnny, don't tense up when you get thrown. Land like a rag doll if you can and tumble over a few yards to get out of the path of the bull. If you stiffen up, you'll get hurt. Okay, boys, it's your turn. Down in the dirt." He pointed.

Three of them obediently went down to start their rolls, but Bobby Blue hung back. "I got a new shirt on."

"Son, bull riding's a dirty sport. From now on save the fancy new duds for Saturday night date night. Now get down there and roll," Cody ordered.

Reluctantly, Bobby Blue went down, and soon he was covered in as much dust and sweat as the other three, which made Cody chuckle a little inside.

Looking at his watch with a sly grin, Cody eventually called a halt to the acrobatics. "Okay, that's enough for now. Time to get cleaned up for lunch."

Huffing for air, Aubrey sulkily got to his feet. "This sucks."

"You can thank me later."

From a standing position, Johnny did a backflip in the air and landed on his feet with a grin.

"Yeah, I'll mail you a postcard some time." Aubrey climbed over the fence and stalked off to the bunkhouse.

Bobby Blue glowered first at Cody and then at Travis and Johnny before he went after Aubrey.

Tommy and Zane stood there sweating and panting, as if they wanted a little space between them and the other two.

"What did Johnny tell you before we started this?" Cody asked.

"Don't stop your forward motion. Let it roll," Zane said.

"Smart man. Holds true for when you're on top of the bull too."

"What does that mean?"

"You'll find out," Cody promised. "Go wash up."

"Uphill all the way," Travis groaned after the two boys were out of earshot.

RJ spat his shredded toothpick into the dust. "Dudes."

"Wow, way harsh," Johnny said. "Even though I kind of agree. Hey, at least that Bobby Blue isn't mad at *you*. If looks could kill…."

"I can feel the death rays flying out from his eyes. Oh yeah, it'll be a fun week." Cody was the only one amongst them who was still clean because he hadn't partaken of the roll fest. He had simply stood over Bobby Blue, making sure he did the exercise over and over until he was coated in dust and grit.

"You just like torturing greenhorns."

"Well, hell yeah!" Cody grinned at Johnny. "There's got to be some upside to getting older and wiser."

AFTER lunch, Cody studied the four boys gathered in the ring again. They looked a bit worse for wear; their hands were clean to the wrists from where they'd washed up before lunch, but they could have used a hose turned on them. However, they didn't need to be clean to learn.

"You may have noticed this ring is set up like a regular one, except it's smaller—"

"And outdoors," Tommy interjected.

"Plenty of outdoor rings where you'll be riding," Cody said. "When you get into the Top Cut, that's when you see the big indoor arenas."

"Can't be that hard to make the Top Cut," Bobby Blue muttered offensively.

"Top Cut's where the elite ride and the rankest bulls are. You have to earn your way there," Cody snapped, his temper flaring for an instant. Then he shook it off. Kid didn't know any better.

He pointed toward where RJ was sitting. "There's the chute. RJ will help you get set and tied up. Travis is the gateman. When you nod, he'll get the gate open pretty damn quick so don't nod 'til you're ready."

"But he's black. There ain't no black cowboys," Bobby Blue said. The other three boys took a step away from him as if to distance themselves from what he'd said.

Travis looked down at his hands and jumped back as if in shock. "Damn! When did that happen? How come you guys didn't tell me!"

RJ grinned around his toothpick and sniggered.

Bobby Blue reddened and tried to backpedal. "Look, I'm sorry. I just never heard of no black cowboys."

"Isom Dart," Travis said crisply. "Google him. Born into slavery. Went west, where he earned his rep as a rider, roper, and bronc buster. I'm just following in his noble footsteps. They used to call him the Black Fox, and he wasn't the only black cowboy on the frontier trail. Also Nat Love, Bose Ikard, Addison Jones, and Bronco Sam, just to name a few."

"Try not to sound more fucking ignorant than you absolutely have to," RJ said to Bobby Blue, his Aussie accent making his rare speech sting just a little more.

"Johnny's the bullfighter. He'll make sure none of you get gored too bad. Unless you piss him off." Cody couldn't help teasing. Newbies were too much fun.

"You mean the clown." It seemed to be Aubrey's turn to take his assholery out for a stroll.

Cody took two quick steps toward Aubrey before he stopped himself, controlling his angry impulse to jack the kid up. He was supposed to be teaching these kids, not beating them into the ground for insulting his partner.

"I mean the bullfighter you might owe your life to one of these days. If you're lucky enough to convince some dumb contractor to let you up on their bull." He controlled his breathing, becoming aware his nails were digging into his palms. Then he laughed it off. "Sure, there's a clown in makeup there for the crowd, but they don't call the bullfighters clowns any more. Try and keep up to date."

"If he's that good, why isn't he riding them?" Aubrey was brave, Cody would give him that, but brave often rode with stupid.

He locked gazes with Johnny and waited for the nod. "RJ, is No Parole handy?"

"Yep." With his usual short answer, RJ jumped down outside the ring and headed for the bullpen.

"Travis?"

"Sure thing, boss."

Together, Cody and Travis helped Johnny into the gear: protective vest, helmet, glove, chaps, and spurs. Cody took the opportunity to impart some information to the students. "The spurs are dull, too blunt to pierce the bull's hide. They're mostly for show. If you spur with your outside leg, you earn extra points. With the vest you'll still get bruised, but it'll keep you from the worst of harm. All that rolling we did earlier, if a bull's coming down on you, the vest can't stand up to it, so don't just lie there like a dummy. Get out of the way, or if you can't, send up a prayer that a bullfighter's there to get between you and the bull. In my opinion, if you go into the ring wearing a cowboy hat instead of a helmet, you're asking for it."

"I don't like the helmet. It cuts down on the visibility," Tommy said.

"It also cuts down on head injuries. Besides, what're you trying to look at? You won't have any time for sightseeing when you're atop a bull."

"But what if he throws me and I have to see where I'm going to hit?"

"Where you look is where you fall. You look at the ground and the next thing you know you'll be down there. You keep your chin tucked and your eyes on the bull's shoulders. That's all you need to be looking at if you want to make eight seconds."

"He doesn't wear one when he's bullfighting." Bobby Blue pointed at Johnny.

"I don't need to—"

"Because when he's fighting he really does need to see everything to save your ass," Cody interrupted. "Good observation. Fighters wear different gear from us because they have to move in different ways. It's your choice of course, but I think any rider who doesn't wear a helmet is an idiot. If not now, then later, when he gets his face removed."

"I'm wearing a helmet to ride," Johnny said.

Bobby Blue scowled at both men. "Sloan Robbins didn't wear one and he's a great rider. One of the best. Or a lot of the Brazilians."

Cody shrugged. "Like I said, your choice when you're away from here. I'm not going to argue about it. Just sayin' is all. While you're on my land, you'll be wearing a helmet, no matter what you choose to do when you're out of here or you'll be watching, not riding."

RJ returned to the ring, leading a buckskin-colored bull into the chute. The minute the bull was shut in, he started getting pissy, ramming his head against the rails.

Johnny climbed the rails with his rope and waited for RJ to get a grip on the back of his vest before he swung a leg over. With Travis helping, he got the rope under the bull and started the wrap.

Cody herded the four greenhorns out of the ring, noticing they all looked a bit paler now that they were up close to a bull. He'd chosen No Parole for a reason. He wasn't his best bull, but he was pretty rank and on the bigger side. And he liked to turn away from the rider's hand. He thought these kids were savvy enough to get it. Johnny wouldn't care; he could ride a bull that turned either way. Even though Cody was having trouble admitting it to himself, he wanted these boys to respect his partner. They could think whatever they wanted about him, but not about Johnny.

No Parole lunged forward in the chute, and only RJ's grip on the vest kept Johnny's head from slamming into the wall. Johnny waited for the bull to settle, then squirmed on the animal's back 'til he was set and gave a quick nod.

As soon as Travis had the gate open wide, it was like a stick of dynamite went off under Johnny. Cody could swear the bull's hooves cleared the gate and the top rail was six feet in the air.

For a moment, his heart stood still. Johnny hadn't been on the back of a bull in the last three months, and no matter how good you were, there was always a chance....

"Come on, boss! Stay up over your rope!" Cody yelled, even though Johnny was having a perfect ride. "Hustle! Hustle it!"

Johnny's timing was right on as he broke at the hips when the bull leaped in the air, his pelvis jutting forward when they jolted to a landing. The pure masculine beauty of his lover always took his breath away, and never more than when Cody watched the lithe swivel of his hips when he was riding and the lean line of his legs hugging the bull's sides.

"Keep it up, boy, keep it going!" Cody took a quick step forward when the bull suddenly stumbled and went down to his knees. Johnny handled it easily as the bull scrambled up, and Cody reminded himself he was no bullfighter. If he raced in there to the rescue, he might make it worse. Johnny could handle himself.

The bull did a belly roll and switched direction to spin into Johnny's hand, and Cody relaxed into the pleasure of watching a good ride. Johnny was as tough as they came, but there was something about the way he moved; he was more flexible than most men, with a fluidity that seemed almost feminine when he shifted to keep his balance. Like water spilling over a dam, beautiful, but with hidden danger and power. Cody swore he couldn't see an inch of air between the bull's back and the seat of Johnny's jeans.

He was startled out of his intense focus when RJ hit the buzzer and Johnny yanked at the rope to release his hand. He stayed on the bull's back for one more second, choosing his moment before allowing himself to be launched into the air, landing casually on his feet and loping for the fence. He pulled himself up on it as the bull charged him. Then he pulled off his helmet and dropped back into the ring to face the bull.

With a confident little smile on his face, he feinted to one side. When the bull committed to charging him, he darted the other way, putting his hand on the bull's forehead, yelling, "Hey, hey, hey!" The bull turned to follow him and Johnny led him into the exit chute. Travis shut the gate behind the bull.

Even Bobby Blue applauded with the others as Johnny sauntered back into the ring, panting a little as he put on his hat.

"Feels funny fighting my own bull after riding. Especially in chaps and boots." Johnny grinned, looking right into Cody's eyes.

Cody smiled back at him before turning to the boys. "I'd say that was a 90-point ride."

"If you can ride like that, why are you only a bullfighter?" It seemed it was Tommy's turn to volunteer an offensive question.

"Man, you can ride!" Zane was staring at Johnny with open admiration.

Cody waited for Johnny to answer, not quite liking the worshipful shine in the boy's eyes.

Ignoring the unflattering way Tommy had worded the question, Johnny answered, "I love bullfighting. First time I did it, I was hooked."

"How'd you get into it?"

"I was riding a bull and not having a very good day. He bucked me off and I got pissed, so I got up and looked him right in the eye. The view's different from down on the ground. It was a question which of us was going to flinch first. Turned out—"

"Turned out Johnny's balls were bigger than the bull's, but we're not here to learn bullfighting. Now listen up, I don't plan to ask each of my men to ride for you to show off their credentials." Cody took control of the ring again. "Just so you know, they all ride better than you, and you'll shut up and listen with respect when they have something to say to you."

As he thought, the authoritative tone got an immediate rise out of Bobby Blue.

"I don't need you all's advice about technique. I learned all that from my daddy. Just give me the secret."

"The secret?"

"Yeah, the secret. How you stay on."

"Superglue," Travis joked. "Spread plenty on your butt before you get up there."

Cody laughed. "So, you want to know the secret, the ultimate keep-it-quiet, lowdown wisdom only a top bull rider knows?"

"Yeah. Give me that and I'll get this done on my own."

"Okay, here it is." Cody leaned closer and lowered his voice to a loud whisper. "Don't fall off."

"Funny. Real funny, dude."

"And true."

"Don't be shitting me, man." Bobby Blue scowled at the four cowboys. Their faces were serious but their eyes were laughing.

"Also, and this is really important, make sure your dick is positioned right in your pants before you get on the bull. Maybe even wear a cup."

"What the fuck? Are you for real?" Aubrey asked.

"For real. It sucks if you're banging around down there when you're pointing the wrong way." Cody nodded seriously. "Truth."

"I'm strong enough to make any bull sorry." Bobby Blue pushed up his sleeve to show off a vein-popping bicep, smirking at the other boys, who were less brawny.

"Doesn't matter how strong you are, the bull is ten times stronger. That bull weighs over a thousand pounds more than you. You're probably, what? A buck forty soaking wet? How you gonna win against a ton of pure muscle? Lifting a few more weights isn't going to do it."

"Well, you could force—"

"Not about force. It's about countering the moves. You do the right thing at the right time and you rob the bull of its power."

"This is all bullshit."

Cody nodded wisely, trying not to smirk. "Yep, there's a whole lotta that in this sport too. Try not to step in too much of it."

Considering the red flush on Bobby Blue's face and the way Aubrey was glaring, Cody thought it was just as well his mom created a diversion at this point. He was in danger of having half of his first class run off on him. Or over him.

"Hey, Cody, hi boys. How's it going?" Val waited for RJ to open the gate for her and walked her pony into the ring.

She sat as straight on the horse's back as if she were a teenager, her silver ponytail streaming down her back from under her hat, surveying the class as if she found them somewhat less than impressive.

"Hey, Mom, right on time. I'm just about ready for you."

Val swung her leg over and slid down from the horse's back. She patted its nose before handing the reins over to Cody. "Don't hurt my pretty baby, now. You boys take it easy on her."

"You're going to make us ride a *horse*?" Aubrey seemed almost as disgusted as Bobby Blue. "A *mare*?"

Jerking his head at Johnny, Bobby Blue said, "He gets to ride a bull and we get a horse?"

"Cajun Spice isn't just any horse," Val scolded him. "She's won more ribbons than you'll ever see in your life." She walked over to Travis and linked her arm through his to stand there and watch.

"You're not sitting on top of one of my bulls until I think you're ready, and none of you have proved it to me yet," Cody said. "You stay on Spice for eight seconds and I'll think about letting you on a bull. How's that?"

"Eight effing seconds on that pony? Let me at it." Bobby Blue pushed forward and went to grab the reins from Cody's hand.

"Just a second. You sure I'm not setting you up here? You don't know anything about this horse or where it's been."

"I don't care where it's been. I been on some rank bulls in my life. I can handle any horse alive."

Bobby Blue grabbed the reins and hoisted himself up and over onto the horse's back. Cajun Spice looked around as if to check he was securely settled, and then she turned into a hurricane, bucking and twisting high in the air.

"Two point three seconds," Cody said, looking from his watch to where Bobby Blue lay stunned on the ground to his mom, smiling gently as if nothing much unexpected had happened. "You all right?"

Bobby Blue sat up and shook his head. "Fine." He got up and brushed the dust off the seat of his pants. "What the hell?"

"Language!" Val rebuked him.

"Sorry, ma'am."

Cody enjoyed the brief exchange intensely. He couldn't make the obnoxious Bobby Blue back down no matter what he said, and here his mom had done it with one word. And also plenty of attitude, but still.

"Cajun Spice is a blue-ribbon bucking bronc. Didn't Cody mention it?"

"No, ma'am. He did not."

"I'm sure it simply slipped his mind. Well, have fun, boys." With a casual wave of her hand, Val sauntered away, heading back to the house.

"How did she ride that horse in here so calm like that?" Aubrey demanded when she was out of earshot.

"It's *her* horse, genius," Tommy said. "It probably likes her."

"It's a fucking horse," Bobby Blue said. "There's no comparison to a bull."

"It's still a smart animal that doesn't want you on its back. Not like riding some tame pussycat," Travis said.

Before it could escalate into an argument about cats vs. bulls, Cody took control. "My mom's probably won more buckles and saddles than all you knuckleheads put together are ever going to score. She's pretty famous in rodeo circles."

"I never heard of no Val Grainger."

"Valerie Kimball. She used to ride under her maiden name." Cody was satisfied when he saw by their nods they at least knew something when they recognized her name. "We were talking about strength earlier. One of the best bull riders I know told me he rides a feisty horse bareback for two hours every day to strengthen his leg grip." He felt the heat slide over his face when he glanced involuntarily over to find Johnny staring at his thighs. "That's advice you can take home with you. Aubrey, you're up next."

Squaring his shoulders, Aubrey approached the chestnut warily and took the reins from Cody.

"THAT Bobby Blue sure has a mouth on him."

Cody glanced over at Johnny's disgusted face and had to laugh. "He reminds me of me when I was younger. Competitive and confident. A go-getter."

"I hope you weren't such an asshole."

"Probably worse, actually."

"Definitely worse," Travis put in. "If Cody'd been my kid, he'd have been up in the hills everyday cutting his own switches and there wouldn't be a tree left on that rise." Travis chuckled as he walked next to the silent RJ.

"Lucky for the trees he got the parents he did." Johnny laughed. "Seriously though, Bobby Blue's got enough attitude for a whole box full of riders. Cajun Spice must need a nice long rest after putting that loudmouth in the dirt eight times."

"I think maybe he's got the moxie to back it up," Cody said. "At least he doesn't give up."

"Because he's too stupid to know when to quit." Travis spat on the ground.

"Imagine if he knew you were black *and* gay," RJ said.

"Oh yeah, I'm not a real cowboy at all," Travis agreed instantly. "Like the bulls care if you're gay or whatever color you are."

"They're equal-opportunity buckers." Johnny snickered as he and Travis knocked knuckles.

"But Bobby Blue stayed on longer each go," Cody pointed out.

"True enough, but it's only the first day. We'll see if he has the balls to make it through the week. See you at supper."

Johnny and Cody split off to go to their bungalow to wash up for lunch. "Please tell me you weren't really such a jerk. And bringing up Sloan Robbins in front of you, for Christ's sake." Johnny let the screen door bang shut behind him as he followed Cody into the house.

"Not everyone's a sweetheart like you, sweetheart," Cody said. He went to the kitchen sink and started the water running while he stripped off his shirt.

"Not a sweetheart," Johnny grumbled. "You're lucky I didn't tell him Sloan's already an idiot and wearing a helmet wasn't going to help him get any smarter."

"Yeah, you are a sweetie, baby." With a sudden laugh, Cody added, "Bobby Blue not only reminds me of me, he reminds me of some of the guys I used to hook up with on the road. He's a good-looking kid. Wouldn't surprise me if he scored a lot of tail on tour."

"You think he's good-looking?" Johnny seemed genuinely surprised.

"Almost as good-looking as me. Not as sexy, though." Cody stuck his head under the faucet and rubbed at his hair.

"And what guys were these you used to hook up with? You went to gay bars on the road?"

"Never went in a gay bar after college. Never had to." Cody's grin turned smug. "Sometimes when I'm in the ready room getting set to ride, it's like a walk down memory lane, looking at some of the guys I used to do."

Looking stunned, Johnny blinked and shook his head a little. "Say what again?"

"It's all supply and demand, baby." Cody kept grinning. Maybe he was feeling a little too pleased with himself, but he couldn't help it.

"You were fucking bull riders?"

"Not that they're gay or anything, but it can be lonely driving from town to town, being away from home for months. Sometimes a guy needs a little fast relief. Hand job, quick blowjob. It wasn't like a romance or anything."

"Some of those guys are married!"

"Now. Not then." Cody shrugged.

"Was Dub one of them?"

Cody sensed a tinge of jealousy and smirked. He didn't want to hurt Johnny, but he liked that hint of possessiveness. "Nope, never was. Never wanted to. He's a friend."

"So if you wanted to do, I don't know, Bobby Blue, you're saying you could get him?"

"Not that I'd want him, but sure. You just fuck with their heads a little, you know, male friendship, remember the Spartans, that kind of crap. Get them thinking with junior, you know?"

"No, I don't know."

"Guys have needs and sometimes a man's gotta do what a man's gotta do. It wasn't ever serious but I got my rocks off and they got theirs."

"Holy fuck, you are blowing my mind. Don't you ever worry one of those guys is going to, I don't know, tell about you?"

"No, because he'd be telling about himself too, wouldn't he?"

"Not if he said he heard it or witnessed it or something like that. You know, if he was pissed because you keep pounding him into the ground on tour."

"I don't know. I never gave it much thought. You going to wash up?" It always made his knees melt when he looked at Johnny without a shirt. Those lean abs!

"Yeah."

CHAPTER 5:

Val Loves Johnny

AFTER lunch, Johnny walked out to the mailbox by the road to put out his letter for pickup. He dawdled on the way back, in no hurry to rejoin the class in the ring.

After the morning teaching session, Johnny was short on patience, both with the boys and Cody. He wasn't sure if it made him madder to find out about Cody's sordid cowboys-with-benefits past, or the fact he thought that mouthy Bobby Blue was good-looking. The boys' ignorance he could overlook; learning the theory behind the riding was important, but nothing would move you forward better than actual experience. It was their disdain for Cajun Spice that got to him. Aside from Zane, they didn't seem to grasp why Cody was making them ride a horse.

You could get hurt falling off a horse, but you could get hurt much worse falling off a bull. Bobby Blue, Aubrey, and Tommy appeared to think once they got on a bull's back, it would all magically come together, but the bulls they'd been riding in the touring division were nothing compared to the higher-ranked bulls.

"That's some rainy-day face, Johnny."

He glanced up and smiled at Val. Her hat was hanging down her back by the lariat, and her hair gleamed silver in the sunlight as she sat on the railing of the log bridge.

"Shouldn't complain. I've got a roof over my head and food in my belly." Even he thought he sounded a bit pathetic.

"It's a sign things aren't all right when you have to remind yourself of your blessings. It's nothing to do with Cody, is it?"

Was it his imagination, or did Val look anxious? He hurried to reassure her. "No, it's those would-be riders. Half of them have too much confidence and the other half not enough."

"They didn't hurt my Spice girl, did they?"

Johnny laughed. "You should have stuck around to watch. She rubbed their noses in it good. You'd have enjoyed it."

"So she didn't hurt them too much. She can always tell who's a tenderfoot. Such a good girl." Val patted the log she was sitting on in invitation. "I'm trying to be delicate here, but if you needed money, I hope you know you could come to us."

Touched, Johnny said, "Well, I wouldn't borrow money if I could help it, but I'm okay. Hell, you already feed me more than I should eat and give me a place to live rent free."

"We love you, Johnny, it's no hardship to keep you around."

Her easy acceptance made him ask a question that had been on his mind. "How did you feel when Cody came out to you? You seem so— casual about it."

"Gay people weren't invented with your generation, you know. Amazing as this may seem, I'd actually heard of it before," Val said dryly. "Travis was one of my best friends on the circuit and he trained me to embrace the gays early. He's my BFF."

"Wow, I didn't realize you'd known him so long."

"We did a lot of driving together, going from one event to the next. I went for bucking broncs and he went for the bulls. Did pretty well too. He made a decent living in a time when it wasn't easy for a black cowboy."

"And you gave him a job when you both retired?"

"Something like that, but he's more a part of the family, and when he hooked up with RJ, well, he became family too." From the amusement in Val's smile, Johnny guessed there was more to the story than he was going to hear right now. "Travis guessed about Cody first. Once he pointed it out it was pretty obvious Cody wasn't too interested in girls, so it wasn't that much of a shock when he did come clean."

"So you didn't punish him when the cops brought him home?"

"That *was* a shock," Val admitted. "I never liked the idea of him hooking up with strangers, especially when he was so young." She sighed. "Listen to me being the protective mother. All kids mess around when they think they're ready, no matter what you say. It's just that once you have kids of your own, you never think they're ready. You want to protect them."

Johnny felt as if someone had hit him in the solar plexus. Her hand over his gave him something to focus on for a moment.

"How did your mother react when you told her?"

"I never told her. She knows there's something 'wrong' with me, but she made it pretty clear she didn't want to know about it."

"Oh dear. What about your father?"

"He's a drunk. They split up a long time ago and I haven't seen him since. My brother's also a drunk. My sister has a kid and lives with my mother. My brother comes by there every now and again. I send them money every month. My mother doesn't earn much cleaning houses." Johnny hoped he'd kept the bitterness out of his voice.

"I'm truly sorry. Life can be so tough sometimes. It's good of you to take care of your mother."

Val's words soothed Johnny even while he appreciated that she didn't probe deeper.

"Have you told Cody about this?"

"No, not really."

"Maybe you should." Val touched his cheek and then stood up. "Well, we'd better get back."

"Why were you out here anyway?" Johnny worried maybe she was stalking him for some reason, as if she could see his rising irritation with Cody.

And maybe she could. Her clear blue eyes seemed as if they could peer into his troubled soul, but if so she wasn't telling.

Val smiled. "I just wanted to check up on Cody and make sure he kept my Cajun Spice safe."

Somehow Johnny wasn't sure that was really it, but when she linked her arm through his, he relaxed enough to walk beside her to the house. When they reached the back door, she reached up to pat his face again and smiled at him.

"There's nothing wrong with you, honey. Nothing at all."

As he watched her go inside, he put his hand to this face, still feeling her touch.

CHAPTER 6:

The Mount

RJ WAS quiet as always while Travis amused himself with stinging little asides that got under the skins of Bobby Blue and Aubrey, probably making them act out worse than ever.

But Johnny was pissed at Cody for an entirely different reason. Cody was downright flirting with Bobby Blue! While Johnny was pretty sure Cody didn't really want to get into the kid's pants, he could see they would have made a cute, all-American-looking couple. Both lean and muscular, with brawny riding arms, both had wavy light-brown hair and chiseled good looks, and both of them had spectacular asses. Not that Johnny was looking at Bobby Blue's ass himself, but he'd caught Cody eyeing it and it was part of what pissed him off.

The one good thing about having these stupid kids around was that Val made them do the dishes. Right after supper, Johnny went directly to the bungalow, where he found himself slamming shut all the drawers and cabinet doors Cody had left open.

He didn't want to break anything, so he went outside onto the back deck to sit and fume by himself. And the worst part was if he confronted Cody about it, the man would just laugh and say he was imagining it all.

He had managed to calm down some when he felt a pair of hands land lightly on his shoulders and slide to the back of his neck to massage muscles tight with anger.

"I shouldn't have made you ride without a warm-up," Cody said.

"You didn't make me," Johnny said shortly.

"You were a good sport about it and I appreciate it. I just hate to see those ignorant jerks diss you." Cody put some muscle into the massage, rubbing Johnny's shoulders now. "You should think about riding again. You could make a lot more than just bullfighting."

Despite himself, Johnny groaned with pleasure. He hadn't realized he was so tense.

"I know you like fighting bulls, but damn, babe, you just look so fucking hot when you ride." Cody leaned down to rub his cheek against Johnny's. "I thought I was going to bust a nut watching you. Maybe you should only do private rides for me from now on. Naked."

"Yeah, right. I was riding a fucking bull."

"And looking hot and beautiful and doing it really fine." Cody sat next to Johnny and grabbed his hand. "What's the matter?"

"Why'd you keep telling me what to do?"

"When?"

"While I was riding. Like I didn't know what the fuck I was doing."

Cody looked surprised. "I was just encouraging you. You know I can't shut up. I'd love it if you changed your mind and started riding again. You were doing great, 90 points at least. If we were in the ring for real, you'd be brushing confetti off your hat."

Johnny bit his lip. Cody was trying to be nice and this was totally the wrong time to bring it up, but he did anyway. "How old you think Bobby Blue is?"

"I told you before, age doesn't make a difference with us. Yeah, I'm older, wiser, better looking—ow!"

It was grim satisfaction to watch as Cody rubbed his arm where he'd punched him. "You're definitely older." Then Johnny regretted the jibe at the fleeting look of pain on his partner's face.

"Gee, I come out here full of compliments and you jump down my throat. What's got you so touchy?"

"Don't keep telling me I'm younger and you get to make all the decisions." Johnny folded his arms and stared into the darkness. "And stop telling me what to do."

"All right. I'm sorry."

Furiously, Johnny tried to hold on to his grudge, but he couldn't in the face of the simple apology, even though he was sure Cody was apologizing for the wrong reasons. "You want to have sex, don't you?"

"Well, I was going to say 'make love, not war,' but I guess I missed my cue."

"Can you ask without putting it in a cliché?"

"Ride a cowboy, save a horse?"

"You gotta trot that moldy old one out every time we have sex?" Johnny laughed. "Geez, sometimes you suck."

"I'd certainly be willing to do that. Or fuck you, baby." Cody leaned closer and leered where Johnny could see him by the light from the window. "You get me so hot."

"You sweet talker. You sure know how to get into a guy's pants." Johnny stood up abruptly. "Okay, let's go do it." He turned his back on Cody and led the way inside.

"The benefits of age and wisdom," Cody said. "One day, my son, you too will have this precious gift."

Johnny undressed silently, watching Cody strip on the other side of the bed, their eyes locked together. Cody used no Chippendale arts when removing his clothes, but his body was so ripped and muscled Johnny was glad he didn't have to pay an entry fee to see it. He stroked himself as they stood face-to-face, examining each other's body.

"I want you so bad," Cody whispered.

"Get on the bed. On your back."

Cody threw himself onto the bed and Johnny walked on his knees on the mattress and bent to lick Cody's cock.

"Oh yeah, babe. You know what I like."

Again a wave of irritation rattled him, but Johnny shook it off. If Cody wanted him to ride him, he wanted it hard. He cupped Cody's nuts and fondled them as he kissed and licked his erection.

"Glove up," Johnny said finally, sitting up and wiping his mouth. He got up on his knees and held out a hand for the lube, twisting to reach behind him to shove lubed fingers up his hole. He didn't bother to stretch much; for some reason he wanted to feel this tomorrow. Most likely Cody wouldn't ask him to ride after today's show anyhow.

When Cody was ready and holding his erection upright, Johnny straddled him and reached behind to grab Cody's cock. The first moment when the head penetrated his hole was painful and he groaned at the burning stretch, but sat down on it slowly until he was fully impaled.

Only then did he lean forward to kiss Cody, enclosing them both behind the curtain of his hair.

JOHNNY'S groan echoed his. The room was cool but the inside of Johnny's body was burning hot like a volcano.

Cody reached to hold Johnny's hips still, watching his partner's face as he struggled to accept his girth. He knew the moment when Johnny relaxed enough to take him, feeling the muscles grab him and pull him in deeper.

Johnny's cock had wilted a little in the entry, so Cody stroked him slowly until it started to rise and point to the ceiling. "Ride me, baby," he whispered.

That afternoon the others had seen an athlete in the prime of life riding a bull, but this was what Cody had seen as he watched Johnny. In his mind, the slim body was naked, impaled on his cock, thighs straining as Johnny ground slowly against him. His hole clenched and worked around him with an insistent rhythm that drove him crazy with lust.

As he watched the slow roll of Johnny's hips and the slide of his skin over taut stomach muscles, Cody ran his hands up and down Johnny's sides. That same fluid, sinuous grace displayed in his ride that afternoon marked his movements now, his body victorious and ascendant as he undulated on Cody's cock.

His hips moved in response to Johnny's movements, rising to meet him. Cody planted his feet on the mattress to give himself some leverage. Usually he would turn Johnny over onto his hands and knees and jackhammer them both home, but he couldn't miss this. Johnny's hips rolled forward, his torso swaying smoothly in a taunting imitation of what he'd done on the bull's back earlier as their slow, deliberate fucking built to a crescendo.

Johnny's head fell back and his mouth gaped open, gasping for air as his hand became a blur on his own cock. Cody was helpless to lend a hand; he felt as though he had to hang on for the ride, as rough as it was, or Johnny might just fly away from him. This was going to be hard and fast. He was thrusting up into Johnny like mad now, both of them slick and glistening with their mingled sweat, until Johnny cried out, the white pearly drops shooting from his cock to land on Cody's skin, hot as lava, burning a brand into his hide.

The feeling of Johnny's hole clamping down on him made him start to shoot, and he just kept on shooting 'til fireworks blinded his eyes. He imagined the roar of the crowd in the stands and the confetti falling around as Johnny finally slumped forward and came to rest against his chest.

His arms were shaking as he circled his partner and held him as they panted for air and their sweat cooled.

"I think that was another 90-point ride," Cody muttered in a hollow voice.

"At least a hundred," Johnny mumbled. "My cheeks are so powerful that when I flex I can shake the world."

Cody chuckled. "The earth certainly moved for me."

"Good," Johnny said. "Hope you're up for the short round."

"I could go another round," Cody protested, but his cock went limp and fell out anyway. "Tomorrow," he added. "You fucked the come out of me."

Johnny slid off Cody to the side and raised his head before immediately dropping it to the pillow and putting his hand to his forehead. He giggled. "I think you fucked me dizzy."

"Bottom takes care of the condom," Cody said.

"You're on your own tonight, cowboy." Johnny closed his eyes as a satisfied smile curved his lips.

On shaky legs, Cody went to the bathroom to clean up. He was too tired for a shower, so he just ran a wet washcloth over his body.

When he came back, he stood looking down at Johnny sleeping for a long time before bending to press a kiss to his forehead. "Am too older and wiser."

CHAPTER 7:

Getting In and Out Quickly

"TODAY I'm going to show you the art of getting in and out of the chute quickly," Cody announced.

The look of disgust on Bobby Blue's face was priceless. "Man, are we *ever* going to get on top of a bull?"

"Absolutely. Why don't you show us all how great you are in the chute right now? Show me that maybe I don't need to go over this basic stuff. RJ?"

"Motherbucker coming right up." RJ's grin did not bode well for Bobby Blue.

"Get your safety gear on," Cody ordered.

"You mean now?"

A quick glance told Cody that Bobby Blue had figured out he was being played somehow, but he was determined to prove he knew more than he actually did know. "No time like the present if you want to ride."

Johnny lounged on the top rail, grinning. Travis covered his mouth, pretending to spit politely but really hiding a smirk. The other three young riders all took a step back as if announcing they weren't lining up behind Bobby Blue for a turn.

"Need help with that gear?" Cody asked.

"No thanks."

As Bobby Blue struggled with his vest, RJ came back leading a handsome animal with a glossy brown hide shading to black at the face and legs to the outer gate. Cody knew all the boys could see was the brown hide moving restlessly behind the bars, but no details. As soon as RJ was set in the chute and Bobby Blue was fully suited up, Cody said, "All right, then, show us some magic."

"I'll show you all right," Bobby Blue muttered. He strode to the chute, swinging his coiled rope in his hand and climbed to the top.

RJ took hold of his vest and Bobby Blue tried to shake him off.

"I got this."

RJ tightened his grip and said, "Boss's rules. Same for everyone."

Gingerly, Bobby Blue lowered himself over the broad brown back, his boots hooked onto the rails, and he let his rope drop to where Travis could catch it underneath and bring it up on the other side of Motherbucker.

Immediately, the animal became angry, shifting in the chute as Bobby Blue drew up the rope tight and wrapped it. Finally Bobby Blue sat down and tried to get a good position. Motherbucker shifted forward and back, kicking a little.

Cody crossed his arms in the ring to watch, a tiny smile tugging at his mouth. "Let's go there, boss! You got less than thirty seconds to get out the gate or you forfeit the ride."

"But this isn't the real thing!"

"It's always the real thing. Hurry it up."

Motherbucker started to kick and knelt down in the front, butt stuck up in the air.

"Ready?"

Bobby Blue shook his head. "Bull's ornery. Let me get him up."

Travis said, "I'll do it." He looped a rope under the horns and yanked.

Motherbucker reared up. All the way up, front legs pawing in the air, forcing Bobby Blue to lean forward and hustle to stay on.

"Running out the clock," Cody called.

"Now!" Bobby Blue yelled back.

Travis got the gate open in one smooth yank.

Motherbucker shot out from under Bobby Blue, dumping him on his ass in the chute and charged wildly around the ring. Cody stood there with his arms folded, not bothering to move out of the way. Johnny jumped down into the ring, put two fingers in his mouth, and whistled. Obediently, Motherbucker trotted straight for him and he put his hand on the animal's neck to guide it from the ring without using a halter.

Cody bent and picked up Bobby Blue's rope from where it fell and coiled it up to return it to him. Bobby Blue was up and slapping the dust from his jeans with the rope, a scowl on his face while the other three boys bent over, laughing their asses off outside the ring.

"What's so funny?"

"You were riding a cow!" Aubrey yelled out. "A fucking cow! And you fell off."

Outraged, Bobby Blue turned to Cody. "What the fuck!"

"Yep, Motherbucker's a cow, but just to make you feel better, she proved she's a real mother."

"You trying to make me look like a fool?"

"You're doing fine with that all on your own, son." Cody clapped him on the shoulder and turned both of them to face the rest of the class. "Okay, comedy's over. Bobby Blue here is the only one out of all of you who stepped up for the challenge, so you can quit laughing at him even though he fell off. One time or another you'll all be on your ass and likely in front of an entire arena, so if you can't stand the heat, it's time to get out of the corral."

The other three stifled their laughter, but Cody could feel the tension in the shoulder under his hand. "So what Bobby Blue did right was volunteering—"

"But he did everything else wrong!" Aubrey shouted.

Cody grabbed the collar of the vest to hold Bobby Blue back as he lunged toward Aubrey. "And we're going to learn from his example. What's the first thing he did wrong?"

"He didn't check for udders?" Tommy cackled at his own wit.

Cody hooked his arm around Bobby Blue's neck and hung on to make sure he didn't go anywhere, like to beat Tommy's ass into the ground. "Very funny. Motherbucker is my prize female. She's the dam of some of my best bulls and she bucks as good as any bull. She doesn't like being ridden any more than they do.

"Remember, once you're in the chute the judges are timing you, so don't forfeit by screwing around. The quicker you get out, usually the better the ride turns out. You won't wear out the bull or yourself. "

"The bull—cow sat down. What was I supposed to do?"

Cody beamed at Bobby Blue. "Good question. By the time a bull hits the show, he knows what comes next as good as you do. That bull is trained to get out and buck and that's what he wants to do. If he goes down in front and you got a good seat, I say go for it anyway. When the gate opens, the bull's gotta come up under you and it's to your advantage. If he bobbles it coming out of the gate, it's an automatic reride for you. If he sits down in back, it's his advantage, so unless you're very good and very experienced, you wait him out. Once he gets up from sitting down, he'll pitch you back on your pockets and you'll be ass over teakettle like Bobby Blue just showed us. If he does that or just lays down in there, you wait for the judge to call a time-out. If he pokes one of your legs through the rails, start praying and get up off him as quick as you can. No score is worth a broken leg."

"Why do we want to get out so quick?" Zane asked.

"Great question! The chute is a dangerous place. A lot of injuries happen in there. Know how you feel all keyed up before a ride? Well, so does the bull. You don't want to use up your energy or the bull's and you don't want to get hurt. But it doesn't mean you should rush out before you're ready. Stay calm. Do a good wrap, make sure you get a good seat. Stay ready and let her rip." Cody released Bobby Blue with a slap on the shoulder. "I like your balls, kid. You did good."

For the first time, Bobby Blue grinned. "Thanks, boss. When do we get to see you ride?"

Cody glanced over to find Johnny frowning at him, and wondered why. "As soon as we work you all through the chute clean." He slapped Bobby Blue on the back one last time and turned to RJ to get a young one brought down.

They'd be riding bulls, even though they were young ones. That would be enough of a challenge for now.

"I DON'T like it when they spin away from my hand," Tommy complained. He groaned as he got up, staring resentfully after the bull that just threw him.

"Well, there's your problem. You got to like it no matter which way they go. It's part of bull riding. You become known as a one-direction rider, you'll be stuck in the lower tier forever."

"There's too much to remember."

"It gets easier as you go along." That time Johnny managed a whole sentence while Cody was taking a swig of water. "The whole drill gets into your muscles and you don't—"

"Johnny's right," Cody took over authoritatively. "Any of you ever played any other sport? Softball? Basketball? It's like that. Your muscle memory gets used to it and takes over. You don't have to think up every move, just go with it when you feel what the bull's doing."

"Do you visualize your rides before you go on?" From having started out mouthy and defiant, Bobby Blue appeared to have made the leap to infatuated admirer with ease, hanging on every word that fell from Cody's lips as if it was money, much to Johnny's annoyance.

"To a point," Johnny said, just to see if Bobby Blue could even hear anyone other than Cody. "You can't plan it all out because—"

"Because you don't know what the bull's going to do. I remember this one bull—" Cody went off into a lengthy story about a bull called Dull Blade on a Chainsaw where the animal had been billed as a one-jump out of the chute, left-turner, and he had turned to the right instead throughout the entire eight seconds, with Cody emerging triumphant of course.

Johnny scowled throughout the story. Somehow Bobby Blue's bull-rider crush was sucking all the hotness out of Cody. Or maybe it was Cody's reaction to it. Or maybe he just never noticed before how much Cody liked to show off. He couldn't see Cody letting him blab on and on telling a bullfighting story. The burst of laughter at the end of the story informed him that Cody had told the funny version. He crossed his arms and scowled as he dug the toe of his boot into the dust.

"RJ! Get Dementia for me."

Johnny realized Cody was looking at him but refused to meet his gaze. There was something about being caught in the laser beam of Cody's attention. It was like walking near a lighthouse; when the beam was on you, it was dazzling. The minute it turned away, you were left cold and dark. Johnny hated that feeling; as if he just didn't exist when Cody was concentrating on something else. Like basking in the adoration of these green youngsters.

"Why's he called Dementia?" Aubrey asked.

"Why d'ya think?" Cody smirked. "Johnny's the only one that can ride that crazy bull."

"Except for you, right?"

Johnny waited to see if Cody would own up.

"That'll have to be a secret between Johnny-boy and me," Cody said.

Despite Cody's attempt at sucking up, Johnny wasn't going to play. His boots made a little puff with each step as he stomped through the dust to get his gear on. The joke would be on Cody if he was too pissed to ride well and let the bull dump him on the ground. Besides, no one was guaranteed to stay on top of Dementia for a full eight seconds except Cody. He didn't know why Cody had chosen him and this bull for his demo when there was no guarantee he could ride Dementia. But then his natural male pride reared its ugly head. No way was he going to fail in front of Bobby Blue and the others. They already thought Cody's shit didn't stink. Johnny suspected Bobby Blue still wasn't convinced that he fought bulls because he preferred it, and Cody kept making him ride bulls as if all his skill at bullfighting wasn't enough.

And calling him Johnny-boy all of a sudden! Did this have anything to do with Bobby Blue? Like everyone had to have double names now to rate? And what got him even more was the subtle undermining Cody was doing whenever he tried to say anything, like whatever a bullfighter had to say didn't count. He knew he was being unreasonable, but so what.

Only when his hand touched the cloud ladder symbol tooled into his chaps was he able to calm himself. No point getting a broken leg because he was pissed. This was man and beast in a contest of wills. Neither would die and both would walk away at the end of it feeling as if he had won. A smile softened Johnny's grim expression. He suspected the bull probably always thought he won; they learned the man on their back would go away after the bell sounded, but they didn't care about the bell. To them it was still a win. They always left the ring free and riderless.

He forgot about Bobby Blue and the other boys; he even forgot about Cody. It was his job to steal the strength from the bull and make it his own, even if only for a short time. He closed his eyes and muttered a short prayer to Brother Coyote to help him trick both gravity and the bull.

He approached the chute from outside the ring, not wanting the sight of Cody winking or smirking to distract him from his hard-won place of calm. As always, Dementia stood placidly within the box. Johnny knew he would have no trouble getting his seat or wrapping the rope. Dementia didn't bother trying to get rid of a rider until he was in the ring. He was a fair bull that way.

When Johnny was set, he gave a quick nod. He felt RJ let go of his vest and caught the swing of the gate in his peripheral vision, but kept his gaze fixed firmly on the bull's shoulders.

And then someone set off a bomb under him. There was no way to be prepared for Dementia, but the talisman of his symbol and the prayer seemed to have woven a magic spell around him. Dementia bucked high but then dipped into one of his swooping, nausea-inducing turns before kicking out with his hind legs. Never one to settle into a predictable pattern, Dementia lurched in the other direction, again swaying almost to his knees before popping his midsection up and stretching out in the air.

When Dementia landed head down, Johnny had to catch himself to avoid a slap or getting pulled off over the bull's head. Then he broke hard at the hips as the bull reared onto his hind legs. He used his free arm to keep his body turning with the bull when they went down like a roller coaster for another dizzying spin. It was almost as if he knew what the bull was going to do next and was always right where his weight needed to be to match the animal's movements. Dimly he heard the bell signifying the end of eight seconds, and tugged at his rope. This time when he dismounted, he missed his footing and rolled in the dust several yards, ending up on his stomach. He recognized the red swirls embossed on Travis's boots as the man pounded by him to distract the bull.

This time he didn't bother to get up to handle the bull himself. He didn't even assess their performance as RJ and Travis eventually harried Dementia to the exit gate, flapping their ropes and shouting while he stood up and followed behind them, lost in his adrenaline high.

Behind him, he could vaguely hear Cody sounding off in triumph, but it didn't matter anymore. He didn't care if the boys were impressed. He needed a moment to enjoy his achievement by himself. He took a drink of water and leaned his forehead against the cool steel of the rail.

"What do you think the bull is doing while you're trying to stay on?" he heard Cody bellow. "He feels what you're doing and thinks about how he can scrape you off. That, gentlemen, was a perfect ride. A rank bull bested by a great rider. Johnny kept making the corrections he needed to. The forward movement gets you leaning back. You gotta stay up over your rope. Keep your chin down. When they go up, you might get forced back, but you have to beat them back over the front end. You don't have to be the best rider in the world if you keep hustling and don't ever give up!"

Johnny's head snapped up. So now he wasn't the best rider in the world, even after he beat Dementia? The strength that had flowed to him from the bull seemed to drain out his boots into the sand as anger boiled within him. He suddenly realized why Cody was so intent on making him ride bulls in front of these boys. Because Cody knew they didn't give a fuck about how good a bullfighter he was. They didn't understand his job or value it any more than Cody did. Only being a good rider had any value in their world, a world he stood outside of. Johnny began to strip off his helmet, chaps, and vest, as if he couldn't lose the outward symbols of being a rider fast enough.

"I can't believe you rode him so well!" Cody called out. "Come on out here and tell these greenhorns what the ride was like."

Without glancing at Cody, Johnny stalked into the center of the ring. "Don't plan it out, just be ready. You gotta stay in the moment and feel what the bull's doing. Don't try to do too much."

"That's it?" Bobby Blue looked superior.

"I think Cody said it all." Johnny had to grind the words out. "He's the bull rider and he's been telling you the same thing six different ways every day. You don't need it to hear it from me. Balance and timing. Everything else is just technical."

He could sense Cody was taken aback by his curtness, but like the showman he was, he snatched the reins back into his own hands to give the kids the big finale.

"Okay, what Johnny's saying is absolutely correct. You got to stay in the moment, feel what the bull is doing. Don't wait for the bull to get something going. You start it yourself, then you can control it."

Zane spoke up, interjecting one of his infrequent requests. "We've seen Johnny ride twice now. We've all learned how to get out of the chute. We're going to be leaving tomorrow. Can we get to see you ride now?"

Cody gave Johnny a private little grin before turning finger guns onto Zane. "You got it. Just remember, anything you can do, I can do better. RJ! Bring out Heartbreak Hotel for me!"

And that went for him too, Johnny thought. He stuck his hair up under his hat and got ready to be a bullfighter again, only half listening to Cody telling the kids about the promising two-year-old, and how he hoped to get some of his bulls contracted out that year to the touring division.

"So you'll probably end up riding one of my bulls at some point," Cody said jovially. "Just remember to show them off for me and make me look good."

Travis brought out Cody's gear and stood by while he suited up in the ring, still flapping his gums the whole time.

Johnny got up on the fence to have a look at the bull. He didn't like how RJ had to tug on the halter to move the animal along. Obviously Heartbreak Hotel was having an off day, plodding into the chute like a tired old cow instead of a contender.

That meant it was going to be up to him to do something about it.

Maybe he was slow, but Johnny was starting to get it. Despite his years of experience riding, Cody still didn't have a clue what a bullfighter did in the ring.

Learning from the best, which was what Vern and Reese were in his opinion, Johnny knew how to read a bull better than any rider. Evidently, today Heartbreak Hotel didn't have its heart into breaking much of anything.

It was important to Cody to show off for these boys. Probably they'd all seen him ride on TV, seeing as they wanted to do the same thing, so they'd witnessed him both winning and falling off. But Johnny was pretty certain Cody preferred they leave the ranch with a vision of him triumphing over the bull, rather than groaning in the dust with an injury. His limp had been getting better since they were home, and Johnny knew how tough Cody was. Stupid tough, like all riders.

It wasn't in Cody to pick an easy bull to ride; his nature was to conquer over all odds. But with Heartbreak flatlining, there was no way Cody could put on his cape and leap over tall bulls in a single bound.

It was up him, Johnny, the only bullfighter in the ring, to make it happen. Most riders were only on a level with the bull after the dismount, and usually they weren't facing them when they took off for the fences with the animal hot on their heels. Most riders faced only four bulls every weekend, whereas each bullfighter took on every bull that stepped into the ring, sometimes over forty depending on circumstances.

A bullfighter didn't run for the fence, except in an emergency. His challenge was to stay in the ring and make things happen, not just save the rider after the dismount. One of the subtler things Johnny had learned how to do was almost imperceptible to anyone not in the know. A lot of riders never tumbled to it. The easy part of the job was getting a bull to leave the ring because it's what it wanted to do anyway.

The art of his job was in knowing how to rev up the bull and make it want to buck. How to suddenly appear in the bull's peripheral vision and vanish at the right moment. How to make a bull turn the way you wanted it to. How to predict where to be for maximum effect and how to not still be there when the bull arrived on the spot with smoke pouring out of its nostrils.

He started teasing the bull when it was still in the chute. Heartbreak Hotel had a new glint of red in its eyes before Cody even nodded the gate open. Deliberately, Johnny stood in the bull's line of sight and silently started moving his hands to get it to pay attention to him instead of what was going on above it.

The bull surged forward in the chute, tossing its head and picking up its feet. Johnny did a little jump in place, one guaranteed to get a bull's attention, and then moved when the bull looked away to make it search to find him.

When Travis opened the gate, Heartbreak Hotel blew out, annoyed with the rider on its back and determined to finish off the man taunting it in the ring. Once again, Johnny darted into the bull's line of sight and vanished.

Enraged with the two irritants and gunning to get rid of the rider, the bull leaped high in the air, practically bending its spine backward. And Johnny was right there on the other side from where the bull expected him, making Heartbreak even more nervous. He let the bull get close and slid away. Finally, a maddened Heartbreak settled into a spin so fast it became a blur. The fringe on Cody's chaps flapped wildly and his free arm was whipping back and forth.

Twisting and breaking on the bull's back, Cody fought to keep his position, sliding too close to the well and pulling himself out. He was even forced to stop spurring, it turned into such a wild ride.

Johnny smiled to himself. He might be invisible to most people, but he knew how to make a bull see him all right.

Of course, Cody handled the storm he'd unloosed. It wasn't just that he was technically a great rider; he made it look exciting. Sometimes other great riders made it look too easy, but Cody could create the illusion of imminent disaster that got people on the edge of their seats, rooting for him. It was that talent that earned him higher scores than a rider who made a bull ride look like plodding along on a placid horse.

The boys were all cheering by the time RJ rang the buzzer and Cody bailed off the back, miraculously landing on his feet for once. He made riding a bull look natural. Johnny could imagine the boys all saying, "I could do that," and then when they failed, "How did he do that?"

Johnny almost felt embarrassed when Cody pumped both fists, his face twisted in a triumphant grimace. "Come *on*, baby! Game *over*!"

For Johnny, the hard part was yet to come. Now that he'd gotten the bull properly riled, Heartbreak Hotel was looking for something to gore, to bash its head hard, to feel flesh and send it flying.

Johnny ran in front of it, putting out a hand to ward the bull off. He stopped and made as if to turn back, waiting for the bull to commit its weight in one direction or the other.

He heard Cody yelling.

"Go left, go the other way, Johnny! Come on, fake him out, ba— boy! Get him spinning!"

It fucking pissed him off. As if Cody needed to instruct him on fighting a bull! He took a couple deep breaths to calm himself, reminding himself to keep his mind on his job. He stared into Heartbreak Hotel's eyes. Usually it was a dance, where first one moved, then the other, a lead-and-follow dance that led to the gate and out.

Sometimes it was a battle of wills. The bull weighed in at over a ton. Johnny was a fraction of that. In purely physical terms, he would always lose. It was a mind game of chicken. He knew how to wait out the bull to see who would flinch first, and he always put money on himself.

The flicker of defeat was so small, Johnny wasn't sure he'd caught it. He moved to his right. The bull turned to follow and he slid left, leaving the ton of muscle charging to where he'd been. The bull stopped, flicking its ears and tossing its head as if asking where Johnny had vanished to. He got within five steps of the bull before he allowed it to spot him again.

Again he heard yelling in the background, but forced himself to ignore whatever pointless instructions Cody was belting out. After all, *he* was the bullfighter and he knew what he was doing.

There was always fear in the ring. He'd seen the damage an angry bull could do. He'd felt it. But this was what he loved, facing the beast and outsmarting it or outrunning it. He knew the exact instant Heartbreak Hotel gave up the ghost. It was as if the bull was saying, "You're too good for me, get me outta here, man."

That's when he started sprinting backward, leading the bull to the gate in a zigzag pattern. The bull was fronting only halfheartedly now, although Johnny knew to the onlookers it looked as if it were still in full attack mode. That was the difference in learning livestock from the ground. You just saw things differently.

Travis had the gate open and Johnny ran into the exit chute, knowing the bull would follow him. He vaulted up onto the fence and over, and it was done. Heartbreak would be given a little time to calm down, RJ would put a halter on it, and the bull would be back to grass very soon.

He heard applause from the ring and Cody's voice saying something about needing confidence to ride. He waited 'til Cody was finished spouting off, glaring at him all the while.

"In a judged sport it's important to have some flare." Cody puffed his chest out. "You gotta have confidence in yourself. You have thirty-two seconds each week to show 'em what you got, *if* you ride in all the rounds."

"It's about timing," Johnny said pointedly.

He walked out of the ring and back to the bungalow. Let them fight their own damn bulls. He'd had enough of teaching for the day.

WHEN Cody walked in, Johnny was on the floor, shirtless and glistening with sweat, doing a seemingly interminable set of sit-ups. While he enjoyed watching the lean torso bunch with muscle and relax, there was a whiff of anger coming off his boyfriend as if he needed to vent his mood other than verbally.

"You don't have to do that. We got three months off for the summer break."

"I don't," Johnny grunted.

"What do you mean, you don't? You'll be riding, yeah—"

"I'm meeting up with Vern and Reese in Chicago next week."

"I thought we decided you were going to stay here for the summer."

"You decided." Johnny's smile was more challenging than happy. "I didn't."

"Look, you know we need to work the young stock, get them trained up. If we're going to make it in stock contracting, I have to get some bulls placed to ride this year. I don't ever want to give up on riding but I have to be prepared for it if the time ever comes."

"You may need to retire, but I'm not ready for that yet." Johnny rolled up onto his feet and went to the bar they'd installed in the doorway and started to do a set of pull-ups. "You're like the Crypt Keeper of bull riders, you're so ancient."

That stung. In an attempt to hide how much it hurt, Cody joked, "Yeah, thirty is usually the hump, but I'm thirty-two and riding better than ever."

"And I'm twenty-three and just starting my run in the Top Cut tour. I've gotta keep my face out there. Vern took a chance on me and I have to prove myself to him and everyone else." Johnny kept doing chin-ups while he talked.

"You could take the summer off and stay here with me. He'd hire you back after the summer. You're great with the stock and I need your help. We don't get to fuck much when we're on the road when I'm—"

"Yeah, I thought this was about you getting your rocks off. You'll say anything to stick it in me, won't you?"

Shocked, Cody took a hasty step toward Johnny and curled his hands into fists, digging his nails into his palms. "I thought you liked having sex with me."

"It's amazing you can still get it up at your age, I'll give you that." Johnny dropped from the bar and glared at Cody. "You're amazing in so many ways."

Cody glared back, his face suffused with color and beads of sweat forming on his forehead. "Listen, I'm trying to make a future for us. I pay for everything when we're on the road because you're just—"

"Just a bullfighter? Besides, I pay my share!"

"You don't even know how much the rooms cost," Cody spat. It suddenly dawned on him. "This is about Bobby Blue, isn't it? You're jealous."

"Don't make me laugh." Johnny crossed his arms contemptuously.

"Because he's a rider and you're only a bullfighter! And he's going to be a good rider! People will know his name. And you're only ever going to be a bullfighter! Part of the scenery." Cody made another mistake and laughed to lighten the mood. "Aw, come on. You gotta stop taking things so serious."

"Yeah, and you're an *old* bull rider. Maybe your claim to fame will be that you trained Bobby Blue, because sure as shooting one day he'll beat your ass. And if he ever found out you're gay—or *did* he find out?"

"You think I—I'm interested in nailing—you're crazy, crazy jealous!"

"I saw you looking at his ass."

"I'm committed, not dead!" Cody shouted. He grabbed Johnny by the shoulders and shook him. "You're being a jerk, dammit!"

"*I'm* a jerk? What the hell are you when you tell me what to do all the fucking time!"

Cody smashed their mouths together, feeling the sharpness of his own teeth dig into his flesh and knowing he'd probably have a fat lip, but somehow he had to prove to Johnny—he drew back when he felt Johnny start to shake and stared at him.

"What's so funny?"

"Why is it when I'm so fucking pissed at you I still can't keep my hands off you anyway?" Johnny was tearing the buttons of Cody's shirt open with one hand and rubbing the front of his jeans with the other. "You are so fucking annoying! But you fill out a pair of jeans nice."

"And you aren't fucking annoying? You're so damned—"

"Shut up!" Johnny snarled. "My turn to fuck you."

"I can't keep my hands off you either." Cody stuck his hand down the front of Johnny's jeans and rubbed the hard bulge he felt. "Is this angry sex or makeup sex?"

"You want to stop and figure it out? Who cares?"

Johnny shoved him down onto the mattress, and Cody decided it really didn't matter as long as they were together. When he had his legs wrapped around Johnny's waist with Johnny's cock buried inside him, his anger melted away as they pounded away at each other.

Afterward, as they lay with their legs tangled together and their arms around each other, Cody said, "I love this."

"What part of this? Fucking? Teaching those noobs?"

"Being able to just be together, hold you. Not having to rush off. Not being so tired after working we fall asleep right away." Cody cursed his own inability to put how he felt into words. It was near impossible for him to say he loved the quiet moments of intimacy after the rush of having sex. Despite all his past experience, he'd never had someone he cared about so much before. Never been in love. "Good thing I've got strong thighs from riding."

Johnny snuggled closer. "It is great."

That made Cody chuckle. Not like Johnny was a great poet either. But they knew what they knew.

"First time I saw you, I said, 'Gotta get me some of that,'" Cody said. Goddammit, he sucked trying to talk about love stuff.

Sleepily but with an edge in his voice, Johnny said, "Like a lost puppy. Put it in a bag and take it home with you. Feed it up so the bones don't stick out."

That made Cody think. He'd never thought of Johnny as a charity case, and it startled him to hear Johnny thought that. "Please stay for the summer. I could really use your help."

"You've got RJ and Travis," Johnny murmured.

"Don't decide 'til after the boys leave, okay?"

Johnny didn't answer and Cody lifted his head to look at him. His boyfriend was asleep. His hair splayed out like his body in total relaxation, lashes fanned across his cheeks, his lips soft. The only sign of trouble was the slight frown that knit his brows together.

ZANE was the only boy Johnny said more than "you're welcome" to when they went down the line to shake the men's hands, Cody noticed.

He wouldn't even look at Bobby Blue when they shook hands, not that it mattered much. Cody knew well enough that he was the only one who had the star power to make much impact on Bobby Blue, but he resented that the kid couldn't see how great Johnny was. The kid never did bother about what any of the hands thought of him, letting their advice slide off him as if he never even heard it. Cody's dad Davis wasn't even on his radar, and Bobby Blue was polite to Val only because under all his bullshit he'd been brought up well. Or maybe it was because she wouldn't stand for any of his crap. When she ordered him to wash the dishes, all he said was, "Yes, ma'am," and did it.

Cody was betting Bobby Blue would be a good rider one day, once his swollen head went down to normal size. That would only happen after he got some actual riding experience under his belt. He was still a blowhard and too impressed with himself, but he worked hard and he had good instincts. In fact, Cody really hadn't paid too much attention to the other three. He'd have to ask Travis and RJ what they thought of the rest of the kids. And maybe that was a problem if he hoped to have a future schooling riders. Something to consider, especially if any of them complained to Sam that he played favorites.

At dinner he sat next to Johnny as usual, but it was as if Johnny had wrapped himself in ice. Cody didn't dare put a hand on him in case it got frozen off. So he did the next best thing he knew how to do—started the conversation.

"I think Bobby Blue came a long way this week," he said.

"Whatever."

It was as though Johnny was miles away, and it scared Cody. He was more used to Johnny looking at him with a glow in his eyes, listening to what he said, waiting to hear how Cody felt about something first.

Luckily Travis was there to take up the slack, taking each kid in turn and dissecting their abilities and lacks with deadly precision. He made everyone at the table laugh except for Johnny and Cody, who was racking his brains to find a way to get Johnny to act regularly again.

Neither of them was much good at talking. Cody would have to fall back on the area where he had the most confidence. Even when Johnny was mad, Cody'd always been able to seduce him so he didn't think too hard. Step one: distract him with sex. Step two: charm him into doing what Cody wanted. It had worked before and it would work this time too.

He couldn't imagine the summer on the ranch without Johnny, and he had to keep him here. They would ride and work out and practice so they were sharp for fall.

Cody never thought of himself as manipulative. The word wasn't even in his vocabulary. He just liked getting his way. And his way was good for him and for Johnny.

CHAPTER 8:
The Dismount

JOHNNY needed a little peace and quiet that morning. It was as if the class of kids had stolen Cody from him. Every time he opened his mouth it felt as though Cody had cut him off, as though he couldn't stand not being the center of attention. It was frustrating. And he still hadn't managed to get Cody to listen to him when he said he was going back to work for the summer. Cody kept talking about how they were going to spend their summer vacation, and he wasn't going to be there.

A couple miles was barely far enough to be out of hearing range of Cody's voice. He had stopped walking and was leaning on one of the fences, looking up into the hills and listening to the distant song of a mockingbird when Davis Grainger found him.

The older man crossed his arms on the top rail next to him and rested his chin on them. It was nice, Johnny thought. They didn't need to talk; he felt close to Cody's dad when they just hung out this way in silence. Davis was a quiet man most of the time, except when arguing with Cody over the technical points of riding. That could really get him going.

Come to think of it, it was odd Val never gave Cody riding advice when she was the one who had won all the buckles in the ring.

"Glad it's over?"

Johnny glanced at Davis. "Yeah. Maybe four was too many to start off with."

"Or maybe it was just those four. That Bobby Blue was a doozy. I started my first class with six." Davis shook with quiet laughter. "I guess Cody never told you I used to train boys to ride. Younger than this group. Kids around twelve, thirteen, just starting out. The only advantage is, even though boys that age still want to strut and look brave, they haven't mastered the bluff yet. It used to get pretty quiet the first time they saw a bull up close."

"You let them ride a bull?" Johnny was amazed.

"No, calves really. Hell, half of them were mounted on heifers and never knew the difference."

"Is that where Cody first learned?"

Davis laughed out loud as if the question jogged some memory for him. "He wasn't like any other kid I ever saw. When he was three I caught him riding a sheep."

Johnny laughed. "A mutton buster, huh? I should have known."

"He never showed any fear, but damn if that confidence of his didn't sometimes trip him up. First time up on a bull was the first time he broke his right arm. After we got back from the doctor, he got right back on again and rode with a cast 'til he healed up. I think the weight of that cast settled him down some. The pain sure didn't."

"I'm not sure he ever is afraid. He likes to take chances."

"Yeah, he lives for the rush. He's still got things to learn."

"How come I never heard you used to ride bulls too?"

"Val's the star in our partnership. She was the best girl rider of her time. Prettiest too. Rode professionally for over fifteen years when sponsors weren't so eager to pin their logos onto a woman. Won so many buckles and saddles we had to buy a bigger house just to have someplace to put them. I was a competent rider, that's about it. Never earned much and rode in the middle of the pack until I cracked a vertebrae in my neck one day." Davis said all this with a quiet pride that told Johnny his ego was intact.

"Was that when you started teaching?"

"One of the board members of the NBR Riders Association took pity on me when I was laid up. When I was on my feet again, he sent a few kids who needed lessons my way. Turned out 'those who can't, teach' was true for me."

"I'll bet you were good at it."

"I turned out to be. Five national champions got their start right here on this ranch, and a whole bunch of other top-flight riders. And then there's Cody. He's one of the best riders I've ever seen. If he keeps his focus this year he might be a first-time national champion with two wins in a row. That'd be something to see." Davis straightened up. "You got time to fix a busted-down fence?"

"You been saving it for me?" Johnny grinned, flattered that Davis valued his craftsmanship that much.

"Yeah, sure have been. I like the way you do it. Patience is a virtue in my book. Give it enough time and you'll have rebuilt the entire run of fence on this place from the ground up for me, piece by piece."

"Sure, where's the break?"

"Ten miles along the southwest stretch. My truck's parked out back behind the equipment barn, loaded up with tools and lumber and such, all ready for you."

"Okay, no problem." Fleetingly, Johnny thought maybe he should let Cody know where he was going, but it was just too nice to pass up a chance to be on his own for a while. Plus Davis had given him something to think about. He couldn't help but see some parallels between them; Val was the star in their relationship, while Cody was the star with him. Davis seemed content to be on the sidelines, but maybe it was just after an injury and a long time getting used to playing second fiddle. Having a broken neck would at least be a good excuse for not being able to do something more, although he suspected Val didn't see it that way. The love between the two of them may not have seethed with excitement, but he could see it steady in their eyes.

He walked back down for the truck and drove the line to search for the bent of broken fence. The rails Davis had loaded into the truck were cut to length, and Johnny figured he could get the work done in a couple hours.

Carefully, he pulled out the broken wood and cleared the splintered fragments from the holes. He dry-fitted the first rail and pulled it out to shave off some excess so it would sit better with the intersecting rail.

There were only two rails left to go when he heard the sound of horse's hooves. Wiping the sweat from his forehead covered by his hat, he stood up and waited for the rider to come into sight.

"There you are," Cody said. He swung down from the horse and wrapped the reins loosely around the sagging top rail.

"Here I am. Your dad asked me to take care of this," Johnny said, moving the reins to a section that was intact.

"It takes so much time to keep up with it. When the ranch is mine, it'll all be replaced with barbed wire," Cody said.

Feeling a little stung by Cody saying "mine" even though he had a perfect right to, Johnny said, "Barbed wire scratches hides. Wood is better."

"Barbed wire keeps the deer out better. We don't need them feeding on our grass." Cody took the hammer from Johnny's hand. "Let me help you so we get done quicker."

"Thanks, I've got it. I was just finishing up." Johnny grabbed for the hammer but Cody swung it away with a joking laugh.

"You're too careful, like dad." Cody picked up a rail and beat on one end to force the other into the slot.

"Hey! Your dad asked me to do it and I'm going to get it done right." Johnny wrestled the hammer out of his hand. "You pounded the shit out of this. It lasts a lot longer if you fit it properly to begin with."

Cody stared at him. "What's got into you? The quicker we finish the quicker we can go back and fool around a little. The kids are gone now. We can swing from the chandeliers if we want."

"Well, go on ahead of me and start swinging. I'm going to fix this first." Johnny couldn't help but grin at Cody's pout. "Besides, I'm driving. I'll beat you back before that old nag can carry your ass down the hill."

"We'll see about that!" Cody swung himself onto the gelding's back and made him rear. "I'll be waiting for you. Naked! And the last one back bottoms!"

Then he kicked the horse's ribs and took off.

Watching the horse bound into the trees, Johnny shook his head. "Everything doesn't have to be a fucking contest. Maybe I like being on the bottom." He went back to work, deliberately removing the rail Cody had ruined and tossing it onto the bed of the truck. When Davis saw it, he'd know exactly what happened, but it could still be salvaged for a shorter section elsewhere. Taking his time, Johnny fitted the last rails to his satisfaction and packed the tools away in the toolbox.

Sliding behind the wheel, even he had to wonder if maybe he'd taken it slower than necessary simply because he needed a little time off from Cody. But that couldn't be it. His cock was twitching thinking about Cody waiting for him naked on the bed. He put the truck into gear and rolled.

WHEN Johnny walked in, the first thing he saw was Cody lying naked on the bed, every line and contour of his body perfect, tight, muscular. Cody was stroking his cock, showing off the length and hardness, a cocky little smile playing over his lips. Damn him. He knew how desirable he looked. Anger flared within Johnny at the confident way Cody assumed he would always get what he wanted, whether he used force or charm. His own urge for sex seemed to wither in the face of what he saw as another surrender in a long line of them.

Being in love was suddenly too much for Johnny. It felt like a heavy chain he was dragging behind him, and he needed to shatter it if he couldn't just slip it off quietly or he'd never get away. Never be free. No matter how much he wanted to rip his clothes off and let Cody do what he wanted with him.

He stopped just inside the door. He couldn't touch Cody now. If he did, he would be lost.

"Like what you see?"

Somehow every word sounded like a taunt, as though Cody was challenging him to defy him.

"Don't you want this big cock? You want it in your mouth, in your ass. You want me to fuck you, don't you? This is what you've been waiting for. You know I'm going to fuck you with this big dick and you're going to like it."

"You're not that big."

Watching Cody's erection wilt, his hand falter, the wounded, unbelieving expression on his face, Johnny took cruel satisfaction in finally striking back, hurting Cody the way he was hurting inside. Being heard.

Apparently Cody couldn't believe he meant it. As Johnny watched, the grin came back and his cock grew hard in his hand again. "Do you want it or not? You want it, I know it. I can see it in your face. Beg me for it."

"Oh yes, sir. I want your mighty cock. Shall I kneel down here and service you? Or would you rather I bow down and put my ass in the air?"

"What the fuck is wrong with you?"

Cody was angry now, but under the anger lurked fear. It hurt Johnny to see it and to know he was the one who put that expression there. The horrible part was that it was so satisfying. No doubt he had Cody's full attention now.

When his answer came out, it stunned him as much as it did Cody.

"I used to be happy to be around you."

SILENTLY, Cody had gotten up off the bed and dressed. He stood clenching his hands helplessly as he watched Johnny pack his bags. "Is this about Bobby Blue? What did I do? Why are you doing this?"

Having broken their trust, Johnny didn't want to have to explain and go over every last detail. He hated talking about feelings, and what good could it do? "Maybe I'm not ready to have you arrange my whole life for me. I've got to make my own plans."

"You can make all the plans you want over the summer. We can discuss them together—and then you can make them." Cody ended lamely, probably realizing it wasn't coming out the best way.

"I've got to earn a living. I have to work."

"Why? You've been earning a steady salary all year up to the break. We eat and sleep for free here, it's on my parents. You've got jeans and boots. What more do you want?"

"What more do I want? I want to go to the finals. I want to fight bulls in Vegas."

"You *are* going! With me!"

"You're not getting it. You're a rider. You're going because you already have the points. You can fall off every bull you ride from now to the finals and you'd still be in the top forty. I'm only a bullfighter. I only get to go if the riders vote for me as the guy they want standing between them and the bull."

"Don't worry about it. I'll campaign for you with the riders. They'll vote for you. They owe me."

If Cody had grinned right then as he usually did, Johnny wasn't sure he'd have been able to control the impulse to wipe it off his face—with his fist. But Cody looked a bit uncertain. While it was satisfying to see him come off his high horse, it hurt. The Cody he knew, *his* Cody, was sure of himself, something he was finding he both hated and loved.

"You better not do that," Johnny said quietly. He jammed his laptop into the padded case. It was one of the few items of value he'd managed to buy for himself.

"I was kidding."

"Yeah? I'm not going to tag along to carry your bags for you. No one even knows we're doing it. You ever tell Dub about us?"

"Not in so many words."

"So suddenly you're going to ask him to vote for me as a favor? If I get to go, I want it to be because the riders want me to be there."

"So you'd rather spend the summer breathing dust with Vern and Reese rather than here with me?"

"I'm the new kid on the team. We've got work to do to make sure it works. It's a trust thing—but I have to be there for it to work. If I don't meet them in Chicago, I'll be sent back down to the touring division and Vern will put someone else in my spot."

"You trust them more than you trust me." Cody folded his arms and glared defiantly.

"I thought you'd understand when I told you I had to go. Most of the riders in the Top Cut have only seen me around for part of this year. They miss Chris Bellow; he's the bullfighter they're used to. They don't know me from a hole in the ground. I've got to show my face, go on the summer tour to show I really care about them. That's what's going to get me their votes, not you leaning on them to do you a favor."

"Summer touring division," Cody scoffed. "Bunch of losers."

"Yeah, some of them may not rack up the points you do, but a lot of the top riders ride all summer, just to keep in practice. Maybe they ride to earn some extra points. And maybe you shouldn't diss them like that. If they found out they might not vote your way."

"When I win the finals, I'll get that big fat bonus check. You'll never have to work again."

"You don't get it, do you? I'm not in this for your money. I love what I do! I'm just starting my career. If I keep working over the summer and through the nationals, I might qualify for the bullfighter finals."

"What, the bullfighters have a competition too?"

"You've been in the sport for over ten years and you haven't heard about it." Cody was always focused on his own goals, but Johnny found this hard to believe.

"Kidding! I was kidding!" Cody bit his lip, maybe realizing his timing sucked. "I didn't mean it."

Johnny didn't bother to acknowledge the lame apology. "I'm a professional bullfighter. With luck and not too many injuries, I'll be doing this for the next twenty—thirty years."

"Yeah, and you pay your own health insurance. And you earn peanuts. Sure, it's a steady paycheck but if you rode bulls instead—"

"A steady paycheck is what I need. I send money to my mother every month to help her out," Johnny said.

Cody seemed stunned and pissed. "I never asked you to account for your money. If you decide to stay the summer, I'll pay you, same as we pay Travis and RJ."

Angrily, Johnny turned away. "Great, that's even more like being a hooker. And then you'll pull strings to get me into the finals. Don't you get it?"

"No, I don't get it. If I pay you, you'll work the same hours as they do and just as hard. I'll see to that."

"And maybe I should move into the bunkhouse too, so no one thinks the boss is fucking me under the table."

"That can be arranged too," Cody said coldly.

"Thanks, but I've already got a job." Johnny closed his bag and picked it up. He paused, struggling with how to say what he was feeling and then that dire sentence came out again. "I used to be happy to be around you."

"We can be happy again. I'll do whatever you want. I'll go to Chicago with you and carry your bags—"

"I was going to hang out here another week but I don't see the point. I'm going tonight. Now." Despite his steady paycheck, Johnny really didn't own much. With his bullfighting gear it added up to a duffle and one small suitcase.

"Isn't there anything I can say to make you change your mind?"

Looking at Cody's face, Johnny wanted to tell him, but another part of him resented that Cody could be that dense he wouldn't know it on his own. "I don't think so."

"You seem like you can't wait to get out of here," Cody snapped. "You're going to regret this."

"I've got to go," Johnny said. He hoisted his bag to his shoulder and picked up the suitcase. "I'm meeting Vern and Reese in Chicago. I don't know. Maybe I'll see you around the tour sometime."

"So that's it? You're leaving?" Cody's voice sounded angry and Johnny didn't want to turn to face him. "Just like that?"

"Yes. I can't stay here."

"You're tearing us apart over nothing!"

"It's not nothing to me."

Johnny walked out and Cody followed him out into the sunlight. Johnny forced himself to look at Cody now, and it killed him to think he was walking away from this beautiful man. He had never thought he'd find love with a guy and never such a handsome one as Cody, and now he figured he had to be going nuts to do this. Cody stood there looking like a little boy whose puppy had just died. Gone was the mischievous look in his eyes and the wide, irrepressible grin. Sunlight glinted off his light-brown hair, almost gilding it against his tanned skin. *A golden boy*, Johnny thought. *He was mine for a while.*

"Please be careful."

Whatever Johnny had expected Cody to say, it wasn't that, especially when his voice almost broke and he sounded... as though he was going to cry. It reminded him of when Cody had told him about being brought home by the police and what his parents had said. And that hardened his resolve. Cody wasn't his parent and that was partly why he was leaving. To get away from that feeling.

"I will."

Johnny hadn't asked for a ride into town. Without a vehicle he would hitch or walk, seeing he was on his own now. Under the anger, guilt started to gnaw on him for walking out without saying goodbye and thanks to Val and Davis, but that just hardened his fury. It was as though his age conspired against him so he was constantly having to thank people for giving him stuff he hadn't yet managed to earn for himself.

Once he reached Route 101, Johnny remembered he also hadn't said goodbye to Travis or RJ either, and sighed. He had no bone to pick with them. When he got where he was going, he'd send them a postcard. Having a great time. Wish you were here. The thought almost made him laugh.

The sound of an engine made him turn to face the road, and he stuck his thumb out. He almost turned around and started walking when he recognized Travis's battered pickup, but resigned himself to the inevitable. He waited 'til the truck pulled onto the shoulder, stirring up a cloud of dust, and peered into the open window, relieved to see it was only RJ at the wheel.

"I'm going to town. Need a lift?"

"Thanks." Johnny threw his bags in the back and got in. After five miles he ventured a sidelong glance at RJ, but the big man didn't say anything. It was one of the more restful things about him. If it had been Travis, he would have talked his ear off and argued with him not to leave until Johnny either caved and went back or shot him to shut him up.

RJ drove directly to the Amtrak station, and Johnny wondered if Cody had told him to come get him. It pissed him off, but it was the last favor Cody could do for him once he was away from here, and he wasn't going to take it out of RJ's hide.

"Thanks for the lift, RJ." They shook hands. "Tell Travis goodbye for me." He didn't dare trust his voice to send a message to Cody's parents.

"Take care of yourself, Johnny."

After he got his bags out of the back, Johnny watched RJ drive away. Somehow it was a fitting end to the whole thing. He knew RJ cared, but appreciated that his habitual reserve had kept him from probing and asking questions. At least Cody would know he'd made it to the station okay and his responsibility was done.

When Johnny went to the window to buy his ticket to Chicago, he felt oddly free. And also completely miserable.

CODY wanted everyone to shut up, just shut the fuck up. He pushed his breakfast around on his plate without tasting it, but he drank his second cup of coffee in a vain attempt to stem the tide of hangover headache he was already drowning in.

Yet his parents, RJ, and Travis all kept chattering as if this were a normal day and there wasn't a huge sucking hole in his chest or an empty place on the bench at his side.

For sure RJ had to know Johnny was gone, as he'd driven Johnny to the train station and left him there, but he was acting as if nothing was wrong. Maybe RJ hadn't told anyone else; that would be like him. Now Cody glared across the table at RJ, who seemed completely unaware of it, as he never looked up from eating.

Travis, on the other hand, could just keep his smug, sympathetic looks to himself! He kept peering over to see how Cody was taking it.

That was the problem with living your life where other people could see it. They could see when things were great as they should be, but also when it was all fucked up too. As long as they realized it was Johnny who had fucked up. Cody was sure they were all blaming him for the break when it was clearly Johnny's fault. Because he'd done nothing but make things easy for Johnny, and even offered him a paying job for the summer.

Now Johnny would have to travel by train and get used to staying in cheap motels again if he wanted to live within his actual salary. Serve him right too.

Still chewing, RJ and Travis rose promptly from the table when they were done and banged out the screen door. Fine! If they wanted to avoid him, just fine. He'd show them by being the most professional bucking-bull trainer and contractor ever, that's all. And top bull rider! He'd ride 'til he was seventy if he wanted to! And if they thought they could get him to talk about it, let them try.

He stared into coffee that had grown cold until his mother called his name.

"RJ told us Johnny left last night, Cody," she said. "From the look of things, I'd say this wasn't your idea."

"No," he grunted. "He just—" Cody shrugged. "Got tired of things, I guess."

"All young colts get a yen to sample their wild oats sometime," Davis said awkwardly.

"I did. He's different. I didn't think he needed to." Cody got up and carried his plate to the dishwasher. "Whatever. I'm over it."

"He's a young man. Maybe he needs to see a bit more of the world before he settles down."

Cody could tell his father was trying to comfort him. "It's okay, Dad. He left. I'm good."

"Right. Well, there's work to be done." Davis got up and went out the screen door with the air of a man who had done his duty and was now relieved to escape a potentially emotional scene.

"Well? You going to tell me what the fuck I ever did to deserve this?" Cody demanded furiously.

His mother had been suspiciously quiet. She looked at him the same way she had when he defiantly shouted the word "fuck" at five because he was mad, not knowing what it meant but knowing it was a bad word and saying it would get a reaction. Then she had laughed in spite of trying to keep a straight face, but she wasn't laughing now. She looked almost sorry for him, but he pushed the thought away. He was not the one who needed her pity.

"You're a grown man, Cody."

It didn't help he could tell she was disappointed. He only hoped it was with Johnny, not with him.

"Look, it's over. I'm moving on. When he does come crawling back, begging me to take him back, I'll just laugh."

"Don't look back," she said in a neutral voice.

"Yeah, never look back. Pillars of salt have crappy sex lives."

Reaching for his hat, he slapped it on and went out to join RJ and Travis in the ring. It turned out to be a bad plan. One after the other, the two-year-old bulls were brought out for him to train, but it seemed as if he was the one who needed schooling. He was riding as if he'd never won a buckle. Hell, he was riding as if he'd never been on top of a horse before, let alone a bull.

Cody gritted his teeth as he pushed himself up off the ground again and dusted his jeans off.

"That's some buckoff streak you got going there, boss," Travis commented. "Five straight falls. Maybe it's time for a break."

"No. Put him back in the chute," Cody ordered grimly.

"I'll get another bull out here for you if you really want, but you're not riding this one again. You're not training him, you're beating your own self up. If you want to run your head into a stone wall, be my guest, but you don't take it out on the stock."

Glaring at Travis, Cody nonetheless felt ashamed of himself. He never overworked his stock, but today he was being a total dick. Shame led to anger, and he felt like taking a swing and smashing Travis's face in even though it wasn't his fault.

If Johnny had been there, he might have swung at him, and then they could have wrestled and maybe had some hot makeup sex. The thought of never making love to Johnny again sent a stab of pain through him, the very pain he was trying to ride out. He turned away from his men so he wouldn't have to face them.

"Never mind. That's enough for today."

"More than enough," RJ snapped.

Cody couldn't blame him for saying it, even though he did. Furiously, he turned on RJ. "Why didn't you tell me he was leaving?"

"Johnny never said anything and it's none of my business."

"You could have stopped him. You took him to the station, you could have made him—"

"Johnny's a grown man, Cody. I'm not his mum. It's not my place to tell him what to do."

"I suppose you think it's not mine either!"

"Cody, there are always two sides. You only ever think about what you want and assume everyone'll go along," Travis horned in.

Cody glared at him. He couldn't remember a time in his life when Travis hadn't been part of it, but that didn't give him the right to criticize. "I'm doing this for him! I don't want to retire, but I'm going to have to eventually. Johnny can't keep going on the circuit without me. He needs someone to take care of him."

"Maybe he doesn't feel that way about it. You ever ask him?"

"He's just a bullfighter, he doesn't make the kind of money he could if he were riding."

"Well, there's your problem," Travis drawled. "You ever ask him his opinion about any of this?"

"We talked," Cody said defensively. "I told him he should ride again. He's good."

"More like you talked and he listened," RJ said.

"You don't know what went on between us!" Cody shouted. "You don't know me!"

Travis promptly opened his mouth to retort, but RJ put a hand on his arm to forestall him. "You're right, we don't know. But something went wrong and neither of you ended up with what you want."

"Shut up! You don't know what I want!"

In a rage, Cody stomped back to the silent bungalow that was so empty with all Johnny's stuff gone. And it was okay. He'd lived alone before and he could get used to it again.

As he searched through one of his messy drawers, Cody's hand hit something flat and hard down at the bottom. He pulled out a framed photo hidden there because he was too embarrassed to have it out on display.

He'd taken it with his phone one day when they were riding. Johnny's long hair was flowing around his shoulders as he rode bare to the waist, his shirt stuffed into a back pocket and flying out behind him like a flag; the bulge at his groin was nicely framed by his chaps. He was leaning back, one hand on the reins, the other on the rump of the horse, his body twisted as he looked back at someone out of frame, laughing. It was probably Travis; he could usually get Johnny going.

The thought of someone else touching the smooth skin of the man he'd thought of as his for the past two years made Cody sad and angry at the same time. He knew someone would take Johnny somewhere. Maybe even tonight. Maybe right now Johnny was smiling up at someone else making love to him.

It was enough to drive a man mad. Cody jumped into the shower and cleaned up.

There was no way he could sit down for supper with his parents and RJ and Travis and act as though nothing was wrong. All of them being careful of his feelings and pussyfooting around, trying not to ask questions, but curious to know what had happened to drive Johnny away.

It was Cody's fault and he knew it was, and he knew they thought he was to blame. The only thing for it was to get drunk or to get laid. Or maybe both. He would go down to his old stomping grounds and get his cock sucked. His big cock.

One of the things he had planned to do this summer was take Johnny down to the beach. After their conversation on the mountain, Cody had wanted to show it to him and show off for him on his surfboard, even though he hadn't ridden one in years.

It was too late to surf today. The sun was going down, but there was still the restroom at the beach. Back in high school, it was one of his favorite cruising spots. Maybe it was time for a walk down that particular memory lane.

In hopes that a quickie would help wipe out other memories, Cody shaved and put on a shirt. He snuck out of his house and put his truck in neutral to coast silently past his parents' house as he used to do when he was underage and went hunting for cock. Not that his parents would or could stop him now. He just wanted to keep it private.

The slight grade downhill to the main road kept him rolling until he had to make the turn, but by then he was out of earshot and popped the clutch. He drove down to the beach, recognizing the salty tang in the air as he got closer.

The red line of the setting sun burned along the horizon when he arrived, making the dark-blue sky look like a fire from reflecting up onto the clouds. Cody made a beeline for the restroom. There were no vehicles parked in the lot, but a man could get there on foot or by bicycle. He couldn't remember ever going into that restroom and not having someone follow him in before too long.

Today was it was different, though. The place was empty. Graffiti, phone numbers, and suggestive comments had been painted over. Even the glory hole had been filled in, although Cody could see signs that someone was working on restoring it to its former glory. After fifteen long, lonely minutes, he wandered outside and found a picnic table and sat on the top with his bootheels hooked over the bench.

The fire on the ocean was gone now and the sky was darker. The moon had risen in the east and was casting a weak, shimmery light on the waves. He put his elbows on his knees, his chin in his hands and sat there waiting.

The bad part about being alone was Johnny kept barging into his brain without being invited. Cody didn't want to think about Johnny. The ingratitude, the misunderstanding, the taking for granted. In fact, he wondered if Johnny had been using him this whole time.

He wanted to believe that when Johnny said he loved him, he'd really meant it. Maybe he had, but changed his mind. People fell out of love, didn't they? Cody's own parents were a bad example, but he'd had friends whose parents divorced. He just never thought it would happen to him. Of course, he never thought he'd fall in love either. In all his sexual exploration and conquest, he'd felt warm appreciation toward a few of his partners, but it wasn't 'til he met Johnny—

"Good evening, sir. May I ask what you're doing here?"

Startled, Cody turned to see a police officer standing a safe distance away, his hands hovering at his sides in case he needed to grab his weapon or his Taser. He'd been so lost in his thoughts he hadn't even heard the cop drive up.

"I'm—I'm just sitting here," Cody answered.

"Truck running okay? You don't need a tow, do you?"

Cody relaxed as he recognized the face. "Jake? Jake Woods? You really did it."

"Did what, sir?" The cop was still suspicious.

"Became a cop. You always said you were going to back in high school. Cody Grainger." Cody held out his hand.

The cop drew nearer and smiled cautiously but didn't take his hand. "Yeah, I recognize you now. May I ask what you're doing here, sir? Cody."

"Just a stroll down memory lane. I was telling a—friend the other day how I used to surf here. I'm home to visit the parents and it was quiet on the ranch, so I drove down here."

"Wait for me right there, Cody, if you would, please." Officer Woods went to the restroom and opened the door and inspected the interior before coming back to stand at a safe distance. "Were you planning on meeting anyone here?'

Cody started to get a little steamed. "Not a soul. Why the third degree?"

"We have a curfew in Santa Rafael now. Beach closes at nine p.m. There was a lot of drugs and illicit sex going on in the restrooms, drunks setting bonfires on the beach, that kind of thing."

"Here?" Cody was so shocked about the curfew he didn't even remember to act shocked about the sex. "Drugs? Back in high school there was a little grass going around, but I never saw any hard drugs down here on the beach."

"Times have changed and we're not getting any younger," Officer Woods said. "Would you mind if I just patted you down? For your safety and mine."

"Knock yourself out." Cody got off the table and held his hands away from his body, all fleeting thoughts of friendliness for Jake Woods gone.

Officer Woods was quick and professional about it. "May I look in your truck?"

"It's not locked," Cody said sourly.

"I would lock it if I were you, sir—Cody, the next time you're down here." Officer Woods did no more than glance inside and lift the mess of receipts Cody had stuffed into the center console to look underneath.

It gave Cody a snide feeling of superiority to note Officer Woods had a bit of a donut going on around the waist. He wondered if Jake had felt jealous when he found out how in shape Cody was when he searched him.

"Happy?"

"You're not feeling like harming yourself, are you, sir?"

That was so crazy Cody couldn't help laughing. "No way, I like myself way too much."

"Part of my job, sir. We get some swimmers out here. Sit staring at the water 'til they make up their minds to go in."

"In these boots? They cost a fortune. I'm not going wading in them."

"Guess you're not suicidal then. I didn't smell any weed or alcohol on you or your truck. Any weapons I need to know about?"

Cody had to suppress a witty reply. "No, I'm unarmed. Just looking at the water."

Officer Woods seemed to relax a bit. "What are you up to these days?"

"Bull riding." Cody grinned expectantly.

"Really? You were always crazy about riding something," Jake said.

It shook him a little that apparently Jake didn't know who he was or anything about the NBR. And he was most definitely not impressed about the bull riding, if he even knew what it was. "Yeah, crazy me."

"Your mom and dad still got that pony ranch? How they doing?"

"They're doing great. Still breeding bucking horses for rodeo."

"Oh yeah. The rodeo. Well, Cody, I'm going to have to ask you to move along. We've got a curfew to enforce on the beach now. Wouldn't want you setting a bad example for our teenagers. Consider this a warning. For the future, I'd stay away from here after dark if you don't want to be inconvenienced again."

"Yeah, that's okay. It's not the same as it was."

"Nothing ever is." Officer Woods stood and waited for Cody to start moving so he could follow. Apparently, despite knowing Cody from high school, he'd learned not to trust anyone. "Take care now."

"Yeah, you too."

Officer Woods stuck out his chest a little. "Thanks. In a dangerous job like mine you can't be too careful. Take good care of the ponies."

Cody got in his truck and pulled out. It was clear Officer Woods wasn't going to trust that he would leave without witnessing it. Somehow running into his old schoolmate gave him the feeling of mild annoyance he got when he ran into an old one-night trick somewhere.

He drove into Santa Rafael to one of the dive bars for a beer or two. He was so far from thinking about finding some action that when it found him, it took him completely by surprise.

He went to the restroom and stood at a urinal, barely noticing when a man came and stood next to him. He did notice, however, when the man put a hand on his dick. He was shaking off when the man reached out to grab him. Shocked speechless, Cody darted a glance at the man's face, but his admirer was staring at the wall straight ahead, as if nothing out of the ordinary was happening. The only movement was one hand wrapped around his own dick and one hand sliding up and down Cody's pole.

Cody didn't usually go for doing it out in the open like this, but the novel approach surprised him so much he was instantly hard. Five minutes later he was spent and sweating but put away, zipped up, and walking out of the bar. He didn't even stick around to see if the guy shot. It was oddly hot but left him feeling empty. He'd get over that, though.

Besides, Johnny only had himself to blame if Cody had to get his needs met somewhere else.

CHAPTER 9:
Riding with Vern

BEING in Chicago in the ring without knowing Cody was back behind the scenes somewhere made for a surreal experience. It wasn't as though they could talk during an event, seeing as they played opposite sides of the fence, but Johnny knew that, when Cody was there, they'd be meeting up at the hotel later, that he had someone to let down his hair with. Now he would have to watch his step.

Close as he felt to Reese and Vern as teammates, they didn't know him. Right now he had to work doubly hard to keep his focus on point so he didn't fuck up and invite questions or a reprimand. Some of the joy had gone out of it for him.

He tried to think back to before he'd hooked up with Cody. He used to enjoy himself just fine when he went to the show, whether as a rider or after he'd transitioned to fighting bulls. Now it was all so difficult. Cody had become so entwined with his experience of bullfighting that Johnny felt off-balance, but he'd get used to it. He'd have to, just like he'd have to get used to the celibate life.

After the show and their usual postmortem analysis of their game, Vern didn't look at him while he asked, "You got a way to Columbus?"

"Taking the train," Johnny said, also carefully not meeting Vern's eyes as he packed his gear.

"You could ride along with me if you want. There's room in my truck."

"Or mine," Reese said.

"You could alternate, so as to keep us from getting our feelings hurt." Vern chuckled dryly.

"I'd be grateful," Johnny said, strangely touched by both their offers. Maybe misery was wafting off him like some toxic aftershave and they'd picked up on it. "I could help pay for gas."

Vern shrugged. "I gotta get to the next venue myself anyway. It's all tax deductible for me. But we're not stopping along the way for a beer."

Johnny smothered a grin at Vern's stern glare. "I'm not much of a drinker."

"Keep it that way." Vern slapped him on the shoulder. "My truck's parked out back. Whenever you're ready."

Johnny nodded and watched Vern and Reese leave the changing room. His running off to meet Cody after shows had made it so he had no clue what his two work partners did afterward. He took one last look in his locker, but he was naturally tidy and had left nothing behind. It had been a while since he hadn't gone to a hotel to meet Cody after the show, but it was his choice. Maybe Cody already had a new boyfriend. In his eyes, Cody was so desirable he could have gotten anyone he wanted. And he was a horndog, so he probably had at least hooked up by now. It had been three achingly long days for Johnny also, but he couldn't even think of a hookup, anonymous or otherwise. But whatever Cody did it was none of his business, not anymore.

He shouldered his bags and walked out to meet Vern at his truck.

VERN refused his offer to help drive. "I'm used to it. Hope you don't mind roughing it. I usually pull into a truck stop along the interstate for forty winks to save on a motel room until I get to the next city."

Johnny nodded. "Okay by me."

"Thought it might be. You get fired from your other job?"

"Quit."

"Uh-hunh."

Somehow, from the tone of his voice, Johnny didn't think Vern was buying it.

"Seems like a funny time to quit."

"He didn't want to give me time off for working the summer in the touring division."

Johnny worried Vern might think he was hurting for money. He didn't need charity or want to take it from the man who hired him onto the team, but he couldn't think of a way to tell the older man that without sounding ungrateful. And he actually was hurting for money. Cody liked staying in nice places, and Johnny never really worried about how much Cody paid for their rooms after he handed over his share, but he was beginning to remember that being with Cody had given him a level of comfort on the road he couldn't afford on his own. While Cody hadn't paid him for helping on the ranch, Johnny still hadn't been pulling his own weight.

He sort of wanted to fume over it in private for a bit and also reject any pity handout from Vern, but he was tired enough from the train and the weekend event that he found himself nodding off and jerking his head upright repeatedly. To cover up, he said, "I could drive for a spell if you want."

Shooting a quick glance at him, Vern answered, "No thanks, we're almost to a good rest stop. Bathrooms and showers. You have to pay to get a shower, but you can piss for free."

"Okay, let me know whenever you want me to drive." Johnny looked out the window, not that he could see more than the shoulder, and beyond that, the blur of bushes and trees rushing past in the darkness. Speaking seemed to have broken his drowsiness, and now he was wide awake. He had to keep reminding himself not to think about Cody.

Vern spoke up again. "If we're going to ride together, we oughta have some ground rules. Like they say, expectations are resentments in training. First off, when I'm on the road, I can't always find a meeting, so first thing in the morning, I call my AA sponsor and then I get down on my knees to talk to my higher power. At night, I speak with the wife. I expect privacy for those conversations."

"No problem." Johnny had been wondering if he would score any privacy himself while traveling with his team leader.

"Second, if you're not ready to go when it's time, I'm leaving without you and you can find your own way to the next event. You're an adult, not my kid. If you get drunk, I'm not going to be pulling your ass out of no bar. I'm not your sponsor. You do what you want as long as you're fit and sober in the ring."

"Okay." In a way it was kind of nice to have someone who wasn't planning his life for him or hovering over him with instructions.

After another twenty or so miles, Vern slowed to pull into a large rest area. The vehicles already parked there consisted of big rigs, pickups, and expensive foreign cars. Johnny recognized a few of the livestock rigs from their logos; some of the contractors who supplied bulls to the tour also seemed to be spending the night here.

Vern guided his truck to a spot under some trees near a fire pit. Both men got out to stretch their legs, Vern with his dopp kit in his hand. "We'll go in one at a time. That way I don't have to set the alarm."

Johnny nodded and hitched his butt onto the picnic table, slapping the air as a mosquito whined in his ear. It was warm and humid at night the way it never was back at the ranch. Even though the air felt heavy, he liked the way it closed around him. At home he would have been wearing a jacket. Here he was fine in just a cotton shirt and his jeans. The cicadas started up after he'd sat motionless for a while, humming to him as he stared up at the stars. Except for the lights on the outside of the block building that housed the restrooms, it was pretty dark, and the stars showed up bright in the sky.

A familiar truck pulled in next to Vern's, and Reese got out to stretch. Johnny lifted a hand in greeting.

Reese said, "Taking turns at the john?"

"Yeah, Vern's in there now getting ready to hit the hay."

"Keep an eye on my truck for me for a minute." Reese stretched again and headed for the restroom.

Even though he missed Cody, it felt adventurous to be out on the road at night with no defined place to sleep. When he heard the crunch of boots on the gravel, Johnny slid off the table and turned to find both Vern and Reese had returned together. "All set?"

"Your turn," Vern said.

Reese only nodded and went back to his own truck. Johnny imagined them hopscotching their way from show to show this way, parking next to each other at truck stops, probably grabbing meals together, living the gypsy life that most of the touring division riders did.

Johnny grabbed his kit and headed for the restroom. It smelled of disinfectant but was surprisingly clean, with a row of white sinks, urinals, stalls, and farther back, shower rooms with pay slots in the doors. He set his kit on one of the sinks and crossed to the urinal where a man in a suit was already standing.

Idly wondering why a man wearing a full-on suit with his shirt buttoned to the neck and his tie perfectly in place well after business hours would stop here at this time of night, Johnny took care of his business.

As he shook off, he glanced up to see the man in the suit trying to catch his eye in the mirror. Purposely, the man dropped his gaze to his cock. Normally Johnny would have zipped up and fled, but he was curious to see if this was a blatant come-on or a misunderstanding on his part. Resolutely, he wouldn't allow himself to think about Cody, but stories of his restroom encounters were swirling in the back of Johnny's mind.

The man looked so normal, so mainstream. After traveling in bull-riding circles for most of his adult life, Johnny found it hard to read a man so far outside his normal experience, but then the man looked up at his face again and jerked his head toward one of the stalls before going inside and closing the door partway. There was no mistaking the invitation.

Johnny was surprised to find that not only was he hard, he was standing out in the open fondling his own dick while trying to decide whether to follow. The man was older, maybe in his early forties, with a shaved head and a body meaty with muscle under the well-cut suit. Despite the man having thirty pounds on him, Johnny wasn't afraid of him. He could handle himself. He just wasn't sure this was what he wanted, a casual suck-off at a rest stop, although at least the restroom was clean.

What if somebody else came in? What if Vern or Reese felt the call of nature again and interrupted? That'd be the end of Johnny traveling with them. Hell, it'd be the end of the team or him being a bullfighter in the NBR.

While his brain was spinning like a rabid hamster on a wheel, the stall door banged open, making Johnny jump.

"You coming in here or what? I don't have all night," the man growled in a loud whisper.

Well, who could resist a sweet-talker like that? Besides, a blowjob was a blowjob. Johnny entered the stall to find the man sitting on the seat, his pants around his ankles, hand wrapped around his short, thick meat. With his free hand, he reached around Johnny to lock the door. Then the businessman grabbed Johnny's ass cheek and pulled him closer.

"You clean? I am," the man said and licked his lips, staring at Johnny's erection.

"Um, what? Oh, yeah, I—"

The man's mouth enveloped Johnny's cock instantly, flooding it with wet heat. The man's eyes closed and he moaned, gobbling the length in hunger until he gagged and withdrew.

Johnny braced his hands on the walls and hoped no one would come in and look under to see four feet in the stall, one pair in cowboy boots, because he didn't think he could move except for the flexing of his hips. The man licked up and down Johnny's shaft before slurping it in again, his stubble rough when he scraped it against Johnny's belly.

Johnny began to thrust harder, aware of the frenzied action of the man's hand on his own cock. The other hand was still gripping his cheek, fingers digging in as if the man feared Johnny might bolt before he got what he came for. He felt sorry for the guy when he pulled off and rubbed his cheek against his cock, as if he didn't get this chance often, before diving in to swallow it again.

Johnny couldn't believe he was doing this, in some stall with a random stranger, but somehow that made it all the hotter. He wanted it fast and dirty so he didn't have to think. When he felt the familiar pulse in his belly, he couldn't hold back. The man managed to take him in deep, and the feeling of hot, tight throat muscles around the head pushed Johnny to the brink.

"I'm gonna—"

Before he finished his sentence, the man pulled off, released his butt, and used his hand to jack Johnny in time to his own stroking until he shot over the man's face.

"Nice cock," the man grunted. He swiped at the strings of come on his face and wiped his fingers with toilet paper.

Dazed, Johnny looked down to see the man had shot also, leaving a white puddle on the tiled floor and his own expensive shoes.

Hastily, Johnny wiped off with toilet paper, ignoring the shreds that stuck to him, put himself away, and zipped up.

"You top?"

"Huh?"

"You fuck? With a dick like that, you should top." The man stood up to arrange his clothing. "Maybe we could fuck next time."

"Uh, thanks." With that, Johnny bolted out of the stall and grabbed for his kit, suddenly anxious to get away without any more conversation.

He heard the man calling after him, "I come here every Wednesday."

Good to know, Johnny thought. He'd make sure to never come here on a Wednesday again, not that he'd be on this highway next week. He hoped the guy cleaned off his shoes before he left, and realized maybe it wasn't that hard to find action after all. Cody was right about that, as he was about so many things. Just not all, Johnny reminded himself.

He walked back to Vern's truck fast, not wanting the guy to follow and see where he went. Vern was sitting inside smoking with the door open, and it annoyed Johnny that the interior light would attract attention to them in the darkened lot, especially from the guy who'd just serviced him. When he got in and stowed his kit, he had a sudden moment of alarm when he wondered if he smelled of sex. Even Vern had to jack off sometimes, though. A man had needs. Johnny decided to ignore it if he did smell, and trust that the smoke of the cigarette would cover it up.

"All set?"

"Yeah, sure," Johnny lied. Now that he was sitting down, his thighs felt weak. And he hadn't brushed his teeth. He'd have to make sure to do a good job in the morning to make up for the neglect, but maybe it was worth it. He wasn't quite sure yet.

Vern got out and shut his door, making the dome light go out. "I usually sleep in the camper. I think I have an extra blanket by me. Tomorrow we'll find an army-navy store and you can buy a sleeping bag. G'night."

Cautiously, Johnny crawled into the back after Vern and turned to stare out the back window. The businessman emerged from the restroom and stood staring around as if Johnny might be waiting for him outside. Then he got into a Mercedes CLS and headed out onto the highway. Johnny watched the red taillights as long as he could see them, and then he closed his eyes and slept.

It wasn't 'til the next morning that he found the one hundred dollar bill the man had apparently stuffed into his back pocket while grabbing his ass. Even though it made him angry, he had to laugh. Maybe if the bullfighting didn't pan out, he had another line of work to fall back on. Lying on the unforgiving truck bed while making sure he didn't brush up against Vern made him miss sleeping with Cody. It was the first night in a long time he'd spent alone, not counting Vern snoring six inches away from him. At least he could afford a sleeping bag.

CODY almost felt sorry for the young guy. Almost. It had been therapeutic to fuck his face that way, jamming his cock down the boy's throat until he came. He'd said up front, no recip, so he felt no guilt about zipping up and walking out right after he came, leaving the boy naked and with a hard-on, spread across the bed, dangling his head back over the edge of the mattress. Maybe it wasn't fair, but what had happened to Cody wasn't fair either.

The boy's voice was hoarse from Cody's cock as he asked, "Can we do this again?"

It felt cruel to say no thanks, but it would be worse if he'd said yes. He had nothing to give the boy and hadn't even cared enough to find out his name. The savagery of the encounter scared him, and had opened a door to a dark place Cody didn't even know he had inside.

There was no feeling of intimacy as there had been when he made love to Johnny. This was nothing more than animal release. He needed it so he couldn't regret that he'd done it, but as he shoved his cock down the guy's throat, images rose uncalled for and unwanted before his eyes: Johnny's shiny dark hair swinging, the slim, strong body, the sound of his gasps, the taste of him, the smoothness of his skin.

It blinded Cody to the blond beauty of the young man whose throat he'd brutalized, and for that he did feel guilty. The guy wasn't only a mouth, a tongue, a throat; he was someone who should be known.

But not by him.

As Cody drove back to the ranch, passing his parents' house and going directly to the bungalow where Johnny didn't live anymore, what was really bothering him struck him.

In the images of Johnny that haunted him, Cody had seen hands on his skin, a mouth over his cock, and they didn't belong to him, Cody. The idea of Johnny being loved, discovered, and known by other men was unbearable, and he had no control over it. No way to stop it.

He stripped and stood under the shower until the hot water gave out, trying to wash the stain of his trick from his soul. It didn't work.

He hadn't cheated. Johnny was the one who'd left. Johnny was the one who had said you're not good enough.

Cody sat on the porch drinking beer, and pitched each bottle out into the grass as he polished it off, even though he knew he'd have to pick them all up tomorrow. Tonight the only thing that mattered was obliterating the images and the gaping void of loneliness. Cody just wanted to forget, for just a few minutes, to get some relief. But it didn't seem to matter how much he drank. All that happened was he was miserable, drunk, and had to pee a lot.

Finally Cody staggered inside and fell onto the bed and stared out the window until the sky was light. He couldn't stay on the ranch all summer, fighting images of Johnny every direction he turned. Tomorrow he would call Dub and ask him to ride the summer exhibition circuit with him.

When he couldn't stand lying there sleepless any longer, he got up. There was work to be done. That was the day he found Johnny's bull-riding gear, his helmet, chaps, and vest. He buried his face in the leather vest as if he could find some lingering scent from his lover.

"AREN'T you going to shave?"

"What's the point?" Cody snarled. The hangover had kicked in and his head was throbbing.

"Just because Johnny's gone is no reason to look like a homeless bum." Val set a plate on the table in front of her son.

"I don't care."

"Of course you care. You don't drink a case of beer just for fun."

Stung, Cody mustered up the energy to yell. "It wasn't a fucking case of beer! He's gone and it's over. There's nothing to say!"

"Don't shout. I'm not deaf." Val sat down with a cup of coffee. "Why did you let him go?"

"He's a grown man. He can do whatever he wants." Cody picked up a fork and pushed the food around the plate.

"And you didn't try to stop him."

"What am I going to do? Tie him up and sit on him?"

"You could tell him you love him."

"I did!" Cody buried his face in his hands. "It's not fair. He just pissed away everything I did for him like it was worth nothing. I tried to help him."

"Maybe he didn't want your help. Maybe he wanted to be an equal partner."

"Who cares what he wanted? I was always walking on eggshells because he was too sensitive. He took things the wrong way. I had plans for us." Cody stopped speaking, just aware enough to realize arguing wasn't going to make his mother let him off the hook and put the blame only on Johnny. He knew it was Johnny's fault, but the knowledge wasn't making him feel any better. He looked at Val helplessly.

"What am I going to do?"

"What do you want?"

"I want him back." Cody had to grit the words out between clenched jaw, as if admitting it made him a loser.

"Get him back."

"Just go after him and drag him back by the hair?"

"Let him get it out of his system first. He might need a little time by himself. Then maybe you can work things out."

"Did you know he was—pissed off?"

"I wouldn't say he was pissed off. I could see he was thinking things over."

"Why didn't you tell me?" Cody sounded accusatory even to himself, but he couldn't help it. He couldn't believe this was happening to him.

"You're not my little colt that I just dropped in the pasture, Cody. You're a grown man. You wouldn't have liked it if I interfered in your business. It never does any good, anyway."

"Yeah. You're probably right." Cody stared hopelessly at his plate. "What am I going to do?" he repeated.

"Is it that hard to pick up a phone, dial his number, and ask him how he's doing? You could tell him you miss him and want him back—"

The words Johnny had used to hurt him rang in his ears, words Cody didn't think he could ever forget. "Hell no! I'm not going to force him to do something he doesn't want to do."

Val sighed. "Then grieve for a while and get over it. Move on and find someone else."

"How long? How long does it hurt?"

"Just because it didn't last forever doesn't mean it wasn't worth it."

"That sounds like a fucking greeting card."

"Actually, I think it was from a fucking calendar," Val said.

Cody couldn't help but laugh before he groaned. "This sucks. I hate drama-queen diva gay guys. I want to know when it gets better."

"I can't give you a timetable. It's going to hurt for a while, and you'll have to bear with it 'til it eases. It's like a broken bone. Hurts like hell at first, then it heals up, and the pain goes away."

Leaving a scar that would always be there, Cody thought, but he didn't say it. He was fucking thirty-two and whimpering to his mother like a kid. "I'd better get to work."

Val didn't say anything to keep him from it, but she gave him the hug he needed before he left.

CHAPTER 10:

How to Find the Action

AFTER the encounter in the men's room on the highway, Johnny became more aware of subtle clues he'd apparently never noticed when he was with Cody. He also learned to recognize the signs earlier and stop a man's advances before it got to the point of a sexual encounter that made him feel dirty or coerced.

Of course, before, he hadn't needed to take notice. Cody was a source of constant hot dick and he never needed to look elsewhere.

Now he had to if he wanted to get some action. He had considered picking out some guy who seemed gay and following him, but the odds of that action leading to sex rather than jail didn't seem that good. He could see himself getting charged as a stalker rather than being led to a great bar full of hot guys. He would have to do this a different way.

On the Internet Johnny discovered a wealth of gay smut; to him, the Internet wasn't made of cats, instead it was a giant forest of cock and ass designed to drive a horny man insane. All you had to do was join one of the cruising sites and type in what you were in the market for. He discovered if a man wanted to top, he could get more replies than he could even answer. It also trained him to question a potential partner's status, something he'd never had to do when he was hooked up with Cody, or before.

There was webcam sex, sexting, IMing, Grindr hookups of every kind: you host, I host, we meet under a bridge for troll sex. Somehow it felt a little too much like a supermarket, where the interchange of sperm was a deal to be made with no human connection desired or necessary. Also he felt uneasy leaving that kind of trail on his laptop. He was no celebrity but he was in a dangerous profession. If the worst should happen and he ended up in a hospital, he would hate for Vern or Reese to retrieve his laptop and God forbid, come face-to-face with who he really was.

Besides, he was curious to see how much action he could scare up in person. He discovered websites that gave the location of gay bars and baths in different cities. He didn't think he was quite ready for the baths; they sounded too intense.

He decided to start with bars and stay out of rest stop bathrooms for a while, except for the purpose for which they were intended.

JOHNNY had never been inside a gay bar before. It surprised him to find one like this in Toledo. Maybe shocked was a better word. Men were practically having sex on the dance floor and literally having sex in the dark hallway that led to the bathroom. He could only imagine what was going on in there.

It was awful and exhilarating. Johnny half turned to say something to Cody, a habit he'd caught himself in more and more recently. Pulling himself together, Johnny lined up at the bar to get a beer. He had a cold one in his hand quicker than he'd thought possible, but then he towered over most of the men, what with his hat and all.

He carried his beer to a table that had just freed up and sat down with his back to the wall to watch.

It was odd to feel so alone and yet totally at home. It must be the difference of a place where being gay was the norm as opposed to sticking out like the rogue bull at the edge of the herd. Johnny wasn't sure he would ever be comfortable enough to whip it out in the back hall to get sucked off, but it was a revelation to be around so many men just putting it out there. Men openly on the hunt for pleasure.

In the darkness, he became aware that hands were groping other men in places not usually considered suitable for polite society. He had to grin at himself. When had he become such a prissy stick-in-the-mud at his age? He needed to get out more.

"Hey, Johnny. Mind if I join you?"

Looking up, Johnny was startled to recognize the young man standing hesitantly by the table. He stood up and offered his hand. "Zane Winslow, isn't it?"

"Right. Actually, I'm Z-man here." They shook and Zane put his beer on the table before he sat down. "I wasn't sure you'd remember me."

"Don't sell yourself short." Johnny felt a little alarm bell go off at the eager look on Zane's face. The kid was cute but he was no Cody. Kid. Zane had to be near his age. Somehow he just seemed a lot younger. "I didn't realize you were legal."

"Twenty-two. I'm a little late getting started in bull riding." Zane hunched a shoulder defensively.

"Sometimes it's better not to start too young. So, how's the riding going?"

"Great! I've really been able to up my game since that week at the ranch. I can't thank you enough."

"It's Cody you need to thank. He's the one who organized it."

"But you're the one who spent time with me one-on-one. I really appreciate it."

Somehow Johnny got the feeling Zane was used to being overlooked in the shadows. He was a pretty quiet kid. He could empathize with that. He also got the uncomfortable feeling Zane wouldn't mind a little more one-on-one time of a different kind with him. "You've got a lot of natural talent. You'll do well."

"Barring an injury, I sure hope to." Zane let his gaze wander around the room. "I've never seen you in one of these places before."

"Never been in one." Johnny laughed at the shock on Zane's face.

"How old are you?"

"Twenty-three."

"Shit! I've been going for years. Waiting for Cody?"

"No."

"Oh, right. He's on break from the Top Cut. Always in the top thirty, right?"

"Yeah, he never rides bad enough to fall out of the top posse."

"You, uh, slipping around on him?"

"We split. Shit!" Johnny could have kicked himself. After all the time guarding their secret, he had just outed Cody without thinking. "Listen, Za—Z-man, forget I said that. Cody—he—"

Zane smiled sympathetically. "Don't worry. I usually hang out in a nice, comfortable closet of my own. I don't come to places like this often except on the road, and I don't mention to people here what I do for work."

For the first time, Johnny realized that although nothing could make Zane look anything but a cowboy to him, he was wearing a tight rock band T-shirt tucked into belted jeans and had left off the cowboy hat. That made Johnny resolve not to wear his again. The Stetson was like a walking advertisement for the rodeo. That is, if he ever had the balls to venture out into a bar again. He had a lot to learn. "Thanks. That was a bum move."

"I'm sorry to hear you guys split. I thought you were great together."

Awkwardly, Johnny asked, "Were we that obvious?"

"Nah. The other guys probably didn't catch on, but my gaydar's pretty honed. Gotta have it juiced up in this life."

"You see the other guys much?"

"Yeah, we all ride in the touring division pretty often. You'll probably see them tomorrow at the venue. So why did you guys split?"

Johnny shook his head in silence. He wasn't going to talk it over with strangers.

"Sorry. I didn't mean to pry into something that's none of my business. It's just a shame. Not too often you see a couple that stays together too long except in the gay rodeo." Zane lifted his chin at the dance floor. "I don't have a boyfriend. With all the traveling I mostly only get one-nighters. I don't suppose you'd...."

Johnny smiled. "Sorry. You're a cute guy but it wouldn't seem right."

"Yeah, I feel you. Well, wish you luck. Nice seeing you."

"Good luck with the riding."

Johnny was surprised at the bawdy laugh Zane gave out.

"Good one. Yeah, I hope I find a good one to ride. You too, huh?"
With a sly wink and a nudge in the ribs, Zane abandoned his beer and
walked over to a good-looking man in a suit who was giving him the
eye.

Being recognized shook Johnny. Being reminded of Cody by
someone outside their family circle who'd known about them made
him sad but also angry. He came here to get laid, and dammit, he was
going to. For a second he regretted knocking Zane back. He was a
good-looking guy and he obviously knew the score both from the gay
end and the rodeo end. But it wouldn't have been right. Johnny told
himself there was no need to worry about whatever Cody might think
now or in the future, as it was none of his business and they were split
anyway, but it still felt uncomfortable to think about doing it with
someone they both knew.

"Hey, cowboy."

Looking up from brooding into his beer, Johnny was surprised to
find a clean-cut guy-next-door type standing by the table. He was
wearing a suit, although his tie was loose, his shirt open more buttons
than necessary, and he looked as though he'd had a few. Still, his
tanned skin and the way his blue eyes crinkled in a smile were
attractive. He wasn't the handsomest guy Johnny'd ever seen, but he
was sort of ugly-sexy.

"Hey yourself."

The man set his beer on the table and started waving his arms
around like semaphore signals.

Johnny stared at him blankly. "You need help or something?"

"'YMCA'? Village people?"

"Doesn't ring a bell."

"Can't win them all." Confidently, the man sat down without
waiting for an invitation. "You're an Indian, right?"

"Native American," Johnny replied automatically. "Diné."

"And that means?"

"Navajo." He sighed.

"Sorry. Let me pry my foot out of my stupid fucking mouth and start over. I'm not usually such a politically incorrect jerk." The man got up, walked away, turned around, and came back with an apologetic grin. "Hey, cowboy. Crowded tonight, isn't it?"

"Yeah. Even the hallway—" Johnny jerked a thumb at the writhing bodies in the shadows.

"So not classy. I've got a big hotel room with a nice big bed just waiting for somebody to warm it up. What about it?"

Johnny hesitated. Then he nodded. Why not? He had supplies. He was single. He was horny and this was what he'd come here for. He knew how to take care of himself, and while this guy wasn't totally plastered, he wasn't exactly sober. He felt his cock throb when a hand landed on his thigh and stroked upward. He looked down and was shocked to see a wedding band on the third finger. Still, it was the guy's business. "You clean?"

"Yeah, but I don't fuck, anyway. I'll blow you and you don't have to do me."

"What are we waiting for?"

The clean-cut guy laughed. "Nothing. If I have another drink, I'll need a derrick to hoist it up. Only so much the little blue pills can do."

IT WAS two in the morning when Johnny silently let himself out of Jeff's room. At least, he'd said his name was Jeff. Without searching his wallet for a driver's license after Jeff passed out, there was no way to know, and Johnny didn't care enough to do it. He would never see this guy again, and if their paths did cross, he had a strong suspicion Jeff was used to looking the other way when he ran into a one-nighter.

Johnny was beginning to feel as though he'd led a very sheltered life before tonight. First the gay bar and then the desperate way Jeff dove onto his cock. The man was starving for dick, almost as if he hadn't seen one other than his own in a very long time. Johnny had never even gotten his jeans past his thighs the whole time they messed around.

Jeff had sucked him off twice and in between times, he'd said enough for Johnny to realize that, for some, the closet was darker and lonelier than he could have imagined. He'd sucked Jeff off, feeling it was only fair to reciprocate, but it was quick. Johnny got the feeling Jeff didn't do this often and that when he was traveling for business was the only time he indulged his impulses. He felt sorry for Jeff. He had a feeling there was a story there, even though the man hadn't been that coherent about his life and why he was in a gay bar if he was married.

After going back to his own cheap little motel room, Johnny lay awake for a while, grinning in the darkness when he thought about what Vern's reaction would have been to his staying out that late on a work night. If Johnny thought it would put a rider or another bullfighter in danger, he wouldn't have done it; that's all, he thought defiantly. Still, it was something he probably should be careful about in the future. He didn't want to be an isolated gay man going from one trick to another in every city he went to. He carefully didn't think about Cody at all.

The sky grew light before he rolled over and finally fell asleep to a weird dream about Jeff and Zane going at it in the middle of the dance floor at the club.

CHAPTER 11:

Bobby Blue Eats Dirt

STANDING at the side of the fence with Reese and Vern, Johnny felt inconspicuous and yet right at home despite the cheering, which wasn't for them anyway. He had gotten more used to the indoor arenas where the top circuit rode, and here they were outside, but it was nice to be under the night sky. It had cooled down after a hot day, and the noise and applause didn't echo out here in quite the same way.

It was time to introduce the riders. Each man had his name read out by the announcer over the loudspeaker and had his chance to run into the ring and wave his hat at the fans. There were more than thirty riders, so it was going to take a while to get through the list as they came out one by one. Each rider ran past the bullfighters, the younger ones without so much as a glance. Most of the older riders high-fived the team as they went by. When he'd first started working for Vern, the lead bullfighter had suggested he clip his braided hair up under his hat to avoid getting his neck broken if it got caught on something, so maybe it wasn't surprising neither Aubrey nor Tommy recognized him. Zane gave him a brief grin and slapped his palm as he galloped into the ring.

Then Johnny's body stiffened when he heard the name Bobby Blue Chandler.

Like any good stock handler, of course Vern noticed. "You heard of this kid?"

Nodding, Johnny tried to be fair. "Raw, but cocky. Shows signs of being good someday."

"Great." Reese rolled his eyes. "Cocky guys are the fuckers that drag our asses into the hurting with them."

"Be careful of the cocky ones," Vern agreed. "Get set and stay on your toes. It's all we can do."

Even though he hadn't gotten much sleep after leaving Jeff's room the night before, Johnny wasn't tired. Just putting on his protective gear pumped his energy, and as the youngest and most athletic of the team, he knew he'd get to handle his fair share of the fighting.

The riding was certainly not of the caliber he had gotten used to on the Top Cut circuit, but neither were the bulls, although there were a few promising young ones. Judging by their riding, he was surprised to see Aubrey and Tommy on the list. He would have thought they would still be on the county fair circuit, but maybe Cody's training had helped more than he'd expected. When Aubrey rode, his buckoff time was three seconds. Tommy went off a little more excruciatingly at just under eight seconds. It gave Johnny a twinge of sympathy pain reminiscent of his own bull riding days.

Neither of the riders appeared to recognize him in his bullfighter role as he jinked and dodged around the bulls. It annoyed Johnny that he kept making a mental note to mention some bit of information about each bull to Cody until he remembered he wouldn't be talking to Cody after the show.

During some of the downtime, his thoughts wandered onto exactly how the bulls were contracted for each show. It was something he might have learned if he'd stuck around the ranch. Val and Davis had been training and contracting bucking horses ever since she retired from riding, so Cody must have gotten some idea from them about how to do it.

At this level, these bulls weren't as challenging as the ones Johnny and his team were used to, but that was no reason to fall asleep at the wheel. The three bullfighters congregated near the exit gate whenever a cowboy was getting ready in the chute so they could hover at a distance that didn't distract him, but be handy to rush in when the rider dismounted, however and whenever he happened to dismount.

It wasn't until Bobby Blue was in the chute that Johnny actually paid more attention to the rider than the bull, even though this bull was demanding notice, bashing around as if it was trying to crush Bobby Blue's leg against the fence.

"You called it, he's an ass," Reese joked, "Seems like he's even pissing the bull off."

"Yeah, that bull ain't normally so bad in the box." Vern touched fists with each of his team members. "Get ready now."

"And not wearing a damn helmet after he's been told. Idiot," Johnny grumbled. He could see his team earning their pay today.

Watching closely, Johnny began to see the raw ability Cody had recognized in Bobby Blue back at the ranch. When the gate opened, Bobby Blue was laid out almost on his back by the speed of the bull, but he appeared to have actually learned something from Cody. He fought his way upright again, but then the bull tossed his head down, almost yanking the kid over his head. Because of the hat Johnny couldn't see his face, but the kid avoided a disqualifying slap of the bull by crossing his free hand in front of his body. Although his movements were awkward and he bounced up and down as though he was churning butter, Bobby Blue managed to stay on top of the bull for the full eight. The buzzer saved him right before he was sent sailing over the bull's head. In midflight its horns caught on his chaps and the bull tossed its head, sending him spinning through the air like a Frisbee.

"Oh fuck." Johnny was already in point position ahead of his teammates and on the spot when the bull charged, trying to present himself as an easier target than Bobby Blue. The arena went dead silent when Bobby Blue landed facedown in the dirt and didn't move, enabling Johnny to hear every snort and blow from the bull coming at him and the distant clang of a metal gate. He tried to lure the bull to the right, but the animal wasn't buying it and Johnny couldn't let the bull trample Bobby Blue into the dust, so he was stuck between them, dancing lightly from one foot to the other and waving his arms in hopes of putting the bull off. Both Reese and Vern were running and yelling in the background, trying to get the animal to turn away.

The bull pranced toward him, stiff legged, and Johnny could feel the damp heat of its breath on his face when the bull suddenly charged.

A flash of orange told him Reese had shot the gap between them. The bull turned its head to look at Reese, catching Johnny's loose shirt on its horns and whisking him off his feet. Then he was flipping through the air for what seemed like hours. The air was forced out of him when he landed, but he scrambled to his feet and darted in front of the bull before it reached Bobby Blue lying prone in the dirt, making himself a human shield for the fallen rider. This time he had no time to maneuver out of the way, although he managed to twist away from the horns at the last moment. When he took the glancing blow, he felt the impact in his solar plexus. He grabbed a horn and the bull shook its head, yanking him off his feet and sending him crashing into its flank.

As he slid down the hard slab of beef, the bull turned to hook him instead of staying on Bobby Blue. Johnny rolled in the dirt frantically, trying to get away, knowing his teammates had his back but still pumped with enough adrenaline that he felt he could tackle the bull on his own and get him under control.

Reese ran in behind him, yelling like a crazy man. The bull's attention wavered for only a moment and then Vern jumped in and shouted, finally making the bull turn away from Johnny. Reese joined Vern as they tried to drive the bull to the gate, yelling and waving their hats.

But the bull was not in a good mood that day and decided not to cooperate. He ran straight at Vern, trying to hook him as he leaped up onto the fence. Johnny had managed to scramble through the dirt on his knees, and threw himself over Bobby Blue before the safety man on horseback cantered into the fray and threw a loop over the bull's horns. Then it was all over as the bull calmed down instantly and was led out by the safety usher.

"You all right?" Still panting for air, Johnny knelt by Bobby Blue but didn't touch his head or shoulders just in case. The younger man rolled onto his back with a groan.

But Bobby Blue's eyes were wide open and he was spitting dirt out of his mouth. The look on his face was one of glowing adoration, and if Johnny could have caught his breath, he would have laughed.

"Thanks, Johnny. You saved my life."

"Or maybe just a bone or two. All part of the service." Johnny grinned at the signs of returning intelligence. "You probably have a slight concussion. Nothing that'll keep you from riding, but the medics are on the way to check you out."

Bobby Blue sat up and put his hand on his neck, shaking his head gingerly. The crowd went crazy, bursting into applause, yelling and stamping for the cowboy, relieved he was up and moving. Bobby Blue lifted a hand in response to the outpouring of emotion. "Hell of a job you have."

"Yeah, just another day at the office. I wouldn't jostle your brain around like that right now."

"What little I have left." Suddenly they were grinning at each other as if they were old friends.

Johnny stood up and offered a hand. Hastily, Bobby Blue grabbed it and stood up before the medics could arrive, which made the crowd cheer louder in grateful relief.

"Here comes the cavalry," Johnny said. "You'll be fine."

"I think the cavalry done arrived already, Johnny-boy," Bobby Blue said and shook Johnny's hand. "I owe you."

"Great. Then do me a favor and wear a damn helmet next time!"

"Yeah, you make a good argument. I might just take it under advisement. Thanks again. Tell Cody I said thanks. He really schooled me."

Unable to answer that, Johnny nodded and went to join his teammates at the gate. "Thanks for having my back, guys."

"We're a team, boys," Vern said.

"All for one, one for all," Reese added.

"There goes one ornery rider," Vern said, bestowing the highest praise he could as they watched Bobby Blue shake off the two medics' helping hands and walk unsteadily between them while waving and grinning at the crowd. "Bet he'll be wondering what happened for an hour or two."

"Yeah, I think he'll learn from it." Johnny nodded. He almost wished Cody could have been there to see how well he'd taught the kid.

Bobby Blue even seemed to have learned some manners, although that should probably be chalked up to Val rather than her son.

"You too," Vern said with a smile. "Don't even try to tell me your ribs don't hurt, but you got a week to heal up before the next event."

"Thanks, but I'm good."

"Here we go again," Reese said as the gate opened for the next rider.

UP IN the sky box, Cody sat back next to Dub, his shoulders unclenching as all the tension melted away. It was Johnny's job and he knew that, but he hated to see him put his body on the line for a loudmouth birdbrain like Bobby Blue. It had been a tense five minutes watching it play out, but there was nothing he could do about it up here anyway. And even if he'd been in the ring, it could have been him on the ground, waiting for Johnny to save his ass.

It was the possibility of Johnny getting hurt that killed him. Cody had been hurt himself often enough and bad enough that watching Johnny get injured was almost more painful than suffering it himself. The time Johnny's shoulder had been dislocated and his collarbone broken had almost broken *him*, and they'd only just started seeing each other. Cody had nowhere near the depth of feeling for Johnny then that he had now. Watching Johnny take the hit, he found himself pleading to some unknown god, promising he'd do anything if Johnny just came through this okay.

And amazingly, once again Johnny had come through unscathed. Cody took in a deep breath. It would never do if Dub noticed him getting his shorts in a bunch over Johnny. He didn't know if his friend harbored any suspicions about his sexuality, but when he'd called Dub and asked him to come along to this meeting with Sam, he'd thought Dub sounded creepily sympathetic for some unknown reason. He hated himself for asking for company, but he'd suddenly lost his nerve. He felt he couldn't trust himself to travel without a companion, especially knowing he was going to see Johnny, if only from a distance. In fact, Cody was exasperated by the thought that maybe he'd asked Dub to come along to prevent him from going near Johnny.

"Looks like Bobby Blue Chandler is going to shake this one off." Everyone could see that, but of course the ring announcer had to say something. "It's only his rookie year, but he's shaping up as one tough cowboy. We'll get a medical update for you as soon as he sees the doc. And I think we should show a little appreciation for the bullfighters. They earned their pay today! Let's have a round of applause for Vern Crocker, Reese Brent, and the young fellow in red who just joined their team. We'll get his name for you—"

Tensely, Cody raised his voice. "Johnny Arrow!"

The announcer continued his verbal tide without glancing up. "I've just been told the bullfighter who took the hit for Bobby Blue is Johnny Arrow. Y'all go to our website now and vote for him for save of the week...." He continued to talk, naming the cowboy and bull coming up for the next ride.

A touch on Cody's sleeve made him turn to face Sam Wells, the stock director for the NBR and the man he'd come there to meet with.

"You trained that rider, correct? Bobby Blue Chandler. Nice job. I seem to recall before he came to you he couldn't sit a bull for eight seconds even if it was standing still."

"You're the one who sent him to me, Sam." Cody smiled as he reminded him, feeling as though he'd passed some kind of test. He had to pull himself together; he was here on business, not to moon over Johnny. It was annoying to find that Johnny was looking better than ever. Maybe he was right to bring Dub along. "You ought to know."

"I like it when an older rider is confident enough to pay it forward to the young ones," Sam said. "Some get too uppity to give back and bull riding is all about community."

"Cody's always been good with the boys coming up," Dub confirmed. "Takes them under his wing, like."

"Mentoring is a big part of our sport. Great to see what a good job you older riders have done. And you too, Dub. I've seen you do your share."

Cody hoped the older man didn't notice his wince at the term "old." How he hated that feeling! He wasn't old, dammit! "That bull Bobby Blue was mounted on now—"

"You're not going to tell me your bulls are better now, are you?"

Actually, that was exactly what Cody had planned, but the sardonic twinkle in the older man's eyes made him stop and think before he replied. "At least as good, I'd say. They're young, I know, but their dam and sire both have great bloodlines: Motherbucker and Fool's Gold."

"Great DNA, but your young 'uns haven't been proved in the ring. Even the best lines don't always pan out when you get them in a noisy ring with all the lights and the noise. Not without proper training."

Dub interjected, "Cody studied breeding in college. Got some kind of degree in genetics. Plus, I've seen his young stock while he was training them. Got some winners there, if I don't miss my guess. I wouldn't mind taking a turn on them my own self."

"Fool's Gold was a high-money bull five years in a row, and had a career buckoff percentage of ninety-two. His get have to start somewhere." Cody hoped he didn't sound like he was pleading.

Sam gave him a shrewd look. "I don't start bulls without stats in Top Cut. Not even in the touring division. If I give you a couple of slots with the county fair rodeos for the summer, can you fill them? That's ten weeks, one day a week. I don't work bulls two days of the week, unless I'm flat out of reride bulls. I pay a quarter of the price earned in Top Cut and no travel unless they start pulling good scores. If they do, I'll bump them up to the touring division at half pay. What do you say?"

Cody would have sent his bulls for free just to get a start in the contracting business, but he wasn't going to tell Sam that. He pretended to consider the offer as if he had to convince himself to settle for the lower fee. "I think I can work with that. It's a good start. You'll see, they'll score high."

"Shake on it." Sam stuck his hand out. "I'll hold you to it."

Cody shook, but from the corner of his eye, he was aware of Johnny's every move down in the ring. He was glad to have a few of his bulls contracted out, but now that he'd seen Johnny, he knew he'd have to stay away from the touring division for the summer even if his bulls were contracted for the tour. At least until his anger died down enough to be polite to Johnny if they came face-to-face.

He missed riding. He needed to get back to it. The NBR Top Cut was on break for the summer, and Johnny was working the summer touring division. Cody could place his bulls with Sam and go ride in the exhibition schedule with Dub. Every point and dollar earned during the off time would just add to his win in the fall. He could get RJ and Travis to travel with the bulls.

That's what he was going to do. But first he wondered if he could ditch Dub to find some action. Maybe it wouldn't be a good move after he'd practically begged his friend to come along with him, but he needed some relief.

Sam Wells left the box, and Dub turned to Cody with a big grin and stuck his hand out. "Well, well, here's to your start on becoming the next big stock contractor."

Modestly, Cody said, "If my bulls work out. It's only the summer fairs. Sam didn't say anything about the Top Cut division, not that I could ride my own bulls. Wouldn't be ethical."

Dub clapped him on the shoulder. "Well, you gotta retire some time. Then you can run your bulls in all the divisions."

"Dammit, why is everyone all over me about retiring? I'm not that old!"

"You can't ride forever, you know." Dub was looking at him with a sappy sympathetic expression that made Cody want to punch it off his face.

"Why not? I'm in good shape—"

"Cody, you're my friend. You're a great rider. You could ride into your forties, like some of the old-timers did, but take a look at their stats. After the age of thirty, the stats are all one way. Downhill."

"Not mine, I'm still riding good."

"This is your year, no doubt about that. All the guys figure you for the winner at finals."

"So next year could be my year too," Cody argued. This felt horribly like when Johnny left. Everything was slipping away from him.

"You're a stubborn man," Dub said. "It's a fine line between confident and arrogant."

"Yeah, well, bite me."

"No thanks. You suck, but it's one of the things I like about you. However, it's coming time for you to give back to the sport. Teach the younger riders how to do it. Get your bulls contracted out. It'll keep your name in the limelight." Dub chuckled. "Hell, with your record your name will always come up whenever they talk about bull riders, just like Sam. He was one hell of a rider and he's still big in the sport. You can be too. Don't hold on so tight you lose everything. Ain't gonna be fun living in a wheelchair if you mess up good."

Cody sighed. "I feel like a fucking target's painted on my back."

"Now you know how the rest of us feel. With you in the ring, ain't none of us got a chance to win unless you get hurt. That's not how I want to win. I want you standing up and healthy when you shake my hand and are forced to admit I'm the better man."

"That's never going to happen. Are they taking bets on me? How long my old joints are going to hold out?" Cody found a certain dark humor in the idea even while he recoiled from it.

"I'm always in your corner, you know that." Dub put his hand on Cody's shoulder and gave him a little shake. "Let's grab a beer."

Feeling grateful for Dub at his side, Cody went with him to find a bar. He sometimes worried Dub had an inkling that he wasn't straight. Dub never mentioned snaring a couple of hotties at the bar, even though Cody had heard him say things like that to other riders. Since he'd met Johnny, Cody hadn't gone to the bars as much after the show. Johnny was infinitely more enticing than drinking with a bunch of straight guys, even if they were his friends. However, he was grateful for Dub's company now, even if he would go out hunting on his own later.

With only one glance back into the ring to see what Johnny was up to, Cody followed Dub to the stairs. People were leaving the stands for intermission. None of the riders or bullfighters were in sight; probably all back in the locker room. It gave Cody an empty feeling, as it always did when he left the ring. Thirty-two seconds a week was all he'd lived for fourteen years. Thirty-two seconds a week to show the world what he was made of. Maybe it was time to find what life had to offer him outside those thirty-two seconds. Without Johnny.

"JUST suck me off." It had become his mantra. He didn't want another man's hands on him, didn't want their willing asses, just a warm, wet, anonymous mouth.

"You sure you don't want to fuck me? You have a great dick."

He had to force the lie out. "I prefer oral."

"Some guys do." The man on his knees before him shrugged and leaned in closer to lick the head of his cock.

Cody braced himself on the wall and closed his eyes. This was the only way he could get off since the fight. The sight of a naked guy bent over in front of him made him wilt faster than a direct hit to the groin.

It's not that big.

The words echoed in his ears, blocking out everything else Johnny had said that day. His face had been impassive, his eyes watchful, as if gauging how much he could hurt Cody. He had been cruel, powerful, and Cody was still cursed with the insecurity and doubt that he'd felt when he went limp that day.

The mouth on him felt good, worshipful. He should have been able to give himself up to the pleasure, but there was a part of him that held back. Worrying. *It's not that big. It's not that hard. You're not that good.*

He'd never failed before. Never failed to please a sex partner, never lost his erection, never doubted himself.

But then it had never mattered before. He was happy if the men he played with went away happy and satisfied, but that was about pride. Performance.

And it was all he'd ever had, mounted on a man or a bull. His performance.

The rush of orgasm took him by surprise, and he drove forward hard enough to bang his hapless sucker's head into the wall, but the man didn't seem to mind. He grunted appreciatively around Cody's cock before he spat into a tissue and wiped his lips.

When he was wrung dry, Cody opened his eyes. "My turn," he said. He needed to fill his mouth with a hard cock.

CHAPTER 12:
Sister Christian

WITH each bar he gained a little more confidence. Like Zane, Johnny tried to look less like a cowboy at night in hopes of preventing an outing, even though the hat, jeans, and boots would have made getting laid a sure thing in almost any gay bar. Since finding out who the Village People were, he also could have opted to dress like a cop or a construction worker. If he had any facial hair, he could have grown a porn 'stache to really look the part, although he would have been laughed out of bullfighting if he showed up with a furry upper lip.

Instead he bought a plain black tank top and wore it with jeans and sneakers. He left his hat at the motel, but with his hair pulled back in a long braid, he still looked and walked like a cowboy. There was no disguising the rolling gait, but it seemed to attract enough attention that he could pick and choose from the men who showed their interest. In fact, he almost wished Cody was around so he could witness his success. Johnny's inner twelve-year-old wanted to stick out his tongue and say, "So there! I am *too* hot!"

The main point was, he looked different than in the ring. So far he'd had only one close call when he recognized a rider skulking in the shadows hitting on a pretty blond. It shocked him enough to see a guy he knew in a gay bar; he was someone Johnny never would have suspected had any impulse to reach for cock, and it was also a wake-up call to be a bit more careful himself. That night he'd left in a hurry without hooking up, simply to get out of there before the guy surfaced and saw him.

After that, he kind of watched that rider when their paths crossed on the summer circuit. He played straight really well and probably was more into girls than boys. It was interesting to know something that private about the man, not that he would ever have blabbed about it. It was a bummer anyone even cared about stuff like that.

He hadn't been planning to go out tonight, but Zane claimed he needed a wingman. Zane had topped his bull for eight seconds and came away with a good score and a nice check for placing in the top ten, so he was up for celebrating.

"I always score better when you're there, just like in the ring. You're my lucky charm," Zane had said, and Johnny let himself be persuaded, even though something felt different the night Bobby Blue needed his help, as if someone was watching him in the ring.

Maybe it was seeing Bobby Blue and the others again. Or covering him with his body. It was odd being that close to someone who knew him in only one way and contrasting it with how well he now knew Zane. In the ring, he and Zane ignored the thing they had in common and simply said hello.

Johnny was observing from a corner as usual, but now he was attuned enough to recognize The Gaze. He even knew how to handle his own gaze to signify interest or say, "Sorry, not interested," without words from across a room. There were a few steamy guys giving him the eye, as well as an obvious young blond who wore makeup and a sequined tank top, surrounded by other similarly dressed boys. "Limp-wristed" didn't even begin to describe him. Johnny crossed him off the list immediately as "too gay."

An arm sliding over his shoulders made him jump, and he accidentally turned his head right into the kiss Zane laid on his mouth. It was just a friendly kiss, and Johnny had seen a lot more kissing between men since he'd been on the road, but he kept his lips closed so as not to send Zane the wrong message.

"Did you see my score today? Highest I ever earned!" Zane was too excited to keep his voice down.

Purposely, Johnny pitched his voice low, forcing Zane to lean in closer to hear him. "I did, Z-man, and you had a great ride! Congratulations. The judges robbed you, you should have won."

"I'll say," Zane agreed. "Damn that Bobby Blue for being such a showy rider. But still, it all helps to build a reputation. They'll be watching me from now on." As he spoke, he swept the room, culling the possibilities. "Anyone you got your eye on? I'll keep my hands off."

Johnny noticed how the blond twink was ogling him with open lust, although he seemed rather crestfallen when Zane showed up. Something about the way most of the men in the bar either ignored the blond, or pointed and laughed at him outright, made Johnny feel sorry for him. "That guy seems interested."

Turning into Z-man on the cruise, Zane instantly dismissed the blond. "That swishy little queen? Too gay."

His words made Johnny feel ashamed about his own automatic reaction to the blond earlier. Something vulnerable about the guy's face kept drawing Johnny's attention back to him, although it might also have been the blinding sparkle of his sequined top.

"I've never done it with a swishy little queen before," he mused. "Could be fun."

Zane did a double take at him. "Listen, traveling with your fighter buds, you don't get that much of a chance for tail on the road. Don't blow a chance with a winner, like that hottie over by the wall. He's cruising you hard."

"You never know, that queen might be the world's greatest cocksucker." Johnny smiled at the blond, who looked dazzled, as if he were either creaming his tight hipster jeans or about to pass out from the attention—at least until the DJ changed the music.

Suddenly the entire group of sparkly queens snapped to attention and started doing a sharp little head tilt and hip shimmy thing Johnny thought of as "gay" while clapping their hands to one side and then the other without actually touching them together.

"What the fuck?"

Z-man laughed. "Lady Gaga. They're doing the dance from the video."

As Johnny watched, more guys joined the group in the energetic dance, although he thought they looked more as though they were having a synchronized seizure rather than dancing.

"Who's Lady Gaga?"

"What the hell kind of music do you listen to? She's the one singing. You know, the one who dresses whack and pops out of an egg when she arrives anywhere? Very popular in gay circles, if you're young and with it." Zane looked impossibly superior as he explained, even though he was only a year younger than Johnny.

Johnny answered, "'Sometimes I think I Get Off on the Pain'."

"TMI, man! What the fuck are you talking about?"

"Country music. Gary Allan, that song he sings about bull riding? That's what C—we used to listen to."

"Well, don't mention it in this kind of bar. Not only is this not a country music place, but there's some leather guys here who would love to hear you say you get off on pain." Zane laughed and flicked a cautious glance at a bunch of bears in leather who were ignoring them and mocking the Lady Gaga queens. "I bet they'd like to find out just how much pain it takes to get you off."

"Nothing like bullfighting pain," Johnny countered.

"True. It's a specialized field. Like theirs."

The song ended with the group frozen in a pose Johnny recognized as being vaguely Charlie's Angel-ish, and then staggering to their table, panting for air while grabbing for their drinks.

The blond he'd been looking at started eye fucking with him again now that the floorshow was over, although only with one eye, as the other was hidden behind the careful swoop of his bangs.

If Johnny was so fucking brave in the ring, why couldn't he go over and talk to the blond?

Because it's completely a different thing, Johnny answered himself. "Nothing ventured, nothing gained," he muttered, and stood up.

"You're not going to do it!" Zane whispered, but then he turned practical. "If you score with that swish, you gotta tell me if he's any good."

"Fuck off," Johnny said good-naturedly. "A gentleman doesn't kiss and tell."

Ignoring Zane's laugh, he walked toward the blond, who seemed to vibrate with excitement as he drew closer.

"Can I buy you a beer?" Too late, Johnny noticed the blond had a drink with a pink umbrella in it, stabbed through some pieces of fruit. Typical.

"I'm good. Let me buy you one, stud." The blond queen beamed at him.

His response made Johnny feel even more ashamed of himself, especially as he was surprised at how much more feminine the guy was up close. He indicated his bottle of beer. "I'm set. Name's Johnny." He held out his hand.

The blond ignored it and leaned in to waft an air kiss beside either cheek. "Christian, and I've had as much booze as I can handle for one night. I'm such a lightweight! And I'd much rather handle fabulous you."

"You might be too much for me to handle," Johnny said, wondering if he was too deep in unfamiliar waters. He stared at Christian's eye makeup. He had on blue eyeliner and mascara, and Johnny found himself wondering if the smoothness of Christian's skin was due to foundation. His perfectly bowed lips were so pink and shiny Johnny suspected lip gloss.

"I don't do restroom sex," Christian announced. "But I can host. I rent a house with a few friends."

"You never do bathroom sex?"

"Restrooms! Ew! Especially in a place like this." Christian ran his hand over Johnny's belt.

Just in time, Johnny twisted his hips away to avoid getting a hand planted on his crotch in the middle of the bar. "I'm not crazy about bathrooms either. Let's get out of here." He grabbed Christian's hand to stop it from roaming and pulled him toward the door, much to Christian's delight.

"Oh, you big strong brute! Using force on me! Too, too hot-making. Bye, girls! I've got a date!"

Feeling intensely embarrassed by the high-pitched squeals of "darlings" and "have fun, ladies," behind him, Johnny plowed through the crowd and out the door. At this point it was Christian who had a grip on him he couldn't shake without hurting the smaller man.

"Where we going?" he growled. The things he was willing to do to bust a nut. The way Christian was hanging on to him, no one could mistake them for strangers or not know what they were about to do to each other.

"It's within walking distance. One of the Victorian houses in the rocking downtown area. I could never afford it by myself, but I got a group of friends together and we rent. We all get along, *most* of the time. They're going to be so jealous when they see you!"

"I thought they already saw us at the bar."

"Oh, that's not them. Most of my roommates are staying in tonight, playing strip Yahtzee."

"Jesus," Johnny muttered. What had he gotten himself into?

Christian kept up a flow of one-sided conversation that made the walk seem shorter than Johnny expected. The house was also the opposite way from his motel, which might prove useful when he wanted to make his escape. Even though Christian wore hot-pink Converse, he didn't seem like the athletic type.

Johnny had hoped Christian might sneak him upstairs, but he guessed wrong. Instead Christian marched him right through the front room, where a group of good-looking, slim young men in various stages of undress all stared at him with frank interest.

"Is he for us? You brought us a prize! Darling, introduce him immediately."

"Hands off, bitches. He's all mine and all man," Christian said, hanging on to Johnny's arm with both hands. "I told you going out was the only way to bag one. The bar is *overflowing* with butch cock tonight. You should go there. Now!"

"Oooh, get a load of the package on her!" said a dark man, staring at Johnny's crotch.

"I'm winning! Maybe she'd like to play with me," blurted another, clad in only a jockstrap.

Embarrassing as it was, Johnny's dick swelled looking at the group of cute, half-naked guys hanging all over each other, so he was relieved when Christian pulled him away.

"Have fun with your game, children, while I have adult triple X-rated fun with a real man! No eavesdropping at the door!" Christian tugged him to an ornately carved staircase. "Up here."

The minute they were inside his room, Christian knelt at Johnny's feet and ran his hands over his thighs. "You must work out a lot. You're so hot. Are you negative? I am. I've got condoms; you want to fuck me?"

"I don't fuck."

"Oh, are you one of the straight boys who pretend not to be queer when they're dicking a manpussy?"

"No, I'm gay all right." Johnny gave him a wolfish grin.

"Then perhaps you've taken a vow of chastity so you can't fuck? Are you a nun, Sister Johnny?" Christian's face was solemn and he held his hands as if in prayer, but his eyes gleamed with wicked fun. "You're in safe hands with me, because blow jobs don't count as sex. Everyone knows that."

"No, my vocation lies in getting a cock in my mouth, pronto. I like it as much as you, Sister Christian."

Christian laughed and started to say something, but it had been hard enough cutting this one out of the herd at the bar and Johnny wasn't here to chat, so he unzipped and pressed his cock to Christian's moving mouth. The glossy lips parted immediately and Johnny filled Christian's mouth with cock to shut him up. However, he couldn't complain about the lavish and expert blowjob that followed. He was nearly unconscious with pleasure by the time he came, and his knees wobbled dangerously because his bones had melted. He sank onto the bed to recover. He was so going to tell Zane about this, and it made him glad he had at least one friend he could talk to freely. Slowly, he became aware that Christian had resumed the interrupted conversation and was asking how he liked it.

"You have a fabulous-tasting cock. I could suck it all day. You're some kind of Indian, aren't you? Oh yeah, I heard about that whole two-spirit thing. Being gay is accepted in your tribe, right? It would be so great to grow up where no one gave a damn that you liked cock. What tribe are you anyway?"

Johnny was beginning to get irritated as always when outsiders used the word "Indian." "Diné, and I wouldn't say it's accepted. All tribes aren't the same, you know. There was no gathering around the fire at night telling ancient stories about homoerotic frolics on the lonely plains. And this two-spirit thing is some romantic fantasy that white guys like to get off on!"

Christian was silent for a moment. "I'm sorry, man. I didn't know."

"It's all right." Johnny felt a little guilty for going off on Christian.

"I hope you still want to do it with me."

To reassure Christian, Johnny started tugging at his jeans.

"Wait, don't rip them! I'll do it. These are designer!"

Patiently, Johnny waited until Christian had managed to force his jeans and skimpy bikini briefs down to his knees after lots of squirming, and then he rolled on top of Christian to take him in his mouth. At first the theatrical moans and shrieks were almost certainly for the benefit of his friends, but soon Christian was moaning for real. He grabbed Johnny's head and held it in as strong a grip as Cody ever had as he thrust, reminding Johnny that for all the affect and makeup, he was still with a man. Besides, Christian had a nice cock and Johnny enjoyed sucking him off.

When he'd drained the other man dry, Johnny reached for the chic designer box of tissues and grabbed one to spit into.

Christian lay motionless for a few minutes before rolling to the side to run a comb through his hair and grab his lip gloss off the nightstand. While applying it, he managed to say, "I've never had an Indian before."

"I've never had a swishy little queen before."

"Oh *snap*! Read me, honey! Too hilarious and on point! So what made you pick me? You're *so* butch. Usually the butch ones don't go for my type of girl." Christian said the words in a flirtatious lisp as he ran his hand under Johnny's shirt.

The idea that he was butch cracked Johnny up. He was known as the skinny guy on his bullfighting team and with Cody—"Butch?"

"Yeah, you know, you're rocking that cowboys-and-Indians chic and all hard and muscly and I'm sort of—fat."

"You're not fat at all. What the hell are you talking about?"

"Not regular people fat, gay-fat." Christian pouted with his newly glossed lips and pulled up his sequined top to tug at the quarter inch of spare skin at his waist. "I'd give anything for a fabulous body like yours."

"Well, my job is physical, so I'm moving around most of the time. What do you do?"

"Art director at an ad agency. Most of the exercise I get is moving my mouse hand a little bit and slitting my wrists over deadlines. What do you do?"

"Construction," Johnny answered. He didn't want anyone to think of him and bull riding in the same sentence, just in case.

"See? That's a butch, macho job. No wonder you're so hard." Christian paused meaningfully before the last word, bending closer to Johnny's groin to blow a blast of hot air over his cock.

"But it's not like I'm twirling my gun and having a shoot-out down at the corral."

"Look at how different we are. I bet you've never seen a boy in makeup and nail polish before, have you?"

"Not up close," Johnny admitted.

"So what did your cute friend at the bar say when you told him you were coming over to pick me up? Is he your boyfriend?"

"How did you know what he said—"

"I spend a lot of time in clubs. I can tell when a guy is trying to talk his wingman out of a date."

"He called you a swishy little queen." Johnny was embarrassed for Zane and ashamed of himself for using the words earlier. He hoped he hadn't hurt Christian's feelings.

Christian giggled in a ladylike way. "Well, it's just telling it like it is. What did you think?"

Slowly, Johnny said, "I thought I've never seen a braver man."

"Get the fuck out! For real?" Christian sat up in a glow of surprised pleasure as he studied Johnny's face. "You mean it!"

"I could never walk around dressed like that. It's like you're out in front, taking the bullets for the rest of us."

"I look good!"

"You look fabulous. You're really cute. I wouldn't have come over if you weren't, but you—uh—do stand out." Johnny shrugged. "I wouldn't have the balls to attract attention like you do. What if some hater bashed you in an alley?"

"What if some smoking-hot butch Native American construction dude brought his dick over and offered it to me? Living dangerously has its rewards," Christian countered. He laid his head on Johnny's shoulder again and snuggled closer. "So, you got a boyfriend? You two play around? If you're in an open relationship, you could bring me home to him. I could do both of you. Maybe he'd like to fuck me and you could watch. You going to be in town long? I could show you around. I know all the good bars."

Even though he admired Christian in many ways, Johnny was a bit relieved that when he told him he traveled for his job and was leaving in the morning, he was telling the truth. Under Christian's relentless questioning, he also offered up some stories about his encounters in highway restrooms just to keep things from getting too personal.

"I always heard they were great places to pick up men, although, bathrooms! Ew!" Christian said. "I may have to break down and give it a try though if it's as hot as you say."

It was another hour before Johnny managed to extricate himself, even though for the last quarter of it Christian had used his mouth for things other than talking. Mindful of Vern's warning that he'd be left behind if he wasn't on time, Johnny finally managed to get his jeans up and zipped and made it out of Christian's room with time to spare to pack and fit in a short nap.

Once again he had to run the gauntlet of Christian's curious roommates giving catcalls and asking provocative questions about what had gone on in the room.

"Did that stud drill you through the mattress? We could hear you *screaming* like a little *girl* all the way down here!"

"Shut up, girls. Let my date leave with a *shred* of dignity," Christian scolded them. His stage whisper of, "I'll dish all the dirt after he's gone!" made Johnny flush with embarrassment again.

In the small entryway, Christian pulled Johnny down for their only kiss. "Thanks, sugar. Don't worry, I'll talk you up good to the girls. I'll always remember this date."

"Yeah, me too."

Christian danced away from him before Johnny was even out the door, so he stopped with the door open a crack to listen.

"Girls! My date gave me the 4-1-1 on where to hunt down grade-A, straight, willing, married cock! Road trip!"

The twitter of raised voices gave Johnny a vivid mental image of a pink convertible crowded with obvious queens flashing sequins and feather boas on the highway. He had to grin at the thought of them descending on an unsuspecting rest area as a group, even though they would probably bring cleaning supplies and have the bathroom sparkling before they started cruising. He wouldn't put it past them to get some action. The desperation of the closeted men he'd met on the road, dying for a mouth on their cock, was pitiful compared to these guys. They might be fey, but they were out and proud. It took real balls to face the world the way they did, but they seemed to thoroughly enjoy their lives. The joyous, exuberant way Christian acted made Johnny think about Cody, but then what didn't make him think about Cody?

"Fabulous," he murmured and pulled the door shut.

He doubted Christian would actually remember him, but he knew he'd never forget Christian.

"IF ONLY Johnny were here, we could get those bulls loaded up in no time, no problem," Travis said provocatively. "Maybe someone should call him."

"Be my guest if you have his number," Cody said stiffly. "Just give me a day's notice so I can clear out."

"You know you want him back," Travis said. "How about if I just help out a bit? I could call him, ask him to—"

Cody stood up and shoved his chair back so hard it hit the dishwasher. "You don't know what I want. Just shut up!" He stalked out and slammed the door so hard the windows rattled. He was so angry he was shaking and had to lean on the door to compose himself if he didn't want to break something. He didn't mean to eavesdrop, but the windows were open, and Cody froze in place when he heard RJ's voice.

"You shouldn't tease him like that, love."

"Someone's got to bring him to his senses. He's been thinking Johnny was just going to come crawling back. Well, he ain't. He's got his pride and Cody's got more than enough for two people. Somebody has to get this party started," Travis said.

"Cody's a proud man," Val said. "It'll take him a little time before he's ready to admit what he wants."

"A proud idiot."

Cody didn't like hearing that, but he was dying to know what his parents thought.

"Thanks a lot for pointing out I raised an idiot," his mother said.

"And you did a great job of it. What would you call him?"

"I call my darling son a handsome daredevil," Val said.

"Okay, a handsome daredevil who's also a top-ranked idiot," Travis said.

"He's so angry," Davis said in a worried tone. "He's not paying attention to business."

"Because he won't give in to what he wants. Stupid male pride," Travis snorted.

"You ought to know," Val said. "I seem to recall when you and RJ once—"

"Ancient history." Travis waved it away hastily. "Besides, RJ came to his senses, apologized, and then I—"

"Funny, I don't remember it that way."

Travis blustered, "We're still together. That says it all. We didn't cross the line like Cody did when we had a difference of opinion."

"Cody didn't cross the line, he floored it and roared past at a hundred sixty miles an hour," Val said. "His normal speed."

Davis sounded anxious as he said, "Maybe I should go after him—"

"No, hon. He's got to work this out for himself, even if he is doing it slower than a glacier," Val said.

"I've never seen him so angry."

"Maybe the ice is beginning to melt. About time too. I miss having Johnny here." Val sounded hopeful, and Cody was glad to hear he wasn't the only one missing Johnny.

"I'm worried he'll get himself hurt, riding a bull in a foul mood like that."

"He hasn't hurt himself yet and he's been riding most of the summer," RJ rumbled. "He's good. Too good to get hurt because he's pining."

"Yeah, but he ain't been scoring." Of course it *would* be Travis who pointed that out.

"Leave it to me, boys. I shall sting like a butterfly and ride him like a bucking bronc when the time is right," Val said. "He just needs a little push in the right direction. What he needs is a woman's finesse."

When they changed the subject to chores for the day, Cody finally was able to tear himself away, tiptoeing so they wouldn't know he'd heard their conversation. At least forewarned was forearmed, but instead of feeling backed into a corner, Cody found himself hoping his mother would confront him soon. It went against his pride to ask for advice, but she was the one person in the world he could consider confiding in.

CHAPTER 13:

Silver Bear

WHEN he was in the ring, sometimes he glanced at the crowd in the stands while they were getting the next ride ready, but usually it was mostly a nameless mass of faces and colorful shirts and hats. No one ever stood out too much, and it wasn't a place Johnny would have thought to scope out for a hookup. He would never have expected to find a gay man sitting there, but if the hottest man in the world had been there, he would have overlooked him because it was usually so jammed.

Tonight was different. It was probably the flash of the silver hair, thick and lush and just long enough to catch the eye, even in a crowd. The man under it wasn't bad either. When he stood up in the expensive box to cheer, Johnny could tell he was tall and stocky, bigger than Cody. Then Johnny turned his eyes away quickly when he realized the man was looking directly at him.

After that he was painfully conscious that the man's gaze was mostly on him, whether he was dancing away from a bull or just hanging at the sides checking in with Vern and Reese. It made him nervous, and he thought up all kinds of lurid reasons some rabid bull-riding fan might be looking at him. Maybe he was a reporter and had spotted Johnny at a gay club. Maybe he was someone Cody knew—but that didn't make sense. There was no need to stalk him; the schedule for the touring division was online.

Someone from his home state? Whatever the man's reason, he paid more attention to the bullfighters than the riders, which was unusual. Johnny tried to stare him down at one point, but the man was irrepressible. He licked his lips with a feral grin that all but said, *Eventually you're going to be in my bed and I'm going to fuck the daylights out of you.* It was as if the man had growled it in his ear, Johnny heard it so clearly.

The unusual attention got him so distracted, Johnny made a mistake that could have cost him dearly. When the bull slammed him back into the fence, he managed to take the brunt of the metal on the fleshiest part of his buttocks, but it was going to leave a mark. It wasn't the worst injury he'd had in the ring, but it was the most avoidable and humiliating and it was all his own fault. He knew Vern would call him on it later, and he would be right.

After the final ride, Johnny sat with Vern and Reese in their changing room for the usual review and prayer. He wasn't surprised when Vern pointed out his mistake first thing.

"Staring into the stands for at least half the night," Vern said with disapproval. "You gotta focus on what's happening *in* the ring. That's where the action is. Our lives and the riders' safety are in your hands."

"We got your back, but you gotta have ours," Reese put in. "Your paycheck is in the ring, not in the stands."

Johnny knew he'd fucked up bad if Reese felt he had to say something. "I'm sorry. I won't let it happen again."

"If there's some cute girl in the audience giving you the come-hither eye, she'll just have to wait," Vern continued. "You're getting paid to do a job and you'll do it while I'm in charge." The implication was clear. Vern had put him on the team and he could kick him off at any time.

"Yes, sir." Johnny made no excuse. There was none that could be acceptable in their line of work. "I fucked up. It won't happen again."

Vern gave a firm nod, as if pleased that Johnny didn't try to defend himself. "I respect that you can admit to it, but don't never let me see you mooning over some filly again. Reese, you did a great job tonight."

Feeling too ashamed to walk out with the other two men, Johnny took a long shower to ditch them. Besides, he needed some hot water therapy on his ass where he'd slammed the rail. He'd wanted to explain himself to Vern, but he knew how it would sound if he claimed his lapse was due to eyeballing a potential stalker, rather than a flirtation. If he wouldn't want to hear it, neither would they. This wasn't like putting a letter in the wrong file; someone could die or get badly injured because of his sloppy performance.

Therefore, when he saw the man with silver hair standing outside the venue and casually smoking a cigar like he didn't have a care in the world, Johnny snapped at him.

"What the fuck?"

"Exactly," the man answered in a deep, growly voice that matched Johnny's imagination perfectly. He held out his hand. "March Avery. And your name is?"

"None of your business."

Ignoring the man's outstretched hand, Johnny walked right past him, but the man showed no sign of irritation. "I was hoping to ask you to join me for dinner and drinks."

"You can ask."

"I'm not stupid enough to ask questions when I know the answer will be no. The art of negotiation is not to ask until the answer is yes." March gave a rich, deep chuckle. "You haven't even known me five minutes and you're already pissed off at me. That might be a new record."

"Great. Guess we can call it a night then."

The man caught up to Johnny and fell into step. "I'd like to have a shot at convincing you to at least let me buy you a beer."

"You're a persistent bastard."

"And that's bad because?" March chuckled again. "I know you'll be in town until tomorrow's show and you probably have nothing much to do. Why not at least have a drink with me? I'm HIV negative and I'm paying the bill. What have you got to lose?"

Johnny looked at his watch. "I might have a whole stable of girls lined up waiting for me to pick them off one by one."

"No, you don't." March was still smiling as if they shared some kind of secret.

"You're making a pretty big assumption here."

It irritated Johnny, but the man's confidence also made him want to laugh. In some ways he was like Cody, the charm, the bullheaded determination to go after what he wanted, the confidence that he wouldn't lose. The good looks. The fucker was handsome. And hot.

"And you might kick my ass if I were wrong, but I'm not wrong."

"I'm already in the dog house tonight because of you."

"Really? Why's that? You seem like you're excellent at your job."

"I wasn't paying close enough attention to the action. I was worrying about why you were staring at me like I was prancing around the ring with no clothes on," Johnny snapped.

"You know what they say. What I think of you is none of your business. Never let an incidental annoyance get in the way of what you love."

Johnny flinched at the words but he wasn't going to let some stranger get his goat. "You were being kind of obvious."

"Maybe I was having too good a time imagining you prancing around the ring with no clothes on." March's chuckle was warm, with no hint of threat. "But if so, it's still none of your business."

"And what I look like without my clothes is none of yours," Johnny retorted, feeling rightfully pleased with his response.

"I hope to make it my business. You sure fill out a pair of jeans nice."

"What about the chance you're taking? You don't know me."

"A straight man wouldn't even have noticed me looking, let alone look back. And if you weren't interested, my cruising wouldn't have bothered you. You'd laugh off the old fart in the stands."

"You mean silver bear," Johnny corrected in a mutter.

March threw back his head and laughed. "Thank you for proving my point. A straight man wouldn't even know the term." He stopped beside a silvery-aqua Jaguar XK convertible. "I'm staying at the Wingate Arms. Would you like to meet me there or can I offer you a lift?"

More used to utility vehicles like the beat-up pickup Vern drove, Johnny was dazzled by the sports car. If Cody won the top prize at the finals, he would be able to afford one, although it would never occur to him to indulge in such a luxury. And for Johnny, at a bullfighter's salary with the heavy health insurance premiums, this might be his only chance to ride in one.

It took a bit of stomping his pride down to accept, because Johnny was sure March would take it as total capitulation to his charms rather than his car's, but he said, "All right. One beer. I can't afford a hangover tomorrow. I've got to prove I'm not a total loser to my boss."

"Hop in."

"Better than wearing out the boot leather. Thanks for the lift." Johnny knew March knew he was saving his face by pretending it was just a ride with no strings, but now he was curious to see what the other man would try next.

Sure enough, the knowing smile on March's face almost made Johnny change his mind, but the older man only said, "I'll put the top down."

Johnny was done at that point. After March unlocked the doors, Johnny got in, grateful at least that March didn't treat him like a girl by coming around the car to open the door for him. They could have a beer, he'd listen to March's pitch for comparison's sake, and then he'd leave.

It was edging toward evening and the sky was showing off a pink-and-gold sunset. Johnny took his hat off so he could feel the breeze blowing through his hair and hung his arm out over the door, catching the wind in his hand. It felt almost solid as it smacked against his palm. He was both relieved and a little disappointed that March made no attempt to touch him, not even a casual brush of the hand that could be passed off as an accident.

Johnny didn't even glance at the tiny rundown motel where he was staying when they passed it and drove closer to the part of the city where the expensive hotels and casinos were clustered.

When they pulled up in front of the valet stand, Johnny decided with amusement that if March didn't care what anyone thought of him in his worn jeans and scuffed-up boots, he wouldn't either. He put his hat back on when the car stopped. March was still taller than him, even with the hat.

It was entertaining to watch March toss the keys at the uniformed young valet, who was practically curtseying he was so obviously panting for a big tip.

"After you," March said, holding out his arm to indicate the double glass doors.

Of course, Johnny didn't have to open the door himself. Some bellhop jumped to it, no doubt also salivating for a tip. It was like getting a free credit report on March.

Once inside, March took the lead, heading toward a bank of elevators with actual operators inside. He showed a key card to one of them, and both men were permitted to enter.

March said, "Derbyshire Lounge, please."

Johnny just went along with it, feeling incongruously shabby next to the impeccably, if casually dressed, silver bear.

The elevator slid soundlessly to a stop on the second floor to let them out into a dark-green marble foyer. March led the way again to a dimly lit bar that had been decorated to look like an exclusive men's club, or so Johnny thought, never having been in one.

March chose a table and Johnny sat opposite him. He took off his hat and set it on one of the empty chairs.

"Name your poison."

Johnny named the beer of his dreams and March told the waiter to bring two.

"I wouldn't think you'd drink beer," Johnny said.

"What should I be drinking?"

"I don't know. Some hundred-year-old brandy that costs its weight in gold."

March gave a big laugh, showing his excellent teeth. "If you'd ever had brandy, you'd know why I stick with beer. It's a very specific taste and I haven't developed mine in that direction. I'm just a regular guy."

"I don't want to poke my nose in where it doesn't belong, but you seem like a rich dude to me."

"I am well-off, but I got rich working. I'm no trust-fund baby; I used to be a contractor. Luckily I got out before the housing crash and I'm able to be a bit more diversified in my interests now."

The waiter set two mugs on the table and withdrew. Johnny was surprised by the mugs. He'd never been served a beer that wasn't still in the bottle it was born in.

"Pretty good," March said in surprise after he'd tried it. "I haven't had this brand before."

"So you can buy pretty much anything you want," Johnny said a bit truculently.

"This isn't a *Pretty Woman* scenario, if that's what you're afraid of," March said. "I think we would enjoy each other, but I don't pay unwilling men to get into my bed. If you end up there tonight, it'll be because you want to."

"Damn! I could have used a few extra bucks," Johnny said regretfully.

March's face froze and then he laughed. "You almost got me. I'm not often mistaken in my assessment of men but you had me going for a minute."

"Am I that obvious?"

"Not at all. I would say you are a very intelligent, cocky, vulnerable, complex young man with a yen for adventure and risk, and excellent taste in men. I aim to offer you sufficient sexual adventure to hold your interest for one night, which I'm fully equipped to do. We could start by having dinner."

"Cocky?" That idea rocked Johnny. Cody was the cocky one.

"We all have it in some way. With you, it's how you move. Confidently, like a sexy wild young panther." March licked his lips. "You know my name. Mind telling me yours?"

"Johnny Arrow."

"For real? Never met a man named Arrow before."

Surprisingly, Johnny found himself explaining. "It's because I'm Native American. Needed a stage name and it was, uh, appropriate."

"I'd like to see your arrow."

"Lame, but still amusing." Johnny snickered and looked March over. He liked the man's appearance; he was older, maybe in his early fifties, but fit, with a light tan that looked good with his silver hair. It was more his face that attracted Johnny, though. He had a nice smile and his eyes were filled with humor and intelligence. He didn't give off the reek of desperation that Johnny had begun to associate with some of the men who'd hit on him. In fact, if it weren't for Cody.... Hastily, he banished the thought.

For the first time since he'd left the ranch, Johnny was attracted more to the man than the idea of getting laid, so attracted that he forgot his initial hostility. "We could start by going to your room."

March seemed only mildly startled. He put a bill on the table and rose. "Well, all right, then. Let's go."

WHILE Johnny was wrestling his boots off, March stripped with a few fluid movements. Naked, he was tanned all over and not quite as trim as he'd seemed in his clothing. He slapped the slight pooch of his stomach. "There's a six-pack under there somewhere, I swear. Do what I can in the gym, I've still got love handles." He leered cheerfully. "However, I earned them fair and square and they're available for you to hang on to when I'm drilling you."

"You look pretty damn good to me." Johnny meant it. Even though March might have put on a few pounds since his prime, it was easy to tell he still worked out. His biceps and shoulders were massive and rock hard. Maybe when he said he was in construction it meant he really built things, not just told other people what he wanted done. They were the kind of muscles a man earned through actual physical labor, not just the toning exercises at the gym. His firm chest was covered with silver hair that matched his head, and gradually grew darker as it trailed down the center of his abdomen to a black cloud between his legs. His cock was long, thick, and hard, encircled by black bushy hair.

When Johnny was naked, he stood up to allow the other man to look him over. During all the dating and tricks since he left Cody, he'd never gotten naked with any of them before. He wasn't quite sure why he wanted to now, but the admiration glinting in March's eyes made him feel good.

March came closer and murmured, "You are so damn fuckable, Johnny Arrow. I'm going to enjoy you."

Johnny might have protested that he wasn't there to get fucked, but before he could, March's mouth took his hostage. Not that the older man jammed his tongue down his throat; his approach was more sensual, licking, tasting, capturing Johnny's lip between his teeth and pulling gently and releasing before sliding their tongues together again. Johnny shivered as their naked skin brushed together and wrapped his arms around March, running his hands up and down his sides.

With a low, shaky laugh, March broke the kiss and said, "You taste even sweeter than I thought."

"You're pretty damn hot yourself," Johnny said.

"I know." March sounded amused. "Sex is more than a hard dick and a perfect body, but damn, boy, your body and face are downright beautiful. I don't say that to too many boys." He ran his fingers over the tattoo. "Stunning. Some tattoos are ugly, but the way this design wraps around your body is perfect. Tight, taut, lean. You'll have to tell me the story later, boy, but right now...."

For some reason it didn't bother Johnny when March called him "boy." Maybe it was the age difference, or maybe he had more confidence in his own ability to control where things were going. It was intensely satisfying to be the focus of such a man's attention because he was quite sure March was interested in *him*, Johnny, not scoring a closeted bullfighter or some random younger man. He decided to enjoy whatever March had to offer.

The next thing on offer turned out to be March dropping to his knees and grabbing his ass to start blowing him. It took his breath away how aggressively March went to town on his cock, licking and sucking him until his balls were wet.

Then suddenly March pushed him to his knees and presented his cock to Johnny's lips for his attention. He did his best, learning the sensitive spots by March's reactions and gasps, teasing under the ridge with his tongue, blowing on wet skin to cool it suddenly and just as suddenly taking him in to the root. March grabbed the back of his head, holding him immobile by his hair while he fucked Johnny's mouth, sometimes plugging his throat with his deep thrusts and making it a challenge to catch a breath. Johnny enjoyed every minute.

Then March lifted him and pushed him onto the bed before blanketing him with his body. The warmth and weight pressing him down felt good. Only now Johnny realized how much he'd prevented other men from touching him, even while getting and giving pleasure. This felt personal, as if March were practically surrounding him with his mass and personality, but not as if he was swallowing him whole. Johnny hadn't felt small or cherished in a long time, and he liked it.

He also liked how quickly March discovered the sensitivity of his nipples, capturing one between gentle teeth and flicking his tongue rapidly over the hard nub until Johnny writhed and cried out with pleasure. Then he gave the same ruthless treatment to the other. Johnny sighed and moaned with each new tactile sensation as March licked his way down his body, using hands and mouth on his cock until he started to thrust urgently. March worked the shaft with his hand and started to kiss him again. Johnny was so lost in pleasure that his orgasm came as a blissful surprise.

He was sweating and still panting when he opened his eyes to find March propped on one elbow beside him, lazily stroking himself and watching him.

"Wow."

March laughed. "Yeah, a man without perfect abs can still work some sexual voodoo."

Johnny reached over and pushed March's hand away, taking over and gently stroking the older man's cock. "You have a great body."

"You have a great ass. Your ass and my cock, I think they're destined to make beautiful music together."

"I don't fuck."

"If you've never done it before, I have a PhD in breaking an untried ass in. I'll be gentle."

Johnny resisted March's attempt to turn him onto his stomach. "I've been fucked. I've fucked other men. I just don't do it anymore."

"I'll use a condom." March licked at one of Johnny's reddened nipples.

"It's not about that. I just don't fuck."

March rolled back up onto his elbow and studied Johnny's face, still with the little confident smile playing around his lips. "I see. You're setting a boundary."

"And you'll respect it." Johnny's voice had a note of steel in it.

"I will respect it. Even though I really want to get inside that exquisite ass and fuck it 'til I make you scream."

This time, when March rolled him onto his stomach, Johnny didn't resist. Somehow, in the space of the hour they'd known each other, he'd figured out he could trust him, and therefore March's hands rubbing his cheeks didn't freak him out. He winced once when March was a little too rough on the spot where he'd hit the fence, and rolled onto his side.

"What is it?"

"Weren't you watching earlier? Bull pushed me into the fence. I'm going to have some bruises tomorrow."

"Tough guy. I admire that. But if it's marks you want, I'd be happy to give you a few love bites." March touched the curve of Johnny's hip. "Maybe here." He bent to kiss the spot. "Or here." This time he pushed Johnny back onto his stomach and bit his ass cheek before sucking hard enough that Johnny knew he'd have a mark tomorrow. "Or here." This time it was the inside of his thigh. Johnny was squirming before March released him and stroked the red mark with a gentle finger. "You look good wearing my marks."

"I'm going to be a mess." Johnny laughed and rubbed his ass. "Just don't give me one where it shows."

"We could stay in bed all day tomorrow and you could call in sick."

Incredulously, Johnny lifted his head to stare at March. "When you're a bullfighter, you don't call in sick unless blood is spurting out of an artery or a bone is poking through your skin."

March threw back his head and laughed. "My apologies. Same in construction, so I ought to have known better." He pressed Johnny back down onto the mattress. "I can make it feel better tonight, though."

Johnny relaxed as the knowledgeable hands worked over his aching muscles, finding the knots and getting them to loosen up, but he felt unjustly pampered. March was still sporting admirable wood, and he hadn't made any effort to equal things up. He almost protested when he felt March remove the rubber band and let his hair spill loose. Johnny purred at the sensation when March ran his fingers gently through his hair.

"Such thick, shiny hair. It suits you. Some guys couldn't carry it off without looking feminine."

Johnny just lay there enjoying the massage, even though he felt unaccountably guilty. It was, after all, *his* hair, but he'd never had it out for sex except with Cody. On the other hand, March was a remarkably sensuous man and seemed to be messing up all his rules. However, he couldn't just lie there accepting all the attention for himself. Johnny was about to take the reins back when March grabbed his hips. He could feel rough, calloused fingers gripping him as March pulled him up onto his hands and knees. A flicker of panic went through him until he felt the unmistakable soft wetness of a tongue against his hole.

Helplessly, he squirmed in March's grip as the other man ate him out almost as aggressively as he'd blown him. A hand reached around and slid up and down on his cock, gently milking him as cool air hit his hole when March blew on it.

Finally March turned Johnny onto his back, and Johnny had to chuckle when he saw March's condition pretty much matched his.

"That's the way I like my boys, hard and ready." March had a hand on each of them, slowly working their erections. "You've got me hot enough I could almost hop aboard and ride you. I bet you could fuck me and make me like it, and I'm exclusively a top."

"No fucking," Johnny reminded him.

"I was hoping maybe you'd forget." March's deep chuckle told Johnny he was teasing. "Trying to tempt you."

"Oh, if you were the one offering the apple, Adam wouldn't have had a moment's doubt." Johnny had a feeling March made a career out of being a tease, and determined he wouldn't be the only one in this bed doing that.

He pushed March's hand away and knelt between his legs, keeping his ass tilted up so March could enjoy the view, and started blowing him. He was no less aggressive than March had been, sucking in his balls and swirling them with his tongue, licking and nibbling up his shaft, following his mouth up and down with a tight ring of his fingers. Moving March into whatever position he wanted, Johnny took pride in the little sounds of pleasure that escaped the other man.

The spurt of salty, hot seed took him by surprise, but he held it in his mouth while March thrashed on the bed, his voice raised to a bellow as he came. Johnny had to grin internally, while still taking care with his teeth, at the thought of people in the next room listening to the deep-bull voice of a grown man bellowing out, "Yeah! Fuck me! Fuck me good!"

When March pushed him away feebly, Johnny spit discreetly into a tissue before he crawled up and straddled him. He leaned down to kiss March. Their tongues danced together languidly now that the initial urgency was gone. March's hands cupping his ass felt good to Johnny, as well as his own dick rubbing in the silver mass of body hair.

"So damn fuckable," March sighed. "And you're still hard."

"Sometimes I don't go down for a while."

"I know you've probably heard this before, but youth is wasted on the young," March said, sounding wistful for the first time.

"Oh, I'll bet you're not a once-a-night man," Johnny teased. He could feel March's cock pressed between their bellies, and ground his hips a little to emphasize the point.

"If I've only got one night with you in my bed, I'm surely not going to waste it." March rolled Johnny onto his back suddenly and pinned him to the bed. "If you're sure I can't fuck you...."

Johnny smiled but shook his head.

"I'm going to put my cock between your legs and fuck you that way," March announced. He reached for the bedside table and rubbed himself with lube before pushing Johnny's legs together. Sighing as he slid his cock between Johnny's thighs, March started to pump.

It was hotter than Johnny could have imagined. With just seductive words, glances and his mouth, March had already made him want to have that cock inside him, filling him. It was a miracle he was able to resist this man, and now, with the big, delicious cock gliding between his legs, rubbing his balls, March's stomach rubbing against his dick, his weight holding him down, Johnny wanted him more than ever. But he couldn't say so; he might break if he did. Instead he let the rhythm and pounding of March's body above him take him into the fantasy of getting fucked through the mattress.

All the while, March talked dirty to him, asking him how he liked his cock, if he liked taking it this way. Johnny gasped out, "Yeah, I like it. Give it to me, give me your cock," without worrying about potential eavesdroppers in the next room.

Suddenly March rolled off and Johnny missed the warmth of the body.

"Turn on your side. I'm going to fuck you from behind." Before he could move, March rolled him onto his side and got behind him to run one slick finger in the crease and over his hole. Johnny's body jerked involuntarily at the tingling sensation, but before he could say anything, March sank his cock between Johnny's thighs again.

Johnny pressed them tight together, wanting to give March as much sensation as he could. Slipping one arm under Johnny's torso, March pulled him back tight against his own chest. Then he circled Johnny's dick with his big fist.

"It's better this way; I can do something for you at the same time."

Johnny gasped and ground his buttocks back against March's hips, relishing the rough slap of flesh against the faint soreness of his cheeks. He let March take control of their movements and pound against him in ever faster rhythm until he felt the slick wetness of come on his balls and between his legs. The feeling pushed him closer until a different twist of March's hand made him stiffen and shoot, his hips jerking frantically.

The feeling of March's breath against his ear as they relaxed, their skins warm and sticking together, was the most intimate thing Johnny had felt since leaving Cody. He snuggled back, anxious not to leave the shelter of the other man's body too soon.

He must have fallen asleep. When he opened his eyes, he was alone in the bed, but before he got too disoriented, the sight of March sitting naked at the table, eating and reading the paper, reminded him of where he was.

Arching in the bed, Johnny stretched, which awakened the dull ache in his buttocks and drew March's attention.

"I called room service. I hope you're hungry."

"Trying to fatten me up?"

"Trying to keep your strength up. The night's not over yet."

Again, the audacious expression gave March's grin a predatory edge, and Johnny liked the hint of danger.

His stomach growled and March grinned. "No dress code up here. Come on over and have a bite before we start on dessert."

Guessing that dessert was probably going to be him, Johnny rolled out of bed and walked to the table. "What'd you get?"

"A winner when I got you in my bed." March ran a hand down Johnny's flat stomach and growled. "Love the way you walk, boy. Like a wolf on the prowl."

"Starving wolf. Feed me." Johnny sat down.

March lifted a silver cover. "Cold stuff. Didn't know how long you'd sleep. Lobster salad. Fruit. Wine. Cheese and bread. If you want anything different, let me know."

"This is on the menu?" Johnny was amazed by the lavish variety on the tray.

"I just asked for what I thought you might like."

"I've never had lobster before." Johnny tried it a bit tentatively and discovered he liked it.

"I hope you like it. I do."

"It's good." Johnny felt a bit awkward eating naked with a stranger.

As if March sensed it, he distracted Johnny. "Tell me about that tat. If you don't mind talking about it."

"It's a cloud ladder. In Diné legend this is the staircase Fire Man used to hang the stars." Johnny looked down and ran his hand over the ink. He liked how the design moved over his muscles, changing as his skin moved. "When I first started working on a ranch back in school, I wanted something to remind me who I was. Where I came from."

Nodding, March said, "When you feel like no one sees you, sometimes you need to do something to set yourself apart. Even if you're the only one who sees it."

"I knew when I decided to work in bull riding, I'd never be able to be out. Diné is another part of me—"

"Trust me. No one could ever overlook you. You're very special and beautiful."

Johnny laughed and tapped his lopsided nose. "Yeah, I don't think anyone is going to ask me to model."

"I would." March watched Johnny eat as if it were the most fascinating sight in the world. For some reason it didn't make Johnny feel self-conscious. Instead he felt proud March was that into him. The intense attention made him hard under the table, a fact he somehow guessed March was aware of even before he went to wash up in the bathroom.

When he came out, March pinned him to the wall and went to work on his nipples until his knees melted and he was practically sobbing for breath.

THE room was dark when he woke again. March still held him within the circle of his arms and was snoring faintly. Johnny grinned. Somehow it seemed to make it more real, like a fart in the middle of a romantic scene where the two lovers were comfortable enough to break up laughing at it.

Even though March's cock wedged between his cheeks, his hips flexing as he rubbed slowly in his crease, Johnny felt safe. He could stop March from fucking him and he knew it, even though the man's arms felt like iron bands around him. He didn't have to use any force; he could do it simply with a word and the strength of his own conviction. It was a gift more powerful than the orgasms March had given him, and Johnny wanted to thank March for revealing something he hadn't known about himself. Even more wonderful was sleeping in a man's arms again. It had been lonely since he left Cody, but he'd never wanted to actually sleep with any of the men he "slept" with until now.

Struggling to face March, Johnny twisted in his arms 'til they were face-to-face. He didn't know how long he had lain there thinking, but March was awake and waiting for him when he got there. Wordlessly, Johnny kissed March, enjoying the taste of him, the sweep of his tongue in his mouth, the way March confidently explored his body.

Their hands roamed over, under, between, avoiding their genitals until the tease was too much. He could feel March's cock beginning to thicken and rise. March shoved a leg between Johnny's and levered his thigh up to get access to his dick. With their hands caressing each other, they made out until they came.

Johnny could feel March's breath in his mouth when the other man said, "Damn, three times in one night. Not bad for a man getting on in years."

"Or for a young one either."

"So fucking hot. Sizzling. How old are you, son?"

"Twenty-three. You?"

"Well, damn. I'm sixty-two." For the first time March seemed hesitant, as if waiting for Johnny to react in shock.

"I bet you were fucking hot at any age."

"True, but I'm naturally uplifted around you."

Johnny laughed at the terrible pun.

Regretfully, March said, "I feel like I lured you here under false pretenses. I never even bought you a proper dinner."

"You fed me well enough." Johnny licked his lips and smiled, thinking of March's cock filling his mouth.

March trailed his fingers through Johnny's hair and toyed with a long lock. "Beautiful. But you need to get some sleep if you're going to escape another tongue-lashing from your boss."

"Mmm, tongue-lashing," Johnny teased.

"In the morning," March promised.

Johnny cuddled closer and fell asleep in March's arms once again.

BY FIRST light, they wrestled for dominance on the bed. Sometimes Johnny was on top, straddling March's sturdy body and rubbing against him, but eventually he ended up on the bottom as March kissed him.

"Where you belong," March taunted with a wolfish grin as he pinned Johnny's hands. "I'm gonna fuck you like I did last night."

"I'm sorry I can't but—"

"Never apologize, boy. Everything has its pros and cons. I'd love to get in that tight little ass, but this way, I don't need to use a condom."

March's cock was already cradled between his thighs, and Johnny arched up to meet the other man's thrusts, wanting the friction of his stomach against his own dick. March kept him firmly pinned, and having to keep his legs together didn't give him much range of motion. Johnny decided he liked a little domination in bed after all, which made him think of Cody. Firmly, he thrust Cody out of his mind, instead focusing on March's face above him, watching it get sweaty and red as he pounded away.

His orgasm seemed to catch him by surprise because March grunted and moved faster, making them bounce on the mattress. Again, the heat of his seed between his legs, coating his balls and trickling between his buttocks, made Johnny squirm with arousal. Then he was pinned for real as March collapsed on him, breathing heavily, his head buried in Johnny's hair.

Johnny was still hard and aching to come, but he didn't want to push March aside even though he hoped the other man wouldn't fall asleep on him. But he underestimated him. March pushed himself up and kissed Johnny's lips. "We're not done yet."

"You're a sex machine," Johnny teased.

"You're right about that, even though you think you're kidding." March did a push-up over Johnny's body in perfect form and rolled off the bed.

Before Johnny could move, March wrapped his hand around his calf behind the knee and dragged him to the edge of the bed. "If you were willing to let me fuck you, I'd deep-dick you on the side of this bed 'til you begged me to come, but since we're not going there—"

Johnny cried out as March cupped his buttocks in both hands and lifted his hips off the bed, and swallowed his dick suddenly to the root. His blowjob was insistent and demanding, as if Johnny owed him another orgasm. He hovered on the edge, the tingle in his balls building slowly after their night of debauchery. March pulled off and stuck his fingers in his mouth before leaning down to lick his dick again. Johnny clenched when he felt the finger circling his hole, but it felt too good to resist the fingering as March worked his way in. Unerringly, he found Johnny's prostate and stroked over it in time to the frantic thrusts of Johnny's hips. It was what Johnny had needed to push him over the edge, and then he was falling into ecstasy. The pleasure was almost piercingly painful as March milked him until he came for the fourth time in twelve hours.

Feeling drained and replete, Johnny lay limp on the bed as March dropped next to him and pulled him closer. "I wanted to give you a night to remember, but damn, you've given me some serious memories to treasure," he said. "And some prime jack-off material for slow nights."

"I can't believe you have slow nights."

"Not often, but not too many nights match up to this." March's voice was wistful.

"I'll never forget you, that's for sure," Johnny said in a hollow voice. "You'll remember me too."

"That I will, darling."

BOTH of them were too drained to come again, but it didn't prevent them from taking a long, sensuous shower, sliding their sudsy bodies together. They ended up kissing for a long time under the stream of water. Johnny was grateful for the water disguising a few embarrassing tears. It had been an unexpectedly romantic, hot, sexy night, and he knew he'd miss March when it was time to leave. Not that he'd fallen in love, but it was a revelation to realize he could have.

It scared him a little to think that he could love someone other than Cody. Even though he was the one who'd left, his feelings for his ex had kept him relatively untouched after the separation. Now March had unlocked that door and charged through, leaving it open behind him.

After they dried off and dressed, March surprised Johnny by inviting him out to breakfast.

"Not a date, just two friends grabbing a meal."

"I really have to get going—"

"You don't have to be at the ring until later, and you have to eat anyway." March took Johnny's arm and guided him to the door. "I'm buying. We had a good time in bed, why not at the table?"

Without resistance, Johnny allowed March to propel him to the elevator. To his relief, March dropped his arm before the doors slid open to reveal other guests. If he'd wanted to, he could have made a break for it and returned to his own motel room, but there was safety in numbers. Out of all his dates, Johnny found himself liking March the most, although on the surface they didn't seem to have much in common other than their raging libidos.

March kept reminding him of Cody in a good way. He was old enough to be relaxed with himself, not controlling or needy or so fixated on his own pleasure that Johnny felt like an interchangeable sex toy. Johnny snorted a little with laughter at the thought.

"What?" March murmured. The doors slid open and he led the way to the restaurant. It was dimly lit and looked expensive to Johnny. He was glad he wasn't paying.

Thinking March would enjoy it, Johnny said, "I was just thinking, you meet a better class of tricks in a ritzy hotel than a truck stop." His body still tingled with remembered pleasure.

As he hoped, March enjoyed the joke, throwing back his head with his nice laugh. "True, although I have met a few good men along many a highway rest stop in my time. One of the best fucks I've ever had was a long-haul trucker with the soul of a poet. The harder I fucked him, the sweeter the sonnet he recited in a voice trembling with lust. Or possibly it was just me shaking the shit out of him as I banged his ass. He had a thing for Shakespeare and asked if I could fuck in time to iambic pentameter."

"And could you?" Johnny was fascinated.

"Of course." March shrugged. "A good top always finds a way to please the man he's making love to."

After a moment, Johnny said, "You are a good man, March. I wish I could have met you some other time...." The compassion in March's smile made Johnny's voice give out.

"That's why I wanted to have breakfast with you. The atmosphere down here is a bit less charged, let's say, unless we're so overcome with lust that we sink under the table to gratify our unnatural desires to the embarrassment of all the guests in the dining room."

Despite himself Johnny laughed. "You definitely know how to charm the pants off a man."

"A talent that has gotten me a lot of ass in my time." Proudly, March winked at Johnny. "I just wanted to tell you to go back to him."

"To who?" He hadn't mentioned Cody to March, had he? He would hate it if he'd moaned the wrong name in a moment of passion. Most guys wouldn't have cared, but March was a man Johnny found himself respecting, and he wouldn't want to hurt him.

"Whoever the man is who holds your heart," March responded. "I was proud of you for not letting me fuck you, even though it was an alarming blow to my ego. I know your body wanted me, but when you wouldn't, I knew this man still has a hold over you. I don't know anything about him, but I know a bit about you. You're a fine young man, son, and you wouldn't have chosen a man who would abuse you or betray your trust. Go back to him. Maybe you two can work it out."

"Your ego can relax, I wanted it too." A flicker of guilt made Johnny clamp his jaw. "What makes you say all this? Are you some kind of a shrink?"

"Well, I do have a degree in psychology now, although I've never hung out a shingle. I used to do long-haul trucking, logging, construction, anything to make a living. Once I earned my pile, I finally got to go to college. And incidentally, locate a new source of willing hot young men." March smiled, perhaps suspecting Johnny was thinking about the Shakespearean trucker. "I've been gay and on the prowl for a long time now. I'm not out drumming up the vote for monogamy, but some people like it. I think you're one of them."

"Maybe."

"I get with a lot of men and there isn't much love in our encounters. In my opinion, it's all too rare in this world. Companionable buddy sex, yes. Love, not so often."

"You don't have a boyfriend, then."

"Not right now. There's one I never should have let get away. He was younger than me. Quite a bit younger. We were in different places in our lives and I made some mistakes and fucked it up. He lost patience."

"Sounds like me and C—us."

March was kind enough not to draw attention to his slip. "Maybe. I don't know your story. We both made mistakes, but I was older and I should have figured it out quicker than I did. Like before he left. But we're talking about you. If you once found love with someone special, you should give it a chance."

"How come you're assuming I'm not fucking around on the side?"

March smiled and shook his head. "You're not."

Respecting March's obvious reluctance to talk about his ex, Johnny said, "I've been thinking a lot about him."

"You miss him?"

Johnny looked down at his orange juice. "Yeah."

"Why'd you break up?"

"It wasn't a big blow-up," Johnny started hesitantly. "It was a bunch of little things. The way he just made plans without asking. He used to talk about his old conquests."

"Ah, the ancient cock notches. It bothered you?"

Johnny nodded. "I'd never been with anyone but him. I didn't know anything other than what he showed me."

"Oh my. He must have enjoyed breaking you in."

"I never told him. He had a lot of experience—he teased me a lot about being younger, and made decisions for both of us. It just—got to me one day."

"Every thoughtless jibe might be as light as a feather but they accumulate until the weight is enough to smother and you can't shake it off anymore. In a long-term relationship, you have to learn to roll with it but also not be a doormat. You have a right to stick up for yourself." March leaned forward and tapped his index finger on the tablecloth. "It may be over for you two, but if you don't go back and find out, you'll never be able to give yourself to another man. If you don't want to end up a sad old queen cruising mall johns, maybe you should give it another shot."

"I'll definitely give it some thought."

"You think about it and do what's best for you. You don't need to take care of him. It's his job to look after himself. But tell him what you told me, especially about not being too experienced."

"I haven't been wasting my time since we broke up." Johnny couldn't keep the smug grin off his face and understood Cody's need to boast. "I've been hooking up, but it's all been…."

"Empty? And you wonder why it wasn't with me?"

"Yeah, I have been kind of."

"It's not because we're in love. It's because I was interested in you and you were interested in me. We clicked. We paid attention to each other in the moment. But we're not going to ride off together into the sunset. This was still just another hookup, maybe with better people. Go back to him." March looked oddly hopeful, but as if the conversation cut too close to the bone for him as well, he changed the mood by wiggling his eyebrows with a lewd expression. "On the other hand, if it doesn't work out after all, you can always give me a call."

"I'll bear that in mind."

"And if you felt like taking care of me again after tonight's show, I could definitely help with that...."

"I'd like to for sure, but Vern—my ride—always likes to head out right after the event," Johnny said regretfully. He forgot all about being in a public restaurant, although it was frightfully discreet and no one could see into their booth anyway, and reached across the table to touch March's hand. "I had a great time with you. I'll miss you."

"I'll miss you too, kid. I told you that you were smart. You know quality when you see it." Characteristically, March started teasing him under the table by playing footsie. As his foot traveled up Johnny's thigh, he asked, "So have you fooled around with Vern?"

Johnny snorted with laughter at the notion. "He's seriously straight and he doesn't know about me. Bull riding is a conservative sport full of the flag and God, and they don't tolerate no homos."

"You'd be surprised." March looked a little smug. "There's a reason I like to go to the rodeo. One hell of a ride, some of those boys. Men who never thought they'd let some guy knock on their back door, let alone an old guy like me."

"Are you going to talk dirty through breakfast?"

"Want me to stop?"

"Hell no! Please continue."

Amazingly, March managed to get Johnny hard again with some of his stories, even though he'd thought his dick was ready for a nice long vacation after the workout it had gotten. His ass wasn't even too sore from the rail slamming, which he chalked up to a lot of healthy exercise with March after the injury.

After breakfast, March drove him to his cheap motel and came into his tiny room to give him another of his soul-searching, tonsil-inspecting kisses before they parted.

Pressing something into his hand, March said, "I'll be there tonight, watching, so do me proud, Johnny Arrow. And keep in touch. I hate losing a good friend."

Expecting to find some bills and beginning to feel pissed, Johnny looked down to see a business card for March Avery, contractor. On the back, March had written, "If you ever want to talk…," and scrawled his cell number.

"Yeah, I just might. I hate losing a good man too. And thanks for everything." Johnny squeezed March tight when he was wrapped in those big arms for the last time.

It had been an interesting night with an interesting man. If things had been different, Johnny could have seen himself with March, but he couldn't deny the little spurt of joy whenever March told him to go back to Cody. In fact, March seemed like a glimpse into the future of what Cody might be like if his cockiness mellowed into confidence.

AFTER a long nap, which he sorely needed after a workout that had been better than any gym visit, Johnny's alarm woke him in time to be waiting outside for Vern to get a lift to the ring. He'd discovered a few more marks March left on his body in the shower, but March had been true to his promise and none of them would show when he was dressed.

It had been a while since he'd worn a man's marks, and he bore these proudly, knowing March was also sporting a few of his. March had given him a lot to think about. Now, he could admit to himself he hadn't been very happy since he'd left Cody, but pride had been a towering wall standing in the way of him calling his ex or even thinking there was any hope for them.

He performed brilliantly that night, outshining his two teammates with his daring moves and athletic saves, but he wasn't showing off even though he was well aware of March watching from his box seat as he had last night. He was just on. He didn't look in March's direction, still wary of Vern's watchful eyes upon him, but he knew his silver bear was there and enjoying him.

Still, as a bullfighter, except for a few exciting saves, he wasn't the focus of attention in the ring to anyone except March, Vern, and Reese. Only when the winner was standing on the platform getting his buckle did Johnny meet March's eyes and smile back at him. He raised a hand and March nodded back, giving him the peace sign.

It was a comforting feeling to know March's card was back in his locker.

AFTER the last high five and one more lingering glance at his silver bear, Johnny followed Vern out to the truck. Reese had already pulled out. Johnny stared out the window in silence as Vern started putting miles between them and Oklahoma.

"So what lit you up tonight?"

Johnny turned his head. "I met someone last night."

"That bimbo that was ogling you in the stands?" Vern's tone was disapproving.

"No, I had dinner with a man, an older guy who told me about his life. He gave me some advice."

"Like what?" Vern sounded as if he felt he was the one who should be handing out the advice to Johnny.

"He said don't let a minor thing get in the way of what you really love."

Vern nodded and pursed his lips. "I'd buy that. I'll bet he meant don't screw up the bullfighting for some girl you'll forget in five minutes when you spot a prettier one in the next town."

"Maybe." Johnny hid his smile by looking out the window.

"Sound advice. Maybe it's time you should get married, settle down. It was a godsend for me. Without my wife and AA, I'd probably be living in a cardboard box behind a liquor store by now. Or dead."

"Sounds like you made a good choice there." Johnny felt awkward about responding. Vern had never spoken so much about his life before, and he was surprised to hear something so personal.

"Choice between life or death," Vern agreed.

When his phone started to vibrate, Johnny looked down to find a text from March.

Good job tonight. Stay well and call me sometime. M.

Johnny smiled in secret reminiscence and texted back.

Thanks. I'll think about you tonight. J.

Dirty thoughts, I hope. I'll hope to see you again sometime.

Filthy. Thanks for everything.

Johnny was about to put his phone back in his pocket when it vibrated again. It felt like his heart practically skipped a beat when Cody's name flashed on the screen.

Great job tonight! Caught you on YouTube. Hope the fence bashing last night didn't hurt too much.

Johnny's thumbs quivered while he decided whether to answer. Finally he did.

Thanks. Last night wasn't my night.

Don't diss yourself. Tonight more than made up for it. See you in a couple weeks.

In a couple weeks the Pro Cut tour would start up again after the summer break. Somehow Johnny hadn't considered that, in two short weeks, they would meet in the ring again. It would be his job to keep Cody from harm, and everyone would expect them to exchange their usual high five if something good happened.

He kept staring at his phone until it went dark without realizing he'd never answered the last text. Finally he thumbed an answer.

See you then.

WITH his elbow hooked over the door, Johnny leaned out to let the wind whip the ends of his hair into his face. The air at the lag end of summer was blistering hot, but the wind made it bearable. Besides, he'd grown up in the desert. Neither Vern nor Reese had ever let him take a turn at the wheel, but Johnny had gotten used to it, and also switching back and forth between them.

Cody's favorite song came on the radio; Gary Allan's *Get off on the Pain*.

The lines about waking up a thousand miles from home hit Johnny hard. Tomorrow and the day after was the last weekend of the touring division before a break of two weeks. He'd been running hard all summer, and suddenly after this he would have no place to go. When he walked out on Cody, he also walked away from the only home he'd known for the past two years. He didn't really know where to go or what to do with himself during the break before the finals, other than that he needed to find work.

Stupid things would suddenly remind him of Cody; seeing a field of grain the color of Cody's hair, the soft moan of the wind that made him hear the sounds of their lovemaking, and a sudden sensory memory would sweep over him, making him long for Cody's touch.

When March told him to go back to Cody and give it another try, it was as if he'd given Johnny permission to miss Cody. And Johnny was missing him badly: his laugh, his scent, the intent way he came after him when he wanted sex. Even the bad parts made Johnny homesick.

He was so lost in his misery, Reese had to repeat himself to be heard.

"So, after Baton Rouge, we got ourselves a little break. Going anywhere fun?"

Johnny shook his head. "Hadn't really thought about it."

"Going to visit with your mother?"

"No."

"Take a vacation?"

"Probably better find some kind of work. I could use the money," Johnny mumbled.

"Well, if you ain't got nowhere to go, you could ride along with me. I'm fixing to go home to my ranch and get a few chores done. Kind of raise up my popularity with the wife a little before I get on her nerves after finals." Reese chuckled. "I can give you room and board and my wife is the best cook around, especially after eating on the road. If you feel like helping out, I could probably scrounge up a few bucks for you."

It was a struggle against Johnny's pride. He hated feeling as though he needed a handout, but the plain truth was that he did. The fact that the money would be going to help his mother didn't make it any easier. "I'd appreciate it," Johnny said stiffly.

"Time'll fly by, you'll see. And Vern lives just down the road. A couple riders live round about too. You'll be all right." Reese reached over to punch Johnny lightly on the shoulder. "Truth is, you need a break. We all do. Man can't just run full steam ahead all the time, much as you might want to."

"Maybe you're right." Johnny relaxed into the heat again and tried not to think about Cody curling up around him in their bed. Or why he had to keep running.

JOHNNY was thankful the break was only two weeks. It was hot, the work was dirty and mostly couldn't be done from the back of a horse, and he was staying in a single-wide with two guys who seemed to live there permanently and didn't know quite what to make of him.

He was used to maintaining a certain level of privacy around Reese and Vern, but he didn't have to share a room with them when they stayed in motels. Here he felt endangered, as if he had to be on guard every minute. Both of Reese's hands seemed to be content with a life of hard work lightened by a little hard drinking on the weekends and mixed with temporary female companionship. It was something Johnny couldn't bring himself to even pretend about, so he stayed at the ranch when they went to town.

He never saw Vern or any of the riders Reese said lived on the same road, and he was glad of it. It was depressing to see what could have been his life if he hadn't discovered bullfighting. And he was missing Cody badly and trying not to think about it.

He was counting the days before they'd get back on the road and feeling as though he might explode with need. He hadn't thought he and Zane got that much action on the road, but two weeks of paranoid celibacy made him feel as though he might deck someone for a blowjob.

The last day before they were due to hit the road, the weather changed. Johnny remembered the slicker he'd left hanging on the hook at the house he'd shared with Cody. Maybe leaving it behind was a sign from his subconscious, but the slicker was there and he was here. He made do with a makeshift trash-bag poncho, shivering when the water dripped off his hat and slid down his neck. His boots were heavy with caked mud, but stock still had to be watered and fed and cows had to be milked.

At the end of the day, he stood next to Reese inside the doorway of the barn, watching the rain sheet down, almost too tired and miserable to make a break for the house.

"Weather broke," Reese commented. "It's fall now. It'll be cooler now when we get back on the road. Good for the bulls. They'll be more frisky. Then we'll be on the upswing to the finals. It'll be exciting."

"You glad to get back to work?" Johnny asked.

"Yeah. Good seeing the wife and the place, but I love the ramp-up to the finals. Most exciting time of the year." Reese stretched and then slapped Johnny on the shoulder. "Supper should be on the table. Let's go get some."

Silently, Johnny followed Reese to the house. Reese chatted with his wife and the hands, but Johnny didn't say much. He helped with the dishes, and leaving the group to watch TV, walked through the rain by himself to the trailer. The sudden vibration of the phone in his pocket sent a jolt through him, and he hoped it was Cody.

CHAPTER 14:
The Fall

CODY couldn't wait two weeks. Watching the touring division on the NBR YouTube channel just to get a glimpse of Johnny in action, trying to concentrate on contracting his bulls and doing exhibition riding when it wasn't the kind of riding he wanted to do... it all made him think about the promise he made to his mother. He finally came to the conclusion he was being a coward, and he didn't like it.

So finally he gave in and texted Johnny. He stopped short of saying he missed him—that would have been cutting a little too close to the bone—but implied he would be in the general area of the next touring event and asked if they could meet after the show.

To his surprise, Johnny had sent him a text, saying he traveled with Vern and Vern liked to hit the road after the final round on the second day, but he'd be willing to meet after the first night's show.

Cody texted back, asking where, and when the answer came back he stared at it in dismay.

A gay bar. Johnny wanted to meet in a gay bar. It confirmed the worst of his jealous fears that Johnny had been out sampling the oats, as his father put it. But it also aroused a perverse instinct to refuse. If this was some kind of test to see if he was brave enough, Cody wanted to text back, "Fuck you!" Johnny had no right—but maybe he did.

Maybe he'd gotten complacent with hiding who he was so it didn't rankle, but Johnny must want someone to know about him, even if it was random guys in a gay bar in west podunk. Cody had given so many other things priority in life, he no longer even thought about being out. But Johnny was younger. And there it was again; they were at different stages in their lives. He'd been expecting Johnny to make all the adjustments because Cody was set in his life, and it wasn't fair to Johnny. But it also wasn't fair to expect him to out himself at this point. If he came out before nationals, he might still win, but there wouldn't be too many fans cheering for him and his sponsors would pull the plug on his contracts.

He became aware time was passing as the text he was looking at dimmed, and he hadn't answered it yet. Maybe this was a test, and if he didn't answer right, he'd lose Johnny forever. His whole future was hanging on a fucking text, where he couldn't see Johnny's expression, couldn't fix it if he said the wrong thing. The fact that he stuck his foot in his mouth so often without knowing made it even more likely he'd blurt out the wrong thing.

He took a deep breath. "I'll be there," he typed in.

There was no answer. Maybe Johnny thought he'd blown him off and turned off his phone. Maybe he'd answer later. Texting sucked. He had no idea whether Johnny had seen his text or not.

Maybe he was too late, but maybe Johnny had had to go do something. He couldn't sit around staring at his phone all the time.

Cody tortured himself for the six hours it took until he finally got an answer. Johnny had typed, "Great. See you then." Except of course he used text shorthand, and it took Cody a minute to decipher it. Another thing that made him feel old despite only a ten-year difference, and he hated it.

All he had to do was shake Dub and get on a plane to Yakima.

NORMALLY getting dressed was easy. Cody thought he was a good-looking man, or at least that's what people usually told him. His mother was probably on the partial side, but Johnny used to like how he looked. Now he agonized between the light-blue shirt and the dark-blue one. As if his whole future depended on which shirt he chose, because if he didn't pick the one that would make Johnny want him enough to come back, then Cody was screwed. Finally he closed his eyes and stabbed a finger at the bed.

The light-blue one. No question about the jeans. He only owned one set of dress pants and one suit, and he hadn't brought them along. In fact, he couldn't remember if Johnny had ever seen him in anything but jeans. Luckily Cody thought jeans looked good on him and set off his ass.

His boots were clean and polished to a high sheen for a change. He'd shaved carefully. His hair was neatly trimmed. His nails were clean. He felt like a damn fool or a girl getting ready for her first date. He was excited, resentful, and anxious, wondering if Johnny was doing his own version of grooming for him.

He had gone out to locate the bar earlier that day so he wouldn't have to ask anyone for directions. At least it wasn't close to the arena where Johnny was working, so it was unlikely any cowboys they knew would stumble in by accident after the event.

Cody wished he'd thought to ask Johnny to meet him for dinner somewhere. He hated eating alone, and it would have been quieter. They could have talked this thing out, gotten it settled, so at the end of the night Johnny would have been his again and come home where he belonged.

"Fuck," he muttered under his breath. It was that kind of thinking that had gotten him to this point, having to go to Johnny with his hat in his hand, asking for a favor. He was used to going after what he wanted. Direct. Forceful. Masterful. He wasn't very subtle, he guessed, and that made him all the more fearful he was going to fuck up royally without knowing it.

Anxiety drove him out of his hotel room to walk the streets of Yakima. He bought a hot dog from a food truck and ate it standing up. He worried about the onions, so he bought some breath mints. He looked at people without seeing them and checked his watch forty times an hour, waiting for the right time to head over to the bar. Maybe he was hoping to wear himself out so he would be calmer when he saw Johnny.

At last it was time. He had to force himself to walk slowly so he wouldn't get there too early. Didn't want to betray how eager he was.

He avoided admitting to himself that he didn't want to give Johnny that power, because then he would have to admit Johnny already had all the power. It wasn't a feeling he was used to.

As he approached the bar, all his senses were heightened like a skittish bull in the chute. The cooler night breeze caressed his skin, and he shied away from looking at the more obvious gay men heading in the same direction, not wanting to meet their glances. The metal handle of the door was cold under his hand.

He pushed his way in, not liking the cigarette smoke but glad of the cover it provided as he stood looking around in the dim light.

And then he saw Johnny. It was like the rush Cody got when the gate opened and he felt the bull gather his muscles under him. The sound of music and men talking faded away; the crowd lost itself in a blur. Only Johnny stood out for him, as if some angel were pouring gold light down over him. Beautiful.

Then Johnny looked up and their gazes met in one of those moments of silent communication where breathing stops, pupils dilate in widened eyes, lips part in unspoken desire. *I want you.* Cody felt as if he could hear Johnny saying it, felt as if he said it aloud himself. In fact, he might have. He wasn't sure.

Without seeing the crowd of men dancing, he pushed his way to the table where Johnny sat. After all his worrying about how he looked, he had no idea what Johnny was wearing. Just seeing his face and his eyes was enough, and how his black hair shone under the lights like the coat of a glossy horse. Cody wanted to pet him, but knew he couldn't assume anything. Maybe Johnny wouldn't want it.

A good-looking man came up to the table, obviously coming after Johnny, and Cody felt a snarl on his lips as he glared at the man. The man noticed him and lifted his hands as if in surrender and walked away.

Johnny smiled at Cody.

"Want to dance?" Cody managed to croak.

Johnny's face was astonished but delighted when he stood up, practically floating into Cody's arms.

Cody didn't know whether this was for him or for Johnny. He'd had sex in the most public of ways when he was a teenager, letting men watch, watching other men in restrooms and movie theatres and adult stores. But he'd never held a man in his arms in a public place simply to dance to music.

Cody circled his arms around Johnny's slender frame and they started to move. It had been so long since he'd held Johnny, it was sublime to simply place his hand on his back, feel the warmth and movement of his muscles under his shirt. Cody could smell Johnny, a scent familiar and filled with memories of sex and laughter and times when they were so tired they fell asleep curled up in each other's arms after only sweet kisses.

He didn't know if it was him trembling or Johnny, or if they both were. He wasn't much of a dancer, but he instantly recognized the metaphor that dancing was for sex. Two bodies pressed together, moving as one with a kind of public intimacy even strangers could share, mirroring the private intimacy of making love. When the song ended, Johnny could thank him as if he were a stranger and return to his table. They could eye each other across the room and part, having shared a moment of magic.

But Cody hoped this would not be how the evening would end. He was afraid to speak, afraid he might fuck it up again. He could feel Johnny was enjoying this as much as he was. He closed his eyes and pressed his cheek against Johnny's and enjoyed the way their bodies touched as they swayed.

When the music ended, Cody stared into Johnny's eyes, seeing acquiescence in the soft black depths. "Come to the hotel with me?"

A quick nod. "All right."

They got their hats and left the bar. The air was cool at the summer's end. They didn't touch as they walked. Cody didn't turn his head to look at Johnny, feeling shy and somehow awkward, as though he'd never met this man beside him. He tried to match his steps to Johnny's, but those long legs strode forward with a confidence he seemed to have lost. He missed their lovemaking desperately, but he wasn't going to rush it. Tonight he would let Johnny take the lead and hope for the best.

When they reached the hotel, he opened the door for Johnny. When the elevator door slid shut behind them, he punched the button for the ninth floor. Then Johnny turned to him and pressed him back against the wall. His face was so close; Cody hoped Johnny would kiss him.

When Johnny's lips covered his, Cody closed his eyes, his hands pressed flat against the mirrored wall as if it could hold him up. He surrendered to Johnny's tongue licking at his lips, opened his mouth to welcome Johnny's tongue inside. Their tongues touched delicately and darted between their parted lips. He could feel the confidence in Johnny's kisses, and it thrilled him as they made out until a soft chime announced they had reached his floor.

Johnny smiled and pushed himself away. He walked out as if his muscles were solid and he wasn't gasping for air. Cody was dizzy and breathless and all they'd done was kiss. He felt dazed, as if his senses were so overloaded with the taste and touch of Johnny he couldn't take in anything else.

He realized Johnny didn't know which room was his. His mind in a fog, his cock hard and bulging in his jeans, Cody walked to his room and fumbled with the key card.

Once inside, Cody dropped his jacket on the floor. He pressed against Johnny and walked him backward to the bed so they could fall down as one. Cody climbed on top to straddle Johnny and bent his head to kiss the enticing lips he'd missed.

The feeling of Johnny arching up under him, their lips meeting, tongues tangling, made him happy and triumphant. Cody felt blindly for Johnny's hands and twined their fingers as they kissed, moving them to pin them by his head. He wondered why he'd never spent more time kissing Johnny. He was always chasing the future, the next ride, the next buckle, the next orgasm. Having what he'd been missing made him regret he'd never savored the taste of Johnny's kisses, the masculine clean scent of him, the solid feel of his body beneath his own.

It was unbearably romantic and yet also unbearably arousing. His cock strained in his jeans, the creases cutting into his flesh almost painfully. Their kisses grew desperate and hungry. Whenever his tongue entered Johnny's mouth, Cody grunted with arousal, but some spirit of caution kept him from making any other move, even keeping his hips still.

Finally Johnny rolled him onto his back. They continued kissing and trading positions, sometimes Cody pressing Johnny down with his weight, sometimes Johnny riding on top. They pressed their bodies tightly together, as tight as possible with all their clothes on.

Cody reached for Johnny's fly.

"Not tonight," Johnny said breathlessly. "Not the first time."

Cody was disappointed, and yet somehow the refusal made it even better. There was a promise implicit in Johnny's words that there would be another time.

Cody pinned Johnny to the mattress and mouthed the hard length of him through his jeans. Johnny's hips were bucking and he pressed his bulge hard against Cody's lips, as if searching for a relief he had denied them both.

His hand rubbed the front of Cody's jeans, outlining the aching shaft. "You're so big," he whispered.

Cody's heart took flight. Their eyes met and he smiled, knowing this was Johnny's way of apologizing. He felt as though his failures were forgiven and he vowed he wouldn't fail again if Johnny gave him another chance.

Then Johnny flipped him so he was facedown on the bed, feeling his strong hands rubbing and squeezing his cheeks. Cody felt the full weight of him on his back as Johnny pressed the welcome hardness of his erection between his cheeks.

Cody reached behind him to grab Johnny's ass and pulled him closer. He had allowed Johnny to fuck him on occasion, even enjoyed it, but he'd never felt the aching need to have Johnny that way. Now he wanted Johnny to be inside him. And then he wanted to make love to Johnny in his turn. The desire to have his cock surrounded in Johnny's heat and tightness made him rotate his hips, grinding back against Johnny's groin as if they were already fucking.

"We'd better stop and slow it down," Johnny said huskily, "before we go too far." He rolled off onto his back and covered his eyes with his arm, as if he couldn't bear the temptation of looking at Cody.

"Yeah. Right. Guess we'd better keep our clothes on." Cody gave a shaky laugh and moved away to face Johnny. He reached for Johnny's hand and began to caress the palm with his fingertips. Stopping was one of the hardest things he'd ever done, especially since they'd had sex so often in the past without any interruption, but this was a new negotiation. It was better to take everything slow.

Johnny rolled into him and Cody slid his arm under Johnny's waist. As if his fingers had their own agenda, they slowly pulled Johnny's shirt out of his jeans. The thrill of a few inches of naked skin made him achingly hard. He ran his hand tentatively under Johnny's shirt, finding the tattoo from long familiarity, tracing the shape with his fingertips from memory although he couldn't see it. His touch made Johnny shiver and close his eyes, letting his head drop back with a low moan. With the thin barrier of their clothes between them, both sets of hips flexed and moved, but Cody was too nervous to take it any further. He ran his fingers over the spine he knew so well, grateful to get to feel even that much.

He felt surprisingly drowsy, even though he was still hard, and all the emotions jostling inside him were too much. It was so nice to simply lie on the bed with Johnny there beside him. It felt right. He didn't want to sleep and miss any of it, but he couldn't fight it any longer. Johnny was back. Things would be okay. His eyelids fluttered shut and he murmured, "Thank God you're back. When we go back to the ranch tomorrow we can talk it over. At least I'll be able to ride again."

The silence seemed ominous to Cody all of a sudden, and Johnny's body stiffened in his arms before he rolled away.

"So this is about you staying on top of a bull?"

"What? No! It's about us, about you coming back to me—"

Johnny jumped off the bed and seemed to tower over Cody as if he were twenty feet tall. "I thought it was about us too, but somehow 'us' always turns out to be 'you'."

Cody sat up. "Listen Johnny, you're the one who walked out on me! I would've been happy to go on just like we were!"

"I wasn't happy, remember? I'm sure it would've been great for you if I just kept giving in to whatever you want."

"What did I say? What's the matter with you?"

"There's nothing the matter with me except I was stupid enough to think you were actually sorry." Johnny stamped his boots on with furious energy.

Cody had to stop him. He couldn't watch Johnny walk away again. His brain spinning, Cody blurted out, "Look, I never wanted a boyfriend. I didn't want to be tied down. I knew I didn't have time for all the emotional stuff. I was fine with one-nighters. I just wanted to ride and win and—"

"And win at everything! You never give a guy a chance! Well, I've got a career too, and I'm not going off to the ranch because you say so! You just go ahead and win your fucking rounds! It doesn't mean anything to me!" Johnny jammed on his hat.

"Wait a second! We need to talk!"

"We never needed to before. You say jump, I ask how high."

"No, you run away!"

"Not like you cared a whole hell of a lot what I did."

"I cared. You didn't stick around to find out. It's your fault I'm in a slump!"

"What the fuck! How is it my fault? You're the one on top of the bull."

"If you hadn't left, I would have been able to concentrate. If you'd just come back, I could go back to winning!"

"And that's all that counts with you—winning."

"Have you been hooking up?" Cody felt like a hypocrite. After all, he'd been hooking up, but it was different. It had been killing him thinking about other men's hands on his lover's body. He had to know, even though it was a hell of a time to ask and a hell of a way to do it. "So now I'm not good enough?"

"You don't get to ask me that." Johnny was staring at him. "We aren't together. It's none of your business what I do, so just fuck off!"

Cody lunged for one of his boots and threw it at the wall, relishing the sound of the smash. Probably everyone on the floor heard it. "You fuck off, you cocksucker!"

Loud pounding on the wall shocked him back to a sense of where they were. "Would you two freaks shut the hell up? If you keep yelling, I'm calling the manager!"

The door slammed shut.

Johnny was gone.

Cody was too angry to go after him. Too proud. Dammit! Johnny was just a bullfighter. Cody had the important job, a chance to make real money. He threw the other boot at the door and the adrenaline died away and with it his anger, leaving him feeling hopeless.

"Shut up!"

"All right, sorry!" Cody managed to yell back.

He sat on the edge of the bed and ran his fingers through his hair, groaning with misery. Karma was a bitch. That's what came of trying to be so careful, and Cody couldn't figure out how he'd managed to offend Johnny again. What the fuck was wrong with him?

After swallowing his pride and saying he was sorry, this is what he got in return.

But then Cody had to be honest with himself. He sucked at saying he was sorry. Even with his emotions reeling, he was going to beg for Johnny to come back, crawl, anything to get him back. One night with Johnny in his arms wasn't enough; Cody needed it for the rest of his life.

He'd fucked up. *Again.* And Johnny was gone. *Again.*

CHAPTER 15:

Riding Out the Slump

JOHNNY was steaming as he jogged toward the motel where he and Vern were staying and where he was supposed to be. He was always afraid he might be caught coming in late and Vern would give him another talking to, or even fire him. Bullfighting was all he had right now that made him feel like a man.

Of course, Cody was right about one thing. Johnny was running away. He had to find a way to deal with this thing by himself. He couldn't tell Cody what was wrong, because all Cody would do was take over and try to fix things by telling him what to do, if he listened in the first place.

Whenever he was with Cody, it was as if his bones melted, his brains slid out his bootheels, and he let Cody take over. The passion between them unlocked such sexual heat that the embers glowed for days. All he could think about was sex, and that's what had gotten them into the fix they were in. If he and Cody were ever going to have a chance, Johnny would have to learn how to stand up to him.

Glancing at his watch, he realized he'd made it back to the motel in record time. It was still before first light, and with luck Vern would never realize he hadn't been there all night. He let himself into the room and started when the phone rang. Could it be Cody? But no, Cody didn't know where he was staying.

He answered the phone cautiously. "Yeah?"

"Good morning, Johnny. Had breakfast yet?"

Was he about to be fired? Usually Vern called him kid. Johnny tensed up. "Morning, Vern. Nope. You?"

"No. What do you say we go out and grab something to eat?"

"Okay, I'll be right out." Johnny hung up and went into the bathroom to splash water on his face. When he stepped outside, Vern was waiting for him.

"There's a good place down this way. My treat."

Sure now that something was wrong, Johnny managed to answer. "It's okay, I can pay my way."

Vern gave him a sharp look as they started walking. "Might as well get this over with."

Johnny tensed up but kept his eyes straight forward.

"Chris Bellow wants to come back." Vern let out a sigh now that the worst was over. "He healed up quicker than the doctors thought he would. This is his last rodeo, so to speak. He wants one last run before he retires after Vegas. I'm going to ask you as a favor to me to stand down and let him take his final bow. I know you were looking forward to this—"

"It's okay." Johnny swallowed hard. "If I were in his shoes, I'd want to go out there one last time too."

"Thanks, Johnny." Vern didn't say any more, but Johnny could sense his relief.

"So I guess I need to find out about getting a spot back with the touring division to finish out the year." He clasped his hands together so Vern wouldn't see how they were shaking.

"We signed a contract through the finals, kid. I'm not tearing it up and I hope you won't either," Vern said in his usual gruff manner.

"But you don't want to pay me for doing nothing," Johnny protested. "And I'm not so sure I just want to sit around getting fat for the rest of the year."

Vern laughed. "You're so skinny, without your vest you don't even cast a shadow. If you packed on a few, maybe you'd look nearly human."

Johnny grinned. "Thanks a lot."

Vern cleared his throat nervously. "Look, kid, you ever repeat this and I'll deny it to my grave. I can't let you go back to the touring division. You didn't hear this from me but I think Chris is making a mistake coming back so soon. I'd bet money you and him are going to be working alternating weekends. He'll want to be in the ring every night leading up to the finals, but he might need a little help getting there."

Johnny nodded. He knew how it felt when he thought he'd be sent back to touring, if he was lucky enough that they had a spot for him. "I'd appreciate it."

"And don't make plans to jet set off to Hawaii for the finals either," Vern said. "All four of us will be in the ring for it. We got new bulls coming in that ain't used to the lights and explosions. We'll have alternate riders up from touring. We'll need a four-man team."

"Thanks." It was a relief to know Vern wasn't ready to get rid of him after the shock of hearing Chris was coming back, but coming right after the fight with Cody, it was a tough hit to take. As if everything were going wrong all at once and he was hitting rock bottom.

The only good thing was at least he wouldn't have to face Cody in the ring next week in Detroit. He needed a little time to think about what his life would be like without him. Being with Cody made him realize he'd always hoped somehow they could work things out eventually.

If Vern thought his distraction was due to Chris taking his spot on the team, Johnny was willing to let him think so. It felt as though he were losing everything.

CODY grunted as he hit the ground and curls of dust covered his clothes and sifted into his nostrils. He rolled over and up onto his feet just in time to sprint for the fence and jump up on the rails right before the bull. The bullfighters at this exhibition were no Johnny. They weren't even Vern or Reese. Granted, even fighters had to start somewhere, but he could have used a little more help at this juncture.

When they finally managed to entice the bull out of the ring, Cody jumped down and found his rope. He refused to look up in the stands, knowing what he'd see: fans who had come to see him, a famous rider known for his ability to stay on board a tornado, disappointed because a green two-year-old had tossed him around like a rag doll.

Cody didn't blame them. They couldn't possibly be more disappointed in him than he was himself. Since that one night with Johnny, he couldn't concentrate on anything but his own failure. Cody knew he could ride, but that sense of being a loser seemed to permeate everything. Fuck, in the box, his own rope had broken and he'd had to borrow Dub's.

Dragging the bell behind him on the concrete to keep the cameraman at bay, Cody hurried to the locker room. He could imagine the ring announcer's comments now, wondering what was going on with him, commenting on the length of his unusual buckoff streak. This was the seventh straight ride he'd blown, and maybe they'd be asking if he would even make it to the finals.

Crap, Dub was beating him to hell and back. Even the rookies were riding better. And Cody had been the last rider today, supposedly the featured star. Those folks in the stands would go home with his failure engraved on their minds.

Dub was waiting for him in the locker room and held out his hand for his rope. "Damn, Cody. You couldn't jump off as fast as that bull bucked you off."

"Yeah, I think you put a jinx on your rope," Cody snarled.

"Right after I broke yours," Dub agreed. "You gotta shake yourself loose, but we can argue about it on the plane. Sam wants to see you upstairs."

"If he's going to tell me I disappointed the fans, he can save it." Cody wished he could dial the attitude down, but he was just so fucking pissed at himself. Blowing an easy ride like that! It should have been a practice bull for him. It was easier to be mad than think about the underlying reason. He hadn't heard a thing from Johnny since the weekend, not even an apology, even though Cody had texted. It was as if Johnny were playing hard to get or something when Cody just wanted to get this damn thing settled before the finals so he could fucking concentrate! Cody didn't even want to hit the bars tonight with Dub. Knowing there would be no Johnny waiting for him back at his room made it seem like a pointless exercise, although getting drunk held a definite appeal. If he could shake Dub—

"So you want to clean up a little before we go talk to Sam?"

Feeling like the asshole he was acting like, Cody pulled himself together. Dub had been great this summer. Cody didn't know if Dub had planned to ride exhibition, but when he suggested it, Dub had come along to be his travel partner. Of course, it wasn't turning out exactly as Cody had hoped. So far he was making Dub look good instead of the other way around.

"Yeah, give me five. Let me just rinse the dust off."

"Go back there, tear the door off your locker, punch a wall, take a shower, and pull yourself together," Dub ordered. "Sam is not a man you want to disrespect."

The solitude of the shower helped him calm himself enough to meet Sam with a smile and a handshake. Feeling defensive, Cody hoped Sam wouldn't ask him to explain how he happened to fall off before the buzzer.

Sam didn't mention his ride, and it made Cody feel irrationally pissed, as if him falling off was so commonplace no one even needed to discuss it.

"Good to see you, Cody. Dub, you too." Sam shook both their hands. "Wanted to get your opinion about some of the stock here tonight."

For a moment, Cody reeled back, thinking maybe Sam had chosen this method to tweak him for falling off a third-rate bull. Then he pulled himself together. No point in making a big show of his own idiocy. Instead he delivered a concise analysis of the strengths and weaknesses of the stock he'd watched tonight.

Sam nodded. "For the most part, I agree with what you're saying. I like how your stock has been performing at the fairs. I think you've really got something with your bloodline. I want to move them up to the touring division, and if that works out, I'd like to see a few of them buck in the Top Cut division."

Realizing Sam was proposing to use more of his bulls in the touring division, Cody reacted with more enthusiasm. "That would be great! I'd be honored to supply the tour."

"I've noticed you've trained most of yours to stay pretty low-key in the box. I like that. Less chance of injury for rider and animal before they even get out of the gate."

"Well, we try with varied success. No fun for the rider banging around in the chute getting bruised up for no score," Cody said, pleased Sam had noticed.

"We'll see how it goes," Sam said. "We can't have you on top of one of your own bulls, but I imagine you're starting to think about retirement about now."

So Sam *had* noticed his crappy rides! "There is no truth to that rumor." Cody tried to make it a joke, but judging by Dub's eye roll it must have flopped, just like his ride.

"You're starting to think like a contractor," Sam pointed out. "Just like I did when the time came to step off the bulls. Even if you don't ride, you can stay involved with the sport."

"Is that why you sent those boys to me for teaching?" Cody demanded.

"You're a big name in the sport, Cody. Boys'll be proud to say they trained with you. And you're also starting to contract out your bulls. Fact of the matter is, I was talking to the sponsors and floated another idea out to them and they liked it. Mentioned your name for it."

Cody stood silent until Dub cuffed him. "What idea?"

He knew he was behaving less than graciously and his mother would be horrified with his manners if she'd been there to witness it, but Johnny was the most important thing to him right now—and he'd lost him. And everyone wanted him to retire and he was riding as if he already had.

"I'm calling it Behind the Box. We've got the arena announcer, and a professional sports announcer up in the broadcast booth with a retired bull rider sitting up next to him, telling the fans at home what everybody's doing right or wrong. I was thinking if we put you in back of the chute, you could give us your views on the bulls and how the riders match up with them. You've rode most of those bulls and you know how they act. Hell, maybe the riders can pick up a few pointers."

"On TV?" The show-off in Cody couldn't help but get excited over a new chance for some face time.

"Yep. Get you wired up for sound, get a cameraman down there. Sound interesting?"

"Well, it would if I were thinking of retiring." Cody took an unexpected step forward as Dub cuffed him again and turned to glare at his friend. "Which I'm not!"

"He's interested," Dub told Sam. "He never met a camera he didn't want to romance and he ain't all that ugly. Give it a little time for the idea to percolate through the granite."

Sam chuckled. "The R-word is hard on all of us, Cody, but there is life in bull riding after you retire. We need experienced riders to stick around and make this operation work like one big family. Give it some thought. Wouldn't be 'til next year anyway."

"Thank you, sir." Cody didn't need the smack Dub aimed at him that time. He'd remembered both his manners and the fact that Sam was the livestock director for the NBR, and that he had better play nice with Sam if he wanted to place his bulls.

As Sam walked away, the distinctive bow of his legs giving away his many years of riding bulls and horses, Dub said, "There goes a real gentleman."

"Yeah, he's all right."

"And you're one cocky, arrogant asshole." Dub rounded on him. "You know, some people actually care about you, God only knows why."

Guiltily, Cody asked, "Why are you even sticking around?"

"Because I knew you before you had to order an extra large in hats," Dub retorted promptly. "Sam's trying to help ease you over the gap, show you a way you can stay in the sport without having to break your neck in the ring every week. And you're acting like he dropped you in the middle of a fucking calf-dressing competition—as the calf!"

"He took me by surprise!"

"Goddammit, I'd slap some granny panties on you myself if I thought it would give you a lick of sense!"

Dub spun on his heel and stalked away.

Watching him go, Cody knew he was behaving badly. Even Dub was getting pissed at him, enough to where he changed seats to sit next to a stranger on the airplane. Although Cody usually hated traveling alone, he was relieved. He couldn't explain the source of his irritability to Dub without talking about the root of it. Johnny. Or rather, the lack of Johnny.

Cody was drowning in failure, and he wasn't used to it. Johnny wasn't talking to him, he kept falling off whenever he tried to ride, and he was acting like to prick to everyone. The more Cody tried to fix whatever was going wrong, the worse he rode. He'd never wanted to retire and generally avoided thinking about it, but if it was inevitable, nothing could be better than to go out with a big win. Not in a slump, dwindling away to a rider people would say used to be great and should have retired before he got past it. The worst fear of Cody's life was to announce his retirement and then fall off the next bull he rode.

If only he'd been able to make some headway with Johnny before the Top Cut tour started riding again, but next week was the first competition after the summer break and things still weren't settled. They might never get settled to his satisfaction.

After that it would be only ten weeks to the finals. Ten weeks of falling off every bull if he couldn't get his shit together. And even worse, the thought of falling off right where Johnny had the best possible front-row seat, right in the ring with him, the better to witness his failures in front of everyone.

Cody needed to talk with Johnny and force a resolution. This wasn't something he could do by text. If he'd been born with a boot in his mouth, surely things would be even worse if he had to type what he was trying to say.

And around and around the whole situation went in his brain, never reaching any answer.

So Cody decided to skip the rest of the exhibition rodeos and go home with his tail between his legs. There actually was stuff he needed to do at the ranch, but he went because he wanted his mother to tell him everything would be all right. Only problem was, he couldn't bring himself to ask her.

He planned to stay only five nights at home. His father tiptoed around him as if Cody was nitroglycerin or something, his mother looked at him with that I-am-woman-I-know-how-you-feel look, and under obvious duress from RJ, Travis was being tactful and not asking about Johnny. They were all so clearly bursting to tell him the answers, the pressure got worse rather than better.

The second night, he went to town and got drunk. Cody considered looking for someone to service him, but nobody could replace Johnny. In the end, Cody drove home, even though he shouldn't have. Maybe Jake the cop was right and he was just waiting for the right moment to walk into the ocean.

Because Cody didn't remember to kill the headlights until after flashing the big house, he didn't bother to turn off the engine and coast either. The old trick wouldn't have made any difference anyway. After stumbling into the kitchen of the bungalow he used to share with Johnny Cody found his mother sitting at the table. Not that he noticed her at first until after he turned the light on.

"Coffee?" she asked mildly, holding a cup up invitingly before she lifted it to her lips.

"Crap, Mom. What're you doing here?" Cody slumped into a chair and jumped at the loud scrape on the linoleum. After listening to her conversation on the porch a month ago, he should have known this was coming, but leave it up to Mom to pull off an ambush anyway.

"Waiting to tell you to cut the crap."

Numbly, Cody rubbed his hands over his face, aware he probably looked as drunk as he felt. "Whatever."

"You're not fooling us, you know. Killing the engine and lights, coasting by the house after you thought we'd gone to bed. Just like you used to sneak out when you were a teenager."

"So I went out for a few beers."

"And a helping of anonymous sex to try to forget Johnny?"

"So I hooked up a few times. What difference does it make?"

"Once you know what love feels like, random, meaningless sex tears you down. After you met Johnny, you were riding better than ever. Now you can't stick on top of a bull for eight seconds if your life depended on it."

"Thanks, Ma. I needed someone to point that out because it totally slipped my notice."

"Have you talked to him? Asked him to come back?"

"Not exactly." Somehow, Cody didn't think the hookup in the hotel room would have ranked high with his mother, no matter how hot it was, especially since all they'd done was rub against each other like sex-starved teenagers and end with a fight.

"You've tried fucking around, you've tried drinking too much. You tried denying to yourself that you miss him. You've been on the road going from event to event to avoid thinking about Johnny," Val said. "How about being honest with yourself for a change?"

Barely aware he was speaking aloud, Cody said, "When I met him, I thought, 'This is perfect. We're in the same biz, he'll understand why I have to do what I do, why I won't always have time for him. We have something in common.' But it wasn't enough. Ah, fuck him."

"So if you can't get him to do what you want you just give up? That's not what got you that rack of buckles in the living room."

"I can't win with him!" Cody knew he was shouting, but dammit, she was picking on him!

"You'd rather win the contest than be happy?"

"Winning is all there is."

"But Johnny isn't a game. And both of you have to win for it to work out. It's not like bull riding where someone else loses so you can win."

"I'm over him."

"Do *not* make me invoke The Saddle," Val warned. "If you didn't care, you wouldn't still be tearing yourself apart."

"How could he do this to me? I offered him everything and he just fucking walked away! Again!"

Cody sprang up, looking around for something to vent his anger. Yanking open the cabinet doors, he grabbed some plates and smashed them to the floor. The crash of broken dishes satisfied something deep inside him, as though he needed to destroy something the same way Johnny had ruined him.

Val sat motionless through the hurricane of shattered dishes until he was left panting and spent. "Again?"

"What?"

"You said 'again'. Did you see Johnny?"

Struggling with his pride, Cody didn't want to tell her, but he needed someone to tell him what to do, even though he hated it.

As if she could read his mind, Val said, "Time wears a path in relationships, Cody. You can't just put someone you love on a shelf until it's convenient for you. Johnny's at a different place in his life. There are ten years between you. You're planning for retirement—"

"I'm not planning for retirement!"

"Bullshit. If you're not, you'd better be. Your body's not going to hold out forever. Being a rider isn't like wine. We don't get better with age, we fall off and get hurt." Val studied his face sympathetically. "Trust me, none of us ever think we're going to get old. If I could still swing a leg over a bronc and ride like I used to, I'd be out there showing the girls how it's done."

"You miss it?" Cody was amazed. He'd thought his mother was totally content with her life on the ranch.

"It was a wonderful and exciting part of my life." Val looked away and Cody saw her fingers clench around her mug. She relaxed them before meeting Cody's gaze again. "I'd be lying if I said I didn't miss it. But life keeps moving forward. Still, there are compensations. Your father and I are closer than we've ever been, once I stopped traveling. And you can't go on doing the same thing forever because you stagnate."

"And mold grows on you."

"You're heading for retirement, not the grave. Johnny's just starting to make a name for himself. Trying to align two separate lives can be difficult, but it's not impossible if two people know what they want."

"I wasn't going to make him give it up," Cody lied feebly.

"Maybe that wasn't clear to him. I seem to recall you talking about the both of you spending the entire summer here when he said he needed to keep working. He needs his salary. He's supporting his mother, his sister, and her child."

"I offered him a salary to stay here all summer."

"He's a man, Cody, with all the male pride you have. Would you accept that kind of handout if someone offered it to you like that?"

"I'm living off you and Dad."

"Please. You earn enough to buy your own place if you wanted to. We're your parents, plus we're in a partnership in the stock business. Johnny doesn't want a handout, especially from his partner. If he feels he must support his mother, he needs to do it himself."

"I make more than he does. I could give him a hand and it wouldn't be a handout. We're equal."

Val tilted her head thoughtfully. "You hear a lot of crap that relationships are supposed to be equal, but equality isn't the issue, it's balance. Sometimes you give more, sometimes he does. The way you two were going on before, he was doing most of the giving, and I don't mean money."

Cody flushed angrily. How he hated hearing it. "It wasn't like that."

"Wasn't it? A relationship needs respect from both sides to be healthy."

"I don't know what you're talking about. I respected him. I do!"

"Maybe he didn't see it that way. A man needs to feel respected to be happy."

Cody thought about his dad. Never once had he heard his mother knock Davis down. "Johnny could be a bull rider if he wanted to. He's really good."

"But he's chosen to be a bullfighter. When Chris was injured, Vern chose Johnny out of all the men with more experience he could have called. He saw something special about Johnny."

"He is special!"

"Yes, he is, in many ways. And capable of managing his own life."

"I did a lot for him. I just had stuff to do. I was planning for our future—you know how it is when you ride. You can't always count on a payday, so you have to be careful and think ahead...." Cody petered out. He wasn't even convincing himself.

"Maybe you were so busy living in the future you forgot what you want here and now. You always get to pay for what you want, one way or another."

"What do I do to fix this, Mom?"

Val shook her head. "You do what you've always done when you want something. You go after it and you don't stop 'til you get it. How many times have you fallen off a bull's back and gotten on again?"

"But how?"

"You'll figure it out." She got up to go and tidily put her coffee mug into the dishwasher, ignoring the crunch of the shards of china under her boots. "Maybe you should ask Johnny what *he* wants."

"What if I ask and he turns me down?"

"Then you'll know for sure, won't you?"

"Really comforting, Mom. Do you think he'll tell me to fuck off?"

"No."

The stark, single-word answer gave Cody a feeling of hope. "I hope like hell you're right."

"Get some rest, dear. And sweep up those broken dishes before you go to bed," Val ordered.

"Yes, ma'am," Cody said.

THE unbelievably loud sound of the phone ringing brought Cody out of his fog. Groaning, he rolled over to answer it. "Yeah."

"Good afternoon, Cody. Sam Wells stopped by to talk to you."

"Tell him I'll see him tomorrow, Mom."

"You get your ass out of bed right now, Cody! Sam's a busy man and he's not going to hang around here waiting for you to dry out."

He winced at the sharp click of the phone and lay back against the pillows, his eyes closing. He must have dozed for a moment because he woke again with a jerk. Screwing up his eyes, he seemed to remember some phone call….

Then he threw off the covers and ran for the shower.

His hair was still wet when he went to the kitchen door to answer the knock, but at least he was fully dressed. Embarrassed, he ran his fingers over his scruff and smiled apologetically at Sam. "Sorry, Sam, just a little under the weather."

Sam looked him up and down, and Cody had a feeling he wasn't fooling the older man. "Slump hangover. Been there. Your mother sent this down for you."

Cody took the glass from Sam. "What is it?"

"Hair of the dog," Sam said. "Got any coffee?"

"I'll make some."

Going through the motions of making the coffee, Cody didn't try to talk. He was pretty sure he couldn't do two things at once, and right now he was fighting to stand upright. When the coffee was done, he poured out two cups and set one in front of Sam. He sat down heavily.

"Sugar?"

"Sorry." Heaving himself out of his chair, Cody labored across the room to the sugar canister and brought the whole thing to the table. At Sam's quizzical look, he went to a drawer for a spoon. When Sam nodded, he sat down and took a swig of the Bloody Mary. Oddly enough, the mixture of spice and alcohol did seem to settle things down a bit.

"Heard you got a bone to pick with me."

"Dub?"

"He didn't rat on you. You gotta realize when you're in this game, there's cameras and microphones all over the place. You never know who will hear what."

Apprehensively, Cody studied the older man. As always, the weather-beaten face showed humor, patience, and intelligence. "I heard you said I was on the downward slope of my career."

Sam chuckled. "Most professional bull riders average out at eight years, so the middle of their career comes at four years. You've already been at this over ten years. How long you planning to ride?"

"As long as I can," Cody gritted out.

"There's no senior championship tour like in golf, son. Maybe you could find a bunch of geriatric bulls to put old riders on, but I'm thinking it won't be much of a draw for the fans. They really don't like seeing injuries."

"Why does everyone want me to retire? I'm not old!"

"Comes a time in every man's life where he needs to learn to compromise," Sam said.

"I don't want to compromise! It sounds so—lame!"

"Take it from me, after forty years in the sport, there's other ways to get the rush."

"Yeah? Like what?"

"You might not think so 'til you feel it, but it's a great thrill watching your bull go out there and raise Cain."

"It doesn't sound the same."

"Never said it was the same. There's more than one kind of thrill." Sam paused for a sip of coffee. "Sounds like you never noticed us stockmen taking buckles for their bulls when they win."

Cody perked up. "No, can't say I ever did."

"Got fifteen gold ones for my bulls in the finals. First, second, or third, you still go home with a buckle when you're the owner of the bull."

"Good thing to know."

"Easier on the old bones too. Injuries add up. Don't get hurt much just leading your bull to the chute," Sam reflected. "I understand where you're coming from. I was just like you when I was a young buck."

"You?" Cody realized that was hardly flattering. "I mean—"

"Your dad was too. Cockiest rider I ever did see. I thought he'd be one of the big stars 'til he started having injuries."

"Dad?" Cody couldn't believe his calm, grey-haired father ever had set the world on fire.

"You didn't get it all from Val, you know, even though she does sport a great set of *cojones* for a girl. Your dad could have been a great rider if he hadn't had that last bad wreck. But he didn't just give up on life after that. You don't hear him complaining about bad breaks; he knew the risks. He moved on. Raises bucking pony stock. Runs a good ranch. Trains kids to ride. Loves his wife." Sam paused. "There's more to life than eight seconds of adrenaline every weekend."

"I guess I'm a competition junkie."

"More'n one way to compete, son. There's nothing more exciting than winning a buckle off a bull you raised up and trained yourself. And it's a hell of a lot easier when someone else is out there riding him."

"So you're rooting against us riders for the bull." Cody smirked.

"Actually, I'm rooting for both. As a former rider, I want a cowboy to do well. As a stockman, I like seeing that fighting spirit in my bulls too. Nothing like a great ride, from either side. Besides, when a cowboy makes money on a good ride, so does the bull."

"I am proud of my stock. Guess maybe I should spend a little more time on that angle." Sam couldn't know, but it was a huge admission for Cody to make. He swallowed hard. No matter what anyone said, this wasn't going to be his last year as a rider if he had anything to say about it.

"Seeing as I'm here, why don't we kill two birds with one stone? Show me around and let me see some of your feisty young stock."

Cody put on his hat and sunglasses to minimize the stabbing pain in his eyes. Even so, he almost reeled back in shock when he opened the door but managed not to groan out loud.

Everyone seemed to be hanging around or at least it felt that way. Val and Davis joined them as they walked toward the field where his bulls were pastured, and Cody fell behind, listening to them chat with Sam. Cody was surprised at how close Sam was to his parents.

Somehow, he'd always seen himself as the connection, but clearly they went way back. Hearing his father and Sam jawing about rides he'd never heard of, Cody had a feeling Sam hadn't just stopped in on his way to somewhere else.

Compromise. A word he hated, but maybe one he was going to have to get used to. He was sure Sam didn't know about him and Johnny, but a lot of what he said hit home there as well.

Travis and RJ were standing by the fence when they arrived. RJ was scratching a two-year-old's forehead, and the bull was grunting with enjoyment as he shifted his head to get the hand where he wanted it.

Sam chuckled at the sight. "Hi, fellas. Hard to believe these bulls will buck you off quicker than a fly on a pile of bullshit when you see them like that."

"Hey, Sam. Yeah, this one will follow you around like a puppy 'til you strap a blanket to his back," Travis said.

Sam rested his arms on the top rail and pushed back his hat. He pointed at a red bull with a patch of white on his forehead. "Like the looks of that one. Great build for it. How is he in the ring?"

Eagerly, Cody said, "Red Snapper. I have high hopes for that one. He's a real fire-eater. Great bloodline and he's coming along."

"You've got an eye for stock, son. I think you might have something here. Tell me about your program."

At first Cody stammered but Travis was more than willing to help out, and soon they were describing the training and feeding regime in detail.

"I like your ideas," Sam said. "If I can be of any help, call on me. Once you put a couple years into a few of these bulls, I expect I'll be seeing them in the Top Cut arena."

"That's my hope," Cody said. "Thanks for coming by to take a look."

"Well, boys, I got to hit the road." Sam shook hands with the men and kissed Val on the cheek. "You must be proud of your boy."

"On occasion." Val smiled as she said it. "He has his points."

"I'll walk you to your truck, sir." Cody glared at his mother, who smiled sweetly at him.

As they walked back to the house, Cody took in a few deep breaths, realizing it was a nice day.

"Feeling almost human again?"

"Yeah. Hair of the dog helped. And the coffee." Cody took a deep breath. "So hit me with it."

"With what?"

"You didn't come out here just to look at a few youngsters. What did you want to say to me?" Cody knew he deserved whatever anyone wanted to say to him. His mother's words from the night before were coming back to him, and he felt ashamed of how selfish he'd come across, even with the best of motives.

"You were riding great before the break, Cody. Now you're in a truly impressive slump. Statistically speaking, I'm not sure I've seen a worse one. I don't think it's physical. You're not a weak man. It's something mental. You can ride so much better than this. You know how."

"You don't know what the problem is."

"True, but if you do, you better fix it if you want that gold buckle as much as I think you do. You were on track to win it all. Now...." Sam shook his head.

"You think I can win?"

"I've learned never to predict anything in this sport, but I'm rooting for you, son. One of the most talented riders I've ever seen."

"Maybe I used to be," Cody said bitterly.

"Man doesn't forget from one day to the next how to do something he loves. If you can't balance on the back of a bull, then something's not in balance in your life. You know how to pull out a win from a ride going south. Seen you do it before. You make the moves on a bull and you hang on like falling off is not an option. Works the same in life. Face whatever problem's holding you back, make the changes you need to, and get on with it."

"Sounds so simple."

"Doesn't it?" Sam flashed him a grin. "Lots of times it is, when you get right down to it. It's running away that sucks all the energy out of a man."

Cody held his hand out. "Thanks, Sam, for coming out here and talking some sense into an idiot."

"Anytime, Cody. Now you go on and win that gold buckle, hear?"

Cody watched the truck as Sam drove away. Everyone was full of good advice and it seemed they were all telling him the same thing. Maybe they were right.

CODY cancelled the rest of his exhibition appearances thinking maybe if he stayed home and got settled down, the slump would work itself out. Or maybe he just wasn't ready to face Johnny yet. He knew there would be a nice slice of humble pie involved. He hoped he'd be back to his usual form when the season started again.

He wasn't. He and Dub had rounded up a few practice bulls at a ranch outside Detroit. He fell off the first practice bull he rode before the event, and it didn't get better after that. He never did get a good seat. He was tossed around, lost his rope, and shot up in the air, spun around, and then came down again on the bull's back, but facing the rear. The bull took one more jump and Cody fell off and landed right on his face.

"Well, that must have been a different view," Dub announced. "Taking time off like you did sure didn't help you any."

"Thanks. I never would have figured that out on my own," Cody said, his voice sour with disgust. He pawed at his face to get rid of the dust.

"What the fuck is wrong with you?"

"I lost some—thing important to me."

"Hey, we all get older, you know? You gotta let go someday."

Cody stared at him. "You saying I'm over the hill?"

"Not yet. But it happens to us all. This is a young man's game. Easier to heal up when you're young. I'm even beginning to rack up the aches and pains, but I've just been hanging in there waiting for you to retire so I could go out on top in one good year. You've got five years on me."

"Gee, thanks for the compliment, I think."

Dub nodded and spat. "No problem, I'm here to help. Thing is, if you don't suck it up, I'm going to beat you this year. Only three thousand points behind, and I've got eight weeks to knock you off the top of the rider board."

"Well, you just go ahead and do it if you're riding so fucking hot," Cody snapped.

"I will if you keep riding like someone shot your dog every week. Fact is, Cody, you're one of the greats, the kind that only comes along every ten years or so. You been a thorn in my side ever since I started riding, always coming in second or third behind you."

"And the Brazilians," Cody said nastily.

Dub waved the Brazilians away. "Frustrating thing is, I couldn't even beat you the year you broke your damn leg. But even if I could do it, there wouldn't be no satisfaction in beating you at your worst. I'd rather you pulled it together and gave me a decent run for my money."

"You think I'm one of the greats?" Cody was honestly astonished.

"You don't listen much, do you? I think so, the NBR thinks so, the sports media thinks so. They've been reviewing your stats. You're in the 70 percent bracket if you don't blow it. You don't ride safe and tame on bulls you know you can top. You take chances and give the fans an exciting ride. You sell tickets. When you retire, you'll be in the ring of honor before ten years is up, you wait and see."

"Ring of honor." Cody's eyes glazed over.

"If you don't keep fucking up. The way you're pushing, you're gonna get hurt."

"I'll keep doing it 'til I get out of this slump," Cody gritted from between clenched teeth.

"You keep riding like you have been and that's all anyone'll remember. Regard this as a friendly pep talk."

For the first time, Cody recognized how much Dub cared, and it touched him that, as a competitor, Dub was still in his corner enough to try to talk him up.

"Thanks, Dub, I appreciate it."

"'Course, if you win, I'm gonna have to kick your butt, but then you can go out as the first back-to-back national winner ever."

After a pause, Cody said, "Yeah. I hope so. Thanks for the talk." He turned and walked away. Without Johnny, did it really matter if he won? Or maybe he should try harder and show Johnny what he was missing out on. His own words came back to haunt him: can't ride from fear. There's got to be joy in it.

That was it. When Johnny walked out, both times, all the joy went away. Riding didn't matter as much to Cody, even while his failures gnawed on his pride. All summer he'd been riding against youngsters he'd taught himself, and they were now scoring points while he was rolling donuts. It was humiliating.

"HEY, Z—Zane. Good luck out there." It still felt embarrassing to Johnny to be backstage in street clothes, but he was glad to see Zane.

"Johnny! Why aren't you dressed?"

"Chris Bellow is back. I'm just standing by." He felt a little comforted by Zane's eye roll at Chris's name. "Congratulations on moving up to Top Cut. Where's Aubrey and Tommy?"

"Tommy broke his leg in Redding and Aubrey strained a groin muscle in Big Sky," Zane answered. "Bobby Blue's here, though."

"Yeah, I saw him. Hope you do well out there."

"Thanks."

They knocked knuckles, and Johnny looked away from the sympathy in Zane's eyes. He really didn't need it. And besides, he had to get out of here and find his seat in the nosebleed section. Vern had done his best, but the venue was close to capacity. They always attracted more fans in the last weeks before finals.

Johnny was anxious to go. If he'd run into Zane backstage, he could just as easily run into Cody, and he wasn't ready to face him after screwing up their date.

Rounding the corner in a hurry, he almost walked into Rex Durham as the TV reporter interviewed a cowboy.

A loud, rather boisterous voice was boasting, "Yeah, Cody Grainger may have trained me, but I can outride him. It's my first year riding professional and I've already made it to the Top Cut."

A sudden sting made Johnny realize he was digging his nails into his palms. He glared at Bobby Blue's back, realizing he was eavesdropping, but the man was giving an interview on camera, for fuck's sake! And lying! And Johnny also felt a twinge of guilt. Ever since he heard about Cody's slump, it had been gnawing at him; he felt as if some of the responsibility for it was his. While he couldn't make Cody ride better, he could terrify Bobby Blue into being less of an irritant. Or at least try.

Rex said, "Cody Grainger has been in a monster buckoff streak. Does it make you doubt any advice he may have given you?"

"Not really. I mean, he was a pretty good rider in his day. He still knows one end of a bull from another."

"Cody's been in slumps before and come out of it. If he were to outscore you tonight, what would you have to say to him?"

"I'll beat you next time, old man. And congratulations."

Rex turned off the mic and nodded to the cameraman. "Thanks, Bobby Blue. Good luck out there."

"Will I be on TV tonight?" Bobby Blue asked eagerly.

"I just ask the questions, I'm not the editor. But if you win or you fall off, I'd say you have a good chance to see it air," Rex said in a friendly but impersonal way. He shook Bobby Blue's hand and started for the locker room.

Johnny enjoyed the startled, almost scared look on Bobby Blue's face as he herded him against the wall. "You're an asshole," he said quietly. "Cody teaches you how to ride and you disrespect him like that?"

If anything, the soft tone of his voice seemed to scare Bobby Blue more than yelling would have. "What am I supposed to say? I gotta make a name for myself. No one knows me from shit."

"You *could* say Cody helped improve your riding. You could thank him. You could give one of those sports speeches about how you depend on support from the fans and how grateful you are to be here before you badmouth a man whose boots you're not fit to spit on before you polish them with your tongue!" Johnny realized his voice was getting louder and took a breath. "But I guess you're too stupid to think that up."

"All right, all right. Give me a break. I just wasn't expecting that guy to come up and stick a mic in my face!"

"Remember Cody telling you that being ready is half the battle? That's good advice for riding or for life." Johnny became aware several people had stopped to watch. He took his hands off the wall and stepped away, even though he still wanted to reinforce his opinion physically. "Keep it in mind for next time. If you're lucky enough to have a next time."

"Listen, man, I owe you. You saved my life. I'll make it up to you."

Now that the first heat of his anger was cooling, Johnny thought maybe he'd made as big a fool of himself as Bobby Blue. "Just don't badmouth Cody. You don't owe me anything. I was just doing my job."

"Whew! For a minute there I thought you might hang me out to dry in the ring if I got in trouble."

Johnny started getting steamed again. "Listen, dickhead, in the ring I'm a professional bullfighter and I wouldn't let my worst enemy get hurt, but I won't mind punching your lights out outside the ring if you keep this shit up."

"Cody Grainger is the best rider I ever saw, probably the best ever. I just thought talking large was part of the game. I won't take his name in vain again. We good?"

"We're good." Johnny wanted to laugh at Bobby Blue's anxious penitence but didn't want to ruin the good effect he was having. "Good luck out there. Don't break a leg."

"Thanks, Johnny. I won't forget." Bobby Blue slid away quick as if he were making a getaway.

It cracked Johnny up because he wasn't used to thinking of himself as particularly scary. It was kind of fun throwing his weight around.

"Johnny Arrow!"

He froze, hearing that voice call his name. He'd hoped to sneak into the stands without anyone catching him. Avoid any awkward moments.

"Johnny, over here!"

Slowly, he turned to face them. Of course they had a perfect right to be backstage. "Hi," he said weakly.

Davis looked as uncomfortable as he felt, but Val looked amused, as if she'd heard everything between him and Bobby Blue and wanted to applaud. She grabbed Johnny and hugged him hard. "I'm so glad we ran into you. You're looking well, but aren't you running late? You need to get into your safety gear. We can talk after the event. Maybe go out for a bite later."

"No, I'm not working today."

Instantly, Val looked concerned. "What's wrong? Are you hurt?"

"No, nothing like that. Chris Bellow came off sick leave and he wanted back in the ring…." Johnny shrugged to show he wasn't upset, although he had a feeling he wasn't fooling her.

"Then come along and sit with us. We have a box. Travis and RJ are here too." Val took a firm grip on his arm. "We've missed you."

Johnny could tell she was dying to find out what was going on between him and Cody without coming right out and asking. She must be pushing Cody into making an effort, but even she couldn't improve his execution. Maybe he'd be hearing from Cody before the weekend was over. Even though he kind of wanted to ask her advice, it felt unfair to take advantage of her kindness. Maybe he ought to stay away from Cody's parents, but he missed them. All of them, not just Cody; his parents, the ranch, and RJ and Travis too. "Missed you too," he mumbled.

"Come on, I don't want to miss anything," Val said. Her voice was excited and her eyes bright, making Johnny remember she used to do this herself.

"You two can tell me later if Cody falls off," Davis said. "I'm going to cover my eyes when he's in the box."

"He won't fall off," Val said confidently. "He's fighting his way back."

Johnny was uncomfortable when he realized Davis was looking him over speculatively, and then hastily turned away before their gazes met.

"I'll keep my fingers crossed and my eyes shut," Davis said.

Val towed Johnny through the gates without having to show any tickets. Apparently the ushers knew her, because they smiled in recognition and waved her party right through.

"Look who I found!" Val announced triumphantly.

Awkwardly, Johnny shook hands with Travis and RJ, remembering he hadn't with Davis and not knowing quite what to do about it now. RJ merely said hello, but Travis pulled him into a ferocious manhug and pounded his back. "How you doing, kid? You been making a name for yourself. Proud of you."

When Travis released him with a final thump, Johnny stared into the ring and blinked, grateful everyone tactfully left him alone for a few minutes.

"Different view from up here, isn't it?" Davis asked.

"Yeah, very." Johnny tried to remember if he'd ever sat in the stands for a show. His place was always on the ground, right by the gate. It was a revelation to look down to see the riders urging the rankest, badass bulls into the ring for introductions. And then he felt bad for the bulls. With all the noise, lights, and the spurts of flame shooting up, they were spooked. In a way it was funny to see his nemeses all meek and skittish in the ring. His job was to rescue riders from their ire and ease them out of the ring when they didn't want to leave, and now each one of the animals was nervously shifting around by the gate, waiting for it to open so they could scram.

On the center platform, Jinks the clown was dancing badly to the music while the ring announcer introduced the riders, beginning with the lowest ranked.

One by one, the riders sprinted into the ring and lined up in front the platform, raising their fists with typical cowboy bravado while the audience applauded. Johnny knew all their names. As each rider came out, he couldn't help but remember the times he'd made a save and the name of the bull each of them had been assigned in the draw.

When Dub Whittaker made his run down the ring, Val grabbed Johnny's hand. "He's next. Here he comes."

Weird. It was just weird to watch Cody run into the ring from up here, raising his hands above his head with a grin. He looked cocky enough, but he wasn't, Johnny could tell. By the way Val's hand tightened around his, she knew too. In a way, he reminded Johnny of how nervous the bulls had been, and he felt sorry for Cody. He must dread his first ride, the way he'd been falling off.

"Does he know you're here?" Johnny asked.

"Of course." Val nodded. Then she said quietly, for his ears only, "That makes it worse for him. Worrying he might fail in front of us."

Johnny was distracted by the bullfighters filing in. It was interesting to sit up here and witness the audience continue to applaud for them. First Vern, then Reese, and then the audience stood up to welcome Chris Bellow back at the urging of the announcer. Johnny got to his feet and clapped also, wishing like hell it was him down there with them.

After the anthem, the riders filed into the back and the ring announcer matched the names of the rider to the bull he was going to ride.

Activity ramped up behind the chute and Jinks told corny jokes to kill the time. Johnny was surprised to hear the audience actually laugh. He'd heard the jokes so often, he no longer paid attention to them when he was in the ring with Vern and Reese going over last-minute game plans. God, how he wished he was down there instead of here.

KNOWING Bobby Blue and Zane had made it onto the Top Cut tour should have made Cody feel proud, considering the improvement in their riding since his class. It hadn't occurred to him to follow their progress, but the stats the announcer gave were impressive. They were riding carefully, not taking too many chances, but staying aboard and making a score, even it if was on the lower end. Not that he had much room to criticize. He wouldn't have minded competing directly with them if he weren't bringing in the same low numbers. Unless he fell off. That would be totally fucking embarrassing, especially as Bobby Blue had been almost lyrical in his praise for Cody when he was interviewed after his ride where he outscored Cody.

This slump was killing him and he blamed Johnny for it. And, if he was feeling generous, himself. If he couldn't even act right enough to get Johnny back, how could he possibly stay on top of a bull for eight seconds?

The ring announcer's voice came over the loudspeakers, stopping after each name to allow the bullfighters to run into the ring and take a bow. "Your bullfighters for tonight are Vern Crocker, Reese Brent, and back with the team is bullfighter Chris Bellow. You remember back in Des Moines earlier this year Chris was hooked by a bull, and he's been out getting well. This is his last year on the tour, but before he retires he wants to look a bull in the eye one last time and tell him who's boss. Between now and the finals, Chris and Johnny Arrow, a bullfighter we've grown to admire here at Top Cut, will be alternating every week. I guess maybe we'll get to see them Indian-wrestle for the right to be in the ring for the finals!"

The announcer seemed all too impressed with his own wit, and Cody scowled. "Diné," he muttered. The unconscious racism annoyed him on Johnny's behalf.

The man kept right on talking, and it made Cody a little hot under the collar that he was blowing Chris Bellow's horn instead of Johnny's. He'd wondered how he would do in the ring with Johnny watching his every move, but now it was even worse. When Johnny was working, he had to watch the bull and look out for his fellow bullfighters and the riders. If he was here, wherever he was, he would be free to see every mistake Cody made. He was surer than ever that his riding slump was far from over as he lowered himself into the chute. If only Dub wasn't hovering, he thought irritably.

"Before the break, Cody Grainger's scores had him right on target to take the gold buckle at the finals, but then he went down into a stunning slump. His outs this summer serve as a stark reminder of how quickly it all can change in this sport. Cody Grainger is pretty dang lucky he wasn't riding for money. If this buckoff streak continues, Cody could slide down in the standings until he's cut from the finals. If that happens, who will take his place? There are plenty of young up-and-comers willing to fill his boots, in fact, there are a few cowboys here Cody trained himself...."

And now the announcer had gotten into his head, making sure everyone knew about his slump.

"As you know, a cowboy only makes it to the finals on dollars, no matter how many points he has. If Cody Grainger rode in the touring division this summer instead of special exhibition events, he might have ridden himself right out of a shot at the finals. The Brazilian contingent is closing in fast on him and they would like nothing more than seeing Cody bite the dust. His good friend and travel partner Dub Whittaker is also positioned to take the lead from Cody unless he can make something good happen here tonight."

Way to put the pressure on, Cody thought. As if he didn't already know all this. He yanked savagely at the rope to tighten it around the bull's girth. He'd show them.

"Take it easy there, partner. Don't want to cut off the circulation," Dub drawled.

"It's got to be tight," Cody grunted. "I need a good grip. Got to hold on."

"And that ain't the way to do it and you know it," Dub said in a low voice. "You can't out-muscle one of these animals. You've been riding all stiff. You bear down like you have been and your hand'll pop out of that rope no matter how hard you try."

"I have to do it my way."

"Well, if you're gonna be stubborn, might as well be tough."

"Just—shut up—please—will you?" Cody ground his teeth, trying to be polite when all he wanted to do was snap Dub's head off. Dub had been great to him all summer and he didn't deserve this.

"Good luck, buddy," was all Dub said, but the steady feel of his hand on the back of the vest was comforting.

He squirmed on the back of the bull, trying to find a good seat. As if sensing his restless energy, the bull banged his leg hard into the wall, making an old knee injury act up. Aware of the clock counting down and the official timing him, Cody gave up and nodded.

The gate opened left and the bull backed out instead of turning out headfirst. The movement threw Cody forward, and he only just managed not to slap the bull's shoulder with his free arm. He tightened up, straining to hang on. This bull was getting near the end of his career and wasn't bucking up to his past glory, a fact that cut Cody two ways. Not only did it make him think about his own career winding down, but he also knew the bull didn't have the snap and power he once had. Embarrassing wasn't the word if he fell off this one.

The bull took off down the ring, throwing Cody back onto his pockets. Cody felt as though he'd never been on a bull's back before. He just couldn't find his center. Then the bull stutter-stepped a few paces.

Cody could feel the rope slipping from his grasp and strained to hang on to the end of it. His hand suddenly went numb but he had tied on well and the rosin held. The bull dove left and Cody slid a tiny bit into the well. The bull might have been old but he was smart. As soon as he felt Cody's weight go left, he ducked and turned right. Cody managed to hang on until just after the whistle when his hand popped out and the momentum launched him into the air. The bull continued to whip around and caught one of Cody's legs, setting him spinning like a helicopter. He came down on both feet and was grateful he kept at least that much of his dignity until he realized he was facing the bull, who didn't seem too happy. The bull charged him and Cody turned and ran for his life, completely forgetting to swerve like Johnny had showed him. He felt a horn slip under his vest and hoist him off his feet before sending him flying again while he wondered where the damn bullfighters were. He curled in a ball when he landed, rolling under the thundering hooves. He braced himself for impact, but miraculously the bull missed him with each foot.

Chris Bellow came puffing up to him just then, heaving for breath and looking apologetic as he caught the bull's attention and drew him off.

"Fucking guy should know when to quit!" Cody muttered. He got to his feet, cringing at the irony of the aging bull, rider, and fighter, all coming together to create a comic moment for the audience. At least they were having a good time laughing it up. The bull was the only winner, but Cody could at least show he was a good sport by dodging when Jinks pretended to be a bull and came at him with both hands held to his head for horns.

Cody forced a grin, swept off his hat, and bowed to the audience and then to Jinks. Still panting hard, Chris came by again, handing him his rope.

"Sorry about that. I was a little late."

A little late. "Yeah, okay, thanks." Cody managed not to growl as he took the rope with his off hand. He realized he was flexing his riding hand in an effort to get some feeling back into it. He was then forced to do the walk of shame down the entire length of the ring, getting sympathetic backslaps from the other two bullfighters, who peered at him anxiously. They knew Chris was a loser, but apparently so was he. At the gate, he looked up at the scoreboard.

"The old bull scored higher than the rider at 44, and with 37 points for rider Cody Grainger adds up to 81" came the inexorable voice of the ring announcer. "At least Cody will make it to the next round, unless somebody knocks him out of the number nine spot. He's on the bubble."

He might be done for the night. It would all depend on how many cowboys surpassed his score. At least he would have something to do helping Dub get ready for his ride.

They were standing by the chute, Cody holding Dub's rope when Dub said, "Say, isn't it that bullfighter Johnny Arrow up in the stands sitting with your parents?"

A fever of heat swept over Cody's body, and he barely managed to keep his head from whipping around. What the hell was Johnny doing with *them*? "Maybe," Cody grunted.

"What the hell? Wonder why they brought Chris back in. I hope they bring Johnny back for the finals. I know I voted for him."

"You did?" Cody whipped his head around to look at Dub in surprise.

"Yeah. Good man to have your back in the ring." Dub shrugged. "I guess we'll find out. Maybe he got hurt."

"I think we would have heard." Lurid imaginings of possible injuries roiled through Cody's mind, but he couldn't let it show. "Whatever."

ONCE the first round started, Johnny felt almost as if he'd be safer down in the ring. Val twitched and moved in her seat along with each rider. Once she even whacked Johnny with her free arm as if she were riding.

"Sorry, Johnny. I get a little excited," Val apologized, but kept her gaze on the ring. Davis laughed while he watched her jump, and Johnny felt a little sadness at the affection in his eyes.

Near the end of the first round, Johnny felt as tired as if he'd been down there working his hardest, and realized he was doing it too. His muscles twitched and jumped whenever one of the bullfighters made a save. Chris Bellow was just a shade slow, and several times Johnny had to bite his tongue to keep from yelling out to him to shake a damn leg as he gripped the rails and leaned forward.

Travis leaned across Davis to say, "Your ass is going to be sore if you don't let up trying to do Chris's job for him. You and Val; she's doing half the riding in this arena." He cackled when Johnny glared at him. "Always sucks to see someone doing your job worse than you, doesn't it?"

"Yeah, I guess it does." Johnny made an effort to relax his tense muscles. "Thanks," he said belatedly, when he realized Travis had been paying him a compliment.

"You're good, kid." Travis nodded to where Chris was trailing after a bull half a step late. "If he elbows you out of the finals it'll be a triumph of sentiment over talent."

Johnny focused on the riders only when it was Cody's turn. It was not a pretty sight, but Cody did manage to make eight seconds. Cody did not look up into the stands searching for his parents, which made Johnny think he must be embarrassed by his low score. It was a humiliating number for Cody, but any other rider would have been equally disappointed at this level.

At the break after the first round, Val asked, "How did you like watching from up here for a change?"

"I hate it! Oh damn— I'm sorry, I meant—" Johnny bit his lip when he realized how rude he sounded, but Val burst out laughing.

"Tell me about it! I'd rather be down there riding myself. At least you get used to it after a while."

"I don't want to get used to it. Maybe I should go."

"Better stay here with us," Val said. "At least you can't beat the crap out of Bobby Blue from up here and the company is good."

So she had been standing behind him in the hall during the whole argument. For some reason that made it seem even funnier to Johnny, and he grinned. "The company's way better." He clenched his jaw on an impulse to ask Val how Cody was doing and how he was feeling, mostly about him. But he couldn't do it. Maybe he didn't want to hear what she had to say, and he really didn't want to put her in the middle.

Val turned her head and smiled at him, as if she knew what he was thinking. She gave him a wink and then immediately stared back at the ring. Travis and RJ went to get everyone drinks, and Johnny groaned over the embarrassing antics of Jinks the clown.

WATCHING Dub ride in the short round was agony for Cody. His competitive nature reared its ugly head when he saw his friend would easily outscore him. Texas Ranger was a smart, athletic bull, and he used his savvy to give Dub a rough ride. At least three times Cody thought he'd be off, but Dub worked to stay on the bull's back 'til the end. The girls in Daisy Dukes waved signs saying, "90 Point Club," and, "Make Some Noise." The audience responded with cheers and whistles.

Unlike him, Dub managed to land pretty much on his feet and stay on them as he ran for the fence. The joy and triumph on Dub's face made Cody ache for the times when he'd felt that way, but in spite of his own failures he was genuinely happy for his friend.

He gave Dub a high five and pounded his back. "Way to go, Dub! Great ride!"

"Thank you kindly, Cody." Dub tossed him a grin as he turned to Rex the reporter for a brief interview.

Cody ducked behind the chute, not wanting Rex to rope him in and ask him about his own lame showing compared to Dub's, but he waited for his friend to come back from the interview.

"You really showed them." When Dub returned, Cody handed him his hat and took the helmet. "I bet you'll take the buckle for this event."

"Kind of a switch, isn't it?"

Cody realized this was Dub's awkward way of being tactful. After a summer of his support, Cody didn't want to minimize his accomplishment. "I hope you win this round, Dub, I really do."

"Thanks, friend." Dub clapped him on the shoulder and they settled in the stands to watch the other rides. "Here come the Brazilians, looking to take me down."

"Juca's been riding pretty good, but I'm betting he won't outscore you." Cody realized his nails were digging into the wooden seat. He had more riding on the result of Juca's ride than Dub did. Dub was ahead in points and he had knocked Cody into tenth place. Juca probably couldn't overtake Dub, as the Brazilian tended to average in the mid-80s, but one good ride would knock Cody out of the second round. It wasn't until the bull dumped Juca in the dirt at 7.91 that he could breathe again. Almost eight seconds of the most excruciating suspense, but by the skin of his teeth he'd actually made it into the second round.

Only then was he willing to sneak a look at his parents' box and saw Dub was right; Johnny was sitting up there with them. He looked oddly out of place sitting in the stands wearing street clothes instead of in working gear in the ring. Cody's parents' box was far enough away he didn't think any of them were looking at him. Bad enough to have Johnny up there watching and sitting between his mother and dad, but it would have been far worse if he had been in the ring. Cody sighed and waited until the draw.

Standing dead last for the second round meant Cody got to ride first on the bull no one else wanted, as the other nine men had drawn names first. The bull he ended up with was an unknown. None of the riders knew much about him, but Comet Dust didn't have a name as a money bull.

Dub was right there at the chute, helping him get ready as usual. "Just remember, the slump is over. You *can* ride. You been riding for over twenty years. You know how."

Cody nodded, too wrapped up in his strenuous effort to visualize a good ride to answer. He pounded his riding hand closed and gave the nod. The gate opened and he hung on to the rail just a second too long, pulling himself off-center as the bull lurched forward.

Somehow he managed to hang on and tighten his abs, feeling the wrench as he straightened up. The bull settled into a spin away from his hand. It felt awkward to Cody. The bull picked up speed, turning faster, kicking and jumping.

Sternly, he told himself, *if this is what they pay you for, you better do your job no matter how you feel.* Comet Dust landed a high kick and switched his rear end around, turning into Cody's hand. It felt better. A little of the old confidence seemed to seep into his bones, and Cody started to smile. He'd lost track of time and was startled when the buzzer sounded, and the bull immediately stopped dead in its tracks and stood completely still, not even switching his tail.

For a second everyone in the arena just stared in silence, Cody down at the bull's shoulders, the crowd at him, and the bullfighters at the bull.

"Hey, you! Comet Dust! Bull!" Vern called out and clapped his hands.

All at once the bull leaped high in the air, and Cody was almost thrown to the end of his arm, but he pulled up, yanking the tail of his rope and twisting off the animal to land on his hands and knees, skidding face-first into the dust as he scrabbled awkwardly to get away. A sudden pain in his bad knee made him wince, but he didn't stop to figure it out.

Mixed applause and laughter sounded as he staggered to his feet, looking around to see where the bull was. The bull knocked into one of the banners on the fence, tearing it loose and flipping it over Cody. He couldn't see where the bull was and batted at the sign, trying to fight it off while the laughter still came in waves. Cody emerged from under the sign, staring around wildly until he saw Vern and Reese had gotten the bull down by the exit gate and he was safe. He swiped at the dirt on his face while the laughter continued. *At least I can make them laugh,* he thought. *I've become a rodeo clown.*

As if he could hear his thoughts, the ring announcer made fun of Cody. "Now *that's* a rodeo clown, folks." Jinks the clown came over and engaged him in a mock battle for his job.

Cody forced a self-deprecating grin to his mouth and gave the audience a sweeping bow before limping to where Dub stood behind the chute. He knew how a good sport was supposed to act.

"That was something." Dub grinned as he helped haul Cody up over the fence. "Never seen that before. That's what I'd call a lunch-bell bull."

"Yeah, like he stopped short like he was saying, 'I earned my feed. Ride's over, you want more, gimme another five bucks,'" Cody said.

"Someone trained that bull. He was smart."

"He sure outsmarted me."

Dub slapped his back. "At least you made a score. Things are looking up for you."

Cody shook his head. Dub couldn't understand this. To have sunk so low where at least not falling off was a good thing…. "At least I broke 80 this time, though. By one stinking point."

"Any time you stay on, no matter how low the score, it's a good ride. Just keep clawing and scratching your way back to the top."

HE'D hoped Rex the reporter wouldn't care about interviewing him, seeing he had the lowest scores after round four, but it seemed he was still news of a sort. Bad news.

"How's it feel to get a score after all these weeks without one?"

"It feels just great, Rex. I hate to show up and lose."

Of course, Rex couldn't resist asking how come he couldn't stay on the bull every time out. "There was a time when it seemed like you could ride anything. What went wrong?"

"I wish I knew," Cody said with a grin, but his eyes were stone cold. He wished he had the power to strike Rex dead with them. "If you find out, let me in on it."

Whatever Rex thought, he turned to the camera with a smile and said, "And there you have it, from the man everyone expected would win this year. Clearly he doesn't know why he's struggling either. As so many have said—"

Knowing it was against the best form of interview etiquette and good PR, Cody walked away while the man was still blowing hot air.

He let a sinister grin twist his lips when he thought of saying, "My homosexual lover left me and I can't ride because I'm always thinking about him." It sure would stir up a ruckus. It was crazy, but he felt almost in the mood for it.

He was almost past them when he heard his name.

"Hey, Cody!"

It was Zane and Bobby Blue. He'd managed to duck any kind of face-to-face with them all weekend, but now he couldn't run away without being outright rude.

"Hi, boys. Congratulations on making it to Top Cut where the elite ride," Cody said, shaking their hands. "I'm proud of you."

"I want to thank you," Bobby Blue said with earnest nervousness. "You're a great rider and a great trainer. I wouldn't be where I am today if it weren't for you."

A little taken aback, Cody laughed. "It was my pleasure. It's great to see how good you're coming along."

"Thank you again. I totally mean it." Bobby Blue shook his hand again and loped off.

Cody stared after him. "What's got into him?"

"He's practicing for his press conferences," Zane said.

"I thought he sounded weirdly grateful. It's good to see you too, Zane."

"Actually, I got here as an alternate. I hate getting to ride because of someone's injury but I'm grateful for the chance," Zane said. "It's a real honor being in the ring with you."

Cody laughed rucfully. "Not much of an honor right now, I'm afraid."

"No. Listen, you're an inspiration to me and to a lot of other guys. It's easy when you're on top, but watching you fight your way out of the slump...." Zane shook his head. "I learned a lot at the ranch, but I'm learning even more now, like how a really great rider never gives up. I'm proud to tell anyone I got trained by you."

"Well, thanks. It means a lot to me to hear it." Cody grabbed the hand Zane offered again and shook it happily.

"It does to Bobby too, for real, even though he sounds like a dickweed. Good luck next weekend."

Cody stared after Zane in confusion as he pushed the door to the back hall open. It hadn't occurred to him that anything but winning could be found admirable. This was something new he needed to think over.

He followed Zane into the back hall just as the door to the locker room opened and he came face-to-face with the bullfighters. Apparently Johnny had come down to join his team, and they were laughing and discussing the event. It was eye opening to see Johnny with his peers. Even though he was the junior member, it was obvious Reese and Vern liked Johnny and having him around. Even Chris Bellow was talking to him.

Watching the bullfighters together, Cody paid close attention to them for the first time. Although Vern was solid with muscle, he was very quick in the ring; Reese was thinner, but still burly next to Johnny. Chris looked old and thick. Johnny was more slender and athletic-looking than the rest of the team. An acute sensitivity to Johnny made Cody notice Chris had an issue with him. In a moment, he realized Chris was jealous, maybe not of Johnny's ability, but of his youth. It was an emotion he could relate to, and he didn't admire it about himself. It was probably why he wanted to dodge Bobby Blue and Zane.

Vern caught sight of Cody and nodded at him. Johnny looked around, and when their gazes met it was another of those moments fraught with fear and suspense for Cody. He couldn't exactly read Johnny's expression, but he knew something was going on for him.

Johnny turned to say something he couldn't hear, and then Chris, Vern, and Reese continued on out into the parking lot.

"Hey, Cody, good ride tonight," Vern said as he passed him.

"Keep it going, Cody, any score is a good score," Reese acknowledged.

Chris still looked apologetic as he passed by. "Sorry about that, still a little slow on my feet."

"Thanks, guys." Cody waited until the outer door clanged shut and went to Johnny. He had a strong notion Johnny wasn't going to come to him.

"Can we talk?"

"Sure, but let's go somewhere where we have to keep our clothes on."

Cody grunted acknowledgement. "There's a place—"

"Let's just walk," Johnny interrupted.

"Okay." Cody jammed his hands into his pockets. He wanted to touch Johnny so bad, but using the fire of their attraction would derail this, and besides, it hadn't worked last time. He knew he could get Johnny in his bed tonight, but he needed more than just a physical connection.

Once outside under the dark evening sky, Cody started. "You know how I like to win. I don't care how much broken glass I have to crawl over to get to that buckle. Even though I've won before, it's like the first time each time. Then I realized I should have done it for you."

"Yeah, I can agree with that."

"Want to go to a bar?"

Johnny shook his head. "Not really."

"Restaurant?"

"Don't really want to talk about this in public."

"My room? We can order something."

"I can't stay long. I'm riding with Vern and we're pulling out early for Boise."

"Just to talk."

They walked in silence to Cody's hotel and stood propped on opposite walls in the elevator, not looking at each other. At least, Johnny wasn't when Cody snuck a glance at him in the mirror.

His heart was pounding as they walked down the hall. He was trying to think of what to say, what words could possibly make Johnny come back.

He slid the card key and the door opened. Once it closed behind them, Cody found himself pressed against the door, being ruthlessly kissed. Hands were unbuttoning his shirt and then slipping inside, fever hot against his skin. Cody slid his hands under the T-shirt, running them up Johnny's back and shoulders, feeling the angular plane of bone and muscle.

They were struggling against each other, trying to get closer, kiss deeper, and Cody pushed himself off the door to take a step toward the bed. Johnny staggered, off-balance from the move. They stumbled into the coffee table, knocking over a silk plant, rebounded off the TV stand, and crashed into the desk. Cody pushed Johnny up onto the desk, bending him back as they continued the kiss, his tongue plunging deeply.

Still kissing, Johnny pushed Cody away and walked him backward toward the bed. They caromed off the nightstand and fell onto the bed together. Their legs tangled and they rolled around in a fog of desire. Johnny's T-shirt was rucked up under his arms and Cody's was pulled out of his pants, but they couldn't let go long enough get them off.

Cody broke away with a moan and dove to suck at Johnny's nipple, causing him to arch up and groan. One of Johnny's hands dropped to the bulge in Cody's pants and pressed it, squeezing lightly. Cody bit down and jerked his hips into Johnny's hand.

Johnny uttered a sound somewhere between a moan and a laugh. "Fuck, you are such a good kisser."

"I'm biting," Cody murmured into Johnny's skin.

"Don't stop," Johnny mumbled back, hands fumbling with the fastening of Cody's jeans. "I'll get this open one of these years."

"Let's get naked, baby." They had to part to deal with their boots and belts.

Watching Johnny take off his shirt was like waiting for the gate to open. Cody could barely control himself. Johnny knelt on the bed, his bulge outlined clearly under his white jocks, his stomach taut and defined as he yanked the shirt over his head. Cody couldn't wait to get his hands on Johnny's smooth, honey-colored skin, suck his luscious nipples, run his hands over his muscular thighs.

There was a teasing smile on Johnny's lips and a glow of challenge in his glittering black eyes.

The sight of the tattoo made Cody start. He'd forgotten exactly how it twined around the slim body, the delicate blue-and-yellow design a startling contrast. He put out a hand and touched it gently with his fingertips, rejoicing at the delicate shiver in response.

"Missed your tat. What is it?"

"Cloud ladder," Johnny said.

Cody almost didn't want to break the mood but he wanted to know. "What does it mean?"

Johnny looked startled, and it wounded Cody to realize he'd never asked before, had just assumed it was some Native American design and left it at that.

"Can we talk about this later?"

Then they were kissing and gasping for air, the heat between them fierce.

"Supplies?" Cody panted.

Wrenching himself away, Johnny dove for his pants. Cody laughed when lube and a bunch of condoms fell out on the floor. Looked like Johnny was hoping to get lucky tonight. Johnny tossed him a condom and the tube and watched as Cody got ready.

Johnny lay on his back, holding his legs up. Cody watched Johnny's abs flutter when he started fingering him, trying to stretch him. It was torture to feel the velvet inside him and have to wait. It had been too long since Cody had had him. He pulled out, turned Johnny onto his knees, and yanked his ass high in the air, watching his hole flex.

When Cody penetrated, the hole felt tight, almost as if Johnny had never been fucked before. Johnny's head reared up and then down, and his spine arched as if he were in pain. The hiss that accompanied his entry and the quick glare Johnny darted at him over his shoulder seemed almost angry, but his body was straining back, craving it. Cody waited patiently for Johnny to adjust to him, even though his impulse was to thrust wildly, to lay down his claim for the body yielding to him.

Even though he was moaning in pain, Johnny reached back with one hand to keep him in place. Cody flinched when Johnny's fingers dug into his flesh.

The harsh angles of Johnny's shoulders curved softly at the moment Cody felt the tight channel relax around him and then adjust, pulsing to suck him in. He waited until Johnny pushed back at him.

"What are you waiting for? An engraved invitation?"

Cody plunged in to the deepest point and held still a moment, enjoying the muscles working around him. He started thrusting.

Johnny groaned and stretched his lean body, looking back over his shoulder again. This time the look he gave Cody was one of deepest pleasure, or at least that's what Cody hoped. He stopped thrusting and leaned down to kiss Johnny's neck, enjoying the full contact of their naked skins. He wanted to keep Johnny under him forever, shielding him from all harm with his body. But he needed to move.

He pounded furiously as Johnny jacked himself in time to each short drive.

He'd hoped it would last longer, that he could dazzle Johnny with his sexual prowess and wow him into coming back, show him what he was missing, but it had just been too long since he'd been inside his lover.

"No one like you...," he moaned as he came. "Love you.... No one...."

Draped across Johnny's back, Cody didn't want to pull out, and even though his head was spinning, he wanted Johnny to come by his hand. He pulled them down onto their sides, still buried inside, and pushed up on his elbow so he could see Johnny's face. He brushed Johnny's hand away from his cock, taking over the task of making him come.

He watched as Johnny's face contorted with the pained rapture of his oncoming orgasm, then softened as he was lost in his own private ecstasy.

He felt the swell of the cock in his hand, the slim body stiffening against him, the clamping muscles on his dick, and then the shoot of hot liquid over his fingers.

Eyes closed and mouth open, Johnny lay panting in the aftermath. Some weird new tenderness moved Cody to press closer and kiss him, feeling grateful for Johnny's willingness to be so vulnerable with him.

"You're really tight." Cody had always wanted to ask Johnny about his past experience ever since their first time together.

"Yeah," Johnny answered. "Been a long time."

Relieved that, whatever Johnny had been out doing while tomcatting around, he hadn't allowed other men to fuck him, Cody wanted to thank him. "I should have asked—I didn't mean to force you—"

"You did great," Johnny assured him. "It was perfect."

"I would have taken more time to—"

"Shut up."

Cody shut up as ordered, even though he had so much he wanted to say. But Johnny snuggled backward against him and he tightened his arms around him, grateful for another chance to hold his partner. Then he yawned. Much as he wanted to savor the moment and think all kinds of deep thoughts about how things would be different this time, male conditioning and emotional exhaustion got to him and all he really wanted was to sleep.

So he did.

CODY woke up to find Johnny pulling on his clothes in the dark. "What's up?" he demanded, instantly on alert. He could have kicked himself for giving in to his stupid need to sleep.

"Sorry, I didn't mean to wake you." Johnny buttoned his shirt and came over to kiss Cody. "I've got to get going. Vern'll leave without me if I'm not on time."

"Stay with me." Cody tried to pull him down onto the bed. "I'll make sure you get to the next event. Buy you a plane ticket."

Johnny pulled away frowning. "Weren't you listening last time? I'm committed to traveling with my team. They helped me out and I'm not going to bail on them without a word."

"Chris is back with them. I'm sure they can handle it if just this once, you—"

"No. I'm going." Johnny shouldered his bag and strode to the door.

"We didn't talk yet." Cody was aware his voice was raised as he got more frantic to make Johnny stay.

"Seems like we had other stuff on our minds," Johnny said. "It was great, but I have to leave."

"We didn't get anything settled. I want things to be back like they were. You have to—"

"I'll see you around."

"Fuck! Fucking running away again!" Cody snapped gruffly.

They glared at each other.

"You're right. I am running away, but you just push too damn hard." Johnny leaned against the door as if he couldn't wait to get out of the room. "Sorry. Maybe I'll catch you at the next stop."

Even though he was glad to hear Johnny admit it, Cody was irked he was the first to apologize. "Yeah, well, you're right too. I don't listen to what I don't want to hear. And I'm sorry for saying my slump is on you. It's my own damn fault I can't stay the course for eight seconds."

"Yeah, damn right about that at least." Johnny checked his watch. "Listen, I gotta go. Vern will pull out without me if I'm not on time."

"I want things to be like they were." Frustrated, Cody smacked his palm on the bed. "How are we going to work this out if you keep leaving?"

"I don't know." Johnny looked sadder than when he'd left Cody at the ranch. "I don't know if we can."

WHY does he always have to push so damn hard? Johnny realized he was running, and his boots weren't built for a race. He slowed to a walk. *Always has to get what he wants.* Before he knew it, he was jogging again. At least he wouldn't be late for Vern. He still had to pack his gear, but it was only 2:20 a.m. and Vern wasn't planning to leave until four.

He stopped and took out his phone, flipping aimlessly through the numbers. He stopped when he reached March's number. Johnny stood staring at it, remembering the night with his silver bear. He guessed he really shouldn't be calling March his silver bear. He hesitated, wanting to call the man but feeling as though it would be disloyal to Cody to discuss their business. And besides, what would he ask March? What did he really want?

Changing Cody was out of the question. Not only was he a stubborn bastard, but Johnny kind of liked how he was, his warmth, his confidence—the word pulled him up short and he realized why he'd been thinking of March.

His silver bear had that same kind of confidence, both sexual and personal; March was self-assured, virile, and had all the attributes of a dominant man. And yet he, Johnny, had had no trouble preventing March from taking what he wanted. He'd said no instead of running away, confident he could stop March.

So what was the difference?

Johnny shook his head at himself. It didn't matter with March; he'd had nothing to lose except maybe one night's hookup. It was different with Cody. He loved Cody. He didn't want to lose him. Johnny leaned against a handy building and laughed at himself. It was like reading a mystery and being unable to wait 'til the end and skipping pages to find out who did it. Just in case Cody might end up kicking him out, he'd gone and done it first. *Way to get what you want*, he thought. "I'm an idiot. I've already lost him. Competitive bastard."

He just couldn't take the heat so he jumped stupidly into the fire. Cody had this way of trying to get what he wanted, joking, teasing, leaning on him, and Johnny hated wrangling. It was one of the reasons he stayed away from his mother. He loved her, but he couldn't take the bitching. He hated saying no to Cody, and yet it had been so easy with March.

He turned his phone off, stuck it in his pocket, and started walking fast. He didn't need to call March anymore; he knew what

March would tell him. Learn to trust yourself. Learn to trust that Cody would live if he didn't always get what he wanted. Even if he did sulk. Johnny had to grin. He was a sulker himself, and the thought of both of them sulking at each other was kind of funny, but at least Cody had a sunnier disposition when he got over his sulks. Johnny tended to brood awhile longer.

But God, the thrill of Cody taking what he wanted in bed was something he couldn't deny he loved. And then Johnny realized he was giving Cody what they both wanted. Cody hadn't taken it from him, and he'd wanted to be fucked just as much as Cody wanted to fuck him.

A moment of doubt hit him. Sliding back to the familiarity of Cody's arms was too easy. It made Johnny's brain turn off and he needed to think about this. He'd worried that this thing between them was just sex, but it was more than that. He had to figure out what he really wanted and if he could even get it. The moment of clarity slipped away as he got lost in a sensual dream of how it felt to have Cody in his arms again.

He shivered as if a shock of cold water had hit him as he replayed the night before. He must have heard it somehow, because he sure wasn't concentrating on what Cody was saying at the time, but now he remembered. Cody had said "I love you." The break in his whisper made it mean so much more. It was something he'd never said in so many words before. He'd probably always assumed Johnny knew.

A secret smile curved Johnny's lips. Cody did love him. It wasn't just conquest. Somehow they had to find a way to make this work.

Johnny was waiting by Vern's truck, his bag over his shoulder before the sky was fully light. A yellow glow on the horizon hinted at the coming sun, but the air was crisp and smelled like fall.

"Why the big grin? You look like you just rolled out of bed, and I don't mean after a good night's sleep," Vern said sourly as he opened the camper back. "Tried calling you."

"You did?" Johnny slapped his pocket. "Crap. I turned it off."

"Don't get twisted around some girl's ring finger," Vern told him sternly. "My daddy always said not to get mixed up with some female woman."

"You're the one who's married, not me," Johnny pointed out. He slung his bag into the back and closed the back of the truck.

"Yeah, well, I never said I followed everything my daddy said." Vern grinned suddenly as he unlocked the truck. "Besides, my wife is a real grown-up woman, not some skank ho who wants to hopscotch from a bullfighter's bed into a rider's. Seen that done before. Don't get your heart broke."

"Oh, I won't. That's one thing for sure you don't have to worry about," Johnny said with his secret smile. While the escapades of the last four months had proven he could enjoy sex with a large number of men, last night had proven to him it would never be as good with anyone else as it was with Cody.

CHAPTER 16:

Back in the Saddle Again

IT STILL felt weird to watch from the stands. It had been a long time since Johnny attended an event where he wasn't part of the action, either as a rider or as a bullfighter. It was weird to smell the dirt and the stock, to hear the music and announcements from such a different place.

Even weirder was sitting next to Davis and Val Grainger in their box again. When they'd met in the hall backstage, Davis had greeted him with a warm grin and a firm handshake, and Val with her usual big hug. She seemed to take it for granted he would sit with them again, and Johnny found he wanted to, even though he dreaded questions about how he was doing or worse, what was going on between him and Cody.

But he underestimated her. She never asked, just seemed very content to have his company. All he hoped was that Cody would be able to get a ride. It would be worse to see their disappointment if Cody fell off, especially after how they left it last week. The announcer was doing his best to make sure everyone in the audience knew how bad a slump Cody had been in, and Johnny felt a little guilty.

It still hurt to see Chris down there, taking his place next to Vern and Reese. Even though Johnny knew he was actually the interloper and Chris probably felt the same hurt and frustration while he was out. At least he got a free seat in the stands. It made him understand a little better how Cody felt about getting older and losing the sport he loved.

Maybe it was the reason for the change in his attitude, why he seemed so arrogant at the ranch when they were teaching those kids.

Val's hand was tight around his as they watched Cody take his ride in the first round. Johnny could tell Cody was riding too tight. Bearing down, somehow Cody managed to make it to the whistle before his hand popped out of the rope. Despite knowing how Cody's pride would be hurt if he knew, Johnny had to laugh when Cody spun around in midair a couple times like a helicopter before skidding into the dirt at the end of the ride. But he felt angry when he saw Chris Bellow moving too slowly to save Cody from getting butted by the bull. It was Cody's own reflexes that made it an embarrassing thing rather than an injury as he was knocked off his feet, but was able to free himself and run for the fence. It wouldn't have been that close a call if Johnny had been down there.

When the disappointing score flashed on the board, Val said, "I hope Cody can pull himself together. He's better than this."

"He is," Johnny said.

Next up was Bobby Blue. Johnny clenched his hands into fists and bit his lip as he watched. It wasn't a pretty ride, with the bull stumbling and hesitating, but Bobby Blue made the best ride anyone could. When Rex stopped him for the post-ride interview on camera, Johnny's frown lightened with surprise as he watched on the ring monitor.

"How did you manage to stay up there for eight seconds?"

"It's all due to Cody Grainger, a great rider and a great teacher. I just want to thank him for the wisdom he shared with me that enabled me to make my ride. It's an honor to be here, and I want to thank the fans and God and our great country for the opportunity."

Even Rex looked a bit stunned by the reply, and Val was flat-out laughing as she turned to Johnny. "I guess you put the fear of God into him. Maybe he thinks the Ring of Honor will come after him for unbecoming behavior."

Embarrassed, Johnny felt his face flush but he had to laugh. "I wasn't really going to knock his block off. It just pissed me off when he dissed Cody. After all he did for him!"

"Hey, don't apologize to me. It was exciting to watch you in action. I was rooting for you." Val touched his arm. "And Cody." Her smile was so meaningful, Johnny had to turn away. He didn't know how to answer her, the unspoken question hanging between them clear as day. He had loved Cody since the day they met; he just didn't know if he could live with him anymore.

The ring announcer started talking. "And here comes the Brazilian contingent and one of their best riders, Juca Matos. For three years he's trailed Cody Grainger in the ring, but this could be his chance to pull ahead. All the Brazilians are great riders, even though Juca Matos has seen some criticism of his game plan. His strength lies in the consistency of his rides, rather than thrills. His scores tend to be average, but he piles up the points by simply not falling off too many bulls. Some say part of his strategy is he won't pick a bull if he knows he can't ride it. And at the end of the year, his consistency adds up in points and dollars, and that's what a rider needs to take him to the finals."

That's where Cody was different, Johnny thought. If a bull had thrown him before or had a rep for being rank, that was the bull Cody would go for. It was part of what made him so exciting to watch.

Juca Matos took his time in the chute, getting his rope fixed the way he liked it. The officials were telling him to hurry it up before he finally gave the nod. The gate opened and the bull shot out, but immediately settled into a predictable spin with kicks and jumps. Another routine ride for Juca. The buzzer went and Juca yanked on the tail of his rope. At that moment, the bull chose to jump and twist in the air, slamming Juca to the ground under his feet. Chris Bellow rushed in to haul the stunned rider to safety.

Johnny saw the disaster coming before it happened and leaped to his feet, straining forward over the rails as if he could somehow get down there in time to avert injury.

Chris found himself backed up near the fence. Vern hustled Juca away to the side while Reese tried to lure the bull away from the trapped bullfighter. The bull swung his head around irritably at the same moment Chris turned his in the opposite direction, just in time to catch a horn under his chin. His head snapped back and he crumpled to the ground, unconscious. Instantly, Reese jumped in front of him, and Vern yelled to distract the bull. The arena usher on horseback threw a rope over the bull's horns and forced him to the gate.

"I've got to get down there," Johnny said tensely.

Davis agreed. "Go ahead, son."

He barely heard Val's words. "Please be careful, Johnny. Take care of yourself."

VERN practically grabbed him by the hair and hauled him to the locker room. Reese already had his bag open and was pulling his gear out.

"I knew this was gonna happen," Vern muttered.

At any other time it would have alarmed Johnny to contemplate being undressed by his bullfighting team, but now it amused him, even as he welcomed the help. "Hope Chris is okay."

"Only a slight concussion and probably a gash on his chin. He'll need a few stitches to close it up," Vern said. "I seen enough injuries in the ring I can diagnose them practically as well as the doc."

"Hurry it up, skinny-bones," Reese said. "I think Jinks is running out of steam. He already told that joke twice tonight. If we don't get out there soon, the crowd'll massacre him."

"His jokes aren't that bad," Vern said.

"Yes, they are." Johnny laughed that he and Reese said it at the same time.

The ring announcer mercifully took over from Jinks, but Johnny would rather have listened to all the bad jokes Jinks knew than what he had to say about Cody.

"It's either money or mud for Cody Grainger. That boy sure loves to take chances. And they don't always pay off for him, but he knows how to get the audience behind him. It all depends on how much he wants to put that gold buckle on his belt.

"He's coming up next on The Remedy: Good For What Ails You, out of Beaver Pond Farms. The Remedy is a great big tough old bull. So far this year he's been ridden only twice out of sixteen outs, both times by Cody Grainger, but that was back when he was riding at the top of his form. This bull can spin either way, but the way Cody's been riding, he might not be able to ride him even using both hands."

Johnny didn't realize he'd made a noise, but Reese said, "Quit growling. The man has to fill up time 'til we get out there. You can kick his butt later."

"Okay, I'm ready." Johnny tucked his braid up and jammed his hat down over it.

"Let's rock and roll," Vern said.

RIGHT out of the gate, Cody knew he was going down. The Remedy caught his horn on the gate and staggered forward, going to his knees for a second. Cody almost went off over his head, but then the bull made a kind of swooping recovery, lurching to the right before he jumped straight up. Cody managed to catch his spur in the rope, knowing it would be his only anchor. Once again the bull staggered on landing and took off down the ring, charging forward but then stopping and pushing back, almost sending Cody off over his head. The drag on his hand was almost unbearable. The Remedy never settled into a spin, jump, and kick and Cody couldn't get situated. They were so far down the ring, he couldn't tell if any red flags had gone down either.

The whistle blew and Cody slid off the back of the bull, only to find himself on his back. A yank pulled him along as he realized his spur was caught in the rope. The bull kicked and flipped Cody over and dragged him along facedown in the dust. A heavy weight landed on Cody's back, and then someone was tugging desperately at his boot. He recognized Johnny's voice above him yelling some direction to him. In spite of the dust going up his nose and in his mouth, Cody couldn't help but enjoy the familiar warmth of Johnny on his back, even though he tortured himself by thinking himself this was never going to be his again.

The pressure on his leg let up for a minute and Johnny rolled off his back, but apparently it was only because the bull had changed direction and was heading back toward Cody. Vern yelled loudly to chase the bull in a different direction. The rope went taut again. Cody dug his fingers in and clawed at the dirt, vainly trying to stop the drag.

Here we go again, Cody thought. He gasped at the sudden weight on his back when Johnny jumped on top of him and tugged at the boot. Reese and Vern were shouting and running alongside the bull, Johnny was yanking at him, and Cody was basically being a toboggan at the bottom of the heap.

And then, relief as his boot came loose and the stretch of tendon in his hamstring was released. He stopped sliding and felt Johnny grab his vest, hoist him to his feet, and hustle him over to the fence, always keeping his body between Cody and the bull. He felt a hand on his ass, pushing him up onto the rails. The crowd was going crazy cheering. He looked down at the handsome face grinning up at him and tried to smile back. "Thanks."

"Getting off isn't your best thing," Johnny told him. "Maybe you should work on that if you're going to keep taking a dive." He handed Cody his boot and ran off to join Vern and Reese.

The medics were waiting for Cody, but he waved them off and jumped down. He put on his boot before he raised both hands to the audience, smiling and nodding, even though he felt like shit. As exciting as his dismount was, the ride was tame and a bull he'd already ridden successfully twice should never have bucked him off. Johnny's words were so impersonal, they could have been said to anyone. As though they were strangers. The whole thing was humiliating, but Cody smiled all the way to the locker room, aware of the cameras on him.

The canned music drowned out whatever the announcer was saying as he avoided the glances of the other riders in the changing room. They all knew he was supposed to be at the top of the leaderboard, and he was riding like a rookie. And Johnny had laughed at him.

After the door closed on the cameraman, Cody hurled his rope at the bank of lockers. The thunderous clang of the bell hitting steel made him feel better. It also made the other cowboys clear out quickly and tactfully leave him alone with his anger.

He sat with his head down, elbows on his knees, hands dangling between his legs. He'd thought one night together would lure Johnny back, if Cody could just make him remember what they had. He was always distracted from the job at hand, thinking about Johnny.

And it wasn't enough. He wasn't enough. Not big enough. Even though he'd managed to turn off the echo of those hurtful words and stay hard, he hadn't managed to conjure whatever magic was required to get Johnny back.

The thought of roping Johnny after the event and dragging him off by force crossed Cody's mind, which made him realize how desperate he was.

He had to pull himself together for the short round. The points he'd racked up all year were keeping him in so far, but if he kept riding like this he was going to lose everything; any chance of winning the finals, the check, and Johnny. How unlucky could one man be?

He sat alone, unmoving, staring disaster in the face. He started when he felt a hand on his shoulder.

"You were red-flagged, you got a reride," Dub told him.

"Whatever."

"Temperamental. That's what you are. One minute you're on top of the fucking world, the next you'd think you was coming from your own funeral."

"Leave me alone, Dub."

"Bull hung up a horn coming out of the gate impeding your forward movement, like they say in the rule book. You got another chance for a score in the long round. Shake it off."

"Tell them no on the reride. I can't do it."

"Don't whine like an irritating dickhead. It ain't like you to give up. You tell them no and you don't get to change your mind two seconds later."

"Just another chance to make a fucking fool of myself. I'll take whatever score I made."

The pause went on long enough that Cody looked up at Dub.

"Go after him, Cody. It ain't worth all this misery."

"Him—who!" Cody stammered, turning away. "You talking about the bull?"

"Come on, I only look like a dumb hick. I'm your friend. If you want to keep your private life private, fine, but a blind man would notice how you look at Johnny. Since you been playing a lone hand, it's been eating you up inside. I know it'll cut to the bone for you to get humble, but you gotta tell him you're sorry, get on your knees, whatever you have to do to get him back. Don't blow your last year. I'll let them know you'll take the reride." With a final pat on the shoulder, Dub walked out without waiting for Cody to argue.

He was through. Dub knew about him and he was a failure, both as a man and a rider. The door squeaked shut behind Dub.

"Last year," Cody groaned, and put his head in his hands.

Then the door opened again. He didn't bother to pretend to be okay as someone came toward him. The someone knelt and put his hands on Cody's thighs.

Startled, he looked up.

"What the fuck is wrong with you?" Johnny said. "You're better than this. This is the last trail to the finals. You've ridden way ranker bulls and you're flopping around up there like you never been on a bull's back before."

"Johnny!" Cody gasped. He couldn't move. Just stared into his beautiful black eyes.

"Stop riding not to fall off. Ride to win! You love to ride, remember?" Johnny kept his hands moving, stroking up and down Cody's thighs, the warmth seeping through the leather of his chaps. "You'd better stick on top of your next ride or else."

"Or else what?"

"Or else we never fuck again!"

"You left me!"

"I'm riding with Vern. I had to leave."

"I thought—I thought—you said—you don't think we can work it out—"

"You're an idiot, Cody, but I love you anyway." Johnny grinned up at him. "Fuck, listen to me, getting romantic right in the locker room. We can talk about it later. I've got to get back out there. And you better stick on top of your next bull or I'll whup your ass."

"You might have to take a number. Dub and Mom'll fight you for the privilege," Cody said ruefully. Cody leaned forward to kiss Johnny but pulled back before their lips could touch.

"Later," Johnny promised. He stood up and stared down at Cody. "Maybe you need an incentive program. Score in the 80s, you get a blowjob, over 90 you get to tap my ass—"

"As long as you come back, I'll ride any bull out there, I'll ride Spinal Tap!" Cody knew he was babbling. He stood up. He wanted nothing more than to grab Johnny, hold him tight, kiss him forever, but this was no place for a reconciliation even though some miracle he didn't understand had happened.

"All right, then. I'll get Sam to truck him in for the short round. He's got ten minutes," Johnny teased. He pointed a finger. "You! Ride the fuck out of your next bull! Make me proud. And rich, because I got money riding on you."

And then he was gone.

The joy that filled Cody made him feel as if he were going to burst, even while he realized that once again, he hadn't paid enough attention. He resolved he would get better at listening to Johnny, he'd do anything—

The music ended and the ring announcer's hyper voice echoed over the loudspeaker.

Cody pulled his glove back on and grabbed his rope. He had to talk the officials into letting him ride The Remedy again instead of another bull. He was going to ride that bull for the full eight, dammit! Waiting for The Remedy to be brought back out, he would have to ride last in the third round. No one would be expecting him to stick on the back of The Remedy after what had just happened, but he would do it for Johnny. He'd show them all, but this was for Johnny. He got up to go talk to the judges.

HE WAS afraid to meet Dub's gaze as he got ready in the chute, but his friend's hand on his vest was comforting, keeping the bull from jerking him forward. "Make him pay for dragging you in the dust, Cody."

"Thanks, Dub."

"Always with you, friend," Dub said.

Startled, Cody looked up to find Dub grinning at him. "I owe you a beer—friend."

"Make it a case," Dub said. "I could use it. My nerves are shot after watching you fall off all summer."

Cody gave the nod, watching the rope slide through the rails as the gate swung open. The Remedy pushed off. He could feel the power as the bull blew up out of the gate, jumping high enough to clear it. Then its back legs went up and the bull twisted, turning left and settled into a spin. Apparently The Remedy felt it had something to prove too. With a toss of its head, the bull went right, turning in ever-tighter spins and throwing in big jumps, rolls, and kicks.

And it was all so easy. Cody wondered why he'd been having so much trouble in the last few months. Like magic, he remembered how to do it. He corrected easily, breaking at the hips, pulling himself forward well up on his rope after each jump. At a sudden change of direction, he felt himself sliding into the well and heard Johnny's voice yelling.

"Toes out, heels down! Keep on it! You can do it!"

Instantly, Cody forced his free arm in front, dug down with his heels, and pulled himself back up again. "You're not getting shut of me, you gol-durned bull," he gritted out.

He strained, tightening his abs to pull himself to center, so focused he barely heard the buzzer. He rode two seconds longer and then yanked the tail of his rope. The bull shot forward and he slid off the side and fell directly under the hooves. Cody curled himself into a little ball and prayed he wouldn't get stomped. Miraculously, the rain of sharp hooves coming down around him didn't hit him and he rolled out from under, assisted by a strong hand on his vest. He grinned his thanks up at Reese, who yanked him to his feet and shoved him toward the fence.

"Get out of here, Cody!"

Cody grinned as Johnny ran by, laughing and shaking his head, getting the bull to chase him to the gate. Cody grinned at the audience and raised both hands above his head. Suddenly he threw back his head, pounded his chest with his fists, and howled in triumph. The dismount might not have been pretty, but he made the whistle. "I am back, baby! Watch your step!" Cody shouted, although with the noise in the ring no one could have heard him. But it felt so damn good.

Rex the reporter was waiting at the gate for him when he limped back. "Looks like you found your riding mojo again, Cody. What was different today?"

Cody wanted to shout out, "I'm in love and he loves me back!" but of course he couldn't. "Guess I'm out of the slump." He knew he was smirking and he enjoyed the hell out of it.

"First you have to make it through the fourth round."

"I'll make it," Cody said, his confidence surging.

"Good luck with it," Rex said, turning to his cameraman. "That's the Cody Grainger people pay to see. It's just like him to demand they bring out the same bull he just fell off and then nail the ride. Now we'll have to wait to see if he's able to ride at this level all the way to the finals."

Dub was waiting for him, looking as happy as if it had been his ride. "Back in the saddle again, Cody. How's it feel?"

"It feels so damn good I can't even tell you."

"You've got it in the bag."

"There's still the fourth round."

"Don't turn modest on me all of a sudden. Don't worry, you've got this one."

They climbed behind the fence into the stands in the rider area to watch the remainder of the rides. He would be up against nine other men who all wanted the buckle as much as he did, including his friend Dub. Cody studied his face while he watched the action in the ring. Somehow he'd never thought Dub could accept the knowledge he was gay, and here he'd known all the time.

"Well, that's all of them. Ready for round four?" Dub asked.

A smile spread over Cody's face. Was he ever. "Yeah, I'm ready."

"Show us how it's done, cowboy."

ROUND four was a blur to Cody. He was still sitting low in the standings, so he had to ride first.

Luckily he still remembered how to ride when his turn came. Zero Tolerance was an ornery bull, and big. So wide across it was easy to strain a groin muscle trying to stay on. For a moment, Cody's courage failed him, and it struck him as totally crazy he should want to climb on the back of a one-ton animal to show the world he still had balls.

Once up there, he nodded, and the gate swung open. The bull backed out and threw Cody forward, but he just managed not to slap. Zero seemed undecided; his head swung left, but when he jumped, he twisted in the air and turned to the right. Being a little extra cautious worked for Cody, and he wasn't fooled. The bull settled into a pattern of jump and kick, spinning into his hand.

His score was 85.75.

Cody was grinning when he made it back behind the chute. He wasn't going to win the round, his hip hurt, and it wasn't his best go around, but it was a decent score, especially after the numbers he'd been looking at over the summer.

Dub was indignant, though. "That was a 90-point ride! They're leaving room for the rest of the field to knock you off!"

"Hey, don't complain too much. You're part of the rest of the field who's trying to knock me off."

"You got this one." Dub shook his head. "You're going to win it. I feel it."

"Don't sell yourself short, Dub."

Now Cody could only wait and see. He'd done all he could. One ride at a time, and the excitement in the ring was growing. The fans were always thrilled to see a good ride, but they wanted to see Cody win. Like dominoes, the eight men who followed Cody fell over, either getting a low score or falling off.

He groaned to see Dub hit the dirt at a little over five seconds, but Cody knew that, even with an average score, by the grace of the other riders doing worse than he did, he'd won. Finally!

Dub came to join him behind the chutes. "You got some kind of voodoo spell going? I should never have fallen off that practice bull."

Cody slapped his friend's shoulder. "That was a rank bull, Dub. I'm lucky I didn't draw him."

"Easy for you to say," Dub complained, but he grinned.

After the last rider failed to cover his bull, Cody bounced to his feet, rubbing his hands. Another buckle!

"Does it hurt?"

"What, that little tumble I took in round three?"

Dub spat in the dirt. "No, always winning over your friends."

Cody gave him a big grin. "Doesn't hurt a bit."

"Could you at least pretend a little?" But Dub was grinning too. "Go on and get your damn buckle."

CHAPTER 17:

Getting on a Hot Streak

IT MADE Cody want to laugh and cry and shout in triumph. That buckle had to be the hardest win in his entire career. Even if he did win the finals this year, no gold buckle would hold the meaning this one did. He'd won it for Johnny. Holding the buckle, kissing it for the cameras, the flashbulbs going off, other riders gathered around clapping for him, confetti, a quick shower, changing into clean clothes for the brief press conference because they were always short in bull riding, then a rather long meet and greet with delighted fans, signing a million autographs. At least, it felt like a million. Good thing Cody wrote with his right, or maybe his riding hand would never have been the same, as so many fans had thrust tickets, hats, and programs at him. Excited fans telling him how they always knew he would ride out the slump, how glad they were he was back, manly thumps on the back, kisses on satin cheeks of pretty girls for the camera, good wishes for the weeks leading up to the finals.

Then dinner with the family. His mother looking so happy, his father so proud, RJ radiating approval in his silence, Travis talking a blue streak, and Dub grinning. Of course, no one commented on Johnny's presence except Travis. He'd waited 'til Dub left the table to speak to a few of his fans before leaning across Val.

"So, you two an item again?"

Val smacked him on the shoulder but at the same time asked, "Well? Are you?"

It made Cody realize how anxious she'd been and how great her self-control had been not to interfere more than she did. "I'll leave that to Johnny to decide."

Johnny had nodded. "We're an item."

Travis passed Val a twenty as she exclaimed, "Told you so."

"That's all we're worth? A twenty?" Cody was grinning.

"There were a few other side bets if it makes you feel any better," Davis said.

"Quit while your head still fits your hat, Cody," RJ said. "Besides, you didn't bet, so what's it to you?"

"It's okay, I feel like I won anyway."

It made him happy his family was behind him, but throughout the celebratory dinner, his attention was mostly on Johnny anyway, feeling the electricity buzzing between them, a heightened awareness that made him conscious of the way his jeans rubbed his groin and thighs.

He couldn't wait for them all to go away so he could be alone with Johnny. Something had happened, something had changed, he could feel it. It felt like being inside the chute, the moment of anticipation before the gate opened and the explosion of energy, the dance of power between rider and bull.

In some ways he knew it would never be the same between him and Johnny, but for the first time he had hope it might be better. Over the past few months, when they met, even when they fucked, Johnny's eyes had been unreadable. Now Cody could see desire, pride, and what he'd missed most, love.

It made him feel proud. He had a lot to be proud of tonight. He'd won the Boise Invitational and a new buckle, and somehow he'd won Johnny back.

Where they sat there was no way they could touch, even if he dared in front of his parents and Dub. For now it was enough to sit there and anticipate.

Eventually the meal was over and people drifted off tactfully. Even Dub slapped his back with a knowing grin. "Congratulations again, you buckle thief. Breakfast tomorrow?"

Cody nodded. "Thanks, Dub."

Johnny waited until they were all out of sight. "He knows. Did you tell him?"

"Didn't have to. He figured it out on his own."

"Guess he won't be holding a press conference to announce it."

"He's my friend," Cody said, and then wondered what he'd done to deserve a friend like that.

Johnny seemed to read his mind. He laughed. "You've been a good friend to him too."

"After all this, I don't see it."

"Remember when he used to ride toes in 'til you told him the right way?"

Cody chuckled. "I forgot about that."

"Guess the boys at the ranch this year weren't your first students."

"Never thought of it that way."

"That's generous of you. You never dwell on a man's failings."

There was an awkward silence. Cody wondered if Johnny felt bad about his cataloging of Cody's failures.

"I'd ask you to come to my hotel, but we can't seem to keep our clothes on long enough to talk."

"What's wrong with that?" Johnny grinned. "We can always talk later."

"Nothing I can see. It's hard enough keeping my hands off you in public." Cody knew he was staring like a starving dog at a juicy bone, but he couldn't help it. All the events of the day seemed to conspire to make him keyed up and horny, and judging by the way Johnny was staring, he was hungry for him too.

"Tell me about it. When I got my hand on your vest and yanked you out from under that bull, I just wanted to pull your shirt up and touch the skin underneath...." Johnny shivered. "There's something between us that's kinda hard to walk away from."

Cody swallowed hard. "Let's get out of here."

When they arrived at his room, he half expected to find himself pushed back hard against the door like last time, but instead Johnny circled his waist with his arms and kissed him softly.

Cody let his hands roam over Johnny, feeling the warmth and firmness of his chest under the thin cotton shirt, the roundness of his ass, the hard length of him pressed firmly against his thigh. He knew he was hard too, but this time it felt as if they had all the time in the world to get to know each other again.

Because Johnny was back.

Slowly, the clothes came off, drifting to the floor as skin was revealed, caressed, kissed. Johnny swayed gracefully in his arms as they kissed, as if dancing to music Cody couldn't hear. Their cocks rubbed together, getting caught between them, rubbing against the hair of their thighs and bellies.

A leg slid between Cody's, rubbing his balls while Johnny's hands stroked his thighs. Cody felt as if he were on fire with sensation; all thought vanished, breathing became difficult, unable to tell sound from touch, pain from pleasure. Feeling the fireworks that come with being in love.

Then they were connected, flesh against naked flesh, hardness nestled in softness, twisting in serpentine patterns against the sheets. Tongues twined together, beating hearts thundered, sweat made their skin slide.

Cody wrapped his arms around Johnny's chest, grasping him from behind, hip to groin, holding him tight as if to keep him from flying away. Keeping them connected, hammer striking iron, sending sparks enough to light up the room.

With every thrust, Johnny cried out, reaching back to grab at Cody, fingers digging into the backs of his thighs, pulling him closer. His eyes stared sightlessly, deep, fathomless as he strained backward, wanting more, wanting it deeper. Cody didn't know if he could be much deeper but if he could he would.

Cody reached to tease a nipple, and then let his hand drift down Johnny's torso light as a feather 'til he found his hard flesh, circling it loosely, teasing. Johnny bucked like a madman, desperate for more friction, taking Cody's hips along for the ride as he clamped down.

Cody tightened his grip and whispered, "I love you."

Hot as molten lava, the eruption spilled over his fingers. Johnny was no longer breathing. He was heaving for air, shaking like an earthquake, straining with taut muscles.

Cody wasn't teasing as he reaffirmed their union with a roar of some emotion too powerful to label. Then there was nothing but the rush of blood, the feeling of pulse and heartbeat, their gasping breaths coming together, the warmth of Johnny's body in his arms.

"I know," Johnny murmured.

WHEN Johnny awoke, he thought for a moment he was back in the room with March, his silver bear. There was a table with candles, food set out, and even a bottle of wine, but the man waiting for him was different.

Cody was sitting there naked, like March had, but instead of reading the paper, he was watching Johnny with an expression of anxious hope on his face.

"Hi," Johnny said, feeling suddenly shy.

"Hi. I ordered some food. Are you hungry?"

"I could eat."

"Good, because you're going to need your strength."

Cody leered, but it was too late. Johnny had caught the slide from vulnerability to confidence. Where once the shift had confused him, now he found it oddly endearing, but perhaps that came along with knowing what it meant. And having the upper hand was something he thoroughly enjoyed. He would have to keep Cody on his toes from now on.

Johnny went to the table and helped himself. "What, no lobster?"

Cody seemed dismayed. "I never thought of it. You like lobster?"

"It's okay, I was just kidding." The food wasn't as lavish as what March had provided, but Cody had remembered what he liked. It touched Johnny.

Cody leaned forward and delicately trailed his fingers along Johnny's ribs. "Tell me about that tattoo."

"I'm Diné, Navajo," Johnny started, as if they were just meeting. "When First Woman put the stars in the sky, Fire Man shot two crooked fire arrows into the sky and made a cloud ladder. Then he climbed the ladder to place the stars at her direction."

"Wow. That's beautiful."

"Part of the creation story. There are four worlds and Diné are the people who live in the fourth world. Diné means 'the people'. The stars were placed to symbolize one man and one woman, so no other stars could approach them. It was the way only one couple lived at one campfire."

"Only a man and woman?"

"It used to be there were four sexes: man, woman, and then there were the two-spirit people, man-woman and woman-man. Sometimes they were visionaries or healers. They were said to be respected, they had a role in the community. People had a less rigid definition of how people should act."

"It must have made it easier for you."

Johnny shook his head. "There was a time when I would have given anything to be 'normal'. These are old concepts. Everything changes, for us and for you whites. I grew up in the same America you did. Bible-thumpers destroyed that part of our culture. I never heard about two-spirit people until I started looking for stuff about my heritage on the Internet." He touched the tattoo as if it were a talisman. "That's when I got this. If there was a time when being gay was acceptable in our tribe, I didn't learn of it from my family. I can't speak for any other tribe, but gay men were seen as lesser, same as in the white world. This romantic notion of the two-spirit people is not my experience. It's not easy being Diné and gay. That's one of the reasons I fell for you. You knew fuck all about this shit and only wanted to get into my pants."

"I still do."

"Yeah, I know." Johnny grinned. "It's good to be able to count on something."

"How did you tell your parents?"

"I've never told them and I never will. My mother does not want to know this and I respect her too much to force her to acknowledge it. It's, like, a private thing. Closed off."

"I'm sorry. And you still support her?"

Johnny tried to smile but could feel his mouth twisting. "I'm the middle kid but my older brother is a drunk. He can't help her. My sister had a baby. The father doesn't want anything to do with them. Someone's got to help them. It's my job."

"I wouldn't give her anything unless she listened to you, accepted you and told you she—"

"It's my culture. Family is very important. I don't want to shame her in her tribe's eyes. Even if they wouldn't think that way, she would feel like an outcast. I have a responsibility to her."

Cody calmed himself visibly. "I can respect that. Admire it, even. I just wish it was easier for you. What about your father?"

"He's a drunk. Haven't seen him in over fifteen years."

"Damn, I knew I was lucky but I didn't realize how lucky. I hit the jackpot on awesome parents."

"Yeah, you did," Johnny agreed. "It's okay. My mother is who she is. It would have been nice…. But she did her best. We visited the reservation to see my grandparents, but she brought us up in Flagstaff because she wanted us to learn how to operate in both worlds. I know she would have preferred to live on the reservation, so I thank her for that sacrifice."

"You ever wish she could see the real you?"

"She loves me. She's proud of what I do. She doesn't think I'm getting whitewashed because I work in a white man's sport. It's just she can't accept some parts of me, and that's how it's always going to be. I've got to stay in the closet so I can earn enough for all of us to live on."

"I didn't know." Cody seemed thoughtful and quiet. "How did you get started in this business?"

Johnny smiled, thinking back to when he was a skinny, gangly boy who didn't know what he wanted. "I always liked horses. Always liked how, in Westerns, the Indians could ride better than the cowboys, even though we always got killed in the end. We lived in a poor section on the edge of the city where it wasn't that far to some of the ranches. I walked out to the Double A one day after school and asked for a job.

"I lucked out by accident. The guy who owned it, Ace, had horses and cows. And bulls. He asked me if I knew anything about horses. I said no, but I wanted to learn."

Cody laughed. "I would have lied and bluffed my way into it."

"True, you totally would have."

"How old were you?"

"Fourteen, but I was tall for my age. Anyway, he liked my answers and he put me to work cleaning stalls. Said he couldn't pay much but if the low wages didn't cure me of loving horses, he'd see about me riding."

"And the rest was history." Cody clapped a hand over his mouth and looked so guilty that Johnny's glare turned to a grin. "Sorry. Go on."

"Didn't care if I had to clean stalls to be near horses. He would let me turn them out of the stalls into the corral so I got to touch them. I have a feeling for animals. They took to me like I did to them. Even his dog, Duke, would wait for me at the end of the driveway every day and follow me around while I worked. Ace used to pretend he was jealous, but he liked that I could read animals. So he taught me to ride. Both Western and English. Said it would make me a well-rounded rider. It didn't matter what he paid, he was giving me a chance to do something I loved."

"You do have a way with animals. Missed you at the ranch this summer," Cody mumbled.

"He had these Mexican cowboys working for him and they would sometimes rope a steer and ride it for fun. One day Ace told me to get on and try it and I did."

"And you stayed on for the full eight?"

"Not even. Bucked off in three. But the Mexican hands and Ace were impressed I hung on even that long. Told me to keep practicing."

"And you weren't scared at all." Cody sounded proud.

Johnny grinned. "Hate to burst your bubble, but I was terrified. Those steers were huge! But I couldn't let them see it. Those Mexicans, they were as good as any of the Brazilians riding today. Like they were born astride a bull."

"It was a macho thing."

"Absolutely. What man is gonna let another man face him down over anything? We'd rather get our necks broke than let on to being scared."

"I'd like to think I was smarter but I have to admit there's some truth in it."

"One day, when I went out to the ranch, Ace told me to hop in the truck. There was something he wanted me to see. It surprised me when he turned around and drove back toward the city. For a minute I thought I'd done something wrong and he was taking me home, but instead he drove to the fairgrounds. Turns out the rodeo had come to town. He wanted me to see the bull riding. And I was hooked. So far riding was just a friendly competition thing with the Mexicans, but then I saw you could actually earn money doing this."

"More these days than back then." Cody nodded.

"Ace helped me out. He found a few retired riders willing to give me some pointers. He fronted me the money to enter a couple of junior bull-riding events, and I earned enough to pay him back," Johnny said proudly. "Pretty soon I was winning, even though some of the white boys didn't like that so much. Oh, sorry."

"It's okay, I understand. I think it's only recently the Brazilians have gotten popular in the States. It's a conservative sport," Cody said. "So how did you switch into fighting?"

Johnny groaned. He hated saying this part out loud. "I'm not that good a rider."

"You are too! You're a great rider! Look at your ride on Dementia when you—"

"I'm not near as good as you." Johnny swallowed hard. It still hurt to admit he would never achieve the dream of being a big-name rider and maybe someone other Diné boys could look up to and say, "I can do that." He couldn't express the bitterness of the realization even to Cody. "I got taller, and the taller I got, the harder it was to stick on top of a bull. You get thrown to the end of your rope and it's hard to pull yourself back up."

Cody nodded. "Yeah, definitely harder for a taller guy."

"You're tall for a rider and I'm not that much taller than you, but a couple inches makes a big difference," Johnny said.

Both of them giggled and Cody cupped his groin, giving Johnny a dirty leer. "That's what I always say."

"Shut up. Anyway, I started slipping down in the ranks, not winning so much. By then I was helping out at home, and when I didn't win, it was hard on my mother. I got desperate."

"That never works. Can't ride from fear. There's got to be joy in it," Cody agreed sympathetically.

"Yeah, that's it. I lost the joy. One day I was having a great ride but the bull threw me just shy of eight seconds. I was so fucking pissed!" Johnny smashed a fist on the table, making the silverware and Cody both jump.

"What was the bull's name?"

"Raindog! Fucking Raindog!"

"Knew you'd remember," Cody murmured. "I remember the name of every bull ever stomped me. You get hurt?"

"Only hurt my pride," Johnny growled, and then he laughed. "I was so fucking pissed off I got up and stared that bull in the eyes. He glared right back at me and pawed the ground to work up to a charge but it suddenly clicked for me. I knew exactly what he was going to do. It was like I could read his thoughts. I put my hand on that bull's head and I *dared* him to come for me. I taunted him and played with him and fooled him. By the end I had the audience laughing at the bull and I got him out of the ring by myself. I *proved* to him, to me, and to that audience that no bull was going to get the better of me!"

"You go, boy!" Cody laughed.

"I started helping out around the touring division, learning the trade. And then Vern came by one day to see if I wanted a job," Johnny said. "I had to make a choice, I had to admit to myself I wasn't going to be a top rider. No glory there. But facing a bull down in the ring was ten times more thrilling than any ride I ever had!" The excitement of remembering made him jump to his feet and stride around the room. "That was it for me. I love fighting more than I ever loved being on top of a bull. I love saving a rider's ass, even if it means taking a hit for him. I love being on the same level with the animals."

"I'm so glad," Cody whispered. He got up and pulled Johnny into his arms so their bare chests were touching. He buried his face in Johnny's long, thick hair and started nuzzling his neck. "I always worried you were jealous of me riding."

"I was. I still am! But I had to face it that I couldn't be a top rider like you, and I found something else I love more. No one's ever going to know my name like they know yours, but I'm doing what I love."

"Believe me, the cowboys know your name, Johnny Arrow."

"And it's not even my real name." Johnny giggled.

Cody pulled back in shock. "Your name isn't Johnny?"

"It's Johnny, all right, but people kept calling me Johnny the Indian. Decided I might as well play into it. So, Johnny Arrow."

"What's your real name?"

"Johnny Begay."

Cody whistled slowly. "I can see why you might change it."

"It's a common Diné name like Smith, but maybe a little too— uh—close to home."

"Is Ace proud to see how you turned out?"

Johnny's mouth had a bitter twist as he answered. "I wish he was still around to see me. Died a few years ago. But he was always proud of me, even when I wasn't riding so well. Said there was a season for all things."

"I'm glad someone cared about you."

"Yeah, my mother loves me, but it's different coming from a man. Ace was kind of like a father to me."

Cody remained silent for a respectful time before he asked, "After tonight you're coming home with me, right?"

Johnny had to smile at the hope and trepidation in Cody's voice. "Nope, I got a job and it's important to me. I'm part of the fighting team now. You've got to understand that. Tomorrow, when Vern leaves, I'm riding with him."

"I do understand," Cody said. "I'm glad you're so in love with what you're doing. I wish I'd known all this earlier."

"It's not all on you. I don't talk about it much, but I'm glad you asked."

"And let me tell you, there's a lot of people who know your name even if you're not a famous rider. Every cowboy you keep from harm is going to remember you. They already trust you."

"Who says so?"

"Bobby Blue, for one. After you saved his bacon in Tulsa, he tweeted about it. Other cowboys picked up on it and are watching what you do. You'll make it to the finals for sure, and you won't be riding my coattails. Dub said he voted for you to be one of the bullfighters."

"It's good to know," Johnny said. "Respect, huh?"

"You know, Bobby Blue *is* kind of a jerk. Travis didn't take to him much either on account of that whole black cowboy thing. But once you point out the error of his ways, the boy can learn."

"Yeah, guess he can." It made Johnny happy to hear Cody finally admit Bobby Blue was a jerk, although it was too late, now that he'd started thinking of Bobby Blue as less of a jerk. Especially after Bobby Blue apologized.

"He's not the only one," Cody said.

"We both fucked up."

"I did more than you."

"I shouldn't have run away. I should have said something."

"If you think I would have listened." Cody sighed. "I guess I have to get better at it."

"You like it when someone tells you what to do?"

"Hate it."

"Makes you want to do the opposite, right? Same goes for me."

"I guess any guy would feel that way. I'm going to be walking on eggshells for a while."

"It's good for the balance. Maybe it'll help you ride." Johnny felt some satisfaction saying that, as if he were evening the score even if it was a little mean.

"Why didn't you say anything?"

"I tried. You just kept talking over me. Telling me what to do. Instructing me!" Johnny reminded himself to breathe.

"Respect," Cody said heavily. "I've always had a lot of respect for you but I guess I didn't show it very well."

"You figure this out on your own?" Johnny couldn't keep the astonishment out of his voice.

"I had a lot of help from your fan club."

"What fan club?"

"Mom, Travis, RJ, Dub, Dad, Sam Wells. I could go on."

Feeling as if the wind had just been taken out of his sails, Johnny couldn't hold on to his anger. His voice was mildly peevish. "You always had to be the star. I'm just wallpaper in the ring, and you can't walk down the street without handing out millions of autographs."

"Depends on the street." Cody laughed and told Johnny about his encounter with Jake the Cop. "He wasn't so fucking impressed. He never heard of me or the NBR. It was a little bit of a wake-up call. We live in a small corner of the world."

"I guess I've got to stand my ground better."

"Like you do in the ring. You know I like sitting in the driver's seat."

"And most of the time I'm okay with that," Johnny said. "But when I speak up, you better listen."

"I can change."

"You have. I have too."

"Not too much."

"I used to be scared it was just sex keeping us together. I mean, we fuck and there's always fireworks. The oxygen gets sucked out of the room and my brain—"

"For me too, but it's more than that for me," Cody said, his face flushed as if it was still hard for him to say the words. "I never wanted to fall in love, especially while I was still riding, but I can't imagine my life without you."

Johnny didn't know what to say. Once he'd thought he couldn't imagine a life without Cody, but he'd managed when they were apart. "It's better with you."

"You don't know. Back when we first met, you were just another hookup. A really hot one, but just another one-nighter. But then I wanted to see you again. I found myself passing up chances to get with other guys just to spend time with you, even if we couldn't have sex. It started to dawn on me I wanted more than just to get in your pants."

"So you wanted to be best buds, eh?"

"Why'd you give me another chance?"

"Last time when we fucked, you said you loved me."

"I did, huh?" Cody laughed self-consciously. "I think I've always loved you, right from the start."

A smile blossomed slowly over Johnny's face. "If that's what it takes to hear you say it, I might have to blow up at you more often."

"I'll tell you every day if that's what it takes to make this work."

"We'll work it out," Johnny said. "You know, you act like we were traveling together for years. Even though we were together, you were riding in Top Cut, I was fighting in the touring division. I only came up to Top Cut three months before we split."

"It felt like forever. It felt right." Cody sighed. "I'm going to miss it."

"It'll be different, that's all. We'll work it out."

IT WAS still dark when Johnny bent over Cody to kiss him goodbye.

Sleepily, Cody rolled over and grabbed Johnny's head, making the kiss deeper before he let him go. "So what do you bullfighters talk about when you're on the road?"

A soft chuckle answered him. "We talk about you."

"Me?" Cody sat up.

"All you guys, all the bulls and what they like to do. Strategy, like what to do if a cowboy gets hung up, how to get a man out from underneath if the bull is crashing around, who takes the point. Stuff like that."

"What do they say about me?"

"You may be a damn fine rider, but getting off is not your best thing."

Cody laughed. "I'll miss you all week. I wish you were coming back to the ranch."

"I'll be back after the finals for the break," Johnny promised. "Get to all the chores. Place won't run itself."

"Yeah, there are fences that need fixing," Cody said.

Somehow Johnny didn't think he was talking about the wooden ones.

CHAPTER 18:

The Win

THEY hadn't worked it all out yet, but they were back together and Johnny was happy. So happy he wanted to share it with someone. Of course the family circle knew—Val, Davis, Travis, and RJ. Zane could tell, judging by the winks and coded jokes, but Johnny didn't want to share details about Cody with him. It was all great, but Johnny wanted someone on his side to know. Vern and Reese were out of the question. There might come a time when they found out about him but now wouldn't be it.

He took the card out of his wallet and fingered it, considering. They'd been broken up when he met March, so there was nothing to feel guilty about. Likely Cody wouldn't be enthusiastic about meeting a man who'd taken him to bed, though, so it was unlikely he would see March again. It would feel too awkward. Besides, March probably wouldn't hesitate to suggest all three of them go to bed together, even if only for a laugh at their expense.

Johnny put the card away and then said, "Ah, fuck it." He took out his phone and dialed.

"Johnny! Good to hear from you" came the throaty growl of his silver bear. "Nothing wrong, I hope."

"No, just the opposite. I wanted you to know I'm back with my boyfriend."

"That's great! I hope it works out for the two of you."

Johnny smiled at the generous pleasure in March's voice. "We've got stuff to work through, but I think we can make a go of it."

"I'm honored you wanted to share the news with me."

"I wanted to thank you, actually," Johnny said softly. "I'm not sure I'd have had the guts to even give it a shot if you hadn't said what you did."

There was a silence while distance hummed over the line. "That makes me feel good. Sort of like a fairy godfather. Want to tell me his name now?"

"No, definitely not." Johnny laughed. "You know the sport. It wouldn't be good to out him first thing after we get back together."

"You can count on my discretion, you know it."

"I know. I count on it for myself."

"Guess there's no chance of one last roll in the hay, then?"

"I'm sure you've got better things to do. How many men have you had since me?"

March cleared his throat. "Well, uh, meeting you and talking to you inspired me to call my old boyfriend. The one I told you I shouldn't have let get away from me."

Johnny grinned. "You too?"

"Yeah. There's something about you, kid, that woke up the romantic in me. I guess monogamy isn't too high a price to pay for love after all."

"That's good to hear. I hope it works out for you too. You deserve it."

"Maybe our meeting was meant to lead to bigger and better things for both of us. Not that if you'd been free I would have let you get away from me. You're a very special man, Johnny."

"So are you, March."

"Give my best to Cody."

Johnny glared at the phone, catching the beginning of March's rich, dirty laugh before he hung up. "You old devil." How had he known? Then he remembered March followed bull riding. Hopefully it only showed to people who were looking for that kind of stuff, but Johnny decided to watch himself when Cody was in the ring. No more dreamy stares and secret smiles. No hanging on to him after yanking him to safety, because even though Cody was riding better, he still couldn't dismount for fuck.

"PUT on your boots."

"But I'm naked."

Johnny leered. "I know."

"Are you getting kinky on me?"

"Kinky as I can. Even though naked with cowboy boots is pretty low on the freaky scale."

"Does it mean I have a lot more to look forward to?"

"If you put your damn boots on."

Cody hoisted himself off the bed and stamped on his boots. "Hot enough for you?"

"Turn around," Johnny directed as he followed Cody. "Lean on the wall."

Cody looked over his shoulder. "I feel silly."

"You look hot. And since when do you not want to show off?" Looking at the defined muscle of Cody's upper back and round cheeks over long, slim legs stuck into cowboy boots made Johnny start to move his hand lazily on his cock. "Stroke yourself for me."

Cody twisted around to face him, still leaning his shoulders against the wall, hips jutting out. His cock slowly rose and hardened under his hand. "Does this mean I'm gonna get lucky?"

"Really lucky," Johnny murmured, his gaze on Cody's lean body. He turned Cody to face the wall again and lowered his body against Cody's to rub himself on Cody's back, letting his erection lodge between Cody's thighs. "My turn."

Cody pushed back slightly and Johnny sank his teeth into the muscle at the conjunction of neck and shoulder, feeling the change in Cody's body from resistance to compliance.

"You're a tease." Cody stretched his neck to give Johnny better access.

"Not really, I plan to follow through," Johnny said, his lips moving against Cody's skin.

"No marks," Cody said.

"Don't worry, you already got enough bruises. No one will be able to tell where they came from."

"I was gonna fuck you."

"We'll take turns. And now… shut up."

Cody shut up, but he rolled them on the wall and pinned Johnny's wrists over his head to kiss him. "Taking turns is overrated."

Johnny spun Cody around to reverse their positions and pinned him to the wall instead. "No, it isn't."

"ALL the excitement of all the arenas the NBR visited for the entire year seems to be packed into the Center here in Las Vegas for the five days of the finals.

"Every year the cream rises to the top, and the world of bull riding ends up here, where we'll see the best bulls and riders match up to compete for the World Championship. It's been a long road to get here, full of triumph and defeat, injury and recovery for most of our competitors, bull and rider alike.

"This year's finals will be the most exciting to date. We've seen the rise of the two great Brazilian riders, good friends Juca Matos and Rinque Tourinho, holding the number two and four rankings respectively. Rounding out the top five is Canadian Tate Klein. We've got cowboys from Australia, Brazil, Canada, and from all over the US of A.

"If the NBR were handing out a buckle for most drama, there's no doubt Defending World Champion Cody Grainger would go home with it this year. At the beginning of the year, he was riding on top and it looked like no one could beat him. He made no secret of his plan to win the finals again this year. He set a new record during the first part of this year for winning at least one round in each event he rode in. It seemed like only a miracle or an injury could bring him down. No bull could seem to get the better of him.

"Then Cody fell into one of the most spectacular buckoff streaks I've ever seen. He blew thirty-four straight rides, although some were during exhibition events. There were lots of missed opportunities to score big and show off his talent, but he never seemed able to convert. Then just as suddenly as it started, and for no good reason we can see, he started winning again.

"Now we'll get to see just what this cowboy is made of, how tough a man he can be. He's taken plenty of hard hits in his career, but none as hard as this slump he's just been through. Will he step up and get that gold buckle he's been chasing, or will he be carried out with dirt on his face and an empty belt?

"Cody is a man who likes to live dangerously. There's no doubt the field of bulls is deeper this year than it's ever been. These bulls are tough, they are big, and they are the meanest ones around. If Cody can put a string of good rides together the way he has the past five weeks, that buckle is as good as his, unless it all goes bad. And when Cody Grainger lets it go bad, it goes bad in a spectacular way."

Speaking out of one corner of his mouth, Dub said, "A man can't even get his name cussed with you around even when you're in a slump. Whether you're winning or losing, you're the headliner, but don't start believing your own hype."

Standing next to him on the ramp, Cody responded, "I wonder if he knows I can hear him. Maybe eventually he'll get over my shortcomings and mention you're riding really well."

The ring announcer went on. "And then there's Cody's friend Dub Whittaker, who's hoping to make that one million-dollar payday his. He's been riding in the top ten consistently most of the year and currently holds the number-three spot on the leaderboard. When he looks back over his shoulder, I bet there's no one he wants to see less than Cody Grainger catching up to him. Some folks are saying when Cody Grainger finally retires, Dub will be the one to carry on his legacy. The two men are close friends and travel partners, so maybe some of that greatness has rubbed off on him."

Cody caught Dub's eye and the two men laughed companionably at this.

"I sure hope some of your greatness rubbed off on me. I deserve a reward after what you put me through this year," Dub groaned. "If you don't retire after winning this, I may have to kill you to get you out of my way."

"You can try." Cody patted Dub's back as the two men filed down the ramp with the other riders and went behind the gate.

"JOHN-NY! John-ny! John-ny!"

The chanting of his name made him turn and search the stands. From the high-pitched squeal, he knew it wasn't Cody, unless he'd gotten kicked bad where it hurt most.

Reese pointed up into the stands. "Looks like we'll have to change over from calling you the skinny one to the cute one."

A group of girls were shouting to him, holding up handmade signs with his name and a bunch of hearts drawn in hot-pink markers. When they saw Johnny looking, they screamed in excitement.

Reese's blow between his shoulders made Johnny stagger a step forward. "Go on, wave back at your fan club. Make them all happy for a night."

Tentatively, Johnny raised his hand and waved. The screaming cranked up a notch and Vern came up to join them.

"Do I have to remind you we've got a job to do here, boys? And what did I tell you about ogling the girls in the stands, Johnny?" His voice was stern, but a tiny smile cracked the usual granite of his face.

Reese laughed at the relief on Johnny's face as he turned away. "You got it wrong, Vern. *They're* ogling him. He seems a little spooked. Our Johnny's a bit shy with the ladies, boss. Guess you don't got to worry about him busting loose."

"No, you don't," Johnny said fervently. "Those girls are scarier than an angry bull."

"At least when a bull chases after you, you know he's not looking for a relationship," Vern said. "Just keep clear of the women and you'll do okay."

"Yes, sir!" It was ironic to know he had orders to stay away from women. If anyone asked, he could always blame Vern.

"Looks like someone's happy you made it to the finals," Reese said. "Been a while since they were calling out my name." He sighed dramatically.

"Okay boys, here we go. Round one," Vern said.

"CODY, you've been struggling these past few weeks, but you're still ahead of the rest of the field in points. How important is it for you to kick off the finals with a good ride?" Rex asked, holding the mic toward Cody.

"It's very important. I'm here to show the bulls, my loyal fans, great sponsors, and most of all the other riders that I mean business."

"You've had a bad slump—"

"I believe it might be the worst in history of bull riding," Cody said with a grin, interrupting the reporter.

"Yes, according to the stats, you set a new Top Cut record with thirty-four straight buckoffs. But lately you've managed to put together a string of good rides. You even broke ninety for one ride last weekend."

"And what a relief it was," Cody said. "But I've been working out, getting on some practice bulls between events, and God willing, I think at least I might not embarrass myself at this event."

Rex laughed. "I hope you have a great ride. Thanks for stopping by and talking to us. Good luck this weekend."

"Thanks, Rex." Cody shook hands, flashed his famous grin at the crowd, and waved before going back behind the fence.

From where he stood, Johnny caught his expression change from the friendly one Cody wore for interviews to the intense concentration he displayed when he rode. Cody switched out his hat for his helmet and began to swing his arms to loosen up. Then came the ritual of pulling on the glove, taping it in place, and getting into the chute with his rope.

When Bonecrusher burst out of the gate, he dragged Cody against the fence before settling into a spin, throwing in a few violent belly rolls for variety. He seemed intent on ridding himself of the rider on his back while Cody was equally determined to stay put. It made Johnny happy to see the fierce grin on Cody's face again as he moved with the bull, his lean body stretched out with his free arm high in the air as the bull picked up speed with each spin.

Then Johnny groaned when he saw Cody twist his body, just as the bull changed direction, and slap the bull's shoulder with his hand as he strained to keep up. Instead of bailing when the whistle signified the disqualification, Cody bore down, staying up over his rope until a full nine seconds passed. The bull launched Cody up and into the air, and seeing its chance for revenge, lashed out with its hind feet, catching Cody's body and slamming him into the signs lining the fence. Cody grabbed on to the top rail and hoisted himself up, and hung there waiting for the bullfighters to get the bull out of the ring.

"And with that DQ for the slap we have another buckoff for Cody Grainger," the announcer said. "Are we seeing the beginning of a new slump, or will that gritty determination Cody Grainger is famous for come into play? Only time will tell. Cody still has the points to move forward, but if he doesn't get a score tonight, it might spell disaster for this year's final for him. And just how long can this cowboy keep riding? You've probably noticed he's got a new elbow brace on his riding arm, but he's used to living with the pain. All the cowboys at this elite level are banged up and hurting at this time of year.

"And there is no other rider on the circuit now who can make dust into diamonds like Cody Grainger can. Whether he wins this year or not, it's always exciting to watch this cowboy ride, but fans will raise the roof if Cody pulls this one out. He's ahead in points but the margin is slim and the other riders sense blood in the water.

"Next up will be Juca Matos vs. Black Diamond."

Johnny could only hope Cody wouldn't let the buckoff get to him as he watched his partner limp to the gate.

CODY bit his lip in pain as soon as the gate clanged shut behind him, but he managed a smile as the medic came over.

"Need a hand? Notice you're limping."

"No thanks, just an old foot sprain. I got stepped on a week ago."

"Well, you don't need your feet to ride." The medic slapped his shoulder and turned away to look at the ride in progress. "Good luck."

It took all he had to keep a smile on his face as he limped into the locker room. He should have been up behind the box, helping Rinque get ready to go, but there was something he had to do first and he knew someone else would step up. Cody stopped at his locker for supplies and went into a stall in the bathroom. He put the stuff on the floor. This was going to hurt. Gritting his teeth, he straightened his leg and slid his kneecap back into place.

He managed not to yell, but he was sweating and panting as he hung on to the door, not daring to put weight on his leg, waiting for the shivering rush of adrenaline and agony to pass. When he felt merely wrung out and damp with sweat, he chuckled to himself. Thank goodness it had been only partially dislocated.

Then Cody lowered his jeans and wrapped his knee with tape. From experience, he knew how to strap it to hold his kneecap in place. And he wouldn't have to ride again until tomorrow. Just as the medic said, he didn't need a good knee to ride. It would only be a little tricky when it came to getting off.

When he pulled up his jeans and buckled his belt, he fingered the buckle thoughtfully. It was the one he'd won for Johnny. He was hoping he could hold out long enough to win the gold. All he wanted was to give it to Johnny.

Cody limped out of the john to the sink and splashed water on his flushed face and dried off. He restored the supplies to his locker and tried to control the limp as he went back out to watch the rest of the riders try to steal his buckle.

WATCHING the dirt Zamboni smooth the ring between flights always had a calming effect on Cody. He took a deep breath before saying to Dub, "Well, that was one jacked-up ride."

"Did you do it on purpose?" Dub seemed relieved Cody was talking and not sulking over the buckoff.

"What the hell?"

"You know, ratchet up the suspense for everyone by disqualifying in the first round. Keep it exciting?"

Cody drew in a deep breath and managed to laugh. "I've had more than enough suspense this summer to last me. No, I did not do it on purpose. That was a really rank, mean bull, and you can't ride them all."

"Well, you seem pretty confident for the guy who was the first one to fall off in the finals."

"Yes, I am feeling confident. Thanks for asking."

"You slapped at 5.3 seconds. Why'd you stay on?"

"Because I could." Cody knew he sounded a little smug.

"Everyone knows you can, why risk getting injured?"

"Think about it. What's the last thing the judges saw before the whistle?"

"You toughing it out and spurring to beat the band," Dub said. "Okay, maybe it's a good strategy."

"I stayed in control even though I slapped."

"You've got a gold buckle in your future, I feel it in my bones," Dub prophesied.

"I didn't know you were psychic," Cody teased. "How are you going to do?"

"Coming in second, right behind you like I always do." Dub shook his head sadly and then grinned. "But next year I'll win. I'm only twenty-six. If you retire after this, I'll still have a few good years left in me to make good."

"You will, I know it," Cody said. He still wasn't ready to think about retiring, especially when things were looking up.

HE WAS sitting on the bed with ice on his elevated knee when he heard Johnny enter the adjoining room. He'd left the door open between them so he wouldn't have to get up again. He might be able to hide this from the medical staff and other riders, but he didn't have a prayer with Johnny. Johnny got to see him naked—at least Cody was hoping he would.

Johnny bounded eagerly into the room and stopped short, taking in the pillow, the strapping, and the towel under the plastic bag of ice. "Fuck! I knew it."

"You saw?"

"Was it the gate or the fence?"

"The gate coming out. The bull kind of knocked me into it." Cody shrugged in resignation. "I've dislocated that knee before. It makes it easier to pop in."

"All the way or partial?"

"Partial."

Johnny came over and sat on the bed, putting his hand on Cody's good leg. "I guess I don't need to ask if you put it back yourself."

"I can't take a chance of the doc striking me off the list. I've got to win this year!"

"You're crazy."

"So are you. I only sit on top of them. You get cozy with them right down there in the ring."

"Do you need something? Chicken soup? More ice? Some morphine?"

Cody laughed. "Morphine sounds great, but I guess I'll make do with some aspirin."

Johnny went to his bag and got aspirin and then went to the sink for some water. "I guess we need room service."

"I guess so," Cody agreed. "I'd better stay off it as much as I can."

"Are you going to be able to ride with that?"

"I actually have a brace I can use from last time. I brought all of them, just in case."

"And that'll keep it from hurting?"

"The brace will remind me to take it easy on that side. Nothing will keep it from hurting."

Johnny took in a deep breath. "Well. What a bummer. I've got to tell Vern about this."

"He'll turn me in! You can't!"

"He won't turn you in. He'll think you're crazy, but he already knows that. You're a bull rider."

Cody slapped the bed impatiently. "So what difference does it make?"

"When a rider is injured, we play it differently," Johnny explained. "Depending on how you dismount, you might not be able to get up so fast. The bullfighters need to be prepared to handle it. I can't let one of them get hurt because you're riding injured."

Furious, Cody glared at him. "You're *my* boyfriend. You should be on *my* side. If the doctors find out, they could stop me from riding! Nothing is going to get in my way this year!" He groaned as he moved his leg.

Johnny jumped up and strode to the door between their rooms, but then he stopped. Deliberately, he turned around and came back. "Listen, Cody, if you want to take the risk, then that's your business. When you put other people in danger, that's a whole other thing and I'm not going to go along with it just because I love you. I can't let Vern or Reese or Chris get hurt because of your decision. You've got to see that."

Cody felt his nostrils flare even as he realized Johnny was right. "You're right!" he shouted, and then he groaned. "I'd feel like crap if I knew someone got hurt because of me."

"Fuck, it's not like you're the first rider ever to ride hurt and refuse treatment. Hell, Vern's probably scoped it out already. He's seen so many guys get hurt, he's like a mobile MRI."

"Sorry. Guess I panicked. It's just—"

"Just what?"

"This could be my last year. It could be my only chance to win back-to-back championships. No one's ever done it before and that was my goal for this year."

"Why didn't you tell me?"

Johnny sat down again and Cody reached for his hand.

"I didn't want to jinx my chances."

Both men laughed.

"Yeah, I know. I almost jinxed myself right out of the finals with my buckoff streak. I do fine screwing myself up. I don't need more help from the doctors and the bulls."

"Why say it could be your last year?"

"I was hoping you wouldn't notice that." Cody bit his lip. "Everyone's on me about retiring." He stopped, unable to speak around the lump that suddenly jammed in his throat, fearing Johnny would also take their side.

He watched as some emotion he couldn't identify flashed over Johnny's face.

"I've been watching Chris Bellow since he came back," Johnny said softly.

"He doesn't like you," Cody said suddenly. "I saw him looking at you once."

Johnny shook his head. "It's not personal. It's not about me. He announced he's retiring but he doesn't really want to. He feels like he's being forced out. He loves bullfighting about as much as you love riding. It's going to be a huge loss."

Suddenly Cody was panting, trying to keep the tears stinging his eyes from flowing down his cheeks. "Huge loss," he croaked. "Like I'm losing my life."

"Yeah, I can see I'll probably feel the same as you when it comes my turn," Johnny said soberly. "But you won't lose your life. When you're on the back of a bull and it feels like you're going to fall off, you do something different. You're always changing it up. Just like life."

"Maybe," Cody managed. "Maybe."

"Once you're a bull rider you're in for life. You may not ride anymore, but you've stomped your footprints all over the record books. You've got more ninety-plus point rides than the four riders right behind you added together. It'll be some time before anyone matches that."

"I guess that's true." Cody felt a little better.

"The NBR isn't ready for you to walk away. You'll contract your bulls, train new riders, tell tall tales about the one that got away, get inducted into the Ring of Honor, and become a judge before you know it. You'll see. People will be talking about I knew him when."

Cody managed to smile. "Sounds great the way you tell it."

"I'll order something to eat and get some more ice," Johnny said. "You'll feel better when you take the gold buckle."

Cody watched Johnny study the menu and pick up the phone. He didn't listen. The ache in his chest overwhelmed him with pain, but he knew Johnny was right. Injuries and age were catching up with him. It was time for a change.

When Johnny returned to the room with a fresh bag of ice, Cody pulled him down and kissed him. "Thank you, babe."

"What's all this, then?" Johnny asked quizzically.

"I'm just so glad we're back together," Cody said. And he was. Contemplating retirement was bad enough; without Johnny, it really might have killed him.

He slept pressed as close to Johnny as he could, holding him tight in his arms with his face buried in his hair.

THE limp was barely perceptible, but the brace was obvious under Cody's jeans. Of course Dub noticed. Johnny saw he stayed by Cody's side, ready to lend a hand if Cody needed it but not making a big deal of it. Dub knew Cody well enough to know when he was hurt.

The second day was round two of the finals. The one that counted for Cody. If he did well tonight, he would stay in the top five positioned where he could take the lead, but to win he would have to ride each of the five bulls left to him. Unless everyone else fell off, which they weren't likely to do. They wanted to win just as badly. At least Cody had the experience and discipline to compartmentalize the pain and focus on his ride.

When the gate opened, Johnny could tell Cody was sure of making the whistle. The ride went by faster than usual, but Cody managed to answer everything the bull threw at him. Johnny could also tell, as usual, Cody was going to make a mess of the dismount, as he seemed to be having trouble getting his riding hand loose. Yanking at his rope, Cody fell off too close and rolled right beneath the bull that was still bucking like a demon. He dodged a kick aimed at his head by inches and covered up, curled in a ball and waited for rescue.

Chris was in the best position, at point closest to the bull's head. Johnny charged toward him but watched appreciatively as Chris got the bull's head turned toward himself. The bull left Cody and took off after Chris. Vern darted in between them and Chris veered away to safety as Reese wove into the mix. Johnny took his turn, getting the bull closer to the open gate. As the bull trotted out, Cody was on up his feet, punching the air in triumph to the sound of wild applause. Some woman in the stands was screaming his name rhythmically. Cody pumped both fists at the crowd, shouting with glee. Then Cody ripped off his helmet and tossed it high into the air, but Johnny noticed he threw it straight up so he wouldn't have to move to catch it. He snickered at the thoughtful strategy.

After Cody was out, the team gathered by the gate and tapped fists. Vern gave him a quizzical smile but said nothing. Everything that had to be said had been said in the locker room before they came out, when Johnny told them about Cody's knee. None of the team had questioned why Cody hadn't gone to the doctor. They knew bull riders were lunatics.

"Thanks, Chris. That was a great save," Johnny said.

Chris looked surprised and pleased. "Thanks a lot. I guess an old guy can still run around the ring once or twice."

"It's not the feet, it's the head," Reese said. "Experience."

"You read that bull right. You know what you're doing," Johnny said. "I respect that."

Chris nodded, and it seemed to Johnny he could see his confidence grow. Because he was the youngest and newest on the team, he'd never thought it was his place to compliment the others, and it surprised him to see his words meant something. Then it was back to business.

When Dub rode, Johnny applauded his ride, thinking once Cody retired and stopped stealing the spotlight, Dub would probably step out of his shadow and people would notice what a great rider he was in his quiet way. He wasn't as exciting, but he was damn good and technically expert.

The next flight came out, and when it was his turn, Bobby Blue fell off his bull and ran to hit the challenge button. The judges denied his challenge and Bobby Blue smacked a sponsor's sign in disgust before slamming through the gate. Johnny was surprised to find himself disappointed Bobby Blue bucked off. He realized, suddenly, that despite Bobby Blue's overrated confidence, he felt almost like a mentor to him. Or maybe it was because he and Cody were back together and Bobby Blue didn't matter anymore. He really did remind Johnny of a younger Cody and it wasn't completely a bad thing, especially as he probably had years of saving Bobby Blue's stupid ass ahead of him.

Surprisingly, Zane finished high enough to move ahead into round three.

When all the interviews and applause were over, Johnny waited to catch Zane behind the gate and walked back to the locker room with him. "Congratulations, Z-man. Good ride. Even nailed your first interview."

"Thanks, Johnny. I can't believe I even made it to Top Cut in my rookie year, and here I am riding in the finals. It's like a dream come true. Thanks to you and Cody, even though I might be cut after the next round."

"It's a chancy sport, but you're doing great. I'm proud of you."

"I'm proud of me too. Don't suppose you'd be up for going out for a beer later to help me celebrate?"

"Sorry, I can't. I've got a date."

"Good to see things working out for you two," Zane said quietly.

"How'd you know?"

"You seem happier." Zane heaved an exaggerated sigh. "And I've lost my wingman. Although lately it seemed like I was the wingman. But I guess I'm too young to get tied down yet."

"You never know. You might like it."

"Yeah, if I scored a hottie like...." Zane grinned knowingly and jerked his head slightly at the locker room door.

"Yeah. Well, they're out there. You'll get lucky someday. Good-looking guy like you."

"Thanks, Johnny. See you around."

"And not under, like, a bull." With a last slap on the shoulder, Johnny went to find his team.

It seemed as if things were going Cody's way again. He'd made it through both rounds, emerging at the top of the leaderboard, trailed by Dub in second and with the two top Brazilians on their tails. Rounding out the top five was Canadian Tate Klein.

And Chris Bellow seemed to be getting back in gear. He was quick, strong, and on the spot. Maybe it was being in Las Vegas in the finals; it was the most exciting week in the most exciting sport in the world.

"WELCOME to the action as round three kicks off. The man who is currently sitting number one at this event is our Leader of the Pack, the California Cowboy, Cody Grainger.

"That winning swagger is back, and Cody Grainger showed in rounds one and two why he's the dynamic rider we all like to watch. He DQ'd on his first bull, although he managed to pull it back and make the whistle on his second. Can it last? That's the question on everyone's mind. Bull riding is a tough sport, and the finals are tougher than anything these men have faced all year. More rounds, ranker bulls, and more mental pressure, because after this week, there are no more chances to make good. The buck really does stop here, and it's make it or break it for the entire year.

"Cody Grainger is not just a tough rider, he's a smart one, but he needs to establish himself as the rider to beat. He's not one of the youngest guys in the field, and the sheer physical pounding takes its toll on an older rider.

"Tonight he goes up against a bull named Renegade Romeo. This pairing could provide some fireworks and he's got a lot riding on this go-around. Cody has drawn Renegade Romeo five times in the past two years. This bull has thrown him twice, but three times Cody has ridden him for a good score. Let's see if he is able to exact some revenge on this bull for the last time he bucked off."

Ignoring the hot air coming from the ring announcer, Cody ran his gloved hand up and down the rope to warm the rosin, aware of Dub's grip on his vest and the buzz of energy in the crowd. The bull was restive, shifting in the chute and trying to mash his leg against the fence. Cody grunted in pain as he pulled his knees up out of the way and went on getting a good sticky mess of rosin on his glove. If nothing else, at least it would glue his hand to the rope long enough. The gateman pushed the bull away from the fence with the padded board, and Cody was able to let his hurt leg back down. He almost felt as if the bull remembered their last trip and was nursing a grudge. They were smart enough to, sometimes, and this bull was definitely smart.

He dangled the rope and the contractor pulled it up on the other side, tugging to yank it tight before the wrap. There was so much riding on this. Cody knew he'd made himself look like a fool all summer and he wanted to prove to the fans he still had it. He was still points ahead of the other riders. The way he calculated, he might be able to miss two rides and still win, but he'd wanted to be six for six. Now the best he could aim for was five for six, but he could still make a big score and get the win.

"He's an honest bull," Dub commented. "Puts his feet almost in the same footprints with each spin, but he's damn strong. He never weakens."

"Yeah, he does the same thing over and over, just better each time," Cody said. He was more focused on his wrap than what Dub was saying. "Wish me luck."

"You know it."

After settling himself down and getting a good seat, Cody gave the nod. The gate swung open and Renegade Romeo jumped forward, giving a big kick and twisting his back end around. Cody felt the jolt of the bull's front feet throw him forward and broke at the hips, swinging his free arm in front to keep centered as the bull flung his rump to the side. Like the honest bull Dub said he was, Renegade Romeo kept doing the same thing, which made him easy to predict. The only problem was, instead of tiring out, he seemed to get stronger and faster with each spin. It felt as if they were going a hundred miles an hour.

Keeping centered, Cody timed it right, leaning back for the kick, using his free arm to stay with the bull when he turned. He was in the air when the whistle came and he rode the bull back to the ground, only then pulling on the tail of his rope. The hind end of the bull came up and popped him off the back so he landed on his ass in the ring. Even though it was a little hard on his tailbone, Cody scrambled to roll into the chute. At least he hadn't landed on his knees. The gate clanged shut behind him just in time to make the bull veer off to chase Reese instead.

Cody pulled himself up by the rails and brushed his butt off, standing on one leg. The gate opened and he took off his helmet, throwing it in the air. "Yeah! Yeah!" he roared.

The crowd was roaring right back and the announcer was yelling over them.

"Cody Grainger does it all on Renegade Romeo for the score of 89.75! Did you see how long it took that bull to come back down to earth when he jumps? But it doesn't matter what bull you put the cowboy from California up on, he knocks them down. Cody is riding like a machine; he can do no wrong!

"Athletes perform better when they feel the energy of the crowd, and this crowd wants to see Cody Grainger go out on top this year. They are sending out one big embrace to the sport of bull riding and to him.

"After that buckoff in the first round, Cody didn't just salvage a score, he shot to the top of the leaderboard. He's proved he's not going to make it easy for the other riders. If you want to beat him, you'll have to fight him every step of the way. Cody Grainger is definitely a legend of the sport!"

Reese came over with his rope and joked, "Good job, Mr. Legend, but you better stop soaking up the glory and get out of the ring. There's other bulls and cowboys left to ride."

Cody limped for the exit gate and was stopped by Rex waiting to grab an interview.

"Last time you met Renegade Romeo, he definitely got the better of you. What was the difference this time?"

Cody grinned. "This time I got a score!"

"You're back on top after a long buckoff streak. What, if anything, did you learn from that slump?"

"One thing I learned is I don't get off very well." Cody rubbed his elbow with a grin. Couldn't rub his ass on national TV. "Gotta work on that."

"You were popped off the back of that bull like a rag doll, but not before you made the whistle and took the lead in another round. Congratulations to you, Cody."

"Thanks, Rex."

"I'VE never seen you pace like this before. Why don't you give that knee a break?"

Johnny enjoyed their new pattern. He got to join Cody and his parents for dinner after his team meeting. They would eat together while Davis gave Cody advice and encouragement. Cody would sign autographs when fans came to the table. Then Davis and Val would tactfully say they had another engagement and vanish. Johnny would walk behind Cody to the elevators, ready to lend a hand if needed. By the time they got to their floor, Cody did need it, and Johnny would help him hobble to the room and get the ice.

"I've never come off a buckoff streak heading into the finals before," Cody said. He paused to stare out the window. "I don't ride every bull, no one can, but usually I get it out of the way earlier in the year."

"'Get it out of the way,' he says." Johnny laughed. "Like it's all in a day's work."

Clearly not hearing a word, Cody swung around. "This feels almost like cheating, but I need your help. Tomorrow they've got me on Failure to Yield and I've never been on him, never even seen him buck. What's he like?"

Johnny laughed. "If that's cheating, they should kick the whole bunch of you riders to the curb. Everyone asks us about the bulls and the owners ask about the riders. Sit down and put your knee up."

Cody looked relieved about the ethics of asking a bullfighter for a tip, and consented to sit on the bed while Johnny applied pillows and ice. "If that bull is here, he's got to be pretty good. Sam doesn't bring in second-tier stock for the finals."

"Failure to Yield is an explosive, powerful bull out of the gate. He usually lands ten feet away, maybe more, from the first jump. He's got so much forward motion that when he digs his feet in under him, he stops short and usually manages to pull the rider off over his head."

Cody was impressed. "That's a pretty specific analysis. How the hell did you figure that out?"

"View's different from the ground," Johnny said modestly. "If he can't get the rider off after the first jump, he burns a hole in the dirt going in a circle, kicking and jumping all the way."

"Left or right?"

"Yeah, left or right. Failure usually starts left, and then if that doesn't work, he goes right. He's got one of the most wicked corners in the business. But sometimes he'll go right. They've got him scheduled for left-hand delivery, so my guess is he'll go left. You just got to be ready."

"I should have asked you to help me all along," Cody said. "When you told me to get my elbow down a few weeks back—"

"Yeah, I could tell you stuff, except you start fixing one thing and then you start fixing things that ain't broke. Sometimes it's better to ride it out."

"And sometimes you just gotta ask someone standing a few feet away for what they see."

"It's hard asking for help."

Cody swallowed hard. "Maybe for both of us."

"Maybe."

"Maybe this really is the end for me. Falling off one bull after another and not being able to cover even a practice bull really shot a hole in my confidence."

"But you're riding good now," Johnny protested.

"I was the first man to fall off a bull in the finals! In the first round! I've always been known for going six for six in the finals." Cody crossed his arms and turned to stare out the window again. "What if I can't do it?"

Johnny wanted to hug him, but somehow he sensed the reassurance Cody needed wasn't from a lover, but from an expert, and if Cody had finally learned to respect him, he just might listen. Maybe Cody always had respected him and it was just hard to see it sometimes. Or maybe once the hard part of saying "I love you" was over, Cody felt safe enough with him to say how he felt.

"There's more to this than just the finals. Even if you lose, you won't fail. There's a purity in what you do, a spirit that transforms you when you're on—when you're in love with being up there. It's what makes you so amazing to watch. Other bull riders are good, but it's like you're flying above them all. It's like you have some kind of magic no one else can touch. Even if you fall, you just keep getting up and doing it again. You make it look effortless when you're loving what you do."

"I'm afraid I'll fuck up tomorrow." Cody covered his face with both hands. "And that'll be what people remember."

"Stop thinking you still have to prove something. Everyone already knows you're the best. You torch everyone else when you don't fuck up."

"I sucked all summer."

"Cody, just go out there and have fun. What do you love most in the world?"

"You." Cody dropped his hands, and Johnny was glad to see he finally cracked a smile.

"Well, you've got me. After that."

"Riding bulls. I love it! It's just—so exciting! I feel so alive."

"Then go out there and ride, babe. Forget about everyone else. Ride because you love it."

"You're right. It's not about the money or the buckle."

"Besides, you're back. I saw you on Renegade Romeo today. Before the bull even left the box, you knew you had him, and he was one rank bull."

"How could you tell?"

"I've watched your replays for years. You can always catch it in slow-mo. You get this cocky look on your face—"

"Me? Cocky?" Cody put his hand on his chest in mock surprise.

"And then if you fall you get all surprised."

"And then I land on my ass." Cody sighed. "I was knocked on my ass a lot this summer when you weren't around. The only good thing was no TV cameras, no interviews. Just exhibition rings of failure."

"Shake it off. That was then, this is now. Tomorrow you'll do great."

"If I make it to the championship round, I'll have first choice. I could pick a bull I know I could win on." Cody took a deep breath. "Or I could pick Spinal Tap."

"You always got to pick the toughest bull?"

"No one remembers 85-point rides. Maybe I'm crazy, but I want to ride Spinal Tap."

"Yeah, maybe you're a little crazy, but you got a right to be nervous." Johnny ran his hand over Cody's arm.

"There's got to be a key to him. He's never been ridden yet in over thirty-six outs."

"Well, you're the guy to do it."

"Thanks, but the two times I tried, he sent me flying like a rag doll."

Cody looked so unsure that Johnny wanted to do something to help him believe in himself. "It'll be different tomorrow. You know what it feels like to ride him and he knows he doesn't scare you."

"Yeah, maybe he does a little, actually. The owner told me he always goes left out of the gate."

"And you never figured the stock contractor might be blowing smoke up your chaps?"

"Yeah, why would he lie?" Both of them laughed. "So tell me, how do I ride him?"

"Whatever you did the other two times, don't do it again," Johnny said.

"That's not real helpful."

"You'll figure it out. Just stay on."

"You just sat here and gave me the technical 4-1-1 on Failure to Yield. What the fuck?"

"Different bull, different trip. You can count on Failure to Yield to do what he does. He's only got so many tricks. Spinal Tap is a whole different story. He's always got it cranked up to eleven. I'd say he's the best bull the NBR has ever seen."

"If I can stay on him, it'll be the ride everyone will remember. Even if I don't win."

"If you cover him, it'll be an automatic 90-plus ride unless the bull's having the worst day of his life."

"That bull doesn't have bad days. What does he like to do?"

"What doesn't he do? He's got more moves than any other bull I've ever seen, and he's wicked smart. If one thing doesn't work, he'll try something else. He'll go down as one of the greatest bulls ever."

"You're just making me more nervous."

Taking in a deep breath, Johnny said, "I could tell you Spinal Tap jumps farther out of the gate than any other bull. I could say he's almost vertical when he kicks, so straight up and down he almost hits a rider in the back with his rump. He twists, he belly rolls, he kicks harder as the ride goes on, and he never gives up. He figures out what you're doing and goes the other way to get you off. You've been on him. Let your muscles replay the trip for you."

He watched as Cody straightened up, swaying slightly as his muscles twitched. "I always feel on edge on Spinal Tap, like I never could find the rhythm to the way that bull moved. If I go out there and take it to him—"

"Someone I know said to stop planning ahead so much. Get out of your head and just react to what you feel under you. Ride what the bull gives you, not what you think he's going to do."

"What smart aleck told you that?"

"You did." Johnny smirked, but then he got serious. "You got one foot in each camp. You think like a contractor, making lists of how each bull is gonna act. You know these bulls really well, but sometimes memorizing their trips gets in your way. A bull gets a rep for going left, so you're all set for him to do that, and then you get caught flat-footed when he goes right. Happens most of the times you fall off."

"Damn. It's a little late in the career to hear that," Cody said. "I learned a lot this summer, but I guess there's always time to learn more."

"You're going to do great, Cody." Johnny gave him a kiss. "It'll be one of the greatest rides ever. The best rider ever on the best bull. You're going to be the one to make the whistle on Spinal Tap. I know it."

Cody brightened up. "That'd be something for people to remember me for."

"Probably make the bull's career too," Johnny cracked. "You'll both make history."

Cody was silent for several long minutes. "I think I'm losing my grip."

After an answering silence, Johnny said quietly, "I know."

"You saw it?"

"You're riding differently. Staying more up on your rope. Did you injure it?"

"I don't know," Cody said flatly, flexing his hand and staring at it, as if he could see the inner workings and figure out what the problem was. "It's been kind of numb for a couple weeks."

"Not broken?" Johnny knew Cody would know if it was. After enough broken bones, you got so you could tell.

"No. I must have strained it."

Choosing his words carefully, Johnny said, "I've heard it happens to riders—after a long career."

"Yeah," Cody said.

AFTER scoring big on Failure to Yield, Cody waited with Dub through the fifth round, watching the rest of the riders try to make their rides. Cody kept replaying the conversation with Johnny from the night before, even while he watched him dart around the ring. "Dancing with the beast," he muttered.

"What's that?"

"What they do." Cody nodded at the bullfighters. "We sit on top but they look them in the eye. In some ways they're beating that bull worse than we do. Look how mad Gunsmoke is."

"You been getting inside information on the bulls from Johnny?"

It was the first time Dub had mentioned him by name since that day in the locker room, and Cody didn't know whether he felt uncomfortable about it or not. He gave Dub a smug grin. "You bet."

"Let a friend in on it then," Dub pleaded.

"He said ride what the bull gives you," Cody replied.

"Sounds like smart advice. Is that why you're so calm, even though you're going up to pick Spinal Tap? I would be shaking in my boots."

"Sure you would. Big fluffy white chicken like you."

Dub chuckled. "Seriously. Never seen you this calm. Usually you're thinking out a game plan—"

"And falling off because I'm not paying attention."

"Yeah, that's how you take the Leader of the Pack spot, falling off all the time. The sponsors admire a rider who never scores," Dub said sarcastically. "It's about time for you to make your choice. Top score, first pick."

"Yeah." Cody grinned at him, but shifted nervously from side to side as he waited for the ring announcer to call his name.

"You still got time to change your mind before the long walk."

Cody took a deep breath. "Yeah, it's a long walk to a short ride."

When the stagehand waved at him, Cody strode out to the shark cage in the center of the ring, limping only slightly, and used the ramp instead of jumping as he usually did.

"Ten great bulls standing ready for the Championship round. Cody Grainger, who's it going to be?"

Cody spoke firmly into the mic. "Spinal Tap."

"Spinal Tap! Cody Grainger has just volunteered, no, boldly chosen to test his fate on the back of the unridden Spinal Tap. That's going to be a ride to remember no matter how it turns out. History in the making!" The ring announcer released his grip on Cody's shoulder and let him walk down the ramp.

Cody got down a bit gingerly and waved at the crowd as he limped out. He felt oddly at peace now the die was cast, but also alive and aware, his nerve endings tingling and a flutter in the pit of his belly.

He heard Dub give his pick and then Juca Matos's halting English as he made his choice.

First to pick, last to ride. The way it had been so often for him the last few years. Realizing he had been taking it for granted there would always be another victory, Cody wanted to savor this moment in time. He didn't want to retire, he was fighting it tooth and nail, but the clock was ticking. He might ride in other finals, but right now he had a sense of real power despite his injuries. Experience, practice, and native ability coming together in a penultimate challenge. He only hoped he'd be able to pull this off.

"As we start the Championship round of the finals, a history-making event with the rankest bulls going up against the best riders, the stakes have gotten higher and higher until the ten best cowboys in the world have risen to the top to face the fiercest animal athletes in the world.

"Every one of these men has the ability to take the title, but despite faltering for several months, Cody Grainger is still out ahead of the pack in points. A spot he is used to being in, but does that buckoff streak signal a weakness? If so, the other men here are circling like sharks, ready to exploit any failure on his part.

"Let's get to the action. First up is Zane Winslow on Snake Whiskey. Let's see how he does."

Later the action would be just a blur to Cody, sitting up behind the chutes, watching nine riders get ready before him, and witnessing their rides. To his surprise, Bobby Blue hadn't made it into the final round, but Zane had. Cody was fighting the urge to pat himself on the back. Two men out of his first class had made it to the finals in the Top Cut, and that was on him. And Travis, RJ, and Johnny, he added hastily. He was beginning to realize one man couldn't do it all on his own.

Sitting in tenth place, Zane was the first to ride. He lost control of the ride at five seconds, his hand popped out of the rope at 7.2, but he managed to keep hold of the tail of the rope while hanging off the bull's side 'til the whistle for an average score.

Cody stood up to applaud, yelling with the rest of the crowd. He felt oddly proud of the kid, almost as if he were watching his own son ride. He felt surprised when he saw Johnny return the rope to Zane and give him a half hug and a thump on the back. He hadn't realized they were friends, but this looked like more than just a bullfighter congratulating a random rider. Vern and Reese both tapped Zane on the back as he ran to the gate, but there seemed to be more of a connection between him and Johnny. Cody wondered if while they were broken up Johnny had—but he wasn't going there. Johnny had ultimately chosen him, not Zane. It didn't matter anymore, especially now. Nothing was going to make him doubt himself now.

Juca Matos made his ride to moderate applause. It was his usual mid-80s score, a ride no one would remember, Cody thought. Especially if Juca didn't win, and he was here to make sure Juca didn't. Too damn bad Juca managed to ride more bulls than anyone else each year.

Cody came off his Leader of the Pack perch on the rail to help Dub get ready. Dub was mounted on a bull that generally stood quiet in the chute, but Cody kept a hand on his vest anyway.

"Any last-minute advice?" Dub asked, his gaze focused on his wrap.

"Don't fall off."

"Painfully obvious, but true."

"You're a great rider, Dub, you know what to do. Ride what the bull gives you. Luck."

The startled look Dub gave him made Cody feel bad. He'd always appreciated Dub's ability, but apparently hadn't found time to tell him so. He groped for words. "You're one of the best, Dub. Show that bull some misery."

"Thanks, I will." Dub gave the nod, and then he was gone.

The smell of kicked-up dust curled into Cody's nostrils as he watched Dub make the most brilliant ride of his life.

The bull made an impossibly tight corner and flung his feet sideways in a frantic effort to get rid of the burden on his back, but Dub timed his counter moves perfectly, riding like a maniac.

Cody was on his feet cheering and being jostled in the mix of riders, staff, and old-timers crowded behind the rails. The cheering was deafening when the whistle went and Dub bailed. The bull gave one last desperate jump, his rump meeting Dub's in midair and spinning him in a somersault to land triumphantly on his feet.

The bullfighters rushed in, but for once Cody was watching his friend instead, laughing as Dub roared his triumph out loud and beat his chest with both fists before raising them. When he ran back to the fence, Cody reached down and grabbed Dub's wrist with his good hand and hauled him up and over to pound his back.

"92 fucking points!" he yelled.

Dub turned to peer through the confetti and past the girls with the 90-point club signs. "92.25! Man, that was a ride! I loved every second!"

"You were great, Dub. Really great! That direction change was as good as anyone could ever hope to do it!"

"Technical praise from the champ!"

"I always knew you had it in you!"

"You did?"

Again, the look of surprise cut Cody. "Absolutely. Hell, you might even beat me yet."

Dub laughed. "That's the cocky Cody I know and love."

"The judges robbed you," Cody declared. "I'd have given you 94, myself!"

"They're leaving room for you," Dub said with a huge grin. "Go out there and win it, because this year will be your last."

The comment cut Cody in a different way, but he wasn't going to spoil Dub's moment. "I'm not going to fall off even for you, friend."

"AT FIRST it seemed like the judges were trying to leave room for someone to overtake Cody Grainger, but now they've fallen in love with him again and his scores have been creeping up with each go-around. Given the rides he's been making, he's beginning to earn the scores he deserves. This crowd is electrified from Dub Whittaker's ride and they're amped to see what Cody Grainger can do on the back of Spinal Tap.

"This bull is a shoo-in for this year's World Champion Bull, and stock contractor Olney Lewis is looking to Cody to show his bull off and win him that stock contractor buckle. Spinal Tap has been on the circuit for three years and has yet to be covered by any rider. Cody has gone up against this bull twice, and both times the bull had it all his own way. But the way Cody Grainger announced he was taking on this Goliath of the sport shows he thinks he has what it takes to ride that bull.

"Rex talked to Cody just a little while ago. What did he have to say, Rex?"

The television reporter took over, speaking to the camera by the gate. "There was no quaver in Cody's voice when he claimed this bull, and no tremble in his step when he came by to talk to me just minutes ago. He picked that bull with conviction! The way he's been riding in this finals, I would say he might have a chance to break Spinal Tap's buckoff streak like he vanquished his own."

The ring announcer said, "I have to remind you Cody bucked off his first bull in round one. Could that signify a chink in his armor?"

"The Cody Grainger I've been watching here this weekend is back to his usual form, doing things other riders can only dream of, but you're right. Only time will tell if Cody can pull this off."

"And Cody is in the chute now, starting his wrap. His good friend Dub Whittaker is helping him get set. Dub just had that great, great ride on High Society, scoring a much-needed 92.25, making him the only one here who might be in position to take that buckle from Cody Grainger this year. In just a few minutes we'll know which man comes out on top."

"Don't listen to that bullshit, Cody. Just go out there and ride," Dub muttered.

"Listen to what?" Cody flashed him a grin. "I can't hear anything but you."

"You know I want to win this thing," Dub said, "but you go out there and ride the crap outta this bull like only you can! It's time someone showed him the righteous way."

Cody said, "I'll do just that," adding, *God willing*, in his mind. Then he went back to making sure his rope was pulled tight, wrapping it around his gloved hand, beating his fingers shut around the handle. Going through the ritual familiar to him since he was a kid, each step had to be completed to his satisfaction to take him one step closer to the moment when the gate opened and it was just he and the bull.

Finally he nodded.

The first leap out of the gate was so explosive, Cody felt the jolt pushing him back onto his pockets, but he forced his chin down and pulled himself forward, glaring at the bull's shoulders. But the opening volley was nothing compared to Spinal Tap's next assault. Up went his hind feet, so high that Cody knew the bull's spine must be practically vertical in the air. He felt the bull's rump push his shoulders forward and forced himself to stay loose instead of giving into his impulse to clamp down. Leaning back even while his hips slipped forward, he flung his free arm up over his head to stay with the bull.

Touching down briefly on his front feet, Spinal Tap did a swooping turn and launched them high in the air, viciously snapping his body sideways until his head almost touched his tail. Cody was well up over his rope and bent at the hips, swinging his free arm to stay with the bull.

Everything came to a shuddering stop when the bull landed and switched direction again without warning. Cody was entirely concentrated on feeling each movement under him, staying centered on the bull, staying loose, chin down.

Another vertical jump, and the bull stumbled almost to his knees when he landed. Spinal Tap pushed himself back and the momentum propelled Cody forward. He barely kept his free arm clear of the bull's shoulders when Spinal Tap surged forward with a sudden burst of speed, rocking Cody back until he was almost lying against the bull's back. Sensing its advantage, Spinal Tap followed up with another huge vertical jump.

But Cody was in the zone. He stayed right with the bull and even started spurring with his outside leg a little to show he was in control. He could feel a grin of pure enjoyment on his face. This was flying! The amazing rush of adrenaline and excitement and physical challenge all rolled into the most astounding, exhilarating, satisfying ride of his life. He never wanted it to end!

Vaguely he could hear Johnny shouting, "Keep riding him! Keep riding him!"

He heard the whistle but it didn't register. Dimly he heard stamping and yelling, and saw the four bullfighters closing in around him. He heard Johnny shouting, "You made it! Get off! Get off!"

Cody yanked at the rope, and suddenly the bull went to his knees. Remembering another time when a bull rolled on him, and the subsequent time out of action for injuries and rehab, Cody yanked harder at the rope, trying to get free.

"Stay on him, stay on him!" Johnny yelled, running toward him.

Cody froze in place, not understanding the conflicting orders. The action seemed to slow down as he watched Johnny slide to a stop and put his hand on the bull's head. The bull lurched up, lashing out with one front foot to sweep Johnny's feet out from under him. As Johnny went down, he yelled, "Bail! Get off *now!*"

Cody dove off the bull, rolling on his shoulder and coming up on his feet with unaccustomed grace, anxiously looking back to see what happened to Johnny.

But Johnny was up on his feet again, playing tag with his team, each of them darting in and out in front of the bull from different directions until the thoroughly confused animal gave it up and went for the gate.

When Cody looked up at the stands, people were standing on their seats screaming. Thirty-nine bull riders were crowded behind the chute, hanging over the rails to cheer and applaud for him. They knew just what it took, and they appreciated his ride for the great performance it was. An overwhelming feeling of joy came over Cody. He'd done it! He'd gotten Johnny back and he had ridden Spinal Tap! He had no idea of his score, although the confetti and screams were good clues it was over ninety.

The burst of emotion was too much for him, and he had to vent physically. Knowing he probably looked like a complete fool, he did a crazy little dance across the ring, kicking his feet out from side to side, the fringe on his chaps flailing around. He didn't even feel his knee as he ran to the shark cage, leaped up on it, and raised his fists in the air, shouting with relief and joy.

He saw Johnny laughing until tears streamed down his face, standing with Vern, Reese, and Chris. Even the usually impassive Vern was grinning and waving both fists back at Cody.

Cody jumped off the cage and ran to the fence to climb up to his parents' box. His mom and dad both grabbed for him and hugged him. He felt the thumps on his back from RJ and Travis. He could see proud smiles and lips moving but he couldn't hear what anyone was saying.

Jinks the clown was there to shake his hand when he dropped back into the ring. He ran over to the gate where Vern, Chris, and Reese gave him a high fist bump in turn, but Johnny gave him a one-arm manhug with a thump on the back. He noticed Johnny was holding his rope for him, and let his cheek brush against Johnny's for an instant before he broke away. With a last glance and a secret smile for Johnny, Cody went for Dub, who hauled him up and over the fence in his turn and pulled him into a ferocious hug. All the other riders crowded around, as if touching him would transfer some riding magic to them, patting him, pounding him, yelling at him.

"Knew you had it, man! This is your year!"

"Thanks, Dub. For everything."

"I didn't teach you to ride, friend."

"Maybe you did, friend," Cody said. "I wouldn't be here this year without you."

The stock contractor who owned Spinal Tap came by and shook his hand with both of his. "Thank you, Cody! You got that gold buckle for me. Any contractor would kill to have you up on his bulls. You make us look good!"

"Thank *you*, Olney. That is one damn fine bull!"

Already he was being pulled away. He had to go back to the shark cage, where the TV reporter Rex and Sam were waiting for him; Rex with microphone and cameraman, Sam with a gold buckle and huge check with a dazzling number of zeroes.

As Cody climbed up, a thousand flashes went off, and the ring announcer was trying to be heard over the mayhem. "Cody Grainger has done it! Spinal Tap has been conquered! That ride was as good as

Spinal Tap ever is! This bull was throwing everything but the kitchen sink at Cody and Cody handled it easily.

"That was a ride to make history! Cody Grainger set the bar high with a score of 96.5, the highest score the NBR has ever seen! It will be a long time until we see a score like that again. He is also the first back-to-back NBR World Champion. Cody doesn't just want to win. He wants everyone to know he's the best, including the bull! In the short space of ten weeks, Cody Grainger has gone from heartbreaking to heart-stopping! He absolutely *dominates* this sport! Cody Grainger has just slayed the dragon! Let's hear what he has to say about his historic win! Take it away, Rex."

Rex managed to get the mic in front of Cody. "You have conquered the titan of the NBR, Cody. This is the first time Spinal Tap has ever been taken to the whistle. How did you do it?"

Cody took a moment before he answered. "To be honest, I couldn't have done it without the support of my family, my friends, and my fans. They always believed in me and told me to do my best, even when my best landed me on my butt in the dirt."

"What a humble answer from one of the best riders in the history of the NBR. What kind of steel backbone does it take to make you persevere and hang on for a high score on a rank bull like that?"

"What was the score? I couldn't hear it over this noise." Cody squinted, trying to see the monitors between smoke, confetti, and columns of flame.

"You made a score of 96.5, a career high for you and a score any rider would kill for," Rex said, smiling. "How does that feel?"

Cody wanted to say something to everyone about how much he owed to Johnny and Dub, standing by him as they had. He looked at the joy on his parents' faces, remembering how they always supported him. Sam was grinning at him with pride. He wasn't sure what he was saying as he spoke, but he meant every word. "I have so many people to thank, but most of all I want to thank my family and friends. I couldn't have made it without them. I want to thank the great sponsors of the NBR who make this competition possible, the stock contractors, and all the wonderful fans who come out at every stop to watch us ride in this great country of ours. I hope you all had a great time tonight, because I know I did!"

To the response of delighted shouts, whistles, and applause, Sam handed him the giant outsized check and buckle as they posed for the cameras. "Thanks for the plug for the stock contractors, son," Sam murmured with a chuckle. "You're learning."

Rex continued on. "Although Cody Grainger is the NBR World Champion this year, as often happens in this wild sport, he's not the winner of this event. He went five for six in the finals, whereas four other men rode six for six. If Cody hadn't had that buckoff in round one, he might be taking home two checks tonight, but his good friend, Dub Whittaker, surpassed him in event points. Dub, get out here and get your check. Here's Dub Whittaker, your event winner for tonight!"

Dub ran out to the cage, both arms raised in victory to more excited applause.

Wishing it could have been Johnny, Cody bent to pull Dub up onto the shark cage. "Get your ass up here, Miss Runner-Up," he teased.

"Always a bridesmaid, never a bride," Dub said in a mocking tone, and then dropped his voice to whisper close to Cody's ear. "Isn't that a little gay?"

"Totally gay." Cody grinned at him. "Next year it'll be you up here as World Champion," he promised.

"We have a check here in the amount of five hundred thousand dollars," Rex said, "made out to the event winner, Dub Whittaker. Dub, you've been on the circuit for seven years. How's it feel to come so close to beating your good friend Cody and then watch it all slip away?"

Dub grabbed the mic and pulled Rex's hand closer. "Slip away? Did you see my ride? This is one excellent final for me. And I won the whole dang event!"

Rex wrestled for the mic and got it back. "Cody, how does it feel to have your good friend Dub nipping at your heels?"

"There isn't a finer man or rider I'd be willing to lose to," Cody said. "Dub's a winner all the way with me and always has been."

"And there's still one other rider we have to recognize. It's time to name the Rookie of the Year and hand over a check for one hundred thousand dollars. It was a close race to the finish between two fine young men, both of whom, it should be noted, received training from the World Champion himself, Cody Grainger. For a while there it looked like Bobby Blue Chandler was going to walk away with the rookie title, but under intense pressure, Zane cowboyed up and took it instead. Your NBR Rookie of the Year, Zane Winslow!"

There was a bit of a jostle at the gate, and then Zane was pushed out into the ring to run the gauntlet of congratulations from more seasoned riders and the bullfighters on his way to claim his prize, looking both surprised and delighted as he came over.

Dub and Cody each grabbed a hand and hauled him up onto the cage. "Getting crowded up here," Dub joked.

"It's where the elite meet," Cody said.

Sam bent to retrieve another check and posed with Zane.

"Zane Winslow is going to be a cowboy y'all are going to want to watch in the coming years," Rex said. "How's it feel, Zane? You've heard of the sophomore slump so many rookies go through. Any worries about next year?"

In a stunned voice, Zane asked, "How did this happen?"

"Points, son," Sam said. "It's in the numbers. You got more points than the other rookies. You're following in Cody's footsteps. He made Rookie of the Year the first year he was called up to the Top Cut, and look at him now."

Zane grinned and held the check over his head. "I don't know how I did it, but I'm glad I did!"

Rex took control. "And now we're going to ask the riders to stand aside for a special presentation. As you know, this was the last final for bullfighter Chris Bellow before he heads into a well-earned retirement. Come on out here, Chris!"

As Cody watched, the three other bullfighters stood and applauded for Chris as he ran out into the ring, waving at the crowd. A shiny new truck was driven into the ring.

Rex shook Chris's hand. "One of the great bullfighters in history. It's been an exciting run to watch you protect the cowboys and stock for almost twenty years. In honor of your great service, the NBR wants you to have this check and the keys to a brand-new truck! How does it feel to walk away from something you love and the team you worked with for so long?"

Chris made his goodbye speech and accepted check and keys while Cody watched in silence. Every word seemed to echo his own pain, and he was the first to shake Chris's hand during the applause that followed.

"And that will be the roundup of the one of the most exciting finals the NBR has seen yet. Thank you all for coming, and don't forget the touring division will be riding every week through November until Thanksgiving. The NBR Top Cut Tour will be back next January to do it all over again. Check the NBR website, Facebook, Twitter, and our YouTube channel for updates, videos, and schedules. Good night and God bless!"

Rex wiped his forehead and grinned when the lights for the camera went off. "See you boys at the press conference. Half an hour in the lobby in front of the curtains." Rex shook everyone's hands in turn and jumped down, assisted by Jinks. They walked off together, followed by the cameraman as the crowd started to file out of the center.

Sam reached for the checks and Cody's buckle. Zane tried to hang on to his check, his face still lit up with excitement.

"Gotta give it back now, Winslow. We'll hand it back to you at the press conference, son, promise," Sam said with a grin.

"Damn. I can't believe this happened!" Zane exclaimed. He let go of the check reluctantly, still eyeing it in disbelief.

"Believe it, kid. You have a great future ahead of you in the ring," Cody said. "Proud of you."

"Thanks, Cody." Zane seemed as if he might burst with pride, and his expression made Cody remember the thrill of winning his Rookie of the Year title, back when dinosaurs roamed the earth.

Sam turned to the other two riders. "Better get a shower and put on some spit and polish. We got to do this dog and pony show again at the press conference."

"Thanks, Sam, for coming out to the ranch to talk some sense into me," Cody said, hanging on to Sam's hand for a beat. "I don't think I'd be up here without you."

"It's good for a rider to have a thick skull," Sam said cheerfully. "Always kept me from too many concussions." He jumped down casually and walked over to the NBR board members.

"Let's go," Dub said. "People are leaving and you need a shower."

"Are you saying I stink?" Cody demanded.

"It is what it is," Dub said.

THE press conference lasted only fifteen minutes, reminding Cody that, compared to football, bull riding was still only a minor blip on the TV sports screen in America.

On the other hand, the meet and greet with the fans went on for over two hours. He was glad he'd strapped on the brace after his shower, but his right hand was almost as numb as his left from shaking hands. It made him glad to see that Dub got just as much attention as he did, while Zane posed for pictures with lots of pretty girls.

It was just about getting to be suppertime when the crowd started to thin out, and finally the banquet room was empty except for other riders.

Dub stretched and grinned at Cody. "I'd buy you a drink, but I got plans. See you next year?"

"Dub, I just wanted to tell you, I feel like I took you for granted," Cody started awkwardly. "You're not just a good friend, you are such a talented rider—"

"Ho, you ain't gonna get all emotional on me now, are you?"

"No, of course not," Cody said. "Anyway, I still beat you."

"Sure you did." Suddenly Dub wrapped Cody in his arms. "Love you, man."

"Love you too, man." Cody patted Dub on the back.

"People waiting on me. Gotta go. See you next year." Clearing his throat, Dub turned abruptly and walked away, raising one hand as he went.

Watching Dub walk away left Cody with a lump in his throat, and for a moment he felt very alone. Dub had done something for him no one else could have when he was at the lowest point of his life. Then he remembered there were people waiting for him as well.

WHEN he entered the restaurant, the feeling of loneliness fell away and he smiled when he saw his family waiting for him: his mother and father, Travis, RJ, and Johnny. All of them formed a circle of love and it belonged to him, as he belonged to them.

He crossed the room and took the empty chair in time to watch Travis hand first Val and then Johnny a twenty each. It must have been what Johnny meant about having money riding on him.

"I guess you were right about Cody. I thought he was going to screw it up this year," Travis said grudgingly.

"Thanks a lot!" Cody protested.

Val very kindly did not say "I told you so," even though she looked as if nothing would make her happier than to rub it in, especially to Travis. "He's a good rider."

"The highest praise a man can have," Davis said, "coming from another World Champion."

"I know," Cody said, surprising himself with the humility in his tone. "I just wanted to thank you all for having my back this year."

"Hey, you're not the only one who likes a challenge," Travis quipped.

"I'm proud of you, boy," Davis said. "Takes a real man to climb out of a slump like that, and you did it. That was one damn fine ride."

"No hints on how to do it better?" Cody teased.

"It was perfect," Val said. "You did what had to be done."

Her eyes were shining with pride, and Cody knew she meant more than just the ride.

"Your mother's usually jumping like a catfish when she watches you ride, but today she was sitting there all calm and serene," Davis said with a broad grin.

"I knew you had it," Val said simply.

RJ spoke up unexpectedly. "It's pushing through when it isn't so easy, that's what makes a winner."

"Thanks, RJ," Cody said. He didn't know what to say to that.

He felt Johnny's foot touch his under the table and looked at his partner. How did he ever get so lucky? He felt as though he ought to get a buckle for somehow managing to be so loved despite himself. He was unusually silent through dinner, watching the faces of his family.

THIS time it was Cody helping Johnny along on the way to the room, even though he was still hobbling a bit himself. "You're limping."

"I know. Spinal Tap almost broke my ankle saving your ass," Johnny said cheerfully.

"Thanks, I'm not sure my ass is worth your ankle."

"Don't go all modest on me now," Johnny said. "I'm not used to it. Might have a heart attack from the shock."

"At the end there, why did you tell me to stay on after yelling, 'Get off'?"

"When Spinal Tap goes down on his knees like that, he does it to pull a rider over his head. Then he hooks him. I just wanted you to stay put 'til I could distract him."

"You sure it's not broken?"

"The medics X-rayed it and taped it for me. Just a sprain."

"You were great tonight."

"Yeah, I'm not the one taking home a million bucks."

"Yeah, you are. You're in it with me, babe. I couldn't have done it if you hadn't read that bull for me."

Johnny chuckled. "I didn't tell you anything about Spinal Tap. I told you about you."

"And for once I listened." Cody flexed his left hand and winced. "Did that bull knock you off your feet on purpose?"

"Spinal Tap is a teddy bear behind the scenes, but he gets really mean in the ring. It was totally on purpose. He's a good multitasker, trying to hook you and knock me over at the same time. Makes him great."

Cody swiped his card and opened the door. "I'll get us some ice. At least I can still walk."

"Get a lot. Get some drinks too." Johnny heaved a sigh of relief as he sat down on the bed and watched Cody leave. Carefully, he hoisted his leg up and worked his boots off. He looked up at the click of the lock when Cody came back.

"Here you go, babe." Cody set three plastic bags full of ice and two sodas down on the table. "I'll get you a towel."

Johnny balanced the bag Cody handed him on his ankle and wrapped the towel around it. "Want me to tie that to your hand?"

"Yeah. Save some for my knee." Cody sat on the bed and scootched closer to where Johnny could reach him. Johnny used one of Cody's shirts to secure the ice to his hand. "At least we have a break in the action to heal up."

"Yeah, we do. That is, if you're coming back."

"I'm coming back to the ranch with you." Johnny smiled at the relief on Cody's face. "Damn, I missed you."

"Not like I missed you. When you left, you said you used to be happy to be around me—it made me think about what it must be like to be around me. I didn't like myself very much while you were gone. I might not be a real nice guy."

"You're a nice guy," Johnny reassured him. "Maybe sometimes your head gets too big to fit through the door—"

"I can be cocky and selfish."

"Everyone is sometimes," Johnny said, thinking of when March called him cocky. "It's not always a bad thing."

"It is when it's bad for you." Cody rested his head against Johnny's shoulder. "I know I'll fuck up again. No matter how careful I am."

"It'll be good practice for both of us. You fuck up and I'll yell at you about it," Johnny said with a grin. "I need to speak up for myself more."

"It was great Dub won the event, huh?" Cody mused. "I always thought he was good but this year he really took off."

"Maybe he'll win the Championship next year."

"Nah, I've still got it," Cody boasted. "I could win next year easy."

Johnny's smile was twisted. "Go out on top, cowboy," he said softly.

"You saw me tonight. I was great, correcting on, timing perfect. I can still do this!"

"Remember Jim Sharp? He rode past his prime, and it's sad hearing old-timers talk about how he never could get his scores up again. You start losing your grip or your knees don't work."

"But I've been riding great! You saw me tonight! I was on top! I can still be on top—"

Johnny was shaking his head slowly. "When I'm slipping downhill, I hope someone will be as honest with me as I'm being with you, because I don't want to die out there in the ring with blood and dust in my mouth, wishing I was here in your arms. Worse yet, I don't want someone else to die because I wasn't good enough.

"And I don't want you to be another Lane Frost. You could ride another five years for sure, and you might even win some of the time. Your muscles are trained, you're in good shape. But it's slipping away. You bore down tonight, you made it happen. But it's not near as easy as it was for you two years ago. When's the last time you had a buckoff streak?"

"I—"

"Be honest. Not with me, with yourself."

Cody groaned as he said it. "You win, I admit it. Something hurts every time I ride. I had to fight my way back on top after this summer."

"That flash of muscle memory gave you a brilliant ride tonight, but it's telling you a lie you want to believe. The reality is you're getting older, you don't heal as fast as you did even two years ago."

"I do the work in the gym to keep flexible and strong—"

"You're stronger than 98 percent of the men in this country. Hell! Stronger than 90 percent of the other bull riders, but it's not enough anymore. I'd rather you could walk in your waning years than me pushing you around in a wheelchair because you broke both legs. Or worse."

"Hey! I'm not on a cane yet! When I'm eighty I'll still be bending you over my walker!"

Johnny laughed at the image of the two of them fumbling to pull that off in old age. "Trouble is, you're not ready to let go of calling yourself a bull rider yet, but it's not the only way to compete. How about setting your sights on Stock Contractor of the Year?"

"It's hard to admit but you could have a point. But it just won't be the same kind of rush."

"You never know 'til you try. Think about when you show up at an event with a bull and people say you know it's a good one because Cody Grainger brought it to the ring. It's a bull you can win on." Seeing Cody still looked unconvinced, Johnny added, "I never would have picked bullfighting over riding to start with and look at me now. Vern made it official tonight. I'm part of the Top Cut bullfighting team!"

"You totally deserve it." Cody looked down and rubbed his hand over his new gold buckle, looking at it proudly. "Want to wear it for a while? It's yours just as much as it is mine."

"How do you figure that? It wasn't me up on that bull's back making the whistle."

"I never would have been able to ride him without you. Not just the stuff you told me about how to ride him, but everything we went through. I think I need you to bring me back down to earth."

"It's a beautiful buckle, but no. It's yours." Johnny covered Cody's hand over it with his. "You earned it. You wear it with pride."

"I thought you'd feel that way." Cody lifted Johnny's hand resting on his and kissed it. "Be right back."

He limped across the room and got a small box out of a drawer. He crossed the room nervously and stood in front of Johnny, looking like an embarrassed little boy.

"This is for you." Cody flushed red as he held out the box.

It was wrapped in manly silver paper with a black ribbon. Their fingers touched as Johnny took it from him. "You didn't have to get me anything."

"I wanted to. Something to show you that you're my champion."

Feeling a bit embarrassed, Johnny took the wrapping off carefully. He lifted the lid. Beneath some white cotton filler was a black leather band.

"Keep going."

He lifted the white cotton square and gasped. "Cody, it's beautiful!"

A relieved grin spread over Cody's face. "You like it? I had it made for you."

Johnny lifted the necklace out of the box. The pendant felt solid and familiar in his hand. "An arrowhead."

"Johnny Arrow, get it?"

"Duh, I get it."

The gleaming arrow was made of gold, with a cloud ladder of silver zigzagging diagonally down to the central point. One side gleamed burnished gold, while on the other a starry sky was made from a field of black jasper inlaid with stars of turquoise and ice opal. His fingers trembled as he closed his hand around the tapered pendant possessively.

"Someone Diné must have made this."

"I found the guy online. Calvin Begay. Any relation?"

Johnny snorted with laughter. "I told you, Begay is like the Diné version of Smith and Jones. I doubt it. How did you ever—" He opened his hand and looked at the pendant in disbelief. "It's so beautiful."

"When the tour went through New Mexico, I went to his studio. I told him about you and this is what he came up with." Cody licked his lips nervously. "I hope it means something to you."

"It means a lot coming from you."

"Let me put it on for you." Cody took the necklace from him and unhooked the cord, leaning over him to fasten it around his neck. "It's almost as beautiful as you are."

Johnny got up to look in the mirror. He unbuttoned his shirt, opening it so the cloud ladder on his skin was visible near the gleaming gold. He stroked the pendant delicately with a fingertip. "I love it. I'll never take it off."

"Maybe you should when you're working."

"Maybe."

"And maybe it's a good thing it's the end of the season so you can get used to it."

"But why? Why not a vest or boots or something?"

"I'm not so good with words. I want you to know what you mean to me. If I could marry you, I would," Cody said with an intense stare, as if Johnny might not believe him.

Johnny relaxed and smiled. "Maybe next time it's legal we should hurry to the courthouse before it gets fucked up again."

"Is that a yes?"

"It's a yes, you idiot. And thank you." Johnny pulled Cody close and kissed him, relishing being in his embrace.

"I'm gonna miss you next year," Cody mumbled into Johnny's hair.

"If you're contracting your bulls to the Top Cut, I'm sure we'll run into each other somewhere along the way." Johnny ran his hands over Cody's firmly muscled back. "Let's go to bed."

"I don't think I could get it up no matter what," Cody said.

"Neither can I. I meant to sleep."

"I guess this means I really am getting old," Cody grumbled. "A hot naked man in my bed and all I want to do is take an aspirin and get some sleep."

THEY made up for it the next morning, and neither of them felt old. The sex was molten and left them limp with satisfaction.

It didn't matter that Cody walked around with a shit-eating grin whenever he thought about it. Everyone chalked it up to his win. It took another day for the event to wind down. For the first time, Cody actually paid attention when a retired rider was inducted into the Ring of Honor. He had a sense of belonging to something with tradition and community instead of being an isolated rider only looking for his own glory.

He stood up and applauded with everyone else, and this time he really meant it. He felt like one of the crowd of riders and bullfighters and contractors.

"You're looking rather exalted," Johnny teased when they filed out.

"Continuity," Cody said. "I guess I didn't fully realize what I belong to."

"It will go on, even if you're not riding."

"Yeah, I guess I'm figuring it out, finally."

IT WAS different going home this time, even though they landed at the same airfield. Cody's truck was parked there waiting for them. The drive along Route 101 was the same. The dirt road and log bridge hadn't changed. The big house was standing open to welcome them, a light on in every window. Beyond, he could see the porch light burning at their own bungalow.

When they stepped inside the screen door, Davis appeared in the hallway, saying, "Val, the boys are home."

Cody went on ahead to hug his father while Johnny stepped into the living room. The saddle was still there on its stand and a new box was up on the wall, empty and waiting for the gold buckle that shone on Cody's belt. It felt like home, and this time Johnny was ready to claim it.

Like last time, Val came up beside him and slipped her hand into the crook of his elbow. "Good to be home?"

"It's great," Johnny said. "I've missed this."

"We missed you, Johnny."

The supper with Travis and RJ, listening to the news of the ranch, and washing the dishes made the minutes count down deliberately until they were able to make love in their own bed once again.

The next morning they saddled up their horses to ride into the hills. Johnny wondered if Cody was trying to recreate the last day they were happy here before it all fell apart. He thought Cody seemed nervous, and had to smile because there was no reason to be nervous anymore.

Cody was silent until they came to his tree and tied the horses. He wrapped his arms around Johnny as he'd done last time and leaned against the tree. "I love you."

"Love you too," Johnny said.

"I told my parents this morning I'm hanging up the spurs."

"What did they say?"

"Dad said it was my decision, and Mom belted out part of the 'Hallelujah Chorus' until I told her I got the message." Cody sniggered.

"I can hear her now," Johnny said.

"Yeah, she doesn't hold back telling how she feels."

Johnny could feel Cody shift his weight behind him and waited.

"It's going to seem weird not seeing you all the time."

"Hey, if you're contracting your bulls out, you'll be around," Johnny said. "Besides, there are breaks for holidays and such. It's not like I'll be on the road all the time."

"It won't be the same."

"We'll make it work."

"You seem so sure."

"I learned a lot this summer."

"Yeah, I can tell. You don't let me push you around anymore."

"I learned to trust myself," Johnny said softly.

"I'm glad of that." Cody hooked his chin on Johnny's shoulder. "I hope you have a long, safe career as a bullfighter. You ever think about what you're going to do when you retire?"

"I thought maybe we'd have a ranch together."

"Yeah, I think we can make that happen."

"I have to earn money while I can so I can pull my share of the load, but one day when I can't fight bulls anymore, I've always wanted to go to the gay rodeo. I want to ride in their Pride parade."

"Wow, I never really thought about that. You think anyone would care?"

"I don't know. I'm only a bullfighter. Maybe no one would even know my name, but it would be like coming out. I'd like it if some kid like me could see you can be gay *and* a manly, macho bullfighter." Johnny laughed at himself.

"Coming out to my parents was like breathing for me. Painless. I never really thought about what it might be like for other kids, even you."

"If it helped even one kid, it would be worth it to me," Johnny said.

"You know, that sounds like a plan. And when you go, I'd like to ride in that parade by your side."

Johnny's face lit up. "You would do that? It would mean so much to have a World Champion rider there, even if you didn't come out."

"I'd be proud to ride by your side. By then I'll be a fat old fart, boring people with stories about my glory days, and you'll be the famous bullfighter. Probably leading your own team by then."

"You'll be inducted into the bull rider's Ring of Honor—"

"Where old bull riders go to die—"

"To be honored. And I'll just be some guy on a horse."

"You'll be my guy on a horse, baby. You're my star."

"It's good to be home," Johnny said softly.

CATT FORD lives in front of the computer monitor, in another world where her imaginary gay friends obey her every command.

She likes cats, chocolate, swing dancing, sleeping, Monty Python, Aussie friends, being silly, spinning other realities with words, and sea glass. She dislikes caterpillars, cigarette smoke, and rude people who think the F-word (as in faggot, or bundle of sticks) is acceptable.

A frustrated perfectionist, she comforts herself with the legend about the weavers of Persian rugs always including one mistake so as not to anger the gods, although she has no need to include a mistake on purpose. One always slips through. Writing fiction has filled a need for clever conversations, only possible when one is in control of both sides, and erotic romances, where everything for the most part turns out happily ever after.

Visit Catt's blog at http://catt-ford.livejournal.com/.

Also from CATT FORD

http://www.dreamspinnerpress.com

Also from CATT FORD

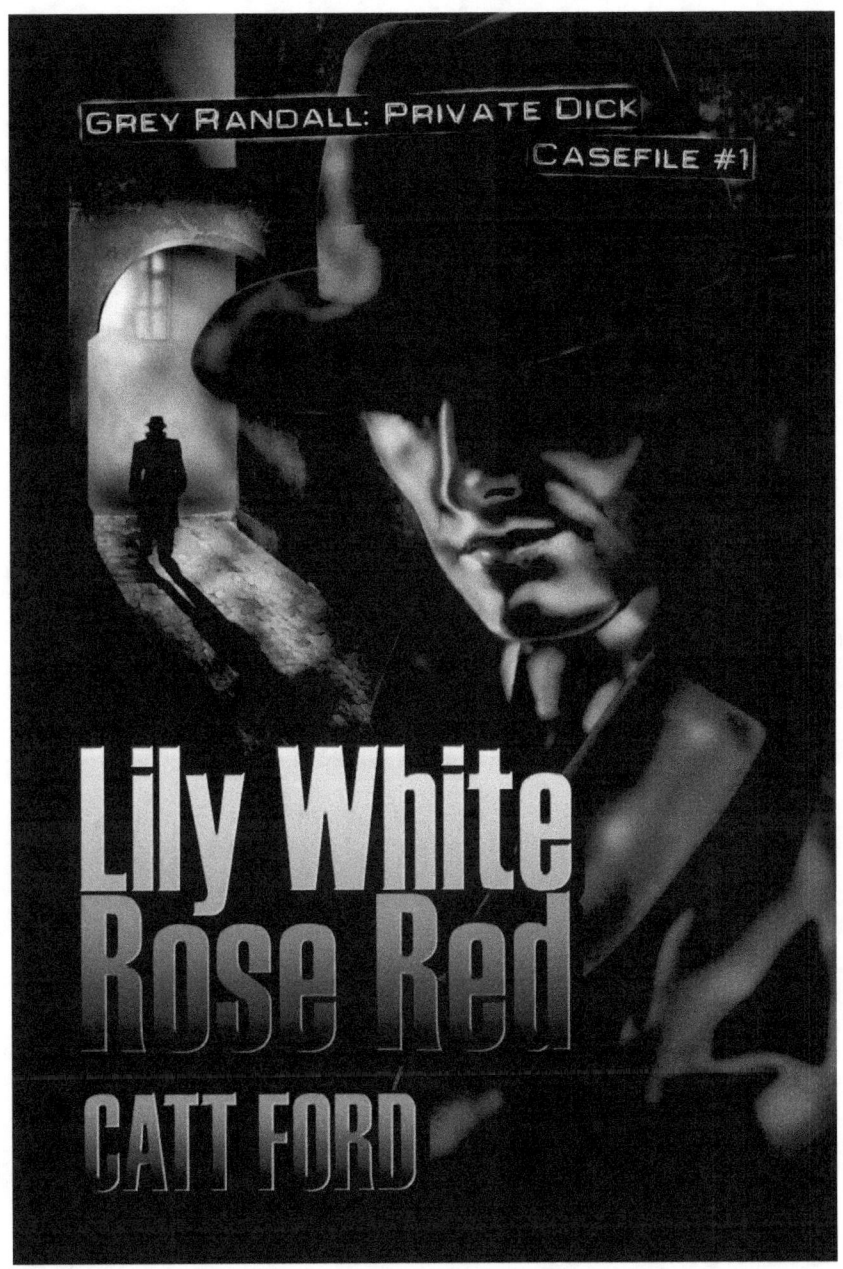

http://www.dreamspinnerpress.com

Also from CATT FORD

http://www.dreamspinnerpress.com

Also from CATT FORD

Also from CATT FORD

http://www.dreamspinnerpress.com

Also from CATT FORD

http://www.dreamspinnerpress.com